"More thrilling than a back-to-back showing of *Top Gun* and *Iron Eagle,* this red-hot piece of military fiction is certain to keep readers riveted . . . some of the most suspenseful battle scenes in recent military fiction."   —*Publishers Weekly*

"There's no doubt that Gandt knows what it's like in the cockpit, and he takes his readers there with flair."
—*The Miami Herald*

"*With Hostile Intent* is especially topical, and you do not need to be a naval aviator to enjoy the description of flight operations and life onboard an aircraft carrier. Gandt is as good an author as he is a pilot, and that's high praise."
—*Aviation Week*

"Bob Gandt is known for a half dozen nonfiction books, including the well-regarded *Bogeys and Bandits* that tracked an FRS class through Hornet training. In his first novel he builds on that knowledge to produce a solid tale about modern carrier aviation, warts and all. . . . It's a roller-coaster ride."

—*The Hook*

"Informative, compelling, and thought-provoking, [*With Hostile Intent*] offers an insider's perspective on what it takes to make the grade, and a number of interesting insights on key events and trends in today's Navy."   —*Sea Power*

BLACK
STAR
RISING

✦

ROBERT
GANDT

SIGNET
Published by New American Library, a division of
Penguin Group (USA) Inc., 375 Hudson Street,
New York, New York 10014, USA
Penguin Group (Canada), 90 Eglinton Avenue East, Suite 700, Toronto,
Ontario M4P 2Y3, Canada (a division of Pearson Penguin Canada Inc.)
Penguin Books Ltd., 80 Strand, London WC2R 0RL, England
Penguin Ireland, 25 St. Stephen's Green, Dublin 2,
Ireland (a division of Penguin Books Ltd.)
Penguin Group (Australia), 250 Camberwell Road, Camberwell, Victoria 3124,
Australia (a division of Pearson Australia Group Pty. Ltd.)
Penguin Books India Pvt. Ltd., 11 Community Centre, Panchsheel Park,
New Delhi - 110 017, India
Penguin Group (NZ), cnr Airborne and Rosedale Roads, Albany,
Auckland 1310, New Zealand (a division of Pearson New Zealand Ltd.)
Penguin Books (South Africa) (Pty.) Ltd., 24 Sturdee Avenue,
Rosebank, Johannesburg 2196, South Africa

Penguin Books Ltd, Registered Offices:
80 Strand, London WC2R 0RL, England

First published by Signet, an imprint of New American Library,
a division of Penguin Group (USA) Inc.

First Printing, January 2007
10 9 8 7 6 5 4 3 2 1

Copyright © Robert Gandt, 2007
Map of Southeast Asia © Robert A. Terry, 2006
Black Star schematic drawing copyright © Jeffrey L. Ward, 2003
All rights reserved

 REGISTERED TRADEMARK—MARCA REGISTRADA

Printed in the United States of America

To Dick Amell,
Buddy, fellow flyer, second dad.

ACKNOWLEDGMENTS

Another hurrah for Brick Maxwell's valiant support crew. Special thanks go to Mark Chait, editor extraordinaire at Penguin; Alice Martell, super agent and friend, and her assistant, Stephanie Finman; Lt. Cmdr. Allen "Zoomie" Baker, fighter pilot and tech consultant; Vernon Lewis, proofreader and factual nitpicker.

Thirty-seven years had elapsed since I last saw Vietnam. Needless to say, a few things had changed, including me. From Hanoi to Da Nang to Ho Chi Minh City, my reception was invariably courteous and hospitable. To my hosts in Vietnam, thanks for the journey through time. *Cam on.*

"O divine art of subtlety and secrecy! Through you we learn to be invisible, through you inaudible, and hence we can hold the enemy's fate in our hands."

—Sun Tzu, *The Art of War* (trans. Thomas Cleary)

PROLOGUE

THE HILTON

Hoa Lo Prison
Hanoi, Socialist Republic of Vietnam
1015 Monday, 2 April

Joe Ferrone hated this place.

For a long moment he hesitated at the main entrance, his hand flat against the stone wall. It had been a mistake to come here, he thought. He knew it would be like this. A flood of memories washed over him. He remembered the coarse feel of the stone, the flaking rust on the iron bars, the concrete floors stained with mildew and blood.

He took a deep breath and went inside.

His guide was a polite young Vietnamese man named Trunh. Trunh kept a respectful silence, allowing him to move at his own pace. They came to the main reception area. Two middle-aged women stood behind a counter. They wore embarrassed smiles, bowing their heads in the way Vietnamese did for their elders and seniors.

"I would be pleased to show you around," said Trunh.

"No thanks," said Ferrone. "I know the way."

Most of the complex had been torn down, replaced by a commercial high-rise. Only the front of the original building remained. Now it was a museum. The public could see where thousands of Vietnamese prisoners had been incarcerated by the French, who built the prison in 1896. Not until later, during what the Vietnamese called "the American War," was Hoa Lo inhabited by Americans. Most were pilots who had been shot down during air attacks on North Vietnam.

Ferrone walked down a long passageway. On either side was a row of barred cells. Abruptly he stopped, transfixed, staring at one of the darkened cells. Without warning a stab of pain shot from below his right knee, up his leg and through his pelvis. He leaned against the wall, his breath coming in hard gasps.

With the pain in his leg came a clarity of recall.

The trees were flashing beneath him at four hundred and sixty-five knots. The undulating terrain seemed benign, void of guns and the circles of SA-2 missile batteries with the telltale Fan Song acquisition radar in the center. No radar warning indication in the cockpit. That was good.

The target was a bridge over a north-south road that served as a night supply route for the North Vietnamese Army. Ferrone knew the bridge. He had bombed it before. The Vietnamese always repaired it, usually overnight. In the repetitive bombing of the bridge, eight U.S. Navy jets had already been lost.

One minute to run. Ferrone checked again that the station selector switches were set for his two thousand-pound bombs. The master armament switch was in the ON position. One of the stupidest mistakes you could make was to place yourself in the enemy's sights and then not release your bombs. If that happened, you faced the choice of making another pass, very likely getting your ass shot off, or jettisoning the bombs and slinking home feeling like an incompetent jerk.

The trees were thinning out. Beneath the nose of his A-4C Skyhawk Ferrone could see open space, the reflection of light on water, rice paddies in the distance.

And something else.

He squinted through the thick flat windshield. He saw movement ahead, dark and squiggly, like insects swarming on a mound.

Troops. Hundreds of them on one of the narrow oxcart paths. They were diving in each direction from the oncoming jets. A battalion, maybe a regiment of North Vietnamese infantry, headed for the war in the South.

Ferrone glimpsed flashes among the swarming insects, tiny winks of fire. The little bastards were shooting at him! It wasn't a serious threat—at least not when you were moving at 770 feet per second directly over their heads. Only the luckiest of shots could hit a—

Thunk.

Someone got lucky.

"Razor Lead," called Ken Schulze, his wingman. "I see you streaming. Fuel or hydraulics or something."

Ferrone glanced at the elapsed time. Ten seconds to go. He'd make the pull-up, drop his bombs, get the hell out. Then he'd deal with the fluid leak.

Five seconds.

Something was wrong. The control stick was frozen. Ferrone tugged on the stick with his right hand. It wouldn't budge. He couldn't get the nose up.

The Skyhawk was still level, flying directly at a hillside.

"Pull, Joe!" came Schulze's voice. "We're at the pull-up."

Ferrone was too busy to reply. Nothing would move the jet's stuck elevator. The trim switch wasn't working either. The goddamn hydraulics were gone, and so was the motor that moved the horizontal stabilizer.

The trees on the hillside were rushing at him. With his left hand he grabbed for the emergency electric elevator override trim.

It worked. The Skyhawk's nose was inching upward.

But not fast enough. Ferrone felt the whap of the treetops on the lower fuselage. He winced, thinking of the three-hundred-

gallon drop tank and the two outboard racks of thousand-pound bombs.

Nothing exploded. The Skyhawk's nose was tilting upward. *Go for altitude,* Ferrone told himself. *Get this thing under control and head for the water.*

The Skyhawk was climbing through two thousand feet. He couldn't budge the stick, but the aileron trim switch on the top of the stick still worked. He reached for the striped handle under the console and yanked. With a lurch, his bomb racks and half-full fuel tank departed the Skyhawk, making the jet instantly two tons lighter. As soon as he'd gotten some altitude, he'd yank the other handle—the hydraulic control disconnect—and that would give him manual control of the jet.

In his peripheral vision he caught a red light flashing on his panel. The radar warning. An air defense radar was targeting him.

Then a growl in his headset. An SA-2 surface-to-air missile was in the air.

"SAM launch, Joe! You've got one coming at you."

A black oily burst of flak exploded just to the left of the Skyhawk's nose. And then another, directly ahead. Ferrone gritted his teeth and tried to hunker down in his seat. Another roiling black burst appeared just to the right of his nose. An instant later he felt the concussion of the blast.

Close, but not a hit.

"Break left, Joe! The SAM's got you bore-sighted."

Ferrone tried to turn the jet. The stick was still frozen, as if it were buried in cement. He was reaching for the hydraulic disconnect handle beneath the console when he felt the explosion. It came from behind. The impact slammed him sideways in the seat, rapping his helmet against the hard Plexiglas.

"You're on fire, Joe!"

The Skyhawk was in a left roll, spiraling toward the earth. Even with the hydraulic controls disconnected, Ferrone was unable to move the stick. The jet was shedding parts.

He tried to reach the handle of the face curtain to fire the ejection seat, but he couldn't raise his arms. The jet's hard rolling movement had him pinned to the side of the cockpit.

Ferrone fought against the panic that swelled up in him. A kaleidoscope of colors whirled across his canopy. Mottled green earth, blue sky, puffs of cloud and flak, green earth again. His right hand groped for the alternate ejection handle, a D ring between his legs at the base of the seat. The earth was whirling toward him.

The tips of his fingers found the handle.

Ferrone knew his body wasn't in the correct position to eject. He was slumped against the left side of the cockpit. His left arm lay on the console like a useless appendage. There was nothing he could do about it.

He pulled the ejection seat handle.

Time slowed to a crawl for Joe Ferrone. He felt as if he were watching a slow-motion movie. The Skyhawk's canopy lifted from its rail and vanished in the slipstream. A hurricane roar of windblast filled the cockpit.

He felt the rocket motor of the Douglas Rapec ejection seat fire. The seat ascended the rail and left the cockpit. The four-hundred-knot wind hit him like a wall of concrete. Ferrone had only a dim awareness of the seat separating, his body flailing like a rag doll. The main chute snapped open with a force that knocked him senseless.

He was at the end of a pendulum swing in the chute when he hit the ground. He landed stiff-legged, all his weight on his right foot. He felt something crack. A jolt of pain shot all the way up his leg.

Then he saw them. Dark figures moving across the paddies.

"Are you okay, sir?"

Ferrone blinked, still immersed in his thoughts. Trunh was standing in the passageway, giving him a worried look. The two ladies from the lobby were peering around the corner at him.

Ferrone's leg was throbbing. A film of perspiration covered his face.

"I'll be okay. It's a little warm in here, that's all."

"I'll get you something to drink. A cold tea, sir?"

"Sure. That'll be fine."

He was alone again. He continued down the passageway.

The place was different, he noticed. Neat and tidy. No stench from the cells. No roaches scurrying across the floors. No screams from the interrogation room.

On the second day they brought in an old man who examined Ferrone's dislocated arm. He took Ferrone's wrist and gave it a yank, twisted it, and reset the arm in its shoulder socket. The procedure lasted only a few seconds. Ferrone passed out from the blinding pain.

It worked. Within a few days he could use the arm again.

The broken leg was another matter. His right lower leg extended from the knee at an unnatural angle. They splinted it with a wooden stake, but it hadn't been reset. The fracture was in the tibia, below his knee. Any attempt to move his foot sent a storm of pain from his ankle to his pelvis.

Even this was endurable. By the time they reached Hoa Lo Prison—the place Americans called the Hanoi Hilton—he had learned to tolerate the pain. The fracture would mend, he told himself. Even if the leg took a slightly different geometry, at least he'd walk on it again. For the next two weeks he kept telling himself that.

Then they took him to the interrogation room.

The interrogator was a flat-faced man with rotten teeth and a right eye that strayed from where he was looking. Ferrone had a bad feeling about him.

"What carrier you fly from?"

Ferrone gave him his name, rank, and serial number.

Flat Face was not pleased. "What carrier? You answer me."

Again Ferrone gave him his name, rank, serial number. Flat Face barked an order to the guard, who came up behind

Ferrone and tightened his bindings, yanking his wrists high up behind his back. The sharp pain brought tears to his eyes.

"What carrier? Enterprise? Or another?"

The questions were just openers, Ferrone knew. By the markings on his downed jet, they had surely learned what ship he came from. They would even know his air wing and squadron. Maybe even the names of his wingmen.

Don't talk, he told himself. That was what they wanted, for him to start running his mouth. That was just the beginning. Then they would pump him for the real stuff.

Ferrone told Flat Face that he was bound by the Geneva Convention. He didn't have to answer questions other than his personal data. Torture was illegal.

Which further angered the interrogator. This time Flat Face himself tightened the bindings. With a two-handed yank he hauled Ferrone's wrists high behind his back. Each of Ferrone's arm sockets made a popping sound. He was unable to hold back a scream of agony.

"You not a prisoner of war," said the interrogator. He showed Ferrone a stack of black-and-white photos. They were pictures of bodies roasted by napalm, buildings reduced to rubble, children's corpses stacked like cordwood.

"You and your friends did this. You a war criminal, kill children and old people. You answer me and it will be much better for you."

Ferrone knew he couldn't hold out. The pain was nearly intolerable. Every man had his breaking point, and he was very near his.

But they would probably kill him anyway. The thought left him hopeless—and defiant. Get it over. Make them kill you.

"What carrier?" Flat Face demanded.

Ferrone peered up at Flat Face. "Fuck you," he said.

It was an unfortunate choice of words, he would reflect later. It was the spark that made Flat Face go crazy.

He watched with a dull fascination as the Vietnamese picked up a rusty, three-foot length of iron bar. It looked like *the kind used to reinforce concrete structures. Flat Face studied the bar, testing its heft, seeming to consider his next move. He raised the iron bar above his head, then hesitated for a full three seconds.*

Ferrone tried to scoot out of the way. He couldn't.

With a guttural yell, Flat Face brought the bar down. His aim was perfect. The iron bar smashed into Ferrone's right leg, just below the knee, at the precise spot where it had been fractured two weeks earlier.

Amid an exploding agony of fire and thunder, Joe Ferrone passed into unconsciousness, which was a blessing.

Trunh was waiting at the main entrance. The two ladies bowed again, giving him crinkly smiles and fluttering good-bye waves.

He stepped into the morning sunlight on Pho Hoa Lo Street. His limo and driver were there, parked amid the mopeds and three-wheeled cyclos.

So were the reporters, over a dozen of them, and a television crew. They snapped away with their digital cameras, asking him to pose here by the main entrance, over there by the sign, down the sidewalk by a barred window.

Ferrone obliged them. The ache in his leg was beginning to subside. He smiled and took their questions. Yes, he was pleased to be here in Hanoi. No, he had no feelings of hostility toward the Vietnamese people. Yes, he thought the U.S. and Vietnam should become allies.

The driver was holding the door of the limousine for him. As Ferrone was about to climb in, a woman came to him with a large bouquet of red and yellow flowers.

"A gift from our people," she said, bowing to him. "Thank you for coming back to Vietnam, Mister Ambassador."

CHAPTER 1

INCIDENT AT
WHITE TIGER

28,000 feet
South China Sea
0745 Sunday, 8 April

Flankers, thought Commander Bullet Alexander.

The images in the radar were still fuzzy, but he would bet on it. These guys were Chinese SU–27s—code-name Flankers. Fifth-generation twin-engine fighters. Four of them, low and fast, directly over White Tiger.

Three seconds later, the controller in the E-2C Hawkeye early-warning aircraft settled the matter. "Runner One-one, Sea Lord. Your bogeys are Flankers, overhead White Tiger." Then she added, "Weeds."

In the cockpit of his F/A-18, Alexander nodded his agreement. The Flankers were northeast of his own position, eighty miles away. "Weeds" meant they were at low altitude, probably making passes at White Tiger.

"Runner One-one confirms the Flankers," Alexander radioed. "Say our weapons status." He needed to know whether they were cleared to arm their air-to-air weapons.

For several seconds the controller didn't answer. Alexander knew she was checking with Alpha Whiskey—the Air Warfare Commander who was a two-star aboard USS *Ronald Reagan.*

"Runner, your weapons status is yellow and tight," the controller said.

Alexander shook his head. *Shit.* "Yellow and tight" meant there was a possibility of a threat but none was yet identified. His master armament switch was supposed to remain off. Alpha Whiskey was playing it safe. Don't get confrontational with our Chinese friends. Not until the little bastards had you in their sights.

"Runner One-one copies yellow and tight." He knew Alpha Whiskey was monitoring the frequency. He hoped the sarcasm in his voice came through. This was bullshit, giving the Flankers the first shot.

Alexander's flight had been vectored from their CAP— Combat Air Patrol—station over the *Reagan* toward White Tiger, the Vietnamese-owned, American-crewed oil drilling platform in the Spratly Island archipelago. The platform manager had transmitted a Mayday: Fighters with Chinese markings were making threatening passes over the installation.

Alexander took a quick glance over each shoulder. To his left he saw the gray outline of another F/A-18E Super Hornet, flown by Lieutenant Hozer Miller. Off his right wing was his second section, Lieutenant Commander Flash Gordon and Lieutenant B. J. Johnson.

He saw that Hozer was flying too far aft and wide. He made a mental note to mention it in the debriefing. Hozer Miller was an okay wingman, but he tended to be a smart-ass. Hozer needed a little training in humility.

But Hozer's attitude was not Alexander's primary concern. A more important question was inserting itself in Alexander's mind: *What do we do when we intercept the Flankers?*

The Rules of Engagement were clear. Don't engage Chi-

nese fighters. Don't light them up with your targeting radar.
Don't go nose hot—point your weapons toward them. Not
unless they do it first.

In other words, bluff.

The trouble with that, thought Alexander, was they didn't
know what these guys in the Flankers were thinking. All it
took was one testosterone-hyped Chinese fighter pilot with
a wild hair up his ass and they'd be the lead story on CNN
tonight.

Only three months had passed since Alexander took command of the VFA-36 Roadrunners embarked on USS *Reagan*. They had just been ordered out of the Middle East and
redeployed to the South China Sea. To Alexander and his
Roadrunners, weary of Middle East combat, it seemed like
a vacation. No more deep-strike missions, no close air support, no air-to-air intercepts.

Until today.

The U.S. had decided to back its old enemy, the Socialist
Republic of Vietnam, in a territorial dispute with the
megapower of the Far East, the People's Republic of China.
Like most such disputes in the twenty-first century, it was
over energy. Recent discoveries revealed that beneath the
Spratly Island archipelago, a cluster of tiny islands in the
South China Sea, lay the planet's fourth-largest deposit of oil.

Ignoring China's protests, Vietnam planted its flag in the
Spratlys. Their first drilling platform—White Tiger—had
just been constructed and was being operated under license
by Midland Petroleum, a U.S. energy conglomerate. Two
more Vietnamese platforms were under construction; more
were on the way.

Which made the Chinese furious. They had already
landed troops on the middle cluster of atolls and were claim-
ing ownership of the entire archipelago. The United
States—and the *Reagan* Carrier Strike Group—was trying
to keep the peace between the two sides. And it wasn't
working.

"Runner One-one," called the controller in the Hawkeye, "single group, bogey, twenty miles south White Tiger, nose hot, climbing."

Alexander squinted at his own display. *Nose hot.* Bad news. The Flankers knew Alexander's fighters were in-bound. The Chinese jets were turning to confront them.

Now what?

He glanced again at his wingmen. "Runners, Runner One-one, take wall."

There was no need for his wingmen to acknowledge. Alexander could see them moving into a wall formation—all four jets spread out abreast to maximize their firepower. Just in case.

"Runner One-one, Sea Lord. New weapons status. Red and free. Repeat, red and free."

Alexander felt his pulse quicken. Alpha Whiskey had finally decided he didn't want to lose any of his jets. "Runner One-one copies red and free." Then he transmitted to his flight "Runners gate." "Gate" meant to select full afterburner.

The flight of Super Hornets accelerated through Mach one, the speed of sound. Alexander toggled the master armament switch to ON.

Red and free. Cleared to engage. Cleared to fire.

"They're leaving," said Evans, the platform shift manager.

Weaver didn't answer. He kept the Zeiss field glasses trained on the last fighter as it skimmed eastward, only a couple hundred feet above the sea. The others were gone now. Maybe they weren't coming back.

Weaver was already feeling embarrassed for having transmitted the Mayday call. A buzz job by a few hot-dog Chinese fighter pilots wasn't a life-threatening emergency. But damn it, he was the OIM—Offshore Installation Manager. He was boss of the White Tiger platform, and it was his job to worry about these things.

In nearly thirty years of working offshore oil rigs, Buck

Weaver had seen his share of trouble: typhoons, tsunamis, ice storms. . . . In the Malacca Strait he had even encountered pirates. He blew them out of the water with grenade launchers and submachine guns. Running an offshore platform was a lot like commanding a warship. You had to have the right firepower.

But there was something about this new threat that unnerved him. When an outfit like China went after you, you didn't chase them away with a few automatic weapons. Sure, he was being paid heavy bucks for taking this job, but now he wished he had stayed back on the ranch in Odessa. Let the Viets and the Chinks fight over the oil. He was too old for this shit.

"Okay to bring the chopper in, Buck?"

Weaver lowered the glasses. He had nearly forgotten about the supply helo. When the Chinese fighters showed up, he'd ordered the helicopter—a Sikorsky S-61 from Cam Ranh Bay—to stay clear and wait for orders.

"Yeah, bring 'em in. The crisis is over."

Evans went back to his radio panel and picked up the microphone. Weaver heard him telling the chopper pilot to bring it in, that the landing deck was clear.

While he waited for the helo to come into view, Weaver peered out the glassed windows of his top deck command post and drummed his fingers on the control console. A quarter mile away, he could see the dark outline of the Vietnamese gunboat, and he could make out the figures on the deck watching them. The red Vietnamese flag with the gold star was clearly visible at the stern.

The gunboat was supposed to be there to protect them from the Chinese, but it just added to Weaver's uneasiness. Putting a Vietnamese warship out here was like sticking a cigar up a bull's ass. It was asking for trouble.

"Here comes the chopper," said Evans.

From the glassed-in top deck of the platform, Weaver and Evans had a panoramic view of the helipad and the approaching helo. The S-61 was a big bird, able to carry more than three tons of supplies or passengers. It was White Tiger's lifeline to home base.

Weaver kept his eyes on the helicopter. It occurred to him that he should call off the Mayday he had transmitted. The emergency was over. The U.S. Navy might even have scrambled rescue aircraft. He'd get around to it in a few minutes, after they'd recovered the chopper.

The helicopter was slowing almost to a hover, swinging around to approach the platform upwind. Weaver watched it closely. Something didn't look right.

"What was that?"

"What was what?" said Evans.

"Behind the helicopter. I thought I saw something." Weaver blinked against the morning glare off the sea. He had seen what appeared to be a blurry streak of light, then it was gone. Whatever it was, it had—

The helicopter exploded.

"What the fuck!" Evans cried out.

Weaver stood frozen in place, too stunned to react. He watched the orange ball of fire pulse outward from the engine compartment of the Sikorsky. The long fuselage folded behind the rotor hub. Pieces of shattered blades sliced like shrapnel across the water, clanging into the skeletal structure of the oil platform.

The front wheels of the destroyed helicopter caught the edge of the helipad. For what seemed an eternity to Buck Weaver, the wheels clung to the deck. He could see the stricken faces of the two pilots staring at him through the cockpit glass.

Then the flaming hulk rocked backward, slid down the side of the platform structure, and plunged inverted into the sea. Smoke and steam leaped from the surface. Within seconds the wreckage had vanished beneath the waves.

Weaver stared at the spreading oil slick where the helo had disappeared. "I don't believe this shit."

Something inside his numbed brain told him it wasn't finished, there was more. He forced himself to take his eyes off the carnage beneath the landing deck.

He gazed back out to sea.

The gunboat was scrambling into action. A rooster tail of spray was kicking up behind the boat's stern. Weaver saw sailors scrambling over the deck.

"What the hell do they think they're going to do?"

Weaver saw the boat's bow tilt high in the water as its powerful engines thrust it forward. The gunboat swung around and pointed directly toward the cloud of steam and smoke that marked the crash site of the helicopter.

Then it stopped. From beneath its waterline appeared a brilliant fireball. As if in slow motion, it levitated from the water. The boat's hull rose upward on a cascade of seawater. A column of fire and debris shot upward through the superstructure, cleaving the boat neatly in half. The long tapered bow pointed downward and dived beneath the surface. The aft section rotated backward and sank from view.

Weaver saw Evans staring at him. Neither man spoke. Evans looked like a man waiting for his own execution. And, thought Weaver, he probably was. They both were.

"Sound the emergency alarm," Weaver ordered. "Get everyone on deck."

Evans kept staring. He seemed paralyzed.

"Move, damn it! Sound the alarm."

Evans turned back to his console and pushed a red mushroom-shaped plunger. Klaxon horns blared from speakers mounted throughout the installation.

It would take several minutes, Weaver knew. Nearly a hundred men and women were working on the platform. They would be skeptical, unwilling to move in a hurry. Another damned drill.

Weaver thought that he should get on the radio, tell the world what was happening out here. Yeah, right. What the hell *was* happening? He had no fucking idea. Nothing was making sense. First the fighters buzzing them. Then the supply chopper blowing up. Then the gunboat.

What else?

In the next instant, he knew. From somewhere below came a muffled *whump*. He felt the deck lurch beneath him, nearly throwing him off his feet.

Another *whump*, followed seconds later by yet another.

The deck tilted at a steep angle. Weaver grabbed the edge of his console but he lost his grip. He felt himself sliding across the teetering deck, colliding with Evans and taking him with him. They slammed into the far bulkhead, which was now almost horizontal.

The floats are going, he realized. A mobile offshore platform rode on an array of undersea cylindrical floats. Without them, the rig would capsize.

Weaver tried to resist the panic that was seizing him like a wild animal. Dimly he sensed the windows crashing inward, a gush of seawater flooding the compartment. As the water enveloped him, he glimpsed Evans wildly flailing his arms, eyeballs bulging, trying to find air.

Weaver felt the pressure building in his ears. As consciousness slipped from him, he wished for the last time that he had not taken this damn job. He should have stayed in Odessa.

"Runner One-one, single group heavy, thirty south White Tiger, climbing, hot."

"Runner One-one, roger."

It was the same picture Bullet Alexander was seeing in his display. His fighters all had Dolly—radar-data-linked information—in the cockpits. Each pilot could see the others' speed, altitude, and heading. They could also see the four Chinese Flankers, whose tracks were being data linked from the Hawkeye.

The Chinese fighters were climbing and accelerating. Coming at them.

Alexander's RWR—radar warning receiver—began a steady chirping.

"Runner One-one spiked at twelve o'clock," he called. His RWR screen was showing the signature of a Phazotron Zhuk-M-S pulse Doppler radar.

The Flankers were targeting them.

Alexander didn't like this. It was four versus four, but in a matter of seconds the Flankers would have a near-certain kill probability with their Alamo or Archer missiles.

He made a private decision. At the first indication of a missile in the air, he was going to command a volley of AM-RAAM—Advanced Medium Range Air-to-Air Missile—shots. The supersonic, radar-guided AMRAAMs were the big equalizer. They were a fire-and-forget weapon. Alexander's flight would shoot, then go defensive against the incoming Chinese missiles.

Forty miles. Instinctively Alexander peered out through the windshield, trying to pick out the telltale dots of the Flankers. Still too far out. He saw only cumulus puffs and distant shadows of the Spratly atolls.

He went back to his situational display. The yellow datalinked images of the Flankers were marching like glowworms across the screen. Still coming at them, still—

No, they weren't. What was this? The picture was changing.

"Runner-One-one, Sea Lord," called the controller. "Tactical range now thirty-five miles. Bogeys in a turn, possible flanking maneuver west."

Alexander studied the display. Maybe they were just leaving. The closure rate of the merging fighters had abruptly reduced. The yellow images were flanking to the west, perpendicular to the track of the oncoming Super Hornets.

The glowworm tracks in the display continued their turn to the north. The Flankers were bugging out, returning to their base on Hainan Island.

Well, give them credit, thought Alexander. The ChiComs

were smartening up. Instead of starting a furball that would get their asses flamed, they were calling it a day.

"Runner One-one, Sea Lord. Take heading one-one-five for White Tiger, distance now sixty-five miles. Alpha Whiskey wants you to overfly White Tiger, check it out. They're not communicating."

Alexander acknowledged. No radio communications? Something wasn't right down there.

He had seen White Tiger a couple of times from the air. The big offshore platform stood out like a silo in a wheat field. You could spot it from fifty miles away.

The Flankers were exiting the sector. Alexander watched the yellow images squiggle toward the far edge of the display. There were no other threats in the White Tiger sector.

Or were there?

Just to be sure, he called the controller again. "Sea Lord, Runner One-one. Say the picture."

She came right back. "Picture clear, Runner. No contacts."

Alexander gave a terse acknowledgment. Okay, the picture was clear, meaning no threats were showing on the controller's screen. Pilots joked that the Hawkeye had scanners so sensitive they could detect birds crapping on a rock. The Hawkeye was also linked to the Purple Net, an integrated real-time feed from Navy EP-3 surveillance aircraft, Air Force RC-135 intelligence-gathering jets, and spy satellites.

So the threat sector was clear of bogeys. Something was still bothering Alexander. He felt a nagging uneasiness somewhere in the back of his brain.

He glanced around. His fighters were still spread out in a wall formation.

On his back radio, which was channeled to the squadron common frequency, he called his wingmen. "Runner One-three and One-four, detach and stay high, above ten thousand, keep us in sight. Hozer and I will drag the surface and have a look at White Tiger. Copy?"

"Runner One-three copies. Do we keep the switches hot, Bullet?"

Alexander thought for a moment. The Flankers were gone from the display. No more threats existed in the sector. Technically, they should go switches safe.

He still felt something tugging at his subconscious. Something about this he didn't like.

"Switches hot. Keep us covered, check for spitters." Spitters were unexpected intruders. It would be Gordon and Johnson's job to confront any Flankers who tried to rejoin the party.

"One-three copies, switches hot."

Alexander watched the two fighters on his right wing pull up and away from the formation. He glanced again at his display. They were forty miles from White Tiger's geographic coordinates. Nothing was showing yet on the radar. Peculiar, he thought. The platform should be making a distinct reflection on the radar.

He nudged the nose of his Super Hornet over, starting his descent to low altitude. He saw Hozer Miller's jet sliding to a loose formation on his left wing.

"Hozer, stay a quarter mile abeam and slightly high. Keep me clear of conflicts." Exactly *what* conflicts he didn't know. He only knew that wanted another set of eyes looking out for him.

Miller acknowledged.

Alexander's radar was painting the chain of tiny atolls directly ahead, hardly more than rocks sticking up in the water. He was even picking up a small rain shower to the right of the track. Still no platform. The thing was all metal. It ought to be glimmering in the radar like a giant reflector. And where were the ships that tended the platform?

Nothing. The screen was empty. *Damn*. Maybe they had the wrong coordinates.

Alexander stopped his descent at a thousand feet. Ten miles to White Tiger's position. Still no image on radar.

Alexander's feeling of uneasiness deepened.

He eased the jet down to two hundred feet. His speed was a comfortable three hundred knots. Slow enough to get a good look. Fast enough to be a difficult target.

He could see whitecaps on the surface. The water kept changing shades as he swept over the undersea ridges and peaks of the archipelago. A mist of salt spray collected on the windshield.

Three miles to White Tiger. It ought to be standing out on the horizon like a marquee sign. Maybe, thought Alexander, he got the coordinates wrong. Maybe he—

There was something in the water. He only caught a glimpse as he flashed over the spot. A sprawling oil slick, flotsam, a peculiar discoloration beneath the water.

"Sea Lord, Runner One-one. Confirm I'm over White Tiger's coordinates."

"We confirm, Runner. You oughta be right on top of the platform."

"I've got news, Sea Lord. It's not here."

Several seconds of silence passed. "Say again, Runner. It sounded like—"

"White Tiger's gone. There's oil and junk in the water, nothing else."

"Runner One-one, you should be seeing a sixty-foot-high offshore platform. There should also be a Vietnamese gunboat close aboard. Are you sure you're looking in the right place?"

"We passed directly over the coordinates. There's nobody home. We're coming back for another pass now."

Alexander pulled the nose of the Super Hornet up in a steep climbing turn, reversing to the right to swoop back down over the spot in the ocean. On his back radio he called Hozer Miller. "Stay high and outside, Hozer. We're gonna do this again. Let me know if you see anything."

"Two copies."

Alexander topped out at three thousand feet in his turn.

He craned his neck in each direction, scanning the flat gray surface of the ocean. He saw the dark humps of atolls, a scattering of cumulus clouds, a rain squall in the distance.

No platform. No gunboat.

Completing the turn, he nudged the nose downward again, swooping back toward the ominous slick on the water. He took a quick glance to make sure Hozer Miller's jet was in position off his left wing. He was.

And then he glanced again. *What was that?* For just an instant, he'd seen a shimmer, a bright blur behind Hozer Miller's jet.

It was gone, whatever it had been.

Alexander returned his attention to the flat gray sea ahead. They were descending again, swooping back down to the place where White Tiger was supposed to be.

In his peripheral vision he caught a flash. A reflection of orange glinted in his Plexiglas canopy.

Alexander swung his head to peer at Hozer Miller's jet. It was gone. In its place was a roiling fireball. Fragments of the Super Hornet's airframe were scattering like shrapnel. A trail of black smoke marked the jet's flight path.

"Eject! Eject!" Alexander called, but he knew in his gut it was too late.

CHAPTER 2

STOU

Hanoi, Socialist Republic of Vietnam
2145 Monday, 9 May

"How does it feel to be in the hot seat again, Skipper?"

Ambassador Joe Ferrone smiled at the image in the video-conferencing screen. He didn't know if he'd ever get used to hearing this guy call him "Skipper."

"Like old times, Mr. President. But when you offered me the job, you didn't tell me the seat would get hot so soon."

"We didn't know. We expected the Chinese to make a fuss, blow some smoke, do their usual saber rattling. This caught us off guard."

Ferrone knew better than to say what he really thought. Getting caught off guard was precisely what military commanders, including the Commander-in-Chief, were paid not to let happen. Someone in the chain of command—the intelligence czar, or the national security advisor, or even the secretary of defense—ought to have his balls kicked into the next congressional district.

"What's the official version of the loss of the Super Hornet off the *Reagan*?"

"Operational accident," said the president. "Cause not yet determined. We want to head off any speculating by the media."

Accident, my ass, thought Ferrone. "What about the oil platform? The Vietnamese lost a huge investment in White Tiger. Not to mention the gunboat and helicopter. And over a hundred people missing, half of them American."

"Accidents happen in the oil business too."

"Wars happen too. Especially in the oil business."

"Not on my watch. Not if I can prevent them."

"You may be too late, Mr. President. Both sides seem willing to blow the other away to get the Spratly oil deposits."

"That's your job. As the ambassador to the Socialist Republic of Vietnam, you have to keep our new ally from overreacting. Keep a lid on the affair while we persuade the Chinese to back off."

Ferrone nodded. "Does that mean we have hard evidence that implicates China?"

It took the usual several seconds for the satellite-relayed transmission to reach the White House. Ferrone saw the president furrow his brow, then turn away to consult someone not in view of the video cam. Ferrone guessed that it was Bradshaw, the national security advisor. Or maybe Watanabe, the White House chief of staff.

The president's face reappeared on the screen. "We're, uh, still checking that out."

"Yes, sir, I understand." No surprise. Whatever they knew or surmised about the involvement of the People's Republic of China in the destruction of the White Tiger oil platform, the Vietnamese gunboat, *A Longh,* or the downing of a U.S. Navy F/A-18 was not going to be discussed over the diplomatic channel.

"We're sending a team out there, Skipper. It will include some people you already know. They'll be aboard in a couple of weeks to help with your, ah, negotiations."

Ferrone knew better than to ask what kind of team or who

was on it. He'd learn soon enough over the Yellow Net, the secure intelligence link.

"Roger that, Beav— ah, Mr. President."

He saw the president grin. Several years before Hollis Benjamin took the oath of office as president of the United States, he had been a junior officer in Commander Joe Ferrone's A-7 squadron aboard USS *Kitty Hawk*. Because of the young officer's obsessive busyness, running about the ship performing multiple tasks at blinding speed, his squadron mates tagged him with the call sign "Beaver."

The name stuck. After Beaver Benjamin left the military to earn a postgraduate degree in international studies, he wound up working again for his old skipper, then Vice Admiral Joe Ferrone, in a Pentagon think tank. When Ferrone retired to join the National Security Council, he took Beaver Benjamin with him. Benjamin distinguished himself as a rising young star.

The party machine from Benjamin's home state of Florida spotted his potential and recruited him to run for Congress. After two terms in the House, Hollis Benjamin handily won a seat in the U.S. Senate. From there, his rise in national politics was meteoric. He became the vice-presidential candidate on the party's losing ticket. Four years later, he won the presidency in one of the closest elections in history.

Benjamin went on. "The country didn't elect me to get us in a Far East war, especially on the side of our old enemy." A wry smile crossed his face. "Hell, they barely elected me at all." Ferrone laughed while he extended his leg on the low stool before him. The goddamn right leg again. The aching had started the day he stepped off the plane in Hanoi, as if his tibia was remembering where it had been crushed forty years ago.

"They elected you to do the right thing," said Ferrone. "Putting the war behind us was the right thing to do."

"You and I know that. But there are still some vets out there who want me drawn and quartered because of the trade deal I signed with Vietnam."

Which is why you put me in this job, thought Ferrone.
Send an old jailbird who'd spent half a decade there.

"Including our friend, Senator Wagstaff?" said Ferrone.

"Especially Wagstaff. Who is not our friend, by the way.
He was raising hell on the floor again today, demanding a
full Senate hearing over our relations with Vietnam."

Ferrone knew Thad Wagstaff well. The senior senator
from Virginia was a crusty ex-Marine who would never for-
give anyone who supported the Socialist Republic of Vietnam. In Wagstaff's view, the U.S. should never have exited
Vietnam without leaving it a smoldering ruin. He regarded
President Hollis Benjamin and his appointee, Ambassador
Joe Ferrone, as collaborators with the enemy.

"Guys like Wagstaff are anachronisms," said Ferrone.
"The more they bluster about the war not being over, the
better it makes you look."

Ferrone could tell by the president's expression that he
didn't really agree. Hollis Benjamin was still in his first
term, and his public approval rating was stuck two points
south of fifty percent. The last thing his administration
needed was an undeclared war in the Far East.

He saw the president rise from his chair. "Give my regards to your lovely bride, Skipper."

"I will, sir," said Ferrone. "Kim will be pleased to hear
that you thought of her."

Ferrone's wife, Li Che Kim, was Vietnamese by birth.
She had been the head of the Australian trade delegation in
Washington when she and Joe Ferrone met. After a whirl-
wind romance, they had married only a month before Ferrone's assignment to Hanoi.

"Hold the fort, Skipper," said the president. "Help is on
the way."

"Yes, sir," said Ferrone. "I'll do my best."

He saw the president rise and leave. The image of his
empty seat remained on the screen for several more seconds,
then flickered and turned to snow.

Ferrone winced as he removed his leg from the stool. As he rose, he felt the familiar stab of pain just below his knee. He tried not to limp as he exited the videoconferencing room.

He reflected again on his conversation with the president. *Help is on the way.* What the hell did that mean?

U.S. Naval Strike and Air Warfare Center, Fallon, Nevada

Where was the MiG?

Maxwell swiveled his head, peering through the top of his Plexiglas canopy. *There.* The MiG-29 was still vertical, shedding energy as it neared the apogee of the vertical scissors.

Maxwell kept the long narrow snout of the F/A-18E pointed straight up. Even with the engines in full afterburner, the digital airspeed readout in the HUD—Head Up Display—was ticking downward.

240 knots.

Through the top of his canopy Maxwell kept his eyes locked on the Russian-built MiG-29—code-named Fulcrum. Against the glare of the afternoon sky, the Fulcrum looked like a sleek gray bat.

220 knots.

180 knots.

Maxwell could see the red-helmeted Russian pilot peering at him from two hundred meters away. The pilot was nursing the jet's nose back toward the horizon, balancing on the Fulcrum's big twin-finned tail as long as possible, trying to lock its weapons onto Maxwell's fighter.

The two jets were in the third cycle of a vertical scissoring duel, zooming upward on parallel paths, crossing noses and diving to recover energy, reversing on the bottom in a high-G pullout to climb once again.

The Russian pilot was good, Maxwell had to admit. Very good. The Fulcrum was an older, less sophisticated fighter than the American Super Hornet. In the hands of a skilled pilot, though, it was still a potent killer.

Maxwell glanced at the airspeed readout. One hundred fifty knots.

He saw the Fulcrum's nose slicing downward, out of energy. It was time to do what the Super Hornet did best: dance on its tail and pirouette.

Maxwell nudged the left rudder pedal and half-rolled the F/A-18 about its vertical axis. The big twin-engine fighter was nearly hovering, not flying, not yet tumbling out of control.

Careful, he reminded himself. *Keep it smooth.* An abrupt yank on the stick, a shove on the rudder, and the Hornet would drop from the sky like a falling safe.

He nursed the nose back toward the horizon. He could feel the airframe humming, protesting the lack of airflow over the thin wings. The two GE engines were rumbling at full thrust in afterburner.

Where was the Fulcrum? The Russian fighter had slid out of view, somewhere under his left wing. Maxwell rolled the Super Hornet farther until—

There. He had to give the Russian credit. The pilot was trying to stay away from the Super Hornet's bore sight, sliding beneath Maxwell's jet, getting the most from the Fulcrum.

But not enough.

Maxwell eased the F/A-18's nose toward the floor of the desert. He increased back pressure on the stick just enough to superimpose the glass of his HUD over the silhouette of the Fulcrum.

He heard the seeker head of the Sidewinder air-to-air missile growling in his ear. The missile was locked on to the MiG-29.

Time to close the deal.

"Fox Two," he called. It was the transmission for a heat-seeking missile launch. The missile on his rail was inert, but the seeker head still worked. "You're dead, Svetlana."

"I don't believe you," answered a woman's voice.

"It's on the HUD tape." The Super Hornet's onboard video recorder captured everything seen through the pilot's Head Up Display. "A bore-sight Sidewinder shot."

"You got lucky."

"It took me three crosses in the scissors to get a shot. I killed each of your colleagues right after the merge."

"I would like to discuss this exercise on the ground."

"We'll use the briefing room."

"Boring. Think of someplace more cozy."

Commander Brick Maxwell smiled inside his oxygen mask. The one-versus-one BFM—Basic Fighter Maneuvering—exercise with Major Svetlana Turin of the Russian Air Force was turning out better than he expected. Maxwell had flown against each of the six members of the visiting Russian Air Force team. Svetlana Turin was the best.

Think of someplace more cozy. Maxwell thought for a moment. Technically, instructors in the Top Gun school weren't supposed to fraternize with the female students. Especially with foxy Russian women students like Svetlana Turin, who had a set of blazing blue eyes and the body of a fashion model.

But technically, he wasn't really a Top Gun instructor. That was the cover job for Maxwell's assignment to STOU—the Navy's Special Tactical Operations Unit—which occupied an unmarked facility in a fenced-off portion of the Fallon air station.

Maxwell saw Svetlana's MiG sliding into position on his right wing. They were forty miles from Fallon, and it was not yet two o'clock in the afternoon. Back in the ready room, he'd finish the paperwork, being sure to give Major Turin high marks for situational awareness and tactical planning. Then a quick shower, change into civvies, debrief the mission.

"How about the club?" said Maxwell.

"Does that mean you're buying the drinks?"

"Sure." Maxwell liked the way this was going. "Maybe even dinner if you—"

"Forget the drinks," said a gruff male voice on the radio.

Maxwell froze. The voice was familiar. He had heard it before, and there was no mistaking that particular inflection.

"Ah, Battle-ax, is that you on the frequency?"

"Affirmative," said the gruff voice. "You can forget dinner too. Land your jet and get over to my office on the double."

"Battle-ax" was the call sign of Rear Admiral Red Boyce, who commanded STOU. That was Boyce: When he wanted something, he wanted it five minutes ago.

Maxwell looked over at the MiG-29, in a tight formation on his right wing. Major Turin had her oxygen mask off. She was shaking her head, gazing at him with those dazzling blue eyes. *Damn.*

"Sorry about that, Svetlana."

He saw her shoulders shrug. "Maybe later."

CHAPTER 3

DREAMLAND

PLAN Submarine Yuanzheng 67
South China Sea
0430 Wednesday, 11 April

Captain Wu Tsien-li could hardly believe his good fortune. "Bearing and range?" he asked.

"Zero-three-five, three thousand four hundred meters," answered the operator at the MGK-400EM digital sonar console. His voice had a high-pitched, nervous ring.

As well it should, thought Captain Wu. They were all nervous. When did a PLA Navy submarine last have the opportunity to sink an enemy vessel? Not since the war in the Taiwan Strait, and that was over before most of the PLAN submarine fleet could even put to sea.

Now this.

The freighter *Ha Long* was steaming eastward across the sunlit surface of the South China Sea as if it were a cruise ship filled with gawking tourists. A fat, unsuspecting target. She appeared to have no screening escorts, no destroyers sweeping the sea around her, no surveillance aircraft overhead.

No enemy submarines patrolling the vicinity. Or were there? Wu felt a wave of anxiety sweep over him. What if the

Americans had one of their attack submarines in the area? Could the passive sonar array aboard *Yuanzheng 67* detect it? What sort of response would an American submarine deliver?

Wu pushed the troubling thoughts out of his mind. He had gone over these same questions a hundred times while they tracked the plodding *Ha Long* from Cam Ranh Bay in southern Vietnam to this point in the South China Sea.

According to the briefing Wu received before leaving their home port in Xiangshan, the *Ha Long* was laden with concrete, steel framing, pipe, pumps—the material with which drilling rigs were constructed. The ship's destination was Mischief Reef, one of the islands in the Spratly group where Vietnam was exploring for oil.

Oil that the People's Republic of China desperately needed.

Wu's orders were clear:

> *Yuanzheng 67 will proceed to station outside Cam Ranh Bay, Vietnam, to intercept and track Vietnamese vessel* Ha Long. *During transit of South China Sea and before* Ha Long*'s arrival at destination in Spratly Island group, sink vessel. Take all measures to prevent detection by U.S. warship or aircraft.*

Wu felt a flash of patriotic pride as he thought of the great honor that had been given to him. As captain of the *Yuanzheng 67*, he would deliver a shock to the impudent Vietnamese.

Technically, of course, the *Ha Long* was not a Vietnamese vessel. Though it sailed under the flag of Vietnam, the freighter was owned by a commercial shipping company based in Galveston, Texas. Her crew was mostly American.

Another wave of excitement swept over Wu. Killing Vietnamese was one thing. Killing Americans was another. What were the consequences?

It didn't matter, he decided. Such matters were not the concern of a submarine captain. He had his orders.

The *Yuanzheng 67* was a Russian-built Project 636 Super Kilo class submarine, delivered to the PLA Navy only a year ago. China now had eight such submarines, but only the *Yuanzheng 67* and its sibling boat, the Yuanzheng 64, had combat-ready crews and operational MVU-110EM computerized fire-control systems.

Like all the Kilo class, the *Yuanzheng 67* was a diesel/electric boat, inferior in many respects to the big nuclear-powered boats of Russia and the United States. But the Kilo had one shining virtue that made it one of the deadliest submarines in the world. At a speed of less than five knots, it was virtually undetectable. The Kilo Class was the stealth craft of the sea.

At the combat information console, the operator called out the data. "Primary target bears zero-four-two, range three thousand, one hundred meters, tracking one hundred and ten, speed eight."

Wu acknowledged. He could feel his pulse rate accelerate. He turned to the planesman. "Ascend to periscope depth."

The planesman gave him a startled look. He hesitated, then said, "Aye, sir."

There was no need to use the periscope, but Captain Wu didn't care. This was too important a moment not to witness it with his own eyes. Anyway, there was no antisubmarine threat in the vicinity. He wanted to do this the traditional way.

It took nearly two minutes to reach the correct depth. The *Yuanzheng 67* was barely making forward headway, slipping through the water at less than three knots. Wu wanted to be certain that no passive sonar in the area would be able to detect them.

"Up scope," Wu ordered.

"Up scope."

It was possible, he realized, that a lookout on the *Ha Long* would spot the telltale object protruding above the waves. But not likely. What was more likely was that their radar would pick up the faint metallic return of the tip of the periscope.

Wu was not concerned. Even if they correctly perceived the danger, it was too late for the *Ha Long*.

He peered through the periscope, adjusting it to clear the waves, then rotating it through 360 degrees to observe the peripheral area.

All clear. He fixed the scope on the target.

"Ready tubes one and two."

"Tubes one and two ready, Captain."

Wu took his time, fascinated by the sight of the plodding, broad-sided shape of the freighter. He could see the rust on her sides, the red Vietnamese flag, the freshly painted lettering on her bow: *Ha Long*.

"Fire one! Fire two!"

"Firing one and two."

A shudder passed through the hull of the *Yuanzheng 67*. There were two deep thuds, one after the other, as the YU-4 torpedoes left the tubes.

Wu waited. He knew it was a violation of tactical doctrine to remain where he was, periscope extended. He was supposed to retract the scope, order a moderate speed descent to below the thermal level, then transition to a minimum-detectability mode.

Not yet. He and the *Yuanzheng 67* had just made history. Everything that happened in his life after this would be anticlimactic.

It took less than two minutes. The YU-4s, adapted from the Russian SAET-60 torpedo, were passive guidance weapons. They moved at forty knots.

The first took the *Ha Long* in her forward quarter. A second later, the next torpedo struck her amidships. Each blast sent a roiling cascade of flame and smoke upward from beneath the waterline.

Wu was riveted to the periscope. In his wildest fantasies he had not imagined such a sight. It was glorious! The freighter was exploding like a New Year's firecracker, rolling onto her starboard side, spouting showers of fire and debris.

It was over in minutes. The *Ha Long*'s hull folded in the middle. In a final gush of smoke and steam, the freighter slipped beneath the surface. The last section to go was the bow with the white-lettered *Ha Long* still visible.

"Should we descend, Captain?" asked the planesman.

Wu stared at the sailor as if seeing him for the first time. He blinked, then returned his attention to the control room.

"Lower periscope," Wu ordered. "Descend to a hundred meters, moderate rate."

"Aye, sir," said the planesman, looking relieved. "One hundred meters, descending moderate rate."

Wu still felt giddy from the rush of adrenaline. He had never killed before, and he found himself savoring the experience. He understood why warriors loved war. It was the visceral satisfaction you received from seeing at close range the death throes of your enemy.

Best of all, thought Captain Wu, he had accomplished the task without being detected.

USS Daytona Beach, *South China Sea*

"That sonofabitch," said Commander Al Sprague. "He's enjoying himself."

"Yes, sir," said the sonar operator, seated at his console. "Looks like he's starting a slow descent now."

"About time. The bloodthirsty bastard could have fired just by sonar, but he didn't. He hung around to watch his victim go down."

"I show the *Ha Long* breaking up. Looks like she's in three pieces now, still going down."

Sprague nodded, trying to suppress his anger. He would love nothing so much as to put an MK 48 into the hull of the murdering Chinese Kilo.

Al Sprague was the commanding officer of USS *Daytona Beach*, SSN-776, a seven-thousand-ton, three-hundred and sixty-foot long nuclear-powered 688(i) fast-attack subma-

rine. At his disposal was enough firepower—MK 48 torpedoes, Tomahawk missiles, Harpoon ship killers—to not only
blow the Kilo to hell but to devastate half the Chinese navy.

But Sprague's orders were explicit: *Intercept, tag, and
shadow PLA Navy Kilo class Yuanzheng 67. DO NOT*—the
emphatic wording was added by COMSUBPAC, the two-star
in Hawaii who commanded all the Pacific Fleet submarines—
*DO NOT interfere with subject Kilo's engagement of foreign
national flagged vessels. Do not engage any PLA units unless
threat is imminent.*

And that was the part that was now causing Sprague the
most discomfort. The little bastards had just murdered upward of a hundred people and now they were leaving the
scene of the crime.

Sprague's orders had omitted any mention of actions he
was to take—or not take—on behalf of the survivors. Only
that he was to keep the Kilo tagged, and now the Kilo was
getting out of Dodge.

Shit. Now what?

Less than a minute later, the Sonar Officer, Lieutenant
Jessup, answered Sprague's question. "Contacts inbound,
Skipper. Two of them, bearing one-one-zero, eleven miles."

"What does the computer show?" Sprague asked.

"Shallow draft. Patrol boats, by the screw noise. Looks
like they're coming out of Mischief Reef."

"Vietnamese," said Sprague. "They'll pick up survivors." *If
there are any.* The *Ha Long* had blown up like a hand grenade.

Well, thought Sprague, at least he wouldn't spend the next
ten years having nightmares about the victims he left floating in the South China Sea. He could stay with the Kilo, stay
passive, keep SUBPAC updated on the Kilo's position. And
maybe, if there really was a God, sooner or later he'd get the
chance to shoot *Yuanzheng 67.*

"Sierra One tracking three-fifty, sir. Depth one-forty,
speed five knots."

Sprague nodded. Sierra One was the sonar designator

they assigned to the Kilo when they first picked it up off Cam Ranh Bay.

"Come left three-twenty. Ahead four knots. I want to stay ten thousand yards offtrack and keep him tagged from a safe distance."

"What if he catches on that we're tailing him?" asked Jessup.

"That's when the fun begins. He might do something stupid."

"Like what?"

"Like take a shot at us."

"What then?"

Sprague drew a finger across his throat. "Then we sink the sonofabitch."

Groom Lake Research Facility, Nevada

Maxwell stared at the sprawling base. The Groom Lake complex—called Dreamland by those who worked there—was the most closely guarded research facility in the United States. The 27,000-foot runway didn't appear on navigation charts or airport directories. Since the early 1950s, almost every ultrasecret U.S. military aircraft—the U-2, F-117, B-2— had been developed and tested at Groom Lake.

Maxwell was still simmering over the canceled evening with Svetlana Turin. Boyce had not offered any explanation, only that they were paying a little visit to Dreamland. The flight from Fallon down to Groom Lake had been in near silence. Maxwell occupied the backseat of the F/A-18F, letting Boyce do all the flying while he made all the radio transmissions. When you flew with Boyce, you always got the backseat.

They were met at the ladder of their F/A-18 by armed security guards and escorted to the screening section. Groom Lake had the most sophisticated security equipment outside the Cheyenne Mountain Complex in Colorado. There were retinal identification devices, ultrasound scanners, metal detectors so sensitive they could read the iron content in a subject's blood.

From the screening section they were led to Hangar 501, a warehouse-sized building on the north edge of the long concrete ramp. Maxwell remembered the building: He had been assigned here on a secret stealth jet project during his test pilot days.

After another ID check at the door, they entered the hangar. The cavernous building was nearly empty except for the object in the middle of the floor.

Maxwell stared at the apparition. The strangely shaped object—it didn't resemble an airplane at first glance—squatted in the middle of the huge hangar like a hulking predator, all angles and facets and blurred features.

"Look familiar?" said Boyce.

Maxwell nodded. "The Black Star. But it's changed."

"Of course it's changed. How long's it been? Six years?"

"Closer to eight."

"Stealth research is an ongoing project here. These guys have been busy."

Slowly Maxwell walked around the diamond-shaped aircraft. From the front, it looked like a wedge. A wedge with sharp edges. Despite the harsh fluorescent glare from the overhead lights, there was no reflection from the lead-gray surface.

It had grown in size since he flew the prototype. The wings were longer, giving it more lifting surface. The jet looked like a reversed kite, with an extended triangular frontal area, and a shallower, delta-shaped aft section.

He noticed that it had landing flaps, which the prototype lacked. The engine inlets were longer and thinner, little more than slits. Same with the exhausts. Almost no infrared signature.

Boyce followed him around. "It has upgraded engines," he said. "Almost twice the thrust of the prototype."

Which it needed, remembered Maxwell. The prototype lacked the thrust to go vertical in a one-vee-one—one fighter versus another.

He knelt on one knee to inspect the underside of the jet.

The belly was slick. No inlets, rivets, or any other protuberances. Zero radar return.

The Black Star's most peculiar feature was that it had no tail. Its directional stability came from computer-commanded spoiler surfaces in the aft section of each wing. Without the fly-by-wire flight control computer, the stealth jet was aerodynamically unstable. It would tumble through the sky like a tossed brick.

"Note the longer and broader control panels," said Boyce. "The flight control computer has a different logic, with more authority. They say the thing has an improved turn rate and a higher G limit."

Which it also needed, thought Maxwell. As a fighter, the Black Star prototype was a dog. He remembered that in a classic hard-turning, G-pulling fight, it bled energy at a horrifying rate. But dogfighting agility wasn't a design priority in a stealth fighter.

Maxwell was still a lieutenant then. He was one of three test pilots on the Black Star prototype. Because of the intense security that veiled the program, each pilot was responsible for a specific area of testing. They didn't compare notes, and none was familiar with the others' test results.

Maxwell's assignment was to test the Black Star's combat maneuvering envelope. Operating mostly at night, he flew the jet through maximum-rate turns, high- and low-speed buffet, accelerated stalls and departures from stable flight, sustained high-angle-of-attack maneuvering.

There was much he didn't know about the Black Star. He had already figured out that it was a potent night air-to-surface attack aircraft, and despite its subsonic performance limits, its radar-elusive design would make it a dangerous air-to-air killer.

He still hadn't learned what made the Black Star the most potent fighter in the world.

On a predawn test flight he was returning to Groom Lake. He was at 1,500 feet, flying down the length of the runway, about to turn downwind and land. In the pale light he glimpsed the shape of the second test aircraft taking off. Never before had he actually seen another Black Star in flight.

He rolled into a turn, keeping his eye locked on the departing jet. As far as he knew, all the Black Star test flights had been conducted in the hours of darkness. It was nearly daylight. Why were they exposing the nation's most closely guarded secret to viewers on the nearby mountain ridges?

And then it happened. The Black Star disappeared.

Maxwell blinked. He thought he had lost it in the gloom of the desert landscape. It would reappear any second. But it didn't. The Black Star had vanished. Gradually the truth dawned on him. He knew why the Black Star was more deadly than any other radar-elusive stealth jet in the world.

It was invisible.

Maxwell abruptly looked up from the shimmering jet in the floodlit hangar. An inner alert was sounding in his brain. Boyce hadn't dragged him down here to show the latest development in stealth technology.

He looked at Boyce. The admiral was gnawing on an unlit Cohiba, wearing the expression he always wore when he was holding back tantalizing information.

"Okay, Admiral. What's it all about?"

"I thought you'd have figured it out by now."

"Give me a clue."

"Look at the Black Star again. Tell me what's *really* different about it."

Maxwell looked again. He had already observed the bigger control surfaces, the stretched wings, the landing flaps. The flaps would allow it to land at a reduced speed.

So what? Every modern jet had flaps. Why would a slower approach speed be a—

He saw Boyce give a signal with his arm. He heard a whirring, the sound of a hydraulic motor. From the aft lower fuselage a seamless panel slid open. A long, striped object lowered to the deck. It looked like a stinger, with a flange on the end.

Maxwell knew what he was seeing. *A tailhook*.

He understood why he was at Groom Lake. And he could guess where he was going.

"What ship?"

"You'll find out in the briefing," said Boyce. He glanced at his watch. "Come on. We're running late."

They headed for the security door. Maxwell looked back over his shoulder at the gray aircraft. "Has anyone actually landed one of those on a carrier?"

"Yeah. You."

"That wasn't a Black Star, it was a Chinese knockoff. And it didn't have flaps or a tailhook."

"They did all the carrier suitability tests here at Groom Lake. The Black Star met all the requirements. Hell, with the flaps, the thing has an approach speed of about a hundred and thirty-seven knots, no more than a Super Hornet. They tell me it's ready to deploy aboard ship."

Maxwell nodded. He noted that Boyce hadn't actually answered the question, which meant that the Black Star had *not* been landed aboard a carrier. The suitability tests were on a simulated deck and field-mounted arresting gear and catapults. It had all been done at night here in Nevada, away from prying eyes and cameras.

"Ah, deploy to where, Admiral?"

Boyce seemed not to hear. They were walking across the sprawling tarmac ramp. The harsh Nevada sun was hovering over the crest of Freedom Ridge, to the west of Groom Lake. Long shadows fell from the rows of slab-sided buildings along the ramp.

Maxwell's mind was processing this latest news. *Ready to deploy aboard ship*. The U.S. Navy was down to eleven attack carriers, with only seven currently deployed. That could mean the Middle East, the Indian Ocean, the South China Sea. Maybe West Africa. Or some other garden spot he hadn't yet heard about. Boyce was being Boyce again, delivering information one snippet at a time.

Maxwell glanced at his watch. The image of Svetlana Turin's dazzling blue eyes appeared in his mind. They could get back to Fallon before dark. She might even still be at the club.

Their escort was a bristle-headed Air Force captain who wore a holstered Beretta and a sour expression. He led them to a two-storied building with covered windows. The sign over the door read STATISTICAL ANALYSIS LAB.

"What statistics are we going to analyze?" said Maxwell.

"Signs here don't mean anything. You'll see."

Another ID check and a retina scan, then they were allowed past the security enclosure, into a long passageway. The Air Force captain escort stayed with them, still showing not a trace of expression. They ascended a flight of stairs, then went down another passageway. At the end was a security door and another scanning machine.

The door swung open. Maxwell blinked in the bright artificial light. The room had no windows. A row of display screens lined one wall, and a long table filled the center of the compartment. On one bulkhead was a large screen on which a map was projected. A pattern of symbols and arrows were arranged on the map.

Maxwell went to the screen. He stared for a moment at the symbols and arrows and the geographic region. The symbols on the screen were of warships. They were arranged around a flat-topped image with the tag: CVN-76.

He caught Boyce watching him, still wearing that smug expression. Maxwell looked again at the screen. The pieces were falling into place. He recognized the symbols. They represented a Carrier Strike Group, led by the USS *Ronald Reagan,* CVN-76. And he recognized the islands and land masses on the map.

The South China Sea.

His thoughts were interrupted by a female voice behind him. "You're ten minutes late for the briefing, gentlemen. Don't let this become a habit."

CHAPTER 4

BULLDOG

Groom Lake Research Facility, Nevada
1610 Tuesday, 10 April

She looked over the late arrivals. The older man, the one with wispy red hair and cigar butt in his hand, was giving her an imperious gaze.

"I'm Dr. Dana Boudroux," she said. "Director of Operations, Electrochromatic Programs."

"Boyce," said the man with the cigar. "Commander, Special Tactical Operations Unit."

For a moment they locked glances, neither showing the slightest bit of deference. Then she noticed the star on each shoulder of his flight suit. An admiral? She hadn't expected anyone of that rank. She was told only that a couple of Navy pilots were coming down for the briefing. He didn't look like an admiral. More like some middle-aged salesman you'd meet at a bar.

"And this is Brick Maxwell," said the admiral, nodding to his taller, younger companion. "Detachment commander."

She nodded her acknowledgment, not bothering to shake hands, not asking what kind of detachment. That was something she had learned about hotshot fighter pilots. They always expected you to go wobbly-kneed and google-eyed in their presence. She knew better. Never give the cretins any reason to think you're impressed by them.

The younger one, Brick something—where did they get these asinine names?—wasn't bad looking. The oak leaves on his shoulder meant that he was a Navy commander. He was tall with a craggy but handsome face and a quizzical smile.

They wore sweaty flight suits with the usual set of flashy patches and leather name tags. Typical fighter pilots, full of themselves, still playing high school games with letter jackets and the silly patches.

"We've been looking at the Black Star," said Boyce. "I wanted Commander Maxwell to see how it's been modified since he test-flew it seven years ago."

She nodded, registering the information but keeping her thoughts to herself. So this one was a test pilot. He must have been here when she first arrived back in the early days of Calypso Blue, the supersecret stealth jet program. He might even have known Frank.

Or maybe not. That was the nature of the stealth program. Outside your own area of responsibility, you didn't know who was working on what. There was a good reason for it, after the original stealth technology had been compromised by a turncoat engineer.

But those were the old days. They were past the research phase. Now it was time for the Black Star to go operational.

She made a show of glancing at her watch. "We're late, gentlemen. I suggest we begin the briefing."

Washington, D.C.

"Have a sandwich, Senator? Those are tuna, and this is ham salad."

"I've already had lunch," said Thad Wagstaff.

"Coffee?"

"Never drink the stuff."

Hollis Benjamin shrugged and poured himself a coffee, then helped himself to a sandwich. Good old Wagstaff, he thought. He was his usual self this morning, meaning that he was a disputatious, supercilious asshole.

Benjamin busied himself with his tuna sandwich while he tried to think of a way to soften up Wagstaff. They were in the Cabinet Room, though none of the cabinet members were present except Dick Greenstein, the secretary of defense. Also at the table was General Gerald Matloff, the Marine four-star who chaired the Joint Chiefs. Half a dozen staffers sat with their notepads a few places removed from the main players.

These one-on-one lunch chats usually worked for Benjamin. Much of his political success was because of his famous ability to disarm the most contentious adversaries with his personal charm. Beltway veterans called it the Benjamin Effect. Hollis Benjamin, they liked to joke, could whack your legs off at the knees and have you thanking him for bringing the floor closer to you.

Well, maybe there was some truth to it, reflected Benjamin, but in the case of Senator Thad Wagstaff, the Effect wasn't working. The senior senator from Virginia was showing no sign of being charmed. If anything, he was being a greater pain in the ass than usual.

General Matloff was giving Wagstaff an update on the situation in the South China Sea. Bringing Matloff along had been Secretary Greenstein's idea, and Benjamin saw now that it was a smart play. Matloff, being a Marine general, could squeeze a certain amount of respect out of Wagstaff, who had been a Marine infantry officer and still looked the part. Wagstaff was a thick-necked man, heavy in the shoulders, with close-cropped white hair and a set of blazing dark eyes that he aimed like lasers.

Matloff finished telling Wagstaff about the Chinese capture of Swallow Reef atoll, in the Spratly Islands.

"What I want to know," said Wagstaff, "is why in the hell we are even remotely concerned about a goddamn reef in the South China Sea."

"Because it could ignite a war between Vietnam and China. It's in our best interest to prevent such a thing."

"And you're telling me, General, that you've sent the *Reagan* into the middle of this pissing contest?"

"Not exactly in the middle," said Matloff. He was a slim, bespectacled officer with a bristly haircut that was even shorter than Wagstaff's. "We have always kept a strike group deployed in the region when tensions are high. Just to discourage the Chinese—or anyone else—from doing something reckless."

"General, my position on this matter has not changed. What we should do is get the hell out of there and let the Chinks finish what we lacked the balls to do thirty years ago. Let them bomb Hanoi back to the Stone Age."

Matloff frowned, unable to contain his dislike of the pugnacious senator. Benjamin forced himself to laugh, just to keep the discussion from getting too serious. Wagstaff was wearing his trademark bulldog expression, signaling that he was ready for combat.

On a personal level, Benjamin had never liked Wagstaff, and he had no doubt that the feeling was mutual. He considered Wagstaff to be an unpleasant, quarrelsome man who made it his life's work to impede every progressive idea in Congress. But there was no denying that the man had earned the right to his opinions, blockheaded as they were. Wagstaff had distinguished himself as a platoon commander during the siege of Khe San, earning a purple heart and a silver star. An embittered war veteran, Wagstaff came home to run for a congressional seat against an incumbent whose credentials included burning his draft card and heading a group called Americans for Nuclear Disarmament. After winning a narrow victory, Wagstaff spent the next thirty years fortifying his position both in Virginia and Washington.

Now he headed the powerful Senate Armed Services

Committee. The wrath of Wagstaff would be directed like a high-yield nuke on anyone, journalist or educator, liberal or conservative, congressman or president, who dared propose a cutback in military readiness. The same wrath would descend on any fool who favored relations with a communist state, particularly one with whom the U.S. had waged eight years of warfare.

"Fifty-eight thousand," said Wagstaff.

Benjamin blinked, returning his thoughts to the breakfast table. He looked at Wagstaff. "Excuse me? Fifty-eight thousand what?"

"Lives," snapped Wagstaff. "American lives. In case you need reminding, that's how many we lost in Vietnam. And if I'm hearing correctly, your administration wants to kiss and make up and pretend it never happened."

Benjamin recognized that familiar deprecating tone in Wagstaff's voice. He forced a smile and said, "I happen to agree that Vietnam was a great tragedy. We shouldn't pretend it never happened, but we should put history behind us."

"If you were a veteran like I am, Mr. President, you would not be so eager to embrace the Vietnamese communists."

Benjamin felt a flash of anger. He gave it a beat, composing himself. "I'll remind you that I *am* a veteran, Senator Wagstaff. The Vietnam War was before my time, but I did serve my country for eight years as a naval officer and aviator."

"Then you should be talking like a veteran instead of a peacenik."

"Not all veterans think the same as you. As you know, Admiral Joe Ferrone, whose war record is as impressive as your own, strongly supports relations with Vietnam and is our new ambassador there."

Wagstaff shook his head. "Something happened to Ferrone. He spent too many years as a prisoner. They must have done something to his head. He's been brainwashed into sleeping with the enemy."

Again Benjamin forced himself to hold back his anger.

Wagstaff was looking for a fight, and Benjamin was almost ready to give it to him. But not yet.

"The Vietnam War was a lesson for the U.S. I want to make sure that we don't repeat the mistake."

"The lesson from Vietnam is that we should never to go to war without the will to achieve total victory."

"Perhaps, Senator. But after our total victory over Germany and Japan in World War Two, we became economic partners with both countries, to everyone's mutual advantage. Doesn't it make sense to do the same with Vietnam?"

Wagstaff shook his head. "We reduced Berlin and Tokyo to rubble before we helped them rebuild. That's exactly what we should have done to Hanoi. Turn the place into a parking lot before we ever considered doing business with them."

"After World War Two, we were in a contest with the Soviet Union. We needed the backing of Germany and Japan."

"The Cold War's over," snapped Wagstaff. "What's that got to do with your sucking up to a commie country like Vietnam?"

"For a similar reason, Senator. The People's Republic of China has replaced the Soviet Union as our greatest economic and military rival. We need partners like Vietnam to maintain balance in the Far East."

"Balance?" Wagstaff snorted. "Is that this administration's secret buzz word for 'oil'? The oil deposits in the South China Sea perhaps?"

Benjamin exchanged glances with Greenstein. Greenstein gave him a barely perceptible head shake. *Don't go there.*

"No," said Benjamin. This was not a time for complete candor. Not with Senator Thad Wagstaff. "The matter of the Spratly Island oil rights is strictly between Vietnam and China. The U.S.'s only role in the dispute is to ensure that neither side uses military force to seize the oil."

"And how are you going to ensure that?" said Wagstaff. "By siding with your new best friend, Vietnam?"

"That's one possibility."

"If we're worried about China violating international law, why not just impose trade sanctions on them?"

"Sanctions don't work. Not with an eight-hundred-pound gorilla like the People's Republic of China. China only responds when confronted with force."

At this, Wagstaff slammed his fist down on the table, jiggling his water glass and sending a notepad scooting over the edge. "Damn it, Mr. President, you don't have the authority to commit U.S. forces to combat over there. Not without my committee's oversight and not without the approval of Congress."

Benjamin nodded, keeping a mask of sincerity on his face. The words of his old mentor, Joe Ferrone, came to him. *If you can't dazzle 'em with brilliance, baffle 'em with bullshit.* It was time for a little bullshit.

"There are several contingency plans on the table, Senator, but no commitment has been made. You can be assured that we would not undertake any military action without the advice and consent of your committee."

Across the table, Benjamin saw Greenstein's eyeballs roll. Matloff was studying some object on the far wall.

Wagstaff took a long drink of water. By his narrow-eyed expression he showed that he wasn't buying it, at least not all of it. He shoved his chair back from the table.

"I'll hold you to that promise." He rose, and two of his aides at the far end of the table jumped to their feet. "In the meantime, know that the ghosts of fifty-eight thousand Americans are counting on you to remember their sacrifice."

"I'll remember, Senator."

Wagstaff nodded to Greenstein and Matloff, who were standing. "Excuse me, gentlemen, I've got work to do."

Benjamin waited until he was gone. He looked around the table. Matloff had stopped staring at the wall and was busy drumming his fingers on the table. Greenstein was rubbing the bridge of his nose with a thumb and forefinger.

"Well?"

"He'll find out," said Greenstein. "Wagstaff has sources everywhere."

"And then what?"

"The proverbial waste matter makes contact with the rotor blades."

"What's the problem?" said Benjamin. "There's plenty of historical precedent for a president authorizing covert military operations. Is that a big deal?"

The secretary shrugged. "Not if it works. You're a hero and you get reelected. If it doesn't work, you're a schmuck and Wagstaff calls for your impeachment. No big deal."

Groom Lake Research Facility, Nevada

Maxwell yawned.

The intelligence briefing had gone on for nearly an hour. The woman scientist, Dr. Boudroux, seemed to be in charge. There were two briefing officers, both civilians. Their names had not been offered, but their demeanor and dress bore the unmistakable mark of the CIA—button-down oxford shirt, khaki slacks, clunky black wingtips.

Maxwell looked across the row of seats and found himself locking eyes with Dr. Boudroux. The research scientist seemed to be appraising him, regarding him over the tops of her narrow glasses.

He returned her gaze. He wondered why she had been so snotty. As if she hated men, or maybe it was just men in flight suits. Maybe it was just a facade.

Maxwell tried smiling at her. She didn't smile back. Okay, maybe it wasn't a facade.

Boyce cleared his throat and interrupted the briefing officer. "In other words," he said, "you're saying this whole damn thing is about oil."

A pained expression passed over the briefer's face. "No, Admiral. Not exactly."

The other briefer said, "It has to do with balance of power." He was a round-faced man with rimless spectacles. "Denying China the right to seize any asset it wants in Southeast Asia."

"Even if the asset happens to be an oil field that's also being seized by Vietnam?"

The briefers exchanged glances. "That's a judgment that goes beyond this level of discussion."

Boyce snorted and inserted his unlit cigar back in his mouth.

"Let me repeat," said the first briefer. "There will be no open provocation of Chinese military units. Our rules of engagement allow only covert operations, meaning Black Star stealth aircraft, certain submarine activity, or special-ops forces operating clandestinely."

"So we're going to engage their invisible jets with our invisible jets," said Boyce.

"Only as a last resort," said the briefer with the rimless glasses. "The objective is to discourage the Chinese from making any further aggressive moves against Vietnam."

"May I ask why we're so committed to helping Vietnam?"

Again the briefers exchanged glances. The first one shrugged. "All I can tell you is that the tasking order comes from the very highest authority."

Boyce's eyes narrowed, then he tilted back in his chair. "Since the highest authority is willing to stick our necks out this far, is it prepared to back us up when we get in trouble?"

"Only to the extent that the operation remains clandestine."

Maxwell saw Boyce nod. They both knew what the officer meant. It was the standard caveat of a black-ops tasking order. Yes, you have the backing of the "highest authority," which meant the president or someone very close to him. Except that the backing stopped short of getting you out of trouble if you fell into the enemy's hands. In which event you were screwed.

Some things never changed.

CHAPTER 5

OLD SOLDIERS

Hanoi, Socialist Republic of Vietnam
1745 Thursday, 12 April

Ferrone's Chrysler limousine glided to a stop at the gates of the Presidential Palace. The afternoon sun bathed the palace in an orange hue. Two sentries in the green and red uniform of the National Security Police stood at rigid attention before the guard towers.

Ferrone's driver, Trunh Bao, leaped out of the limo and rushed around to open the back door. Ferrone extended his right leg, then stepped outside, ignoring Trunh's outstretched hand. He winced. The goddamn leg. It was giving him fits again.

With Ferrone was his Deputy Chief of Mission, Mike Medford. Trunh would serve as his translator. Since Ferrone's arrival in Vietnam, he had grown fond of the young Vietnamese man. Trunh was fluent in four languages, and he had displayed an amazing ability to get Ferrone through Vietnam's labyrinth of red tape.

"You've been here before, yes, Mr. Ambassador?" said Trunh.

Ferrone smiled. He was tempted to give the wiseass

fighter pilot's answer when someone asked if he'd visited somewhere in Vietnam before. *Yeah, but I was just passing through.* But he'd not passed through—or over—Ho Chi Minh's palace because it wasn't on the list of approved bombing targets.

"Only once," he said. "To present my credentials as the new ambassador. I've never had a real meeting with the president."

The big iron gates swung open. Ferrone's party entered the front courtyard. The palace was an ornate, colonial-style edifice built by the French when they ruled Vietnam at the end of the nineteenth century.

Standing at the entrance to the palace were a half dozen Vietnamese of varying ages. Ferrone recognized the older man in the middle of the group. He was small in stature. He wore a dark suit with a bright red tie.

President Van Duc Chien smiled, revealing a gold tooth. "Welcome to the Presidential Palace, Mr. Ambassador."

Ferrone bowed his head deferentially. "I am grateful that you have agreed to this meeting on short notice, Mr. President."

Van's interpreter repeated Ferrone's greeting in Vietnamese. Van smiled his gold-toothed smile again. "It is I who should be grateful that you have come to help us with our problem."

Ferrone kept a blank face while Trunh translated it into English. His Vietnamese was still rudimentary, but he had understood everything Van had said. The homework with Kim was paying off.

"Will the Chinese ambassador be joining us?" Ferrone asked.

"He's waiting in the conference hall," Van said.

They walked down the long, carpeted hallway to the conference hall. Ferrone tried not to limp, but he couldn't help it. The goddamn leg was still aching from being bent during the fifteen-minute limo ride. He caught Van watching him with a curious expression.

Inside the square-shaped conference room, Quian Shouyi, ambassador from the People's Republic of China to the Socialist Republic of Vietnam, was waiting. Quian was a plump, thin-haired man with what seemed to be a permanent scowl on his round face. He lowered his teacup and gave Ferrone and Van an appraising look as they entered the room.

After the ritual bowing and exchange of introductions followed by the necessary translations into English, Vietnamese, and Chinese, the principal parties took seats at the large rosewood table. Tea was served in flowered china pots. The translators took their places at the sides of their respective emissaries.

Van opened the meeting by looking directly at the Chinese ambassador. "To begin this discussion, we would be grateful for a complete explanation of why the People's Republic of China has perpetrated acts of war on the Socialist Republic of Vietnam."

The Chinese ambassador's face didn't change expression. "You have no grounds for making such a preposterous accusation."

"And China had no grounds for destroying the White Tiger oil-drilling facility."

"Despite the fact that Vietnam has no right to install such a facility, the People's Republic denies any involvement with the loss of Vietnam's illegal oil-drilling platform. The loss of the platform was clearly a natural calamity, probably due to inept construction."

Van's face reddened. "Would you also blame the destruction of three of our aircraft and the torpedoing of a fifteen-thousand-ton freighter on a 'natural calamity'?"

"These are more reckless statements. I must warn you, such irresponsible accusations by a head of state will not be tolerated by the People's Republic of China."

Ferrone watched, fascinated, as the argument heated up. At the urging of President Benjamin, Ferrone had brought the parties together to broker an armistice. Some broker he was. Two minutes into the meeting, and it was in meltdown.

Ferrone loudly cleared his throat. A silence fell over the table, and Quian and Van both stared at him. "Excuse me, gentlemen. We've gotten off to a bad start. I believe we're here to seek an agreement, not to expand on our differences. The president of the United States has directed me to assist in a negotiated settlement between your two countries of the Spratly Island matter."

Quian said, "May I ask what reason the United States has for interfering in a dispute between Vietnam and China?"

"The United States does not wish to interfere, Mr. Ambassador. Our interest is in preserving peace and stability in Southeast Asia."

"Does the United States intend to preserve peace in the same way it has in the Middle East? By attacking a sovereign country?"

"No, Mr. Ambassador. We do not."

Quian seemed to be enjoying himself. He sipped at his tea, then said, "Does the United States deny its own clandestine involvement in the recent conflict in the South China Sea?"

Ferrone had known this was coming. "The United States does not wish to become involved in any armed conflict in the region. But . . ."—he waited while the translator caught up—". . . the U.S. will lend support to any beleaguered nation who is threatened by another."

"That is very interesting, Mr. Ferrone, but you didn't answer my question. I will ask again. Do you deny that the United States has engaged in clandestine military operations against my country?"

Ferrone met the Chinese ambassador's hard-eyed gaze. *Okay, the sonofabitch wants to play hardball.* "It is not my position as the ambassador to Vietnam to deny or affirm your allegations."

"Which I can only interpret to mean that the United States

is lending military support to Vietnam. Is that not true, Mr. Ferrone?"

Ferrone felt all the eyes around the table on him as he composed his answer. *Damn.* Who the hell's idea was it to send an amateur like him to play diplomat? He knew the answer. The president of the United States, whose brilliant notion of brokering a deal between the Viets and the Chinese was going straight down the crapper.

Ferrone said, "Vietnam and the United States have a mutual security pact, just as we do with many other nations of the world."

Quian listened to the translation. "Your devious answer simply makes it clear to me, Mr. Ferrone. You are telling me that the U.S. will make war on China on behalf of Vietnam. True?"

Ferrone shook his head in frustration. "What my president has instructed me to tell you, sir, is that the U.S. will not condone the use of a powerful country's military forces against a weaker nation. There must be a peaceful solution to the Spratly Island dispute."

Quian's eyes narrowed, and he paused to scribble a note on the pad before him. Ferrone glanced around and saw Van Duc Chien looking at him with the same curious gaze. *What is he thinking?* Ferrone wondered.

Abruptly Quian shoved his chair back from the table. "It is clear that this meeting is a sham. Neither Vietnam nor the United States has any intention of recognizing the rights of the People's Republic of China in the Spratly Island dispute. I regret that I must report to my superiors that my efforts to reach a reasonable agreement have failed."

With that, Quian rose, gathered his pad and spectacles from the table, and marched out. His translator and two aides scurried out behind him.

A heavy silence hung over the table. Ferrone felt a sense of gloom coming over him. His first shot at international diplomacy had lasted less than five minutes. Beaver

Benjamin should never have expected an old warhorse like Ferrone to pull off a stunt like this.

Van was giving him that curious look again.

"You speak Vietnamese," Van said in English.

Ferrone tried not to show his surprise. "And you, sir, speak English."

Van's wrinkled face broke into a smile. "Only when I want to. Like you, I find it convenient to let the translators do their work."

"This meeting did not go well."

"It went as we should have expected. The Chinese ambassador did not come to negotiate a settlement."

Ferrone's mood darkened. More damned surprises. He had the growing feeling that he was just along for the ride. "Okay, so what did he come here for?"

"I'll explain," said Van. "In private. May I suggest we take a walk in the palace gardens?"

Ferrone glanced around the table. He saw Trunh watching him with a rapt expression on his face. So was Mike Medford.

"With our translators?" Ferrone said.

"No. Just you and I."

"Bugs?"

"I believe that's what you call them," said Van. "Listening devices. We've recently found them in the offices and meeting rooms of the palace."

Ferrone and Van were alone. They followed a wide gravel path that wound through the gardens. On either side grew a stately row of mature ficus trees. The afternoon had turned warm and sultry. The two men had left their suit coats in the palace.

"Who planted them?" said Ferrone.

Van shrugged. "Spies are common in Hanoi. Chinese, Korean, Russian." A smile came over his face. "Even American. The palace is so infested with listening devices that I cannot conduct sensitive meetings there. Only here in the garden can we can talk in privacy."

Ferrone had to concentrate to follow everything the Vietnamese president said. Van would begin in English, then shift without warning to his own language. Ferrone was getting a headache trying to keep up. Worse, his goddamn leg felt like it had a flaming hot poker stuck in it.

"So why did the Chinese ambassador show up today if he didn't intend to negotiate?" Ferrone said.

"To test you. And to hear what you would say when he challenged you. Quian has no authority to negotiate. His orders from Beijing are very specific. He is to deny any involvement with the actions in the South China Sea and accuse the U.S. of giving military support to Vietnam."

Ferrone nodded. He knew better than to ask how Van knew what orders the Chinese ambassador had received from Beijing. *Spies are common in Hanoi.* Vietnam obviously had some of its own.

President Van Duc Chien, Ferrone knew from his briefing dossier, was a longtime Communist Party official and member of the Vietnamese National Assembly. He had just been elected to his second five-year term as president. Van was sixty-six, the same age as Ferrone, which meant that he had almost certainly fought in the long war with the U.S.

"What will it take to make them negotiate?" said Ferrone.

"More than diplomacy. The Chinese leadership must understand that they cannot seize the Spratly Islands without a serious challenge from us."

"I've already explained to you the position of our president. The United States will not engage the Chinese in open warfare. Not over the Spratly Island oil rights."

"It doesn't matter. Vietnam will fight to the death."

Ferrone was surprised at Van's change in tone. His voice had a hard ring to it. "With all respect, Mr. President, I don't think fighting to the death is a productive strategy."

"There is no other strategy for us. For a thousand years

China has been our traditional enemy. Fighting them to the death is the only way we have prevailed. It is how we prevailed over the French. It is also how we won the war with the Americans."

Ferrone didn't reply. The subject of the war was one that both he and his Vietnamese counterparts had learned to treat with extreme delicacy.

As if triggered by the thought, another stab of pain flashed down Ferrone's right leg.

Van was watching him intently. "Your leg has been injured?"

"A long time ago."

"In the war?"

"Yes."

"When you were a prisoner." It was a statement, not a question.

Ferrone nodded. He wondered how much Van knew about his years as a POW.

"It was a terrible war," said Van. "You should hate the Vietnamese."

Ferrone shrugged. "I've gotten over that." *But I'll always hate the evil bastards who did this to me.* He made an extra effort not to limp. It was time to change the subject.

"Sometimes I still hate the Americans," said Van.

"Because?"

"Because of this." Van stopped and turned his back to Ferrone. He pulled his shirttail up, exposing a mass of gnarled scar tissue. "My back, shoulders, my legs. All scarred like this."

Ferrone stared at the destroyed flesh on Van's back. He had a good idea what had caused it.

"It was 1968," said Van, "soon after the Tet Offensive. We were operating near Lao Bao, just after nightfall. We thought our convoy was safe, crossing a valley. A flight of American jets spotted us and dropped napalm. Over two hundred were burned alive, and only a few in my battalion escaped with their lives. It was the end of the war for me. I spent five years in constant pain, hating Americans every minute of the day."

Ferrone had to avert his eyes from Van's destroyed flesh. Van pulled his shirt down and stuffed it back inside his trousers.

"But we Vietnamese no longer have the luxury of hating former enemies. We have to reserve our hatred for the current adversary."

"The Chinese?"

"Our oldest enemy. For a thousand years the Chinese have threatened Vietnam. They have seized territory, sea-ports, fleets of ships, islands, even our culture. Now they want our oil."

"And that's the problem, Mr. President. They don't agree that it's your oil."

"It doesn't matter. It *is* Vietnam's oil, and we must challenge them."

Ferrone knew what Van meant. The only serious challenge to the Chinese would have to come from the United States.

"You know the position of our president. We will not engage the Chinese in open warfare. Not over the Spratly oil rights."

"Then Vietnam will fight the Chinese alone."

"President Benjamin sympathizes with your position," said Ferrone. "But he and I urge you not to provoke China any further. We believe that we can persuade China to negotiate."

"Vietnam has just lost an investment of over fifty million dollars in the White Tiger platform."

Ferrone nodded. This wasn't a good moment to remind Van that the majority of the funding for the offshore drilling rig came from the United States. "The platform can be replaced. So can the lost vessels and aircraft. Those are small losses compared to what may be lost if Vietnam goes to war with China."

"China only understands force."

"Force can be applied," said Ferrone, measuring his words carefully. "But in an invisible way. As invisible as the weapons they are using against you."

Van peered at him with new interest. "Invisible? You mean—"

"There are means at our disposal," said Ferrone. "I'm not at liberty to describe them. In order for this strategy to work, it is critical that Vietnam avoids engaging China in open warfare."

For a while Van didn't reply. His face wrinkled into its contemplative expression again, and he trudged along the path, hands clasped behind his back.

Finally he stopped and looked at Ferrone. "As president of the Republic, I am in direct command of the military. It will cause me many problems with the National Assembly, but I will give the order to our commanders. No direct offensive action will be taken—unless China commences open aggression against us."

Ferrone nodded. For the first time today, he was beginning to feel a sense of optimism.

As quickly as it came, the feeling passed.

"But only for two weeks," said Van. "Then we go to war."

CHAPTER 6

DRAGONS

The White House
0905 Thursday, 12 April

"Two weeks?" said the president of the United States into the video cam. "You gotta be kidding, Skipper."

"That's what the man says," Ferrone said.

After the usual three-second delay, he saw Beaver Benjamin shake his head. "Shit, it takes longer than that just to get the Chinese to answer the phone."

"Yes, sir, I know."

"And Van knows it too. Sounds to me like blackmail. Is he trying to coerce us into a shooting war with the Chinese?"

Ferrone glanced at the two clocks on the wall. The hands of the Hanoi clock were at ten minutes before four in the afternoon. The other clock, the one displaying Washington time, showed ten till five in the morning. Beaver Benjamin was still an early riser.

"I doubt it," said Ferrone. "He's under the gun from his own legislators in the National Assembly. They're the ones who elected him, and they'll throw him out if they think he might be getting soft on the Chinese."

"Sounds familiar," said Benjamin. A wry smile flashed

over his face. "Except that on this end, I get the sack if they think I'm too hard on the Chinese."

"Speaking of Senator Wagstaff, how's he behaving these days?"

"No change. Like a pit bull in a meat locker. He wants a full Senate inquiry into what he calls 'the Spratly Island coverup.' Says he'll sponsor an initiative to impeach me if necessary."

"What about our other diplomatic efforts? Will we get any support from the United Nations?"

"Are you kidding? The United Nations wouldn't support us if we offered the world free condoms. The Security Council votes this afternoon on Resolution 1705. You'll get a copy of it on the Net. It's an inspirational document mandating 'free and unencumbered' access for all Southeast Asian countries to all mineral rights in the Spratly Island archipelago."

"It's a joke. As a voting member of the Council, China will veto it."

"That *is* the joke. China is the country sponsoring the resolution. They're just reinforcing the illusion that they're not carrying out any offensive military ops in the region. They didn't dump the oil platform. They didn't shoot down the Vietnamese aircraft or our F/A-18. They're innocent because there's no visible evidence, and they're sticking to their story."

"What about Swallow Reef? Pretty hard to hide the fact that they've overrun the island and captured the Vietnamese garrison there."

"They claim they were already there. It was the Viets who landed illegally, not them."

Ferrone thought for a moment. It was preposterous—but perfectly logical. "The good old United Nations. At least they're consistent."

"You have that right, Skipper. What it means is that it's going to be up to us. You and me and Red Boyce."

Ferrone nodded. He knew that was as far as Benjamin would go with the details about Boyce and his black-ops boys. Nothing of extreme sensitivity was ever discussed on the videoconferencing net, even though the satellite-relayed signal was scrambled and passed through an NSA—National Security Agency—cryptologic processor.

"Can we expect help to show up soon?"

"The players are in motion as we speak. In the meantime, persuade our Vietnamese friends to stand down."

"Yes, sir. I'll try."

"I'm counting on you, Skipper."

With that, the president seemed to notice that his coffee cup was empty. He gave the video cam a wave and left his desk.

31,000 feet, northern Nevada

A moonless night.

They were flying back to Fallon the same way they had flown to Groom Lake—Boyce in front, Maxwell in the back. A canopy of stars covered the night sky. In the distance were the lights of Fallon, Nevada.

"Well?" said Boyce, breaking the silence on the intercom. "What did you think of Dr. Boudroux?"

"It's obvious that she holds you in high regard."

"I noticed that she took a real shine to you too."

Maxwell had noticed the same thing. He could still feel the imperious green eyes blazing at him. But beneath the frosty demeanor and the no-nonsense jumpsuit was an attractive woman. The tortoiseshell glasses and swept-back red hair masked a pretty face. He wondered if she ever smiled.

"Why was she at the briefing?" said Maxwell.

"She's one of the researchers who developed the Black Star's visual cloaking technology. Now she's the head bureaucrat, director of something or other. You'd better be nice to her."

"Because?"

"Because you're moving down there tomorrow. You're going to get qualified in the Black Star, including field carrier quals."

Maxwell groaned inside his oxygen mask. He knew what Groom Lake was like. Hidden in the middle of the desert, it was like a maximum-security prison. He folded his arms across his chest and watched Boyce fly them back to Fallon.

It was nearly nine o'clock when he reached the Fallon Senior Officers Quarters, his temporary home for the past three months. He'd been promising himself he would start looking for a condo in town. No reason to bother now.

A message was waiting at the front desk.

Sorry, Brick. Some friends showed up last night, and I went out. Perhaps we debrief another time.
Cheers,
Svetlana

He dropped the message in the trash basket. Win some, lose some. Good-looking Russian women didn't wait around. Even if he could tell her where he'd been, she wouldn't believe it. He wasn't sure *he* believed it.

At 0945 the next morning, duffel bag in hand, he boarded the Gulfstream C-20 that would fly him to Groom Lake.

Groom Lake, Nevada

"A liii-iiitle powerrrrr," called the landing signal officer on the radio. He was using his LSO sugar talk, a lilting, encouraging voice.

Maxwell nudged the throttles forward. He saw the glimmering yellow ball rise back up and settle between the rows of green datum lights on the Fresnel lens. The lens with its ball that rose up and down was the visual cue that guided pilots down the glide path to the landing deck.

Maxwell was back on the glide path. No more sugar talk.

The LSO's name was Slim Chance. He was a lieutenant commander on temporary duty from his air wing job at Lemoore Naval Air Station. Like everyone attached to the

Black Star program, Chance had signed a document swearing to divulge nothing about what he saw here at Groom Lake.

The center-line lights on the blackened deck rushed up at the approaching jet. In the left corner of his peripheral vision Maxwell saw the dark form of the LSO watching him from the port deck edge. Just forward of the LSO station was the Fresnel lens, abeam the target touchdown point.

Whump. The wheels of the jet slammed into the deck. Maxwell shoved the throttles forward, and the Black Star leaped back into the air.

"Shit hot," said Sharp O'Toole from the backseat. "Another okay pass. You're getting the hang of this, Boss."

Maxwell concentrated on the HUD, keeping the Black Star climbing straight ahead in the blackness over Groom Lake. No lights were showing on the 27,000-foot runway, nor were any lights visible from the complex of buildings. Only when he rolled the jet onto final approach did he see again the pattern of deck edge and center-line lights that simulated an aircraft carrier's deck.

This was Maxwell's third night of FCLP—field carrier landing practice. Sharp O'Toole was right—he *was* getting the hang of it. Landing the Black Star on a carrier wouldn't be any more difficult than landing a Super Hornet. Not with the improved engines and landing flaps.

Major Sharp O'Toole, USMC, was Maxwell's wizzo— weapons systems officer. O'Toole was a test engineer who came to Dreamland three years ago on the Black Star project. As a backseater, he had more flight time in the stealth jet than anyone, including the test pilots.

Maxwell and O'Toole had been flying together for nearly two weeks. Even though the Black Star's electrochromatic cloaking made it invisible in daylight, the cloaking was effective during takeoff or landing. Every flight in the Black Star, even the FCLPs, was conducted at night to hide the secret jet from prying eyes in the hills around the base or from spy satellites overhead.

"Hey, Boss, that's eight straight okay passes. The low-beer-level light is flashing. Whaddya say we land and debrief at the bar?"

O'Toole, Maxwell learned, ran his mouth. Like most fighter pilots, Maxwell preferred being alone in a cockpit, but he'd gotten used to O'Toole and his nonstop talkativeness. The Marine was good company.

"One more. Then the beer's on you."

"Deal."

The last pass was rock solid, drawing no comment from the LSO. The Black Star's wheels thudded down on the pavement. Maxwell pulled the throttles to idle and let the jet roll out on the row of dim white lights that defined the center of the long runway. A set of green turnoff lights led him onto the taxiway and back to the darkened tarmac. As the massive shape of Hangar 501 swelled in the gloom, Maxwell saw the front door slide open. He rolled the Black Star into the gaping black cavity. Not until the door had closed again did the bright overhead fluorescent lights snap on.

"Spook City," said O'Toole as the Black Star's engines whined down. "Is this place weird or what?"

And getting weirder, thought Maxwell as he unstrapped from the front seat. Conspiracy theorists never stopped speculating about what was going on at Groom Lake. Theories ranged from UFOs, antigravity propulsion systems, hypersonic pulse jets, and teleportation devices. And stealth technology. Some of the theories were close to the truth.

O'Toole was already scrambling down the boarding ladder, unfastening his torso harness as he went. He yelled up at Maxwell. "Come on, Boss. Twenty minutes left of happy hour."

The club was called, appropriately, the Black Hole. It was hidden beneath the concrete apron of the Groom Lake base, part of an immense underground warren of living spaces and shops and laboratories.

"Attention on deck," shouted Lieutenant Commander

Crud Carruthers when Maxwell walked in. "The commander cometh."

The whole Dragon Flight team—the name Boyce concocted for the Black Star unit that would deploy to the *Reagan*—was assembled in the bar.

"Never mind the commander part," said Maxwell. "I can't command anything until I've finished quals." His title—it would be official when he'd completed the carrier qualification—was Commander, Flight Evaluation Team. It was mostly an honorific title. Boyce had overall command of Dragon Flight.

"A done deal," said Slim Chance, who strolled into the club just behind Maxwell. "The FCLP write-up is already in the computer. You're good to go, Brick. You're now one of the Dragons."

The Dragons was the name the group had given themselves. Someone had even designed a patch for their flight suits—a red dragon emblazoned on a green background. Gypsy Palmer, an Air Force captain who was Carruther's wizzo, stepped forward to attach one of the Velcro-backed patches on Maxwell's flight suit.

A cheer went up from the group.

Gypsy took the stool between Maxwell and O'Toole. She was a petite woman with a pretty, oval-shaped face and a gymnast's compact build. Like O'Toole, she was a test engineer who held two graduate degrees. On the next stool was Duke Wayne, another lieutenant commander and test pilot. With him was his wizzo, Marine captain Plug Heilbrunner. Heilbrunner's call sign came naturally: He was five feet four, with the barrel-chested build of a sumo wrestler.

The fourth Black Star crew was all-Navy. Lieutenant Commander Otis McCollister was a tall African American with the lanky frame of a running back, which he had been at the Naval Academy. He came from the F-14 Tomcat community, via the Navy's test pilot school at Patuxent River. His wizzo, Lieutenant Foxy Wolfe, was a sinewy triathlete who had three degrees, including a PhD in physics from Cal Tech.

Each of the Dragons was wearing the standard olive-drab flight suit. It was a Groom Lake custom, Maxwell learned. It was how the flight test crews distinguished themselves from the scientists and technicians.

Maxwell ordered a Foster's, which was served on draft along with eight other beers at the Black Hole bar. Mug in hand, he leaned against the bar.

"Check nine o'clock," said O'Toole in a low voice. "The Ice Queen."

Maxwell looked. At the end of the bar, sitting by herself, was Dana Boudroux. She was reading a *Scientific American*, sipping something that looked like a martini.

"Ice Queen?"

"That's what the crews call her. Cold as a glacier."

"What's her problem? Some kind of man-hater?"

"Didn't used to be. When I got here—that was nearly four years ago—she was friendly. Several guys, myself included, tried to get in her knickers. She was involved with an older guy, a civilian named Cummock."

"Mad Dog Cummock? I remember him. He was ex–Air Force, one of the contract test pilots when I was flying the prototype Black Star."

"That's him. Well, he and Boudroux—we didn't call her the Ice Queen then—were an item. Never touchy-feely in public, at least not around the flight crews, but you could tell."

"So what happened? They split up?"

"One night Cummock and his wizzo, an Air Force guy named Williams, planted the Black Star smack into the southern slope of the Groom Range."

"I don't remember hearing about that."

"You were gone by then. The report never went public be-cause the Black Star didn't officially exist."

"And Boudroux became the Ice Queen."

O'Toole nodded. "Overnight. She got real snotty with the

crews, like she blamed us for what happened to her boyfriend."

Maxwell watched her for a while. She seemed oblivious to the scene in the bar, the laughter and animated conversation.

As if reading his thoughts, Dana Boudroux lowered her magazine and met Maxwell's gaze across the room. For a moment she regarded him through the tortoiseshell glasses. Still watching him, she finished her drink, then rose and left the bar.

By now O'Toole was into another of his stories. It was one about a Marine, a Navy officer, and an Air Force pilot. Sharp O'Toole was a natural storyteller. With his dark-eyed, Irish good looks, he also had a mesmerizing effect on women. There was no mistaking the look in Gypsy Palmer's eyes. The Air Force wizzo seemed to be riveted on O'Toole, following his every movement.

The other crews, Carruthers and Palmer, Wayne and Heilbrunner, McCollister and Wolfe, were experienced Black Star aviators. Carruthers and Wayne had been test pilots on the Black Star prototype, and Carruthers had flown the carrier suitability trials. Otis McCollister and Foxy Wolfe had joined the Black Star program six months ago.

Watching his fellow Dragons, Maxwell couldn't help wondering how they would do in combat. By definition, these were smart young people. Each had at least one postgrad degree. They were brilliant analysts of data, skilled test pilots, accomplished engineers.

And that was the problem. He'd seen too many test pilots return to combat squadrons—and fail miserably. They were good at analyzing data, but short in the hand–eye skills. A fighter pilot, by definition, was a risk taker. In the tumult of battle, good decisions had to come from the gut. Too much analyzing got you killed.

"Hey, Boss, don't look so serious."

Maxwell looked up to see O'Toole grinning at him. The Marine signaled the bartender for a fresh beer. "We'll have plenty of time to be serious later."

CHAPTER 7

SWALLOW REEF

4,500 feet
South China Sea
0445 Tuesday, 24 April

Captain Tran Van Duong didn't like anything about this mission. In fact, he didn't like anything about this job.

Tran could be as patriotic as anyone in the Vietnamese Air Force when it came to asserting their independence and their right to exist as a free socialist republic. He didn't even mind flying into a combat zone. At least not when he knew where the enemy happened to be. And that was the trouble. *Where* was the enemy?

The four Ivchenko turbine engines of the Antonov AN-12 rumbled like the growling of a beast. He had the ungainly cargo plane almost to its red-line limit, nose slanted downward, descending in the darkness toward the island group ahead.

Tran didn't dare remove his eyes from the instruments. At this altitude, less than five hundred meters, it would be easy to fly into the water. In the gray gloom outside the cockpit, there was no horizon, no hint of the surface, no visual reference whatsoever.

"Are they still with us?" he asked over the intercom.

The young man in the right seat, Lieutenant Nguyen Trai, looked into the round, green-tinted radar screen. Then he craned his neck, peering up through the small eyebrow glass panel above his side window.

"Yes, I think so."

"All four of them?"

"I can't see them all in the darkness."

Tran nodded. His fighter escorts were still there. He wished their presence made him feel more secure, but it didn't. The Vietnamese pilots in the cockpits of the ancient MiG-21s were no match for the SU-27s of the PLA Air Force. Even if they possessed the necessary tactical skills—which they didn't—they were flying obsolete fighters, armed with obsolete air-to-air weapons, vectored by an even more obsolete ground-controlled intercept site.

Junk, thought Tran. Everything in the Vietnamese military was junk left over from the Cold War. When the Soviet Union collapsed, Russia had abandoned Vietnam like an unwanted relative.

This was Tran's third flight in a week to Swallow Reef. A week ago, Vietnamese troops had occupied the island, evicting the small Chinese garrison that maintained the base. Now they were being reinforced and resupplied by air from the mainland.

"Fifty kilometers to go," said Nguyen, peering again down at the console.

And still no sign of trouble, thought Tran. *Where were the Chinese?* It was too much to expect that they wouldn't come back to reclaim their precious runway. There were three other runways in the Spratly Island complex, but Swallow Reef was the only one with a hard surface long enough to accommodate large aircraft. Ownership of this ribbon of concrete was critical to the development of the oil-drilling rigs.

Tran intended to keep his speed up until he was almost over the end of the runway, then make a hard 360-degree turn to the left while he slowed and extended the landing gear and flaps. The maneuver would minimize his exposure to any lurking Chinese fighters or gunboats offshore. It would also increase his chances of accidentally flying into the water. The thought made him grip the big knurled control yoke even tighter, keeping his eyes riveted on the attitude indicator and the altimeter.

Though Tran had been trained as a pilot by the Vietnamese Air Force, he never considered himself a professional military officer. Early in his career he had been selected for one of the prestigious jobs with the national airline, Vietnam Airlines. Now Tran was a captain on one of the new Airbus A-321s.

Or at least he had been until two weeks ago. Now he was back in the air force. The crisis with China had prompted the mobilization of thousands of his countrymen, including over a hundred pilots like himself.

"Swallow Reef reports the runway operational," said Nguyen. "Temperature seventeen, wind calm, altimeter setting ten-twelve millibars."

Tran grunted his acknowledgment and adjusted his altimeter to the current setting. He knew the report from Swallow Reef was transmitted in the blind, knowing there would be no reply from the incoming transport aircraft. Without question, the Chinese would be monitoring the frequency. Even though they would have no trouble spotting the fat transport and its escorts on radar, there was no sense in helping them with a radio transmission.

Twenty kilometers. Tran leveled the Antonov at four hundred meters above the water. He took a quick peek out the windshield. Nothing. The same bleak grayness.

He knew the runway lights would not be illuminated until they were within ten kilometers of the island. After he plunked the big transport down on the relatively short runway—it was two thousand meters long—he would slam the propellers into full reverse to bring the Antonov to a shuddering stop. At the far end of the runway was a narrow apron where they would unload.

The turnaround would be quick, he hoped. Roll the cargo pallets—food and water for the troops, tools and building materials for the construction workers—out the back ramp, then get the Antonov back in the air before sunrise.

The heavy cargo—drilling equipment and new platform components—was on its way aboard surface freighters. The loaded ships bore the flags of Cambodia, Laos, Myanmar—anything but the Socialist Republic of Vietnam.

Tran banked the Antonov to the right, changing heading by thirty degrees. He wanted to be aligned with the runway when the lights—

A flash illuminated the cockpit through the right side window. An orange glare came from somewhere above them.

Tran's heart nearly seized. "What was that?"

Nguyen was peering out the window. "I—I think it was one of the fighters."

The glare seemed to descend past the right wing of the Antonov, then extinguish. Tran's heart was pounding like a hammer.

The radio channel filled with a torrent of hysterical chatter, all in Vietnamese. The MiG-21 pilots were breaking radio silence, screaming that they were engaged.

Engaged? Tran tried to make sense of what was happening. *Engaged by what?*

Then another flash, this one to Tran's left. This time he had a clear view of the fireball through his own side window. He could make out the silhouette of the wrecked MiG. It was shedding pieces as it plunged toward the water.

Two MiGs down. Tran fought back the panic that was growing inside him. Someone—*something*—was attacking his escort fighters. That could only mean—

In the next instant he knew. He felt a lurch, as if they had been rammed from the rear left quarter. Tran stared in morbid fascination at the swelling ball of flame on his outboard left wing.

The number one engine had exploded. It was trailing flame like a comet. As Tran watched, the turbine engine tore away from its mount and vanished in the Antonov's slipstream. With it went the outer portion of the left wing.

Captain Tran Van Duong knew with a dreadful certainty what would happen next. Despite the piercing scream from Nguyen in the right seat, Tran felt a sense of calm come over him. There was nothing more he could do. The Antonov was rolling out of control, no longer suspended in level flight by its severed left wing.

Tran closed his eyes and waited for the darkness of the South China Sea to take him.

Groom Lake, Nevada

Chuff, chuff, chuff.

Maxwell heard the sound coming from behind him. Rubber soles on hard desert dirt. Someone running along the path, moving at a good clip.

He had just rounded the corner of Hangar 503 on the northern ramp. The sun was perched on the rim of the high ridge to the west of Groom Lake. A final blanket of orange light lay over the desert.

He looked over his shoulder. In the fading light, he couldn't make out a face, only the level, sure-footed stride of a runner. A serious runner overtaking him.

Not until they were twenty feet apart did he recognize her. He waited until she came alongside, then sped up to match her pace.

"I didn't know you were a jogger," he said.

"I'm not," said Dana Boudroux. "This is called running."

"I see. A good eight-minute-mile pace."

"More like seven."

She kept up the pace, head not bouncing, covering the ground with the easy grace of a dancer.

"How many miles do you run?" Maxwell asked.

"Five in the morning, five at night when I can break free."

Running beside her, he took a sideways glance. She looked different without the baggy jumpsuit and severe hairstyle. She wore Polaroid glasses, black headband, red hair tied in a ponytail that bobbed as she ran. A sheen of perspiration covered her face. Her tank top was damp with sweat. Maxwell couldn't help noticing the lean, freckled legs, moving in a smooth rhythm.

Maxwell was already feeling the faster pace.

"You run marathons?" he asked.

"One. Seattle a couple years ago. That was enough."

"Bad experience?"

"I don't like running in a crowd."

That figured, thought Maxwell. They continued in silence for another two hundred meters. He could feel her notching up the pace. He was sucking in the dry desert air, making a hard raspy noise.

"Are you okay?" she asked.

"Oh, yeah. Never better."

"You sound like a dying whale."

"I always sound like that when I'm having fun."

A knowing smile passed over her face. "Tell you what. You go at your own pace. I'll just run on by myself."

"I've got a better idea. Why don't we turn around and run to the club? Drinks on me."

"No, thanks."

"Why not? No strings attached."

"Not my policy."

"Policy? What's that got to do—"

"Nothing personal, Commander. It's just that you and I work different sides of the street. I'm a scientist, you're a trigger puller."

"Why does that mean we can't have a drink? Call me Brick, by the way."

"In this business, it's best if we keep our communication strictly professional."

"Sorry, Dana. That's your name, right? I must be missing something. I thought we were working on the same project."

"Not really. To scientists like me, projects like the Black Star are the culmination of our lives. This is what we dreamed about in high school physics class. Most of us wanted to go into space, but this is the next best thing. Jet jockeys like you don't relate to that. To you, the Black Star is just another toy."

Maxwell felt a flash of annoyance. "I *can* relate to that. I used to dream about going into space."

"So why didn't you?"

"I did."

She slowed the pace to a jog. "Explain, please."

"STS 71, a five-day orbital mission aboard space shuttle *Atlantis.* I was the pilot. And for the record, I used to have drinks with the scientists who built the thing. They didn't mind that I worked the other side of the street."

She was looking at him with fresh curiosity. "You were an astronaut?"

"Two and a half years."

"Why'd you leave?"

He hesitated. Why he resigned from NASA after one shuttle mission was a subject he didn't discuss with anyone.

"Personal reasons," he said.

She nodded, peering at him through the Polaroid glasses. For a while they ran together in silence. Their shoes drummed a staccato beat on the hard path. Then she slowed and reversed course, running back toward the complex of hangars in the east.

Finally she said, "I need a shower."

"Me too."

"One drink, that's all."

"Fine."

Swallow Reef, Spratly Islands

Hurry, sunrise.

Maj. Phan Tien stood with his hands on his hips and frowned at the darkness over the sea. He could see a faint pinkening on the horizon. Dawn was still an hour away.

Not soon enough.

Something was happening out there. Something very bad. The radio operator at the makeshift control tower had reported that the inbound aircraft—the resupply plane and its fighter escorts—were under attack. And Phan believed it because he had seen the explosions and the ribbons of fire arcing toward the sea. *Something* had shot down three airplanes, including the Antonov and its precious supplies.

Two of the MiG-21 fighters had escaped, but neither of the shaken pilots was able to give an accurate report of what had happened. Only that something had caused two of the MiGs and then the Antonov to explode. The MiGs were already on their way back to their base in Vietnam.

Now Phan wanted the sun to rise. In his experience, most bad things in war happened at night. Darkness was the friend of the predator, not the prey.

He should know. It had been under cover of night that he and his little force of three hundred had landed on Swallow Reef and overwhelmed the Chinese garrison of nearly a thousand troops. The firefight had been quick and surprisingly bloodless—fewer than a hundred casualties, all but twenty of them Chinese.

That was the day before yesterday. Now Phan's force awaited resupply and reinforcement. The essential supplies were on the big lumbering Antonov. A reinforcement battalion of 250 troops was supposed to arrive by surface ship sometime after sunrise.

"I can seize the island," Phan had assured his regimental commander, Gen. Bui, on the eve of their departure from Haiphong. "And I can occupy the facility. But there is no earthly way that I can hold it against the PLA when they come to take it back."

"It will not be necessary," said the general. "The capture of Swallow Reef will be a symbolic operation only. It will validate our claim to the Spratly oil reserves. You may be sure that before it comes to an open war, the conflict will be resolved."

Phan didn't like what he was hearing. "Resolved in what way, General?"

"By the United States. They will not allow China to make war on us."

Phan stared at the general, wondering if he actually believed this nonsense. The United States? It was true that the United States and Vietnam had signed a security pact. But would the United States go to war with China over an insignificant flea speck of a country like Vietnam? General Bui and the leaders in Hanoi were delusional.

Standing on the rocky outcropping, he tried to pick out the gunboats that were positioned around the reef. That was the extent of Vietnam's navy—a fleet of fast but fragile little gunboats. This was the force with which they would repel the PLA Navy's armada of missile-firing destroyers and nuclear submarines.

Another delusion.

What Phan and his troops needed most urgently was for the sun to rise. With the coming of daylight, they would live another day. Even the Chinese, clumsy as they were, were not so stupid as to land on Swallow Reef in—

What was that?

A bright flash illuminated the sea a kilometer from where Phan stood. Then another. Seconds later came the dull *whump* of explosions.

More flashes. It took Phan a moment to comprehend what he was seeing.

The gunboats. Something was happening to the gunboats. Mixed with the *whumps* of the exploding craft came another sound, sporadic at first, then more insistent. And closer.

Phan was a trained commando unit leader. He knew what he was hearing—the sound of automatic gunfire. Chinese AK-74s and Type 67 machine guns, mixed with the chatter of American-made M-16s. The gunfire was coming from the north side of the reef, where the water was most shallow.

An excited voice crackled from the transceiver clipped to Phan's belt. He heard the voice on the radio—it was one of his platoon sergeants—blurt out the news. An amphibious landing, troops storming the reef, gunboats exploding, incoming mortars.

"How many landing craft?"

"Many, many craft, Major. They are here. The Chinese are here."

Phan whirled and began running back toward his command post, knowing by the closeness of the exploding mortars that he was too late.

Groom Lake Research Facility, Nevada

The Dragons were clustered at the bar. Their chatter abruptly stopped when Maxwell and Dana came in. Maxwell caught O'Toole studying him with narrowed eyes.

He had showered and changed into a clean, pressed flight suit. Dana Boudroux wore a blue velour warm-up suit. Her hair was wet, tied back in the same ponytail. But she looked different, Maxwell thought. Softer somehow, less severe.

Then he saw it. The tortoiseshell glasses were gone, revealing her strikingly large hazel eyes.

"Vodka tonic, Dr. Boudroux?" said the bartender. He was an older black man with a thin mat of gray hair.

"A tall one, Bert. With an extra lime."

After she'd sampled her drink, she turned to Maxwell. "You didn't tell me the whole story."

"Excuse me?"

"About your career at NASA."

"What about it?"

She sipped at the drink. "I stopped by my office and looked you up in the database."

"What database?"

She smiled, showing a row of very white teeth. "As a project director, I have next to the highest level of access. I can look up the background file on anyone assigned here at the facility."

Maxwell nodded, not sure where this was going. "So you looked me up. Pretty boring stuff."

"Not at all. BS in aero engineering, cum laude, from Rensselaer. Top of your class in test pilot school. Three years of test and engineering duty, including early eval work on, ah, certain stealth technology platforms."

"You didn't have to look it up. You could have asked me."

"And then selection for astronaut training. One space shuttle mission, then you resigned."

"You already knew that."

"But not why."

"Like I said, it was personal." *And private*, he wanted to say.

She took her time, sipping at the vodka tonic through the straw. "You must have loved her very much."

He felt a stirring inside him, like the pain of an old wound. He had almost—but not entirely—shoved the memory into a far recess of his mind.

"My wife is in the file too?"

"Only the report of the accident. She and the other mission specialist—his name was Feldman, I think—died in that crew compartment fire two days before they were supposed to launch. You disagreed with the accident report and made yourself persona non grata at NASA."

"That's putting it diplomatically."

"There was something about threatening a Houston newspaper reporter with physical harm? What was that about?"

Maxwell had almost forgotten that one. "The guy was

bugging me for an interview. One day he followed me to the parking lot. He wanted a photo of the grieving astronaut, mourning his lost wife."

"That's when you threatened him?"

"Not exactly. What I did was grab him by the collar and tell him if I saw him again I'd shove his digital Nikon up his ass."

He saw a smile flit over her face. "And that was when you left NASA."

"Seemed like good timing."

"Hmm. Guess I couldn't really—"

She stopped. Her eyes swung to the front of the bar.

Maxwell saw a familiar figure shambling toward them. He wore running shoes, a pair of wrinkled chinos, and a beat-up Navy G-1 leather flight jacket. The stub of a well-gnawed cigar protruded from his mouth. With him was a broad-shouldered man in creased BDUs—battle dress utilities—and spit-shined black boots.

"Figured I'd find you here," said Admiral Boyce. "You ready for a drink?"

"I was just leaving," said Dana.

"No need," said Boyce. "I want you both to meet Lieutenant Commander Wedge Flores. He's the officer-in-charge of the SEAL unit that will be attached to our mission."

Maxwell shook hands with the SEAL officer. It was easy to see where Flores got his nickname: His torso tapered from a narrow waist to a massive set of shoulders. Flores maintained a stony expression, his dark eyes seeming to evaluate Maxwell.

"SEAL unit?" said Maxwell. "Why do we have a—"

"To do dirty jobs you Airedales don't know anything about," said Flores. "And to pluck you out of the messes you get yourselves into."

"Airedale" was the derisive label surface sailors liked to apply to aviators. For a moment Maxwell locked gazes with Flores. He appeared to be about Maxwell's age, maybe a couple of years older. Maxwell guessed that he was a former enlisted man who had graduated to commissioned rank. And he had an attitude.

Boyce watched them and chuckled. "Wedge is like most SEALs. They think that aviators are a bunch of pampered prima donnas. Am I right, Wedge?"

A momentary smile appeared on Flores's face, then vanished. "You said it, Admiral, not me."

Boyce signaled the bartender and ordered a Stoli martini for himself and a beer for Flores. He turned to Maxwell and Dana. "Glad to see you two are getting along."

Maxwell shook his head. That was Boyce. He never stopped inserting himself into Maxwell's private life.

Dana said, "We were just having a drink after a run in the desert, Admiral."

Boyce nodded and gave Maxwell a knowing smile, which further annoyed Maxwell. His martini and Flores's beer arrived. Boyce removed his cigar and sampled the drink, rolling it around on his tongue, then flashed a thumbs-up to the bartender. Flores accepted his beer and stood with his back to bar, scanning the room with his dark, hooded eyes.

Boyce turned to Maxwell. "Congratulations are in order, I understand."

"For what?"

"For completing the training syllabus here. In only two weeks, which is probably a record. Now you can go to work."

Maxwell took a quick glance at Dana. As a civilian engineer not directly involved in Dragon Flight, she wasn't supposed to be hearing this. Boyce didn't seem to care. Dana was sipping her drink, studying them over the rim of her glass. It occurred to Maxwell that the Ice Queen had thawed a little—but just a little. He could still sense the chilly demeanor just below the surface.

But it no longer mattered, he reminded himself. Boyce was back, which meant they'd soon be leaving. And that was fine with him. He'd had enough of Groom Lake and the Ice Queen.

The cluster of flight-suited pilots and wizzos—all junior officers—had just awakened to the presence of a flag officer in their bar. They were in a subdued huddle, talking in a low buzz. Wedge Flores was standing by himself down the bar, sipping his beer and returning the aviators' curious look with a cold-eyed glare.

"I was in Washington this past week," Boyce went on. He lowered his voice. "For your information, there's a lot of high-level interest in what we're doing out here."

Maxwell just nodded. He could always tell when Boyce was leading up to something.

Boyce sipped his martini and said, "Beaver sends his regards, by the way."

Maxwell blinked, momentarily confused. "Beaver?"

"The president. I spoke with him yesterday."

Maxwell had almost forgotten. President Hollis Benjamin was a former naval aviator who had once served under Maxwell's father. Maxwell remembered Beaver Benjamin as a young lieutenant, drinking beer in their backyard in Jacksonville. And then it came back to him that Boyce and Benjamin were contemporaries from flight training days.

"Does he know about—" he caught himself. Dana Boudroux was sipping her drink, watching them with a studious expression. Wedge Flores's dark eyes were peering over the rim of his beer glass. "Sorry," said Maxwell. "Wrong place to discuss it."

"Yeah, Beaver knows," said Boyce. "And don't worry about Wedge or Dr. Boudroux. They're both cleared." He turned to Dana. "I take it you haven't told him."

Maxwell was more confused. "Told me what?"

"That I will lead the support crew of Dragon Flight," said Dana.

"Which means—"

"I'm going with you."

Maxwell didn't know whether to cheer or groan. "That's swell," he said. "So when do we leave?"

"Tomorrow night," said Boyce. "A C-17 will take the Dragon Flight team as far as Guam, and a pair of C-5s is going to haul our hardware. While it's being transported by surface out to the *Reagan*, the three of us are going to take a little side trip."

He knew Boyce. Boyce was waiting for him to ask the next question.

He gave it a beat, watching Boyce play with his olive. "Ah, side trip to where, Admiral?"

Boyce took a sip of his martini. "Hanoi, of course."

CHAPTER 8

GWAI-LO

Lingshui Air Base, Hainan Island
0615 Thursday, 26 April

Kill symbols, thought General Zhang Yu. They would be an appropriate touch on the side of his fighter. Too bad that it was not possible.

General Zhang stood beside the *Dong-jin* admiring the jet's oddly beautiful lines. The big bifold door was already closing over the entrance to the hangar. Through the narrow space remaining beneath the door, Zhang could see the horizon glimmering in the east. He and his wingman, Major Tsan, had landed back at Lingshui air base just before sunrise. The missions were ridiculously easy. Even though he detested low-altitude flight over the water at night, killing Vietnamese aircraft made it worthwhile.

It was a great pity that he couldn't paint a tally of all his kills on the unblemished skin of the stealth fighter. His total aerial victories—eighteen after this morning's mission—would cover the entire fuselage beneath the cockpit. The trouble was no one would ever see them. No one except the handful of select technicians allowed to work on the secret *Dong-jin* stealth jets.

The hangar door closed, blocking Zhang's view of the coming dawn. His systems officer, Lieutenant Po, was still climbing down the ladder from his seat in the aft cockpit. As usual, Zhang didn't bother waiting for Po. He turned and strode across the hangar bay, out the exit, and down the long hallway to his office bunker.

It was not unique in the PLA Air Force for an officer with the rank of general to fly operational fighters. It was rare, however, that a general like Zhang Yu would not only fly combat missions but would do it in the air force's most secret weapon, the *Dong-jin.*

But Zhang himself was a unique commodity in the PLA. He wore two hats—commander of the secret *Dong-jin* unit, and the commanding general of the Hainan Island military sector. All the units of the PLA on Hainan—over fifty thousand troops, air defense batteries, six air force squadrons of SU-27 and F-7 fighters as well as the invisible *Dong-jins*— all reported directly to Zhang.

Zhang arrived at his office door, waved away the sentry who quivered at full attention in the passageway, and let himself inside. Not until the door was closed and he was alone did Zhang do what he always did when he returned from a mission in the *Dong-jin.* He went to the mirror mounted on the wall beside his desk.

For a full minute Zhang stared at the face. He had to force himself not to turn away in revulsion.

Hideous. The waxen mask leering back at him was all that remained of what had once been a handsome face. Reconstructive surgery had left him a stub of a nose, which was set above the diagonal slash of his mouth.

Somehow Zhang's eyes had been preserved. They glowered back at him now like embers in a bed of ash, reminding him of what happened three years ago.

Zhang Yu's ascent through the ranks of the PLA Air Force had been meteoric. Early in his career, he was assigned the task of ferreting out the politically untrustworthy members of the PLA—dissidents, collaborators, rumormongers. His methods were harsh, meant to discourage others from breaking ranks. As a reward for his diligence, his mentor and patron, General Tsin, chief of staff of the PLA, had given Zhang command of the vital *Dong-jin* project, even though he was still only a colonel.

When the war with Taiwan erupted three years ago, Zhang was ready. His *Dong-jin* fighters, developed from technology stolen from the United States, were the deadliest weapons in the sky. Zhang alone destroyed eleven Taiwanese aircraft and sank more than a dozen warships. Because of his brilliant success, he was assured of future high command in the PLA. Perhaps even a seat in government.

And then something happened.

One night a Taiwanese commando force, guided by traitors from within the PLA, struck the Chouzhou Air Base where Zhang's three completed *Dong-jins* were hidden. One of the precious jets was destroyed inside its protected hangar. Zhang managed to get airborne in another. The third *Dong-jin* was commandeered by an enemy pilot, who somehow possessed the skill and knowledge to take off and fly the exotic jet.

The stolen *Dong-jin* was halfway across the strait when Zhang intercepted it. In a swirling, fuel-consuming, low-altitude duel over the water, the enemy pilot managed to bring his cannon to bear on Zhang's jet.

With the *Dong-jin* exploding around him, his cockpit filling with a torrent of flame, Zhang ejected. Seconds later he was in the water, horribly burned, more dead than alive. He drifted for half an hour before a PLA Navy vessel rescued him. No trace was found of his weapons systems officer, Captain Yan.

During the months of rehabilitation and surgery, Zhang had time to reflect on what happened. A thousand times in his memory, the dogfight with the stolen *Dong-jin* replayed itself. The questions kept repeating themselves like an end-less tape.

Who was the pilot?

How did he know enough about the *Dong-jin* to fly it in combat?

Was he a PLA defector? Or a Taiwanese?

Or was he a *gwai-lo*—a Westerner?

The pilot who stole the *Dong-jin* almost certainly had ex-perience in a similar aircraft. And the only similar aircraft in the world was the one from which the *Dong-jin* was copied—the secret American stealth jet called the Black Star.

In tiny increments, like the dripping of water into a ves-sel, the level of knowledge began to rise. Chinese operatives in the U.S. supplied facts about secret projects and those who worked on them. PLA agents planted inside the Tai-wanese military high command brought back snippets of in-formation about American activity during the short war between China and Taiwan.

What happened to the stolen *Dong-jin*? Extensive com-puter simulations of the flight path, time aloft, and available fuel aboard the jet proved that the *Dong-jin* could not have reached an air base in Taiwan. An exhaustive search turned up no evidence that it crashed at sea.

Which led to only one ominous likelihood. Cruising in the eastern strait, within range of the fuel-starved *Dong-jin*, was an American aircraft carrier—the USS *Ronald Reagan*. It would be technically very difficult to land such an air-craft aboard a carrier—the *Dong-jin* had no tailhook or high lift devices to give it a slow landing speed—but it was the-oretically possible if the pilot were an exceedingly skilled carrier aviator.

The Americans had captured the *Dong-jin*.

Then came more tantalizing clues. A U.S. Navy pilot was observed by a PLA agent at the Chingchuankang commando base in Taiwan during the time of the raid on Chouzhou. If the reports were true, he was an experienced carrier aviator, the commander of a fighter squadron aboard USS *Reagan*. Even more tantalizing was his background. He had once been a test pilot assigned to a secret project at the U.S. base called Groom Lake. The place where the American Black Star and its Chinese sibling, the *Dong-jin* were developed.

The war between Taiwan and China abruptly ended only a few days after Zhang's crash. In the purge that followed, Zhang's former patron in the PLA, General Tsin, was arrested and executed. Zhang himself escaped the recriminations. He continued his fast track to high command. Though his facial disfigurement would have disqualified him for a more public role in the PLA, it didn't matter in the invisible world of the *Dong-jin*.

Zhang's promotion to general and his appointment to command the Hainan military sector were not without controversy. During his year of convalescence, two of his rivals, both air force colonels, had risen to prominence in the PLA high command. Just as he had done in the old days when he led the purge of the PLA's dissidents, he eliminated these threats to his further ascent in the PLA rank structure.

The first was easy. Using his old connections in *Te-Wu*—the PLA secret police—Zhang exposed a classic case of corruption and bribe-taking by his archrival. The man, a newly minted general, was summarily removed from his command. A few days later it was reported that he had committed suicide.

Eliminating the second rival took a bit longer. Again using agents of the *Te-Wu*, Zhang planted evidence linking the officer, also a new general, to a dissident group with links to Taiwan. It didn't matter that the charges were never proved. The officer disappeared from view and was also reported to be a suicide.

Now Zhang commanded the *Dong-jin* squadron, the most elite unit in the PLA Air Force. Even better, he was responsible for all military operations on the island of Hainan, which was the hinge point of the war in the South China Sea.

But his face was still hideous.

Abruptly Zhang swung away from the mirror. He could feel the same old pounding in his temples, his scalp tingling as it always did he when he thought of the *gwai-lo* who shot him down.

Zhang sat at his desk and pulled out the sliding wooden tray beneath the desktop. On it was taped a clipping from a magazine. As he had done a hundred times before, Zhang stared at the photograph in the clipping.

A smiling Caucasian man was wearing a blue naval uniform with three stripes on the sleeves. He was shaking hands with another officer, a burly black man who also wore three stripes. The smiling man appeared to be taller than average, with the lean build of an athlete. He had a dark mustache and the angular, oversized nose that uncivilized *gwai-los* considered attractive. Judging by the expression, Zhang could see that this man was confident, proud of his looks, accustomed to being admired by other men and, probably, desired by women.

But the most telling item in the photograph was parked in the background. It was an F/A-18 Super Hornet. Visible on the fuselage beneath the canopy were three silhouettes.

MiG-29s. Kill symbols.

In lettering just below the canopy rail was a name: CDR BRICK MAXWELL.

Zhang stared at the photograph, his eyes blazing. He knew the caption by heart:

Aboard USS Ronald Reagan, *Cmdr. Samuel J. Maxwell USN, CO of VFA-36, is relieved by Cmdr. Felix B. Alexander. In an earlier ceremony, Cmdr. Maxwell was presented the Distinguished Service Medal by Commander, Carrier Strike Group Three, Rear Adm. John H. Hightree.*

Prior to assuming command of VFA-36, Commander Maxwell served as the squadron's operations officer and executive officer. A graduate of the U.S. Naval Test Pilot School, he was assigned as a special projects test pilot before receiving orders to NASA, where he trained as a space shuttle pilot and flew one orbital mission aboard the shuttle Atlantis.

Commander Maxwell's new duty station will be the U.S. Naval Strike and Air Warfare Center at NAS Fallon, Nevada.

Zhang shoved the tray with the photo back inside the desk. *Maxwell.* Learning the man's identity had taken nearly a year of intelligence harvesting. The scraps of circumstantial data gradually came together like pieces of a complicated mosaic. But it was still circumstantial. There was no hard evidence to prove that it was Maxwell who stole the *Dong-jin* and shot Zhang down.

Zhang no longer required hard evidence. If he had gained anything from the terrible agony of the crash, it was a new and intuitive vision. Zhang needed only to look at the cocky, unscarred face of this *gwai-lo* to know.

It was Maxwell.

And now the PLA's intelligence service had just presented Zhang with another tantalizing scrap of information. The man who stole the *Dong-jin* was back. According to a report from a reliable and highly placed source in Vietnam, a man fitting the profile of Commander Samuel J. Maxwell had just arrived in Hanoi.

Why?

It was too much of a coincidence that he would choose this moment to visit Vietnam. But it didn't matter. It was an opportunity Zhang did not intend to pass up.

Hanoi, Socialist Republic of Vietnam

"I told you help was on the way," said the president.

Joe Ferrone looked at the grinning face in the videoconferencing screen. "You didn't tell me it was Red Boyce and his gang of burglars."

"I wanted to be sure they had their act together before they went out there. You do have it together, don't you, Red?"

Red Boyce, seated on the couch next to Ferrone, said, "You bet your ass we do, Mr. President."

President Hollis Benjamin laughed. "I still don't know how a guy like you ever made admiral in the U.S. Navy, Red."

"Same way Joe Ferrone did. Baffled them with bullshit. It just took me longer."

Watching the exchange, Ferrone had to shake his head. He was sure that no one else got to talk to the president of the United States this way. No one except the president's old Navy buddies.

"And it's good to see you again, Brick," said the president. "How's your old man? Still full of piss and vinegar?"

"Yes, sir," answered Maxwell, sitting on Ferrone's right. "I spoke with him just before I left the States. He's doing fine, puttering with his old cars, rebuilding a Porsche now."

The president smiled; then his face took on a sober expression. "It was my idea to get you guys together in Hanoi. I want everyone reading from the same page before we start the next phase of this, ah, operation. And I wanted Red and Brick to get their feet on the ground in the country we've befriended in this dispute."

The three men watching the screen nodded their understanding.

The president went on. "Ambassador Ferrone is doing his utmost to bring both sides in this disagreement to the negotiating table. The mission of Red Boyce's STOU team will be to discourage, ah, certain parties from overstepping the limits of . . . let's just say, ah, acceptable behavior."

Ferrone understood that the president was being deliberately vague. Even Ferrone didn't know exactly what Boyce and his STOU team were tasked to do, or what kind of exotic equipment they brought with them. Only that they were staging from the USS *Reagan*, on station now in the South China Sea. Ferrone had been around long enough to know how covert operations worked. No one was supposed to possess all the pieces of the puzzle. Especially an old civilian bureaucrat like Joe Ferrone.

But another side of Joe Ferrone objected to being left out of the picture. He was, at heart, a military officer. He had commanded an aircraft carrier, a battle group, and for a while an entire fleet. At his fingertips had been enough firepower to demolish an entire nation. Now he was an outsider.

But he had already figured out most of the obvious stuff. It didn't take an intelligence expert to deduce that the Chinese were employing some kind of stealth aircraft. The ChiComs were indulging in invisible warfare, both above and below the surface. Ferrone knew too that the U.S. possessed advanced stealth aircraft of its own.

The arrival of Boyce and Maxwell supported his belief. Boyce was running a black-ops unit out in Fallon. He knew that young Maxwell, who worked for Boyce, had once been a test pilot on one of the spook projects at Groom Lake. And he knew that a supply ship from Guam had just loaded some large items cloaked in wraps aboard the *Reagan* at sea. It had to be stealth jets.

Ferrone wished he could see. Someday the wraps would come off, and he intended to get a close look at the thing that Maxwell was flying. Old pilots never got over their love for exotic toys.

On the video screen, a young woman in a business suit was whispering something in the president's ear. Benjamin nodded, then looked back into the video cam.

"They're nagging me about another damned meeting I'm late for. The truth is, I'd rather spend the time with you guys telling war stories."

He pushed himself away from the console and tossed a salute to the video cam. "Carry on, gentlemen. Good luck to you."

The camera remained focused on the empty chair. Then the screen flickered and filled with snow.

Boyce said, "I still have trouble picturing Beaver Benjamin as the Commander-in-Chief. Back in flight training, the guy was a social klutz. He was too tongue-tied to ask a girl for a date."

"I think he's gotten over that," said Ferrone.

Ferrone led them out of the videoconferencing room, back toward the embassy reception room. As he walked, he had to force himself not to limp. The goddamn leg again. Aching like a sonofabitch.

Two women, deep in conversation, looked up as the men entered the reception room. One was a slender Vietnamese woman with swept-back black hair, brown eyes set above high cheekbones. She wore the traditional *ao-dai*—a slitted dress over long silk pants. The second woman was taller. She had red hair and tortoiseshell glasses. She wore a yellow pantsuit, clasped at the waist to reveal a slim, athletic figure.

"There you are, Kim," Ferrone said to the Vietnamese woman. "I see you've met Dr. Boudroux."

CHAPTER 9

MAGIC SWORD

Hanoi, Socialist Republic of Vietnam
1545 Thursday, 26 April

"Lime?" said Ferrone.

"A twist," said the American woman. "Just one."

Ferrone applied the lime, then slid the vodka tonic across the bar to her. The white-coated bartender—the *real* bartender—watched indulgently while the ambassador mixed drinks for his guests.

Ferrone was enjoying himself. Playing bartender was something he had done when he was a flag officer with stewards assigned to his staff. It lowered barriers, he believed, allowing junior officers to communicate with him on an informal level.

They were in the lounge wing of the reception hall where Ferrone received visiting dignitaries. Dark wooden panels covered the walls. On all sides of the room were tapestries, displays of Vietnamese art, vases and urns in each corner. Ferrone's cat, an overweight tabby named Maynard, observed the gathering from his own stool at the end of the bar.

They'd gotten through the introductions, the Americans

meeting Li Che Kim. Now they were into their second round of drinks.

"Ah, you're from Vietnam, Mrs. Ferrone?" said Boyce. He was working on a bourbon and Coke, playing with an unlit cigar.

"I'm Australian," she said, "but I was born in Ho Chi Minh City."

Behind the bar, Ferrone winked at Kim. He'd warned her about Boyce. He would be nosy, fishing for information. Kim was being discreet with the facts, causing Boyce to be frustrated.

A couple of stools away, Maxwell was keeping up a polite conversation with the American woman, Boudroux. She was sipping at the vodka tonic—just one twist—while Maxwell nursed a Halida, a local beer that Ferrone himself favored.

Ferrone had been surprised when the woman arrived with Boyce's group. She was some kind of scientist—no one was saying exactly what kind, but Ferrone could guess. It had to do with the technology of the secret airplane they also weren't saying anything about.

Watching her now at the end of the bar, swizzling her drink and chatting with Maxwell, Ferrone wondered if the two were an item. For young Maxwell's sake, he hoped not. The woman was good-looking enough, that flaming red hair and *Vogue* model figure. Probably a fitness freak, judging by the tight body. Definitely smart, tough as nails.

And a nutcracker. He'd already picked up the signals. She was the kind who would chew you up for breakfast and spit you out before lunch.

He knew about such women because he'd been married to one. His ex-wife used to think it was she who wore the stars instead of her husband. He knew that "Mrs. Admiral" was the not-so-secret name his staff used for her. By the time she and Ferrone divorced, she had pissed off most of the officers in his command staff and all their spouses.

That was ten years ago. Ferrone had assumed he would live out his years as a crusty but content old bachelor. That was before he met Li Che Kim.

He was still at the National Security Council. Her official title was Deputy Director of the Australia–American Trade Council. They were introduced at a cocktail reception at the Australian embassy. She was a dozen years his junior, still a teenager when Ferrone's ordeal as a prisoner of war began in the autumn of 1967.

With the fall of Saigon, Kim and her parents fled to Brisbane. She started a career in advertising, married a lawyer, had a daughter, divorced the lawyer, accepted the post in Washington with the Trade Council. And met Joe Ferrone.

Boyce was still fishing. "So you and Joe—ah, Ambassador Ferrone, I mean, are—"

"Having dinner with you tonight," said Kim. She smiled.

"That's right," said Ferrone, looking at Maxwell and Boudroux. "You're all invited to join us here at the embassy."

"That's very sweet," said Dana Boudroux, "but I'd like to see something of Hanoi before we leave."

"You're leaving so soon?" said Kim.

"In the morning."

"That's too bad. Back to the U.S.?"

Dana hesitated. "Mm, yes, eventually."

Kim caught Ferrone's glance and asked no more questions. She was a fast learner. She knew that more went on in the embassy than cocktail parties and polite chatter.

"But you shouldn't go out by yourself," said Kim. "In Hanoi, you need an escort."

"I have one," said Dana. "Isn't that right, Commander Maxwell?"

A look of surprise flashed over Maxwell's face.

And then he recovered. "Sure," said Maxwell. "Let's see Hanoi."

"Good idea," said Ferrone. "I'll send my driver with

you." He signaled for Trunh Bao, who was watching them discreetly from the entrance of the lounge. "He'll keep an eye out for you."

The streets of Hanoi were chaotic. Thousands of mopeds flowed in an endless stream through the city.

Trunh showed them how to cross the street. It was an act of faith—walking slowly into the stream, letting the cyclists flow around you like water around a rock.

"Only in Vietnam," said Trunh. "Please do not try this in America."

The sidewalks teemed with vendors, beggars, cyclo drivers, all competing for their attention. Sellers of *bia hoi*—freshly made draft beer—beckoned for them to sample the brew. Maxwell tried one. It was warm, foamy, and not bad at all. Dana stopped at another stall and bought dried squid and pork rolls.

Before leaving the embassy they had changed into street clothes. Maxwell wore chinos, a polo shirt, and deck shoes. Dana had put on a designer T-shirt and jeans, which, he couldn't help noticing, nicely accented her derriere as they strolled the sidewalk.

They continued walking until they came to the shore of a lake in the center of Hanoi.

"A very symbolic lake," said Trunh. "Legend has it that in the fifteenth century, a magical sword was sent from heaven to our Emperor, Le Thai To. He used the sword to drive the Chinese away from Vietnam. One day after the war, he came upon a giant golden tortoise swimming in the lake. The tortoise seized the sword and dived to the bottom of the lake with it. Since then the lake has been known as Hoan Kiem, which means lake of the restored sword, because the tortoise returned the sword to its heavenly owners."

"Maybe that's what Vietnam needs," said Dana.

"What would that be, madame?" said Trunh.

"Another magical sword to drive the Chinese away."

Trunh smiled.

They walked through the old quarter, stopped for another *bia hoi*, then they told Trunh he could leave.

Trunh looked skeptical.

"Not to worry," said Maxwell. "We'll take a taxi home."

The driver bowed politely and left them. They continued through the market district, then kept walking through the Old Quarter.

"This place gives me a funny feeling," said Maxwell.

"Because?"

"Because my dad dropped bombs all over here. He and Joe Ferrone and their squadron mates. Now we're walking around here like tourists."

"We *are* tourists," said Dana Boudroux. "Wars don't last forever."

"They do for some people. A lot of the old guys think we should have turned Hanoi into a parking lot."

"Joe Ferrone doesn't."

"Neither does the president."

She kept her silence for a while. "I felt that way about Beirut for a long time. I wanted to see it made into a parking lot."

"Why?"

"Because my father was killed there."

Maxwell nodded. "Sorry to hear that. What happened?"

"He was a Marine officer, a captain, assigned to the U.S. mission in Lebanon. The militia kidnapped him and executed him. They made a video of him hanging from a ceiling. I was twelve years old." She said it in her dry, matter-of-fact scientist's voice.

"That had to be a tough thing for a kid to go through."

She shrugged. "I learned."

"Learned what?"

"That life is provisional. It gets snuffed out"—she snapped her fingers—"like that. No matter how much you love someone, you lose them."

Maxwell didn't reply.

They had walked for nearly an hour since detaching Trunh. Darkness had come to Hanoi. They came to another market area. The vendors were closing down their stalls, loading pots and griddles and vats onto pushcarts.

Maxwell had only a vague sense of where they were. He stopped and pulled the Fodor's map from his shirt pocket. In the thin light he couldn't make out the street names.

"Maybe we should take a taxi," said Dana.

"That's a cop-out. It can't be more than a few more blocks to the embassy."

He squinted at the map. The U.S. embassy was in the Ba Dinh district, on Lang Ha Street. It had to be west, near the shore of another lake, Hoy Tay.

"That way." He pointed across the market area, to a narrow side street.

After they'd gone another two blocks, the stream of pedestrians and bicyclers thinned. The narrow street ahead appeared to be empty. On either side were shuttered windows of rickety buildings, laundry hanging limp in the still air, darkened entrances.

They kept walking. Something—a cat or a rat—scuttled across the darkened surface ahead of them.

"I don't like this," said Dana. "Let's turn around."

Maxwell tried again to read the map. The light was too dim. "It's farther to go back than to go on ahead. I'm sure this street comes out by the lake. Then we'll be close to the embassy."

They continued down the empty street. Dana clutched his arm.

Another two blocks. The street was still deserted, still dark.

"Okay, navigator, what kind of mess have you gotten us in?"

"Don't be negative. You wanted to see Hanoi, didn't you?"

"Not this part. This is a black hole."

"Hang on. We're almost out of it."

He saw lights ahead. Vehicles were passing at the end of the street. It had to be the street that bordered the lake.

He could feel Dana's grip on his arm relax. It occurred to him that in the course of their evening together she had shed some of the old hostility. Dana had become almost friendly. Almost.

"Remember that little bar we passed down the street from the embassy?" he said.

"What about it?"

"We should stop there for a—"

A scuffing sound. Light, barely audible.

"Maxwell?" said a low voice behind him.

He whirled around. He saw only a dark silhouette. A man in the shadow of a doorway.

He felt Dana release her grip on his arm.

"Brick. Behind you."

He turned again. There was another man, standing in front of them. Both were dressed in black, arms out in front of them. In the dim light, Maxwell saw something metallic.

The glint of a blade.

"Run!" he yelled to Dana. He faced the closest of the attackers.

He took a quick glance over his shoulder. She was still there.

"Run, damn it!"

She wasn't running. In his peripheral vision, he saw her moving forward. Toward the shadowy figure closest to her.

"Dana, get the hell away. He's got a—"

The man he was facing lunged at him. Maxwell dodged, seeing the knife blade slash at his midsection. The man was a head shorter than Maxwell. He was lithe and fast.

He slashed again, holding the knife low, thrusting it like a fencer. Maxwell sidestepped, swinging the edge of his left hand around, nearly missing. His hand glanced off the side of the man's head.

The attacker stepped back, shook his head, then lunged again. Maxwell got a glimpse of his face. He had gleaming brown eyes and a round, unlined face that looked neither young nor old. A bristle of coarse black hair covered his head.

Maxwell had only rudimentary martial arts training. He had been a middleweight boxer, not a knife fighter. He balanced on the balls of his feet, trying to weave and dodge the knife thrusts.

The attacker was too quick. Maxwell felt a stab of pain in his right arm. He glanced down and saw a remnant of his sleeve hanging loose. Blood was spurting from his upper arm.

The sight of Maxwell's wound seemed to spur the attacker. The dark eyes flicked over Maxwell, measuring him, deciding where to thrust the blade.

Maxwell's arm throbbed. He was right-handed and now his goddamn right arm was useless. Timing was critical now. He had to catch this guy off balance. Surprise him. It was their only chance.

He heard scuffling noises beside him, feet scraping cement, heavy breathing. Dana didn't run away, and now she was in trouble. He had to do something very soon or—

Too late. The attacker was coming at him, feinting left, stepping to the right. Maxwell lurched back. He caught his heel in the broken pavement, and fell backward. He saw the black form sweeping down, the knife going for his chest.

Out of the darkness swelled another shape. Maxwell heard a *thump*. The man with the knife lurched to the side, hitting the concrete on his back.

Before he could get up, a foot lashed out, connecting with his chest. The air left him in an audible *umph*, and he skidded across the crumbling cement.

Maxwell shoved himself to his feet. The man who had attacked him was also back to his feet. The man glanced around, then turned and ran down the darkened street.

Maxwell heard a scuffing noise and whirled. The other attacker was running away too.

It took Maxwell a full second to comprehend what happened.

"What did you do to that guy?" he said.

"Kicked him in the crotch," said Dana. "Same as I did to the first one."

She wasn't even breathing hard. Maxwell stared down the street. The two men had disappeared in the darkness. He could still hear the pounding of their feet on the broken pavement.

"Where'd you learn how to do that?" he asked.

"You don't want to know." Then she saw the blood streaming from his right arm. "Uh-oh. How bad is it?"

"Not bad. Help me tie something on it. Then let's get the hell out of here."

CHAPTER 10

EMBARKED

Hanoi, Socialist Republic of Vietnam
0750 Friday, 27 April

"Unbelievably fucking stupid," growled Boyce.

Maxwell nodded and continued eating his oatmeal. Boyce was letting off steam.

"I should have restricted everyone to the embassy compound," said Boyce. "This mission is too critical to be compromised by getting two key players killed in some damn alleyway."

Joe Ferrone was sitting across from Maxwell at the breakfast table. He had been alerted last night about the attack on Maxwell and Boudroux. He'd called the embassy physician, who dressed Maxwell's wound and gave him a tetanus shot. It turned out to be only a shallow gash in his upper arm, bloody but not serious.

"It's my fault," said Ferrone. "I thought Hanoi was a safe city. Tourists get hassled by beggars and vendors, but there's hardly ever any violent crime."

"Maxwell and Boudroux weren't tourists," said Boyce. "They're players in a sensitive operation. They shouldn't have been someplace where they could get mugged and robbed."

"It wasn't a robbery," said Maxwell.

"How do you know?"

"One of them knew my name. It wasn't money they wanted: They wanted me dead."

"And they damn near succeeded," growled Boyce. "Sounds like our lady scientist is tougher than we gave her credit for."

Maxwell nodded. Dana Boudroux was tougher than the would-be killers, too. Otherwise Maxwell would have been found in the alleyway with his throat cut.

"What did the Hanoi cops have to say about it?" said Boyce. He'd already wolfed down his breakfast and was pacing the room with a fresh Cohiba in his hand.

"Clueless," said Ferrone. "Or else they're not talking."

"How would they have known Maxwell's name?"

Ferrone shrugged. "Easy. The Chinese have operatives all over Vietnam, especially in Hanoi. They like to keep tabs on foreigners. I get tailed sometimes when I go walking in the city. It goes with the territory."

"Tailing isn't the same as killing," said Boyce. "Sounds like the game is ratcheting up to a new level."

Maxwell peered out the window. The sun was breaking through the early morning haze. In the courtyard outside, two Vietnamese orderlies were loading bags into a van.

"Ten minutes," said Boyce, looking at his watch. "Time we said good-bye."

Maxwell nodded, still finishing his oatmeal. The van would carry them to the Noi Bai International Airport. A Navy C-2A Greyhound was standing by to fly them out to the USS *Reagan*.

Boyce and Maxwell were wearing plain gray-green flight suits with the black rank symbols on the shoulders. Sanitized and subdued. No name tags, no Dragon Flight patches while they were in Vietnam.

Ferrone and Kim walked them out to the courtyard where the van was waiting. Dana Boudroux was already in the van, wearing a khaki jumpsuit. She didn't look up or smile.

Ferrone shook hands with Boyce and Maxwell, wished them luck, then stood watching the van carry them out the front gate, past the Marine sentries, off to the airport.

Maxwell waited until they were at the airport and through security. They were walking across the ramp toward the C-2A COD. Boyce had gone to chat with the COD crew.

"Something the matter?"

"No," said Dana. "Why?"

During the drive from the embassy, across the Thang Long Bridge, through the countryside to the airport, she kept herself buried in a newspaper.

"You haven't said a word since we left the embassy."

"Why do men always think something is the matter if a woman doesn't participate in banal conversation?"

"Sorry," he said. "I must have missed something. For a while last night I actually thought that you and I might be friends."

She looked at him through the tortoiseshell glasses. It was the same frosty glare she had given him when they first met at Groom Lake. The Ice Queen look.

"Look, Commander Maxwell, I think we should—"

"It's Brick, remember?"

"Whatever. I think we should keep our relationship on a professional level, and not let our, ah, emotions complicate our jobs."

"Would it complicate our jobs if I thanked you for saving my life?"

"Yes. Don't bother."

Maxwell suppressed the anger that rose in him. He was an idiot. In a weak moment he had let himself think that he and this redheaded automaton had something going. Boudroux was as human as the computer in the Black Star.

"Okay," he said. "I won't."

She didn't hear him. She was already walking toward the airplane.

USS Ronald Reagan

That smell.

Maxwell stopped inside the door at the base of the *Reagan*'s six-story-tall island structure. He stood transfixed, inhaling the evocative scent—a mixture of paint, steel, oil, sweat, hydraulic fluid. Every ship had its own distinctive inner atmosphere. This one belonged to the USS *Ronald Reagan*. He was home.

Maxwell had followed Boyce out the clamshell doors of the COD. A thirty-knot wind swept over the deck, carrying with it wisps of steam from the bow catapults. On either side of the island were parked F/A-18 Super Hornets, wings folded, looking like tethered birds of prey.

He was still wearing the protective Mickey Mouse headset and float coat—survival helmet and inflatable vest—that all COD passengers had to use. Outside the door, fifty feet away, the COD's port engine was still turning.

In the compartment just inside the door to the island, Rear Admiral Jack Hightree, the *Reagan* Strike Group Commander, was grinning and pumping Boyce's hand, welcoming him back to the *Reagan*. Until a few months ago, before being promoted to rear admiral, Boyce had been the commander of the *Reagan*'s air wing.

Half a dozen staff officers and enlisted personnel stood around them, awed by the presence of two flag officers. Maxwell saw Dana Boudroux coming through the door. She was peeling off her float coat and headset.

She glanced around, then sniffed the air. "This place smells like a locker room."

"It *is* a locker room," said Maxwell. "One of the world's largest."

"Why are you just standing around here? Didn't we come here to work?"

"Are you always this snotty, or is it just me?"

"You haven't seen anything yet, Commander Maxwell."

"It's Brick."

"Whatever. Is someone going to tell me where I'll be living?"

"You'll have to be escorted until you've learned your away around the ship. I'm sure someone has been—"

"I know about ships. All I want to know is where my stateroom is located."

A baby-faced young woman in dungarees stepped forward. "Petty Officer Miller, ma'am. I'm here to show you to your quarters. Don't worry about your bags: Someone will take them to your room."

Dana flashed a glacial smile at Maxwell, then turned to follow the young woman. The petty officer led the way through the first knee-knocker—the hard steel enclosure positioned at every bulkhead along the ship's passageways.

"Owww, damn!" Dana was clutching her shin with both hands.

"Oh, sorry, ma'am," said the petty officer. "I forgot to warn you about the knee-knockers. Happens to everyone the first time."

Maxwell caught Dana glowering down the passageway at him. He tried to turn away before she saw him laughing, but he was too late.

The ready room hadn't changed. Over the door was the same old sign: HOME OF THE WORLD-FAMOUS VFA-36 ROADRUNNERS.

The leather-upholstered, airline-style lounging seats, all facing forward, were the same. By longstanding tradition, the aisle seat on the front row was the Skipper's seat. *His* old seat.

For a while Maxwell stood in the front of the room peering around, letting the memories wash over him. This was where he'd checked in as the new squadron operations officer after leaving NASA. Within a few months he'd replaced the executive officer, who was lost in an accident. Not long after that, Maxwell took command of the Roadrunners when the skipper, Killer DeLancey, was shot down in Iraq.

For two years the VFA-36 Roadrunners had been his life, his responsibility. In this ready room he'd briefed over a hundred missions, mourned pilots lost in combat, celebrated the squadron's victories in peace and war.

On the port bulkhead was the Greenie Board with the grease-penciled carrier landing grades of each Roadrunner. Maxwell noted that the current Top Hook in the squadron was Lieutenant B. J. Johnson. Bullet Alexander was in a respectable third place on the grade ranking.

"What's this?" said Maxwell. "The squadron skipper isn't number one?"

"It's called leadership," said Alexander, standing beside him. He was wearing his battered leather jacket. "Have to let the junior officers share a little of the glory, you know."

"Oh, yeah. I forgot."

He remembered when Alexander checked into the squadron as the new executive officer. His logbook contained not quite three hundred carrier landings, a paltry number for a senior squadron officer. Alexander had spent tours of duty as an instructor in the Hornet training squadron, then as a member of the Blue Angels, the Navy's aerial demonstration team. They were shore-duty jobs, and they'd caused him to miss most of the combat operations in the Middle East and Afghanistan.

Like Maxwell before him, Alexander had faced the prejudice against officers who hadn't worked their way up through all the junior- and middle-grade squadron jobs before getting their own command.

Alexander surprised everyone, including Maxwell. He learned quickly. Going one-vee-one against all comers, he established himself as the undisputed king of the hill in air-to-air combat. And though it took him a little longer, he'd worked his way from the bottom of the Greenie Board.

They walked down the aisle between the rows of seats. Maxwell stopped to shake hands with some of the pilots who had once served under him.

"Hey, Brick," said Lieutenant Commander Flash Gordon, jumping up from one of the computer terminals. "We thought you had a cushy job back at Fallon."

"They sent me out to check on you. We heard Bullet has been too soft on you guys."

Gordon rolled his eyeballs. "That'll be the day."

Lieutenant B. J. Johnson was sitting in the last row, pecking on a laptop computer. She glanced up, saw Maxwell, and thrust the computer aside. Her cheeks reddened.

"Skipper Maxwell," said B.J. She thrust her hand out. "You coming back to fly with us?"

He shook her hand and gave her a smile. B. J. Johnson was the only female pilot in the squadron. During her first year in the Roadrunners, she had carried a not-so-secret crush on her commanding officer.

"If Bullet wants to give me his seat," said Maxwell, "I'll take it."

"No way," said Alexander. "It took me too damn long to get this job. I'm not giving it back."

Alexander steered Maxwell on down the aisle to the back of the ready room. The fluorescent glow from the overhead lights glistened off Alexander's shiny brown scalp. He glanced around, making sure they were out of earshot of the flight-suited pilots watching them.

"They're still bummed out over losing Hozer Miller," said Alexander. "No one is buying that 'operational accident' bullshit, and neither am I. Hornets don't just blow up without a good reason."

"You were there," said Maxwell. "What do you think?"

"A missile. No question. But where did it come from? Why didn't we get a radar warning?"

"What, then?"

"You tell me." Alexander was giving him a hard look. "How about something Chinese, something invisible? Same thing that's been whacking the Vietnamese airplanes and gunboats. How about it, Brick? Am I close?"

Maxwell didn't answer. Alexander had a good idea of what happened to Hozer Miller. And Maxwell could tell that he had a good idea of why Maxwell and the STOU team were aboard the *Reagan*.

He glanced at his watch. "I've got to get down to Intel. When I have the answer, I'll let you know."

"Red, don't even *think* of lighting that thing here."

Boyce had the lid of his Zippo open, ready to ignite a Cohiba. "You never bitched about cigars when I was the Air Wing Commander."

"You're not the Air Wing Commander anymore," said Rear Adm. Jack Hightree. "You're just another freeloading admiral and a guest on this boat. No cigars on my bridge."

Boyce sighed and snapped the lighter closed. Hightree was still a pompous pain in the ass. Boyce gave the Cohiba a loving look, then stuffed it back in his leather flight jacket.

Boyce and Hightree had been friends for twenty years, though Hightree had always been senior by at least one pay grade. As the *Reagan* Strike Group Commander, Hightree wore two stars versus Boyce's one. In Boyce's opinion, Hightree was a competent but overly conservative commander. His ascent through the ranks had been accomplished in a risk-averse manner, and he made it no secret that he was earning a third star the same way.

They were in the flag intel compartment. At the front table with Hightree was his intelligence officer, Commander Harvey Wentz. Seated at a second table were Maxwell and the rest of the Dragon Flight team, all in flight suits.

An illuminated screen glimmered on the bulkhead. On it appeared a photograph of a gray, diamond-shaped jet.

"Hey," said Sharp O'Toole. "That looks like our Black Star, sort of. Close, but not exactly."

Harvey Wentz flashed an indulgent smile. Wentz never bothered to conceal his distaste for aviators. In his view, they were single-purpose gladiators who became dangerous if given too much information. Wentz made it his business to parcel out only what they absolutely needed to know, nothing more.

"You're looking at the *Dong-jin*, ladies and gentlemen. The Chinese stealth jet based on technology stolen from the United States. This is the prototype, the only version on which we have current information. We consider it probable that the aircraft has been upgraded in the past two years, just as our own Black Star has been improved.

"The intelligence consensus is that the PRC has inserted the *Dong-jin*—probably several—into the conflict with Vietnam. Evidence suggests that all the aerial losses sustained by the Vietnamese—a transport aircraft and two Fishbed fighters—as well as numerous surface craft were caused by *Dong-jins*."

"What about the F/A-18 off the *Reagan*?" asked Crud Carruthers. "Was that a *Dong-jin* shoot-down?"

Wentz hesitated, glancing at Boyce. Boyce gave him a nod, and Wentz continued. "From the small amount of debris recovered from the downed F/A-18, we determined that the F/A-18 was probably hit by a PL-8 heat-seeker missile, an item the Chinese adapted from the Israeli Python 3. Since there were no Chinese fighters in the area at the time, we're assuming it was fired by a *Dong-jin*."

"Why shoot a U.S. jet?" asked Gypsy Palmer. "Are the Chinese trying to start a war with us?"

Again Wentz hesitated. Before he could answer, Boyce rose to his feet. "One side of our intelligence community is of the opinion that the ChiComs are sending us a little message. They want us to stay out of this little dispute they're having with Vietnam. Another side thinks that the PLA commanders have just gotten reckless. They're sure enough of their strength that they're betting that the U.S. will back down."

"Well, Admiral?" asked Sharp O'Toole. "Will we?"

Boyce fixed O'Toole with a piercing look. It had always been Boyce's style to encourage his junior officers to be open with him, even disagree—up to a limit. As usual, O'Toole had exceeded the limit.

"Button your lip, Major O'Toole, and you'll find out."

Boyce nodded to Wentz, who picked up a stack of red-bordered file folders. He began distributing them to the team members. Each folder bore a TOP SECRET stencil.

"This is the fact file on the *Dong-jin*," said Boyce. "Read the standard caveat on the cover, including the item about not removing it from this compartment. Bear in mind that the currency of the data is questionable. During the war with Taiwan, the Chinese lost all their existing *Dong-jins*. But their technology and research facilities were left mostly intact, so it was only a matter of time before they resurrected the program. Since then, we have to assume they've made advances in stealth technology, just as we have."

Hightree watched the exchange, his lean, patrician face showing no reaction. As the Carrier Strike Group Commander, he had overall responsibility for operations from his ships. But he and Boyce knew this was a unique situation. Though Boyce was junior in rank, his authority came from a higher link in the chain of command.

"If the ChiComs have, in fact, sent us a message by shooting down one of our Super Hornets, then our Commander-in-Chief intends to send them a little reply. But instead of an eye for an eye, it's gonna be two eyes. Or in this case, two jets, or two ships, or two of anything they whack that belongs to us."

The illuminated screen behind Boyce went blank for a second, then another image flashed onto the screen. It was a still shot of a stubby-winged, bulbous-nosed jet aircraft. The long fuselage was slick, unmarred by the bulge of a crew cockpit.

Boyce gave it a moment, enjoying the curious stares of the audience. "For those of you unfamiliar with our latest UCAV technology, let me introduce the Chameleon."

UCAV was the military's acronym for Unmanned Combat Air Vehicle. The Chameleon—the UAV-17—was a single-engine, unmanned reconnaissance aircraft equipped with a configurable radar and IR signature. Using its own electronic emulation equipment, the Chameleon could present itself on enemy radars and infrared sensors as a high-altitude bomber, fast-moving fighter, or surveillance aircraft.

"All you need to know about this little bird is that we have them aboard the *Reagan*. One will be launched tomorrow, configured to display the electronic signature of an F/A-18G Growler."

The team members stared at the image on the screen. The Chameleon looked nothing like a Growler, which was a variant of the Super Hornet developed to replace the aging EA-6B Prowler. The mission of the Growler, like the Prowler before it, was to suppress enemy radar and communications.

Boyce went on. "The Chameleon—posing as a Growler—will make a feint at Hainan's airspace. We want them to think a strike might be imminent. Our Rules of Engagement preclude an actual overflight of Chinese territory, but the ChiComs won't know that. We expect them to send up fighters, probably SU-27 Flankers."

"What about our CAP fighters?" asked O'Toole.

"They'll be on station, presenting plenty of radar presence, but they won't go in to cover the Chameleon."

"Then the decoy's gonna be dead meat," said O'Toole. "How else are you going to cover—"

He saw the answer in Boyce's face.

"Very good," said Boyce, smiling at his audience. "Now you know why you're here."

CHAPTER 11

CAT SHOT

USS Ronald Reagan
South China Sea
1015 Saturday, 28 April

Maxwell peered around the *Reagan*'s flight deck. It was nearly deserted. So were the viewing decks in the island and most of the compartments that overlooked the carrier's massive flight deck. Gone from the open deck was the swarm of plane captains, fuelers, aircraft handlers, and ordnance crews.

Only essential personnel—catapult crew, asbestos-suited firefighters and rescue men, the captain, helmsman, and officer-of-the-deck on the captain's bridge, the air boss and his staff in Primary Flight Control, Admiral Hightree and Boyce on the flag bridge—were permitted to observe the strange craft on the *Reagan*'s flight deck today. Each had been required to sign a nondisclosure statement.

Maxwell and O'Toole had ridden the number-one elevator from the hangar deck up to the flight deck with their shroud-covered Black Star. Crud Carruthers and Gypsy Palmer accompanied their own shrouded jet upward on the number-two elevator aft of the island structure. Not until the jets were towed forward and spotted on the bow catapults were the shrouds removed, revealing the shape of the stealth jets.

Maxwell saw the Chameleon positioned on the number-three waist catapult. The unmanned jet's single turbofan engine was already whining. It was ready to be catapulted.

"Look at that thing," said O'Toole. "Are the Chinese stupid enough to believe that's a Growler?"

"Maybe not," said Maxwell, "but we're betting they'll come up and take a look."

"I'm betting they'll laugh their asses off."

"Are all Marines as optimistic as you, O'Toole?"

"Marines expect every operation to turn to shit. That's why we're never surprised when it does."

Since their final briefing an hour before in the intel compartment, O'Toole had been jabbering nonstop. His vocal cords seemed to be hardwired to his adrenal gland.

Maxwell ducked under the nose of the Black Star and gave the exterior of the jet a final preflight inspection. Following him was Senior Chief Petty Officer Rodman, one of the Black Star technicians who had accompanied the Dragon Flight team from Groom Lake.

"Talky one, that Major O'Toole," said Rodman.

"He's a little pumped right now."

"Guess I would be too if I was flying in this thing."

Maxwell had known Rodman since his early test pilot days. The senior chief was a veteran of nearly thirty years' service, most of it in black-ops programs like the Black Star and its predecessor, the F-117 Nighthawk.

Maxwell continued around the jet, peering into the wheel wells, checking the underbelly for fluid leaks or signs of skin damage. At the jet's rear fuselage, he ran his hand over the wing's trailing edge as if it were a living thing. It was a habit of his, like a rider stroking his horse.

The Black Star was still an unknown quantity to him. Even with the qualification flights and the field carrier landing practice, he had less than a hundred hours flying time in the jet. But he had already figured out that the Black Star was not a fighter pilot's dream machine. Compared to fighters like the F/A-18 Super Hornet, it was a dog.

"Five minutes, Commander," said Rodman.

Maxwell nodded. Rodman was prompting him to wrap up the preflight and man the cockpit. A window of sixteen minutes had been allotted for the mission package—the two Black Stars and the Chameleon—to be exposed on the open deck. Outside this time frame the jets were vulnerable to observation by Russian and Chinese reconnaissance satellites that were scheduled to pass overhead. And though the sea around the *Reagan* Strike Group was constantly screened for alien submarines, a sighting by a Chinese vessel couldn't be prevented.

He climbed the boarding ladder and settled himself into the front seat. O'Toole was already strapped into the back. He was busy setting up his station, running the systems checks.

Standing outside on the ladder, Rodman helped Maxwell fasten his harness and plug in the life-support and communications connections.

"Bring this bird back in one piece, Commander," said Rodman. "I've gotten attached to her."

Maxwell nodded. "I'll take care of her, Senior Chief."

Rodman clapped him on the shoulder, then disappeared down the ladder. Seconds later he reappeared beneath the nose. He was rotating his hand, giving Maxwell the go-ahead to start engines.

In less than a minute, both turbofan engines were running. O'Toole read the check list over the intercom, and Maxwell responded. When the checks were complete, Maxwell signaled that they were ready. The mission would be conducted in an Emcon—emissions control—environment. No electronic signals to give away the Black Stars' presence.

In his peripheral vision, Maxwell sensed a blur of motion from his left. The Chameleon was hurtling down the track of the number-three catapult, off the angled deck. The pilotless jet rotated smoothly and accelerated into the hazy sky ahead of the *Reagan*.

The fictitious Growler was on its way to its station.

Following the aircraft director's signals, Maxwell eased the throttles forward and rolled toward the catapult.

"Hey, Boss," said O'Toole over the intercom. "I just had a thought."

"It better be important."

"You know we're about to be the first crew ever to make a catapult launch from a ship with the Black Star?"

"Terrific. Now shut up."

O'Toole was right, he thought. They had made half a dozen launches from the mobile catapult at Groom Lake. But that was dry earth, without a sixty-foot drop from the deck to a churning ocean below.

He felt the jet lurch as the nose-tow bar clunked into the slot on the catapult shuttle. The shuttle—the only moving component of the mighty steam catapult visible above deck—would travel the length of the catapult track towing the jet with it. With a sixty-thousand-pound jet attached, the shuttle could go from zero to one-hundred-fifty knots in two and a half seconds.

Maxwell saw Dog Balls Harvey, the *Reagan*'s shooter—catapult officer—giving him the power-up signal. Maxwell shoved the throttles forward to the full-thrust detent.

The shooter was peering at him, waiting for the salute—the traditional signal that he was ready to be catapulted. Maxwell glanced back inside the cockpit, giving the displays one last scan. No lights, no warnings, no cautions. Over the open intercom he heard O'Toole's heavy breathing.

He gave the shooter a salute, then shoved his helmet back against the headrest.

A second ticked past.

Another. And then—

Whoom. The Black Star hurtled down the catapult track as if it were in the grip of a giant hand. The gray mass of the flight deck blurred past. Maxwell felt his eyeballs flatten, his spine pressing into the hard contour of the seat back. From the backseat he heard O'Toole grunting against the force of the acceleration.

The acceleration abruptly ceased. The bow of the carrier swept beneath him. Ahead lay the whitecapped surface of the South China Sea.

He nudged the stick back. The jet responded, tilting its nose a few degrees above the horizon. Maxwell raised the landing gear, then the flaps.

"Shit hot!" said O'Toole. "Imagine that. This thing is actually flying. That makes us the first guys ever to catapult in a—"

"O'Toole?"

"What, Boss?"

"Shut the fuck up."

"Okay. But isn't it just amazing—"

"That's an order."

"Yes, sir."

Lingshui Air Base, Hainan Island

General Zhang peered into the green-tinted screen of the situational display. The screen was a repeater of the master display in the air defense command post. Sitting inside the fortified revetment at his headquarters, Zhang had been alerted by the air defense controller at Lingshui.

A lone F/A-18 jamming aircraft flying directly toward the Hainan air defense boundary.

Why? It was very peculiar, thought Zhang.

The Americans routinely sent electronic surveillance aircraft to the edge of PRC airspace. Since the American aircraft carrier, the *Reagan*, entered the South China Sea a few weeks ago, they had kept fighters and jammers and data-collecting aircraft in the air almost round the clock. Though such activity was an irritant to PLA air defense command-ers, it was not overtly hostile.

Already a flight of SU-27s was taking off to engage the intruder. Zhang could hear the muffled thunder of their afterburners as they leaped from the runway at Lingshui. Led by Major Chun, the four supersonic fighters were being vectored toward the incoming American jet.

It should be a routine response to the American provocation, Zhang reflected. Just another of the Americans' games, probing the PLA air defense network, causing the acquisition radars to light up and identify themselves so that the Americans could plot them. Before the interceptors actually got close enough to engage the incoming Growler, the American jet would turn away.

At least, that's what usually happened.

Zhang's fueled and armed *Dong-jin* was also ready to launch, and so were two more in the adjoining revetments. Though the *Dong-jin* wouldn't normally be used for such a routine operation, he had alerted the *Dong-jin* crews to ready themselves. Just in case.

There was something different about this encounter. What was it?

For several seconds Zhang stared into the greenish display. And then it came to him. He'd seen this scenario before. It was a ruse the Americans had attempted just before the war between China and Taiwan. The incoming jet had been a decoy—an unmanned aircraft emitting the electronic profile of a jamming aircraft.

The trick had worked—almost. Not until Zhang had fired a missile from his *Dong-jin* did he realize that it was a trap. In the next few minutes, he found himself engaged with a swarm of U.S. Navy Super Hornets. Only because of the *Dong-jin*'s near invisibility was he able to elude the fighters. He had managed to put a few cannon rounds into the lead F/A-18, puncturing a fuel cell, but the enemy jet was lucky and escaped.

But Zhang's intuition told him that it was more than luck. The enemy pilot demonstrated the same sort of cunning that

Zhang encountered later when the *gwai-lo* devil stole one of the precious *Dong-jin*'s and then shot Zhang himself down with it.

And caused his face to be hideously disfigured.

Could it have been the same man? There was no proof, but it didn't matter. Zhang didn't need proof.

So now they were trying it again. But what did they want? A skirmish between their fighters and the PLA's? Did they wish to avenge the Super Hornet they lost a few weeks ago? If so, then there would indeed be an exchange of missiles and each side would shed some blood. It would be another event in an ongoing series of events—the U.S. and the PRC jabbing and testing each other like two bulls in a pasture.

Each nation would righteously blame the other in public, then the diplomats would resolve the dispute in private. The rival nations would continue to glower at each other, waiting for the next skirmish. All very predictable.

But why were the American fighters keeping such a distance from their jamming aircraft? At this far range, they would be unable to protect it from the intercepting SU-27s.

Over the tactical frequency monitor, Zhang could hear Major Chun, the SU-27 flight leader, responding to the vectors of the radar intercept controller. If the intruder turned away and showed no hostile intent, Chun and his fighters would merely parallel his track, warning him away from Chinese territory. If he actually violated the air defense boundary, then Chun was authorized to shoot him down.

Zhang frowned at the display. He could see the symbols of the SU-27s accelerating on the screen. The symbol of the Growler—or whatever it really was—continued to bore straight toward the air defense boundary.

The American combat air patrol fighters—they were tagged on the situational display as F/A-18 fighters—were still in their orbit. They had to be aware of the SU-27s streaking toward the unprotected Growler.

In the green-tinted glass, Zhang could see the reflection of his face. A wave of revulsion swept over him.

And then, as if triggered by the memory of his ravaged face, a thought struck him like a thunderbolt. *Could it be him? The man who shot him down? The* gwai-lo *who destroyed his face and his life?*

Zhang needed no further prompting. He snatched up the red telephone at his console. "Alert the crews. Ready the *Dong-jins* for takeoff."

CHAPTER 12

IRONJAW

27,000 feet
South China Sea
1055 Saturday, 28 April

"Ironjaw, this is Sea Lord. You have bogeys airborne off Lingshui, range sixty-five, angels twenty and climbing."

"Ironjaw copies. We tag the contacts as Flankers. Confirm?"

"That's confirmed, Ironjaw. Four Flankers, nose-hot, fifty-five miles."

Maxwell had to smile at the bogus dialogue. It was being transmitted for the Chinese eavesdroppers on the Navy's tactical frequencies. Sea Lord was the controller in the orbiting E-2C Hawkeye. The voice of Ironjaw, who was an intel officer back aboard the *Reagan*, was being relayed via a satellite to appear as if it were coming from the Growler. Directing the scam from his padded seat in CIC—Combat Information Center—was Rear Admiral Red Boyce.

In his multifunction display screen Maxwell could see the data-linked symbol of the pseudo-Growler, thirty miles ahead, and the symbol of Crud Carruthers's Black Star a mile off his left wing. Also on the screen were the symbols of the four F/A-18Es on their CAP station. The CAP jets were there for theatrical effect, but Maxwell knew they could be summoned if the engagement with the Chinese suddenly turned sour. The squadron mates of Hozer Miller were eager for a payback session.

Other symbols swam into view on the display. Sure enough, there were the bogeys, each showing the telltale ID of a Russian-built SU-27 Flanker, now the PLA Air Force's premier fighter.

Maxwell peered out the left side of his canopy, at the place in the sky where his display showed Carruthers's Black Star flying in a wide combat spread.

Nothing. Not even a glimmer of the stealth jet.

Maxwell lowered the chromatic frequency–detecting goggles mounted on the top front of his helmet. Instantly his world was bathed in a soft greenish glow. The CFD goggles were similar in shape and weight to night-vision goggles, which enhanced available light to permit seeing objects in darkness. The goggles permitted the viewer to see an object like the Black Star, whose skin was chromatically altered as to be invisible. If the goggles were calibrated to the frequency of the stealth jet's skin cloaking, they could reconstruct the image for the viewer.

Again Maxwell peered out beyond his left wing. He blinked, still seeing nothing. Nothing but the greenish sky and—

There. Shimmering into view a half mile away was the spectral shape of the Black Star.

Okay, he had the Black Star. What about the *Dong-jins*? Did the Chinese send their stealth jets up to play? Would the CFD goggles penetrate the cloaking of the *Dong-jins*?

No one knew. It was a missing piece of the puzzle. CFD goggles, in fact, had been developed by the Chinese after they acquired stealth jet technology from the U.S. When Maxwell commandeered the *Dong-jin* during the raid at Chouzhou, he took a set of the Chinese goggles with him. In a rare instance of American reverse-engineering, scientists at Groom Lake developed their own chromatic frequency–detecting goggles and tuned them to the specific wavelength of the Black Star's skin cloaking.

"Ironjaw, Sea Lord. Your bogeys bear zero-two-zero, forty miles, angels twenty-five. Whoa, looks like they're bracketing now, Ironjaw."

Maxwell saw it too. A bracket—splitting the flight of Flankers into two elements and attacking from either side of the target—was an obsolete but sometimes effective tactic. Especially if they were concerned about the CAP Hornets coming to the rescue of the Growler.

"Ironjaw, roger, we see the bracket. We're maintaining track."

More bogus dialogue. The guy playing the role of the Growler pilot was good, thought Maxwell. His voice had an edge to it, the right mix of tension and professional cool as the enemy fighters closed on him.

Neither Maxwell nor Carruthers had transmitted on their UHF radios since catapulting from the *Reagan*. Except for the data-link connection, which was relayed via a coded satellite downlink, the two Black Stars were emission-free.

Or so Maxwell hoped. The Chinese were full of surprises. The existence of the sophisticated *Dong-jin* came as a shock when the jets were first deployed in the PRC–Taiwan war. China's advances in stealth technology continued to surprise U.S. intelligence analysts.

The Flankers were almost within heat-seeking-missile range of the Chameleon. Almost close enough to get a visual ID.

And then what? Would they realize they'd been scammed and go home? Or would they hose it with a missile anyway?

"Ironjaw, your distance to the boundary now twenty miles. Take heading three-five-zero to parallel."

"Ironjaw, roger, coming to three-five-zero. That puts me nose-hot on the left pair of bogeys, confirm."

"Sea Lord confirms. Your weapons status red and tight, Ironjaw."

"Ironjaw's status red and tight."

Maxwell listened to the exchange between the Sea Lord controller and the fictional Growler pilot. Red Boyce was a puppet master, pulling the strings from his padded chair in the *Reagan*'s CIC.

"Red and tight" meant that the Growler—normally armed with two AIM-9X Sidewinder air-to-air missiles, a loaded M61A2 twenty-millimeter cannon, and at least one AIM-120 radar-guided missile—was not cleared to fire on the incoming Flankers. To Chinese monitors, it would seem that the Growler was changing course to parallel rather than to penetrate the Chinese air defense boundary. His intentions would appear not to be hostile.

Now it was up to the Chinese. Would they—

Yes. Maxwell saw it in his display. The left element of Flankers was climbing, taking a perch from which they could cover the second pair. As the Chameleon/Growler changed course to the left, the two Flankers on the right swung their noses into a hard pursuit curve.

They were going to shoot.

"Ironjaw is spiked, four o'clock!" The Growler pilot's voice sounded authentic. He sounded like a pilot being targeted by a Chinese air-to-air radar.

The Flankers were rolling in on the Growler, lighting him up with their fire control radars—causing the "spike" on the fake Growler's radar warning receiver.

Maxwell shoved his throttles forward. Any second now the Flanker pilots would get a visual ID. They'd know the Growler wasn't a Growler.

He saw the Flankers. They were high and fast, in a loose fighting formation, separated by a quarter mile. They were in a hard turn, carving toward their target like lions chasing a wildebeest.

In his HUD Maxwell saw the AIM-9 Sidewinder seeker

circle superimposed over the silhouette of the Flanker on the right. The tone in his earphones confirmed that the missile was locked onto its target. An illuminated SHOOT cue was flashing above the target designator box. He knew that Carruthers was tracking the Flanker on the left, waiting until he saw Maxwell's missile in the air.

The image swelled in his HUD. For an instant Maxwell felt a sense of revulsion: Shooting an unsuspecting enemy jet from behind gave him no pleasure.

He shoved the thought from his mind. *Remember Hozer.*

He squeezed the trigger.

The airframe of the Black Star shuddered as the missile bay door opened and the 190-pound missile was ejected from the launching rail. Half a second later, the door snapped shut again.

He saw the blur of the missile accelerating to its Mach 2.5 attack velocity. In his peripheral vision, he caught the flash from Carruthers's weapon leaving its rail.

He resisted the impulse to transmit "Fox Two"—the announcement of a Sidewinder shot. No announcements today. Let the Chinese figure it out for themselves. While he waited for the seconds to tick by, he kept the Flanker superimposed in the seeker circle in case a follow-up shot was necessary.

It wasn't. Through the HUD, he saw a bright orange plume erupt where the Flanker had been. *Splash one Flanker*, Maxwell thought, again omitting the radio call.

Two seconds later, another plume erupted where the lead Flanker had been.

Splash two.

"Ironjaw, this is Sea Lord. Say your status." The playacting continued. The controller in the Hawkeye was querying the Growler.

"Ironjaw is naked," replied the bogus Growler pilot, reporting that he was no longer receiving a radar threat. "I've still got two contacts—I show them as Flankers—eight o'clock high, twenty miles."

The two remaining Flankers were still out there.

"Sea Lord confirms the Flankers, Ironjaw. We show them turning nose-cold. Suggest a heading of two-nine-zero to keep you defensive."

"Ironjaw coming to two-nine-zero."

The controller was vectoring Ironjaw to a heading that would keep it in the rear quarter of the retreating Flankers. Maxwell wondered if either of the Flankers reported a visual on the Chameleon before they were shot down. If so, the Chinese controllers now knew that *something* had slipped through their radar and killed two fighters.

Beneath Maxwell's right wing were the carcasses of the two destroyed Flankers. One had exploded, leaving a wide debris field, and the other had its tail knocked off by the Sidewinder. The billowing gray canopy of a parachute appeared above the tailless Flanker. Maxwell shoved the CFD goggles up on his helmet and peered through the glass of his canopy. One Chinese pilot had survived, and one hadn't.

Too bad, thought Maxwell. The Flanker pilots had thought they were about to kill a Growler crew. He had shown them the same consideration they gave Hozer Miller. Payback was a bitch.

But it wasn't a Flanker that killed Hozer Miller.

With that thought, Maxwell sensed the presence of danger. *Could a* Dong-jin *be out here?*

He snapped the CFD goggles back in place. He scanned the area from behind, across the front of the jet, to the other side. The Chameleon was turning to the new northwesterly heading. The last two Flankers were exiting the area, probably returning to Lingshui. Carruthers was on station a quarter mile abeam and slightly aft of Maxwell's left wing.

Nothing else in the area.

Or was there?

Maxwell blinked, squinted to refocus his eyes, then scanned again. Nothing.

It would have been a lucky accident if the CFD goggles were able to pinpoint the chromatic frequency the Chinese had selected for the *Dong-jin.* Anyway, why would a *Dong-jin* be there if they sent SU-27 Flankers to kill the Growler?

Peering into the empty green haze through the CFD goggles, Maxwell didn't have an answer. He only knew that he was getting a loud and clear gut feeling.

Something was out there.

General Zhang Yu watched the fireballs plunge toward the sea.

From his perch high and outside the SU-27s' pursuit curve, he had expected to observe the destruction of the enemy jet. Instead, one of the attacking SU-27s exploded. While Zhang stared in shock, the second fighter erupted in a roiling ball of fire.

What happened? He hadn't seen even the metallic glint of an air-to-air missile. Did it come from the jamming aircraft, the one the Americans called a Growler?

No. He was certain that nothing came from the direction of the target, which was still in a turn away.

Zhang and his wingman, Captain Tsan, had arrived only a minute before Major Chun, leading the flight of SU-27s, had received authorization to kill the enemy jet. It was an American Growler. It could be on a mission to jam the Hainan air defense network.

Now Chun's SU-27 was a heap of debris. So was his wingman's, and at least one of them was dead. Zhang had glimpsed the flutter of a single parachute canopy.

Like a computer processing a problem, Zhang's brain began assembling the disconnected bits of information.

Something killed the two SU-27s from behind.

Zhang rolled his *Dong-jin* into a steep left bank and peered into the sky where the pair of SU-27s had been. With his naked eyes, he saw nothing. Nothing but the falling debris of the destroyed fighters.

He reached for the spectrum-sensing goggles that were hinged to the side of his helmet and swung them into place over his visor. Again he peered into the sky, sweeping from side to side.

Still nothing. He kept scanning, peering up, down, directly behind the decoy. Nothing out there. No visual clue to—

What was that?

Something below his left wing, perhaps three kilometers away. A faintly visible object, shimmering like a mirage.

As Zhang stared, the object disappeared. A second later, he saw it again, but in a different place. Were there more than one?

The pieces of the puzzle were falling into place. With a rush of clarity, Zhang knew what happened to the SU-27s.

The enemy Growler wasn't a Growler. The SU-27s were lured into a trap.

Zhang knew now what the shimmering objects were. If only he could get a clear view, he would turn them into the same kind of hellish fireballs that they had made of the SU-27s.

But couldn't they do the same to him? Zhang reversed the *Dong-jin* into a hard right bank, keeping his jet high and inside where he'd last spotted the ephemeral objects. Could they see him? Did they have spectrum-sensing technology?

There was no way to be sure. The only prudent thing to do was to remain out of range and exit the area. The order of battle had just been radically changed. The one-sided conflict was now a two-sided stealth war.

Zhang's turn was taking him behind and above the Growler, which was just rolling out of its turn on a northwesterly heading. Zhang had a good view of the aircraft's bulbous-nosed, stubby-winged shape.

It wasn't a Growler. Zhang had encountered such an aircraft before. It was an unmanned decoy, something the

Americans had developed that could imitate a real warplane. They had employed the decoy before during the war in the Taiwan Strait.

"It is not too late," said his systems officer, Captain Po, from the back cockpit. "We can kill the enemy jamming aircraft." It was the first time Po had spoken since they witnessed the downing of the SU-27s.

For a moment, Zhang considered. Po, incompetent idiot that he was, still hadn't figured out that the aircraft was a decoy. But at least he had the spirit of a warrior. And perhaps he was right. They could fire a heat-seeking missile and be gone before the Americans detected them.

No. It would play into the hands of the enemy. The invisible jets—they were undoubtedly some version of the American Black Star—were waiting for such an opening. Even if they couldn't spot him, a single bullet or missile from the *Dong-jin* could mark his position. It would set him up for a kill shot.

Zhang took another glance at the decoy aircraft. It was a tempting target, fat and vulnerable as a low-flying goose. The words of Sun Tzu came to him: *He will win who knows when to fight and when not to fight.*

This was a time not to fight. He swung the nose of the *Dong-jin* toward the safety of Hainan.

CHAPTER 13

GUT FEELING

USS Ronald Reagan
South China Sea
1140 Saturday, 28 April

"Three-oh-one, Rhino ball, five-point-two," called Maxwell.

"Roger, ball," answered the voice of Slim Chance, the LSO.

More radio playacting. Maxwell had just reported that he had the ball in sight and that his fuel remaining was five-thousand-two-hundred pounds. He identified his aircraft as a "rhino"—an F/A-18 Super Hornet.

Gear down, hook extended. He rolled the Black Star's wings level in the groove a quarter mile behind the USS *Ronald Reagan*. A white ribbon of foam trailed behind the hundred-thousand-ton carrier.

The flight deck and the viewing platforms in the island were again empty of nonrequired personnel. Instead of the usual half dozen assistants and LSOs-in-training on the LSO platform, Slim Chance was alone. Even the PLAT—Pilot Landing Aid Television—that videoed every carrier landing was blacked out. The Black Star would return to the *Reagan* the same way it left—in secret.

Maxwell forced himself to concentrate on the Fresnel Lens—the glowing yellow ball mounted to the left of the landing area. The ball was slightly beneath the row of green datum lights that marked the correct glide path to the carrier deck. It told Maxwell that his flight path was below the optimum glide slope.

He nudged the throttles an increment forward. The Black Star's descent rate flattened. The ball eased up between the datums. On glide path.

The ramp swept beneath him. In his peripheral vision he saw the LSO platform blurring past the left wing. On the right, the carrier's massive island structure loomed like a granite outcropping.

The Black Star's wheels slammed onto the steel deck. By habit and training, Maxwell shoved the throttles forward in case the hook missed a wire.

It didn't. He felt the hard, reassuring bite of the straps into his shoulders. The jet lurched to a stop on the center line.

"Hey, Boss," said O'Toole. "We just made history. First crew to land a Black Star aboard a real ship."

O'Toole's mouth was engaged again.

"Don't expect to get your picture in the paper. This thing doesn't exist yet."

"Oh, yeah. I forgot."

"Run it," said Boyce.

Commander Harvey Wentz pushed the play button on the video machine.

While they waited for the plasma monitor to come to life, Boyce gazed around the intel compartment. Seated at the long steel table, still wearing their sweat-stained flight suits, were the Black Star crews. By the bulkhead were Adm. Hightree and Wentz. Dana Boudroux was wearing her blue jumpsuit, seated at the far end of the room. Cool and aloof as ever.

It was strange, Boyce thought. When they were in Hanoi, he had detected signs of a thaw in the Ice Queen. To his critical eye it looked as if she was warming up to Maxwell. But something happened.

A black-and-white image appeared on the monitor. It was from the digital tape recording of Maxwell's head-up display. In the foreground was the standard HUD symbology—the velocity vector showing the direction the aircraft is flying, the horizon, and the digital readouts for altitude, heading, airspeed, Mach number, angle of attack.

A grayish object was squiggling in the corner of the HUD view.

"That's the Chameleon," said Wentz. He aimed the red beam of his laser pointer at the image of the decoy jet. "He's just been given the heading that would penetrate the Hainan air defense zone. Any moment now you'll see—ah, there they come."

Two long twin-finned shapes swept into view, in a steep bank to point their noses toward the Chameleon.

"The Flankers," said Boyce.

The audience watched in silent fascination. Through the HUD they could see the Flanker on the right. The illuminated seeker circle on the display enclosed the Chinese jet like the loop of a lasso. The SHOOT cue was flashing.

The blurred image of the Sidewinder air-to-air missile appeared in the bottom right corner.

Seconds ticked by. Boyce, who had already watched the tapes, realized that he was holding his breath.

The aft section of the Flanker exploded.

Then the second Flanker.

"Pause it there," said Boyce. He stepped up to the screen where the image flickered, the motion frozen. He peered at the screen, studying the debris pattern. "Now advance it three seconds at a time."

The image started, stopped, started and stopped. "Anybody see anything else there?" said Boyce.

The screen was empty except for the debris pattern of the Flankers.

"Just the Chameleon and the Flankers," said Boyce. "And the Black Stars, who are not visible to the cameras. No sign of any *Dong-jins*, which are also invisible. None of the Black Star crews picked up anything with the CFD goggles either."

"That doesn't mean anything," said Dana Boudroux. It was the first time she had spoken during the briefing. "The goggles are fine-tuned to the precise chromatic frequency of the Black Star. Even a very slight wavelength variation, and they'd be ineffective."

"Why don't we have something like the spooks in signal intel use?" asked Boyce. "You know, some kind of device that scans an entire spectrum until it finds something?"

She shook her head. "Electrochromatic sensing doesn't work that way. I could explain the technical reasons for it, but it would be best if you just took my word for it, Admiral."

Boyce shot her a baleful look. "I'll be the judge of what would be best, Doctor. Just tell me this. Why don't we have a set of goggles that can see the *Dong-jin*?"

"Without having the *Dong-jin*'s new skin-cloaking generator to study, we'd have to build a thousand sets of goggles with different frequency sensors. And then we would still probably miss."

"You're saying there's no way to penetrate their cloaking without actually having that piece of equipment to study?"

"That's what I'm saying."

"Shit," said Boyce. He saw Hightree giving him the look again. "Umm, pardon my French, folks, but I'm frustrated. I need to know whether the *Dong-jins* were at our party today."

"They were," said Maxwell.

Every head in the room swung to him. The room went quiet.

"Excuse me?" said Boyce. "You saw them?"

"I didn't get a visual on them. But I know that something was out there watching the show."

"If you didn't see them," said Harvey Wentz, "how do you know they were there?"

"A gut feeling," said Maxwell.

Wentz chuckled. "Since when do gut feelings count as intelligence reports?"

"Since I took command of this unit," snapped Boyce. "I know about gut feelings. If Maxwell says something was out there, it would be extremely dumb of you to discount it."

Wentz made a sour face and folded his arms over his chest.

"For what it's worth," said Sharp O'Toole, "I had the same gut feeling. I thought I saw something shimmering out there, but when I focused on it with the CFD goggles, it was gone."

"Okay," said Boyce, "If it's true, then what does it mean?"

"That they can't see the Black Stars any better than we can see the *Dong-jins*," said Maxwell.

"Stalemate," said O'Toole.

"Negative," said Boyce. "We achieved our first objective. The Flankers took the bait, made a pass at the Chameleon, got hosed by Brick and Crud. If the *Dong-jins* were out there, it means they couldn't do anything about it. Two Flankers splashed, which is a little message from our Commander-in-Chief to the ChiComs. That should give them something to think about before they target any more of our assets."

"You achieved one other objective, Red," said Admiral Hightree.

"Sir?"

"You saved Captain Stickney's UCAV from the Flankers. Sticks sends his thanks."

Boyce nodded. The Chameleon cost upward of five million a copy. It had gotten back to the *Reagan* in one piece and was now nestled in its enclosed berth off the hangar bay.

"Oh, yeah," said Boyce. "That thing."

Shahezhen Capital Air Base, Beijing

This is undignified, thought Gen. Han Jianli.

Han swiped at the trickle of sweat that ran down the inside of his shirt. Through the glare of the afternoon sun he watched the fighter taxiing across the ramp. In the shimmering heat waves, the twin-finned jet looked like a bird of prey.

In normal circumstances it would have been beneath the dignity of the commanding general of the PLA Air Force to be standing out here like an enlisted peasant from the provinces. Han Jianli was not only the third-highest-ranking officer in the PLA, he was a member of the all-powerful Central Military Committee. It was not the habit of such a figure to wait in the midday sun for an ordinary wing commander to arrive in his jet.

But this, of course, was no ordinary wing commander. General Han squinted against the harsh glare, watching the SU-27 jet roll toward him then lurch to a stop. While the engines whined down, a flag-festooned *bei-jung*—an open-topped military utility vehicle—wheeled up to the jet's boarding ladder.

The pilot tossed his helmet to a waiting ground crewman, and climbed into the *bei-jung*. Thirty seconds later, the vehicle rolled up to the long red carpet where General Han and his staff stood waiting.

The pilot hopped out, drew himself to attention, and snapped a salute. "General Zhang Yu reporting as ordered, sir."

Han returned the salute. As always, he had to force himself not to wince at the sight of the man's wrecked face. Every senior commander in the PLA knew Zhang by personal acquaintance or by reputation. His face was one that many knew in their worst dreams.

Zhang shook hands with Han, then with the staff officers. Each bowed deferentially to Zhang, even though most out-ranked him.

With the courtesies out of the way, Han turned and led the procession inside the sprawling headquarters building. General Han's command complex filled one entire wing of the building. The Shahezhen Air Base was twenty kilometers outside Beijing and served as the central command base for the PLA Air Force. Beneath the hexagonal building lay a rabbit warren of fortified chambers that could survive the discharge of medium-yield nuclear weapons.

Han led them to the thickly carpeted conference room where he conducted meetings with his unit commanders. In the center stood a long table. The walls were covered with framed photos of PLA Air Force aircraft. At the far end of the room, smiling down like a benevolent cherub, was a bust of Mao Tse-tung.

Han waited until the white-coated stewards had served tea and placed dim sum trays before each of the seated officers.

"It was kind of you to come on short notice," said Han.

"I welcome the opportunity to confer with my commanding general," said Zhang.

"We expected you to arrive by transport aircraft, not in an SU-27."

"I command a fighter wing. A commander should set an example for all his airmen."

Han kept his face blank, pretending not to notice the veiled insult. Few senior officers in the PLA Air Force still flew operational fighters. Han himself had abandoned the cockpit years ago, preferring the upholstered cabins of the PLA's executive transport jets. In his opinion, it was foolish for commanders to put themselves at risk by flying super-sonic fighters.

He knew better than to order Zhang to remain on the

ground. Zhang was a legendary figure in the PLA Air Force. Flying the *Dong-jin*, he alone had visited more carnage on the enemy than the rest of the PLA Air Force combined.

Although the true story behind his disfigured face had been skewed to protect the secret of the *Dong-jin*—the official version had him flying SU-27s—Zhang's exploits made him a cult figure in the briefing room of every PLA Air Force unit. Even his ghoulish face was seen by junior fighter pilots as a mark of patriotic honor.

But there was a more basic reason why General Han would not chastise Zhang. Not only was Zhang Yu a legendary war hero, he was reputed to still be an officer of the dreaded *Te-Wu*, the secret police of the PLA. The *Te-Wu* was a nearly autonomous unit whose role was to cleanse the PLA of traitors and dissidents. Such a connection gave Zhang an influence far in excess of what his relatively junior rank would confer on him. Officers in every branch of the PLA, including Han himself, shuddered at the thought of a late-night visit from the *Te-Wu*.

General Han was afraid of Zhang Yu.

No, thought Han, he wouldn't order Zhang to stop flying. Gen. Zhang Yu would be permitted to fling himself into more battles. If his reckless spirit should eventually bring him to an untimely end, then so be it. With the rest of the PLA, Han would publicly mourn the loss of a national hero—and then privately rejoice. He could sleep without fear of the *Te-Wu*.

"Two of your SU-27 fighters are down, General Zhang. One pilot dead, one recovered. Both fighters lost to air-to-air missiles. Were there eyewitnesses to this encounter?"

"There was one very reliable witness."

"And who was that?"

"Me. I was airborne in a *Dong-jin*. I observed both jets explode."

"So? Was it American fighters? Super Hornets from their aircraft carrier in the region, *Reagan*?"

"No, General. I must report that it was something more dangerous. I have reason to believe the Americans are operating stealth jets in this region. Probably the one they call Black Star."

Han blinked, surprised at this news. "The jet from which our *Dong-jin* was, ah, adapted?"

Zhang nodded.

"You actually saw this Black Star?"

"No. And that is what is most worrisome. It means their cloaking technology has evolved beyond what we acquired from them."

General Han sipped at his tea while he considered this news. He had seen the *Dong-jin* up close, but he had only a rudimentary understanding of the technology that made it invisible in daylight.

"This would also mean that the United States has become directly involved in our dispute with Vietnam?"

"So it would seem," said Zhang.

"From where are they operating these stealth aircraft? Vietnam?"

"It is possible. I consider it more likely that they came from an aircraft carrier."

"The same aircraft carrier that sent the Super Hornets to engage us?"

Zhang nodded. "The USS *Ronald Reagan*. In the South China Sea."

Han lowered his teacup. Zhang was reporting what the Central Military Committee had already confirmed at their high command meeting yesterday in Beijing.

He turned back to Zhang, who was helping himself to the dim sum. "The Central Military Committee has issued explicit orders. Any attempt by the Vietnamese—or anyone else—to interfere with our efforts in the Spratly Islands will be countered with military force."

Zhang plucked a pork dumpling with his chopsticks. "This force, I presume, is to remain covert?"

"In the air and beneath the sea. Since the Americans have chosen to insert stealth aircraft into the region, your *Dong-jin* unit will play a crucial role in the air war."

Zhang displayed no reaction. He continued eating from the dim sum tray. He swallowed another dumpling, then picked up a spring roll. Han had to avert his eyes. Watching Zhang stuff food through the hideous slash in his face was making Han's stomach roil.

"The Americans have placed unmanned surveillance aircraft over Swallow Reef," said Han. "They wish to obtain photographic evidence of the PLA occupation of the reef. The Central Military Committee has ordered us to eliminate one of the aircraft."

"And they want us to do it with a *Dong-jin*?" asked Zhang.

"Yes. It will transmit a warning to the U.S. that they should not interfere."

"And when is this mission to be accomplished?"

"Tomorrow. The targeting information will be waiting for you when you return to Lingshui."

They concluded their meeting, and Han escorted Zhang back to the flight line. He stood again on the broiling ramp while Zhang's SU-27 roared down the runway and climbed into the hazy sky.

Zhang was dangerous, thought Han, watching the speck disappear in the west. Han sensed that the day was coming when Zhang would use his *Te-Wu* connections to try to displace him as commander of the PLA Air Force. Before that day came, Han would have to eliminate Zhang.

But not yet. Not while Zhang was indispensable.

CHAPTER 14

HAWKEYE

33,000 feet
South China Sea
1340 Sunday, 29 April

An easy kill.

So easy, in fact, that Zhang had almost assigned the Global Hawk intercept to Major Tsan's crew. There was nothing difficult about shooting down the high-flying unmanned reconnaissance jet. The slow-moving UCAV had a wingspan of 116 feet and weighed more than twelve tons. It stood out on radar screens like an elephant in a pasture. Even though the big lumbering jet operated at an altitude of nearly twenty thousand meters—over sixty-five thousand feet—well above the *Dong-jin*'s service ceiling, it was a simple pitch-up maneuver.

At the last minute he removed Tsan and assigned the mission to himself.

He had no problem locating the target. The PLA's coastal air defense radar had picked up the jet as it lifted from the runway at Kadena, the U.S. base on the island of Okinawa.

From almost directly beneath the target, Zhang pulled the *Dong-jin* into a nearly vertical climb. He obtained a lock on the big UCAV, then fired his PL-8 missile. He could have fired two missiles, just to be sure, but that would have given the enemy *two* chances to compute and locate the IR source.

The heat-seeking missile had no difficulty tracking the Global Hawk.

"Impact," announced Po. "The missile has struck the target."

Zhang didn't need confirmation. Through his canopy he could see the orange-and-black smudge of the explosion high above them. The Global Hawk carried enough fuel for forty hours' endurance. The ingredients of a spectacular fireball.

"Where are the enemy fighters?"

Several seconds passed while Po obtained a data-link update. "They have left their station, General. They appear to be inbound, accelerating."

The *Dong-jin*'s nose was almost back to the horizon. The jet was gathering speed, almost back to normal flight.

Zhang wasn't worried about the F/A-18s that had been flying combat air patrol near the UCAV. Even if they had obtained a fix on the source of his missile, they wouldn't be able to detect him.

On his center display he could see the blips of all the enemy aircraft—the four fighters in a combat spread coming directly toward him, their controlling ship in an orbit behind them.

His mission was accomplished, Zhang told himself. The Global Hawk was dead. His business here was finished.

Or was it? He studied the blips of the American aircraft in his display.

He still had missiles left.

USS Ronald Reagan

It had to be a *Dong-jin*, thought Boyce.

He stared at the situational display. Something had just

hosed the RQ-4 Global Hawk UCAV over the Spratly group. Something invisible, and he had no doubt what it was.

Boyce considered for another half minute. There was a very good chance that the *Dong-jin* was still in the vicinity. He had CAP fighters close by—Bullet Alexander's four Runners—but they were useless against a *Dong-jin*. He had one crew—Maxwell and O'Toole—on ready alert in the enclosed Black Star bay off the hangar deck. Two more were suited up and ready as backups.

Boyce turned to the petty officer seated at his console. "Launch the alert crew."

Six and one-half minutes later, he stared down at the flight deck of the *Reagan*. Maxwell's Black Star was sizzling down the track of the number-one catapult.

It took eight more minutes before they were in the vicinity of the downed Global Hawk. He heard Maxwell talking to the controller in the E2-C Hawkeye.

"Sea Lord, Dragon One-one has a visual on the debris field."

"Sea Lord copies." Boyce recognized the controller's voice. She was a lieutenant commander named Deb Abruzzo. The Black Star and the Hawkeye were transmitting on a discrete tactical frequency. Except for the controller in the Hawkeye, none of the other airborne aircraft knew the Black Star was there.

The controller said, "Dragon One-one, the datum point on your missing bandit bears 020, thirty miles, level. That was his missile origin point, but those numbers are now—let's see—nearly ten minutes old."

The datum point was the firing location of the missile that killed the Global Hawk. Boyce knew that was all they had. Even the Hawkeye's sophisticated sensors and detectors were unable to find the *Dong-jin*. It could be anywhere in an eighty-mile radius. It could be loitering in the area. Or heading back to Hainan.

Or setting up another target.

The thought caused Boyce to frown. He stared at the display. There were other aircraft out there. The Hawkeye, Alexander's Runners, a pair of orbiting tankers. They were all exposed.

Boyce keyed his transmitter. "Sea Lord, this is Battle-ax. Vector all CAP birds out of there. Now."

24,000 feet, South China Sea

"Target one o'clock, eighteen kilometers, General."

"I have a lock," answered Zhang. He also had a visual ID. He could see it silhouetted against the opaque surface below.

A fat goose waiting to be shotgunned.

For a moment Zhang considered the wisdom of this engagement. He'd just shot down an unmanned surveillance aircraft. As provocative as it might be, shooting down the Global Hawk was a legitimate response to an intruding spy plane. Zhang was following a direct order.

This was different. Killing a manned American warplane, especially over international waters, was outside the scope of his orders. In fact, he had received specific orders *not* to engage the enemy's aircraft.

But such orders were subject to interpretation. He was a senior commander in the PLA Air Force. Was it not his prerogative—*his duty*—to make tactical decisions during the fluid conditions of combat?

General Han would be furious. Let him be, Zhang decided. Han was an impotent lackey. Zhang knew how to deal with Han.

He returned his attention to the tactical display on his center console. The little yellow triangle of the target was pulsing like a firefly in the center of the display. He felt the old excitement swelling inside him, just as it always did when he was about to pounce on an unsuspecting prey.

Zhang toggled the switch that armed the number-two

missile station. With his left thumb he slewed the acquisition box so that it covered the pulsing yellow target symbol.

He wrapped his finger around the firing trigger. He hesitated, taking a deep breath, savoring the moment.

He squeezed the trigger.

USS Ronald Reagan

"Missile in the air!"

At his console aboard *Reagan*, Boyce felt a chill run through him. It was the voice of Deb Abruzzo, the controller in the Hawkeye.

"Who's targeted?" someone called.

"Say the threat zone!"

"Runner One-one, turn to—"

Bleep.

"Sea Lord, say again the—"

Bleep.

"Flares! Flares!"

Radio discipline had gone to hell. Everyone was stepping on each other's radio transmissions.

Boyce knew that each fighter was spewing a trail of flares—incendiary decoys to lure away the heat-seeking missile. Even the Hawkeye had flares.

A missile was tracking someone. Who? Boyce wondered. In the next moment, he knew.

22,500 feet, South China Sea

The explosion lit up the horizon.

Maxwell saw the trail of flame arcing across the sky. A section of wing was blazing like a Roman candle, tumbling end over end. The aft half of the fuselage was still intact, the fins on its tail clearly recognizable.

An abrupt silence filled the tactical frequency. Over the guard channel—the emergency common frequency—

sounded the warble of a locator beacon. It was an automatic signal generated when an aircraft was in distress.

"Sea Lord, Alpha Whiskey, how do you read?"

No answer.

"Sea Lord, Alpha Whiskey, answer up."

"Alpha Whiskey, this is Blaster Four-one." It was the voice of Spike Mannheim, the Hornet pilot who had been covering the Hawkeye. "Sea Lord is down."

Maxwell studied the descending wreckage. It was almost directly below him. Swooping over the debris pattern were the twin-finned shapes of the two Blue Blaster F/A-18s who had been covering the Hawkeye.

The frequency was quiet for several seconds. Then Hightree's voice came on the radio. "Roger that, Blaster Four-one. Blaster and Runner flights, are you engaged?"

Good question, thought Maxwell. Hightree was asking whether they were in a furball with the bandit. "Negative," called Bullet Alexander, leading the CAP fighters. "Runner One-one, clean. No contact, no spike."

"Blaster Four-one clean."

"Runner One-one clean."

No one was targeted with a hostile radar. No surprise. Whoever just killed the Hawkeye was remaining invisible.

Seconds later, Mannheim called, "Blaster Four-one has a chute. I've got one chute from the Hawkeye."

Someone had managed to bail out. Maxwell was amazed.

"Another chute!" called the Blaster leader. "We've got two good chutes."

"Alpha Whiskey copies the chutes. Keep counting, Blaster. Blaster and Runner flights go to RESCAP stations."

RESCAP fighters—rescue combat air patrol—were assigned to cover the rescue of downed airmen. It would be the job of Blaster flight to cover the SAR—search and rescue—HH-60 Seahawks as they searched for the downed crewmen. Give Hightree credit, Maxwell thought. Having just lost a high-value asset—a precious E-2C command and control ship—he was putting more high-value assets on the line to rescue the survivors of the Hawkeye.

Several minutes ticked past. The spewing wreckage of the Hawkeye was splashing into the ocean below. Blaster Four-one and his wingman were still orbiting the crash site.

Hightree's voice came over the frequency again. "Talk to me, Blaster Four-one. Any more chutes?"

"Negative," said the Blaster flight lead. "I still have the two. They're going into the water now."

Maxwell shook his head. Two out of five crew aboard the E-2C. He wondered who didn't make it out.

Boyce's voice crackled over the discrete frequency. "Dragon One, Battle-Ax. The datum point on your missing bandit bears 020, fifteen miles, level. That was his missile origin point. The numbers are two minutes old."

"Dragon One copies," Maxwell answered.

"I'm plugging it in now," said O'Toole from the backseat. "Looking for an IR return in that sector."

None of the pilots swirling around the wreckage of the Hawkeye knew the Black Star was there. The presence of the Black Stars aboard *Reagan* was still a secret.

"Hey, we're getting something," announced O'Toole. "Not much signature, but something. It's on your display, Brick."

Maxwell peered at the multifunction display on the right console. It was selected to show infrared returns from one of the six IR sensors mounted in the skin of the Black Star. The screen looked blank. Nothing there but—

He saw it. A curly red line, like a sine wave. It was on the twenty-mile range circle.

Then it disappeared.

"I had something at two o'clock," said Maxwell. "It popped up and—whoa, there it is again."

"That's our guy," said O'Toole.

"Get a Dolly update. Make sure we haven't got friendlies out there."

It took ten seconds. "No one in that sector, Brick. It's gotta be the bandit."

"Terrific. Except he's not emitting now."

"He's a stealth jet, right? We were lucky to get any IR signature. Keep closing on him. We'll pick him up again."

Maxwell cranked the Black Star's nose twenty degrees to the right and added thrust, notching up the airspeed. The tiny IR trace from the *Dong-jin* had to come either from his exhaust or some minuscule reflection from his forward quarter.

"Ten miles, ten o'clock," called O'Toole. Maxwell could hear the excitement in the wizzo's voice. "He's crossing right to left."

On the weapons select panel, Maxwell had already armed a pair of AIM-9X Sidewinder heat-seeking missiles. The Black Star's flush-mounted IR sensor linked its signal to the Sidewinders' seeker heads until the missiles were off their rails and flying on their own. Then the Sidewinders would go on their own search-and-destroy missions.

Before Maxwell could fire, the red trace faded.

He stabbed the REFRESH button. Still nothing. *Shit.* What now? The Chinese pilot might be going through his own target acquisition process. About to shoot again.

Maxwell hesitated. He could fire a missile anyway, letting it track on memory until the seeker head picked up a fresh signal. It was dangerous because, once launched, the Sidewinder would lock onto *any* heat-emitting signal.

Let it. He squeezed the trigger. Then squeezed it again.

He felt the rumble of the firing sequence. In the space of one and a half seconds, the right weapons bay door opened, the missile rack extended into the slipstream, the Sidewinders roared one after the other into the sky ahead.

Then a smooth stillness again. Each missile was flying its own zigzag path, searching for a target.

One missile stopped zigzagging and veered hard to the left.

"Bingo," said O'Toole. "We have a lock."

*   *   *

"Missiles inbound!"

Po's shrill voice cut like a knife through the stillness of Zhang's cockpit. "Seven o'clock, heat-seeking missiles!"

Zhang stared at his own display. It was impossible. None of the enemy F/A-18s was in a position to fire missiles.

He rolled the *Dong-jin* into a left vertical bank and pulled hard. In a conventional fighter he would be dispensing flares—old-fashioned decoys—to thwart the missile. The *Dong-jin* carried no decoys: It was immune to radar-guided and heat-seeking missiles.

But there was a missile coming at them. He glimpsed it, but just for a second. It was in a pursuit curve, like a cheetah tracking a gazelle.

Zhang kept the Gs on, turning hard into the path of the missile, trying to make it overshoot. Po's labored breathing sounded like the gasps of a dying man.

By the time Zhang had completed ninety degrees of the turn, he knew what had happened.

Nothing. The missile no longer had guidance, and it had gone ballistic. It would rocket off into empty space until its fuel was gone. The advanced stealth technology of the *Dong-jin* had prevailed.

He drew a deep breath and considered the close encounter. *Who fired the missile?*

In a flash of clarity, the explanation came to him. Of course. It could only have come from one source.

"They went dumb," said O'Toole. He couldn't keep the disappointment out of his voice. "The Sidewinders lost the emission source."

The wavy red trace of the stealth jet was gone on their screens.

"At least we scared the shit out of him," said Maxwell.

"Or pissed him off so much he's gonna come after *us*."

That thought had already occurred to Maxwell, but he dismissed it. If the *Dong-jin* had detected the Black Star, the

Chinese pilot would already have taken his shot. They were playing blindman's bluff. The *Dong-jin* crew was as blind as Maxwell and O'Toole.

"Keep scanning with the sensors. If we pick him up again, we'll take another shot."

For another twenty minutes they swept the sky between the last trace of the *Dong-jin* and the area where the helicopters were searching for survivors of the Hawkeye. They had rescued the two who managed to bail out. No others had been found.

"Who'd they pick up from the Hawkeye?" Maxwell asked Boyce over the discrete frequency.

"The aircraft control officer and the radar officer." Boyce's voice was somber. "The pilots and the Combat Information Center officer, Deb Abruzzo, didn't get out."

Maxwell shook his head. He knew most of the E-2C crews. The Hawkeye squadron shared the Roadrunners' ready room. Deb Abruzzo was one of the best intercept controllers in the business.

After the CAP fighters and the tanker, a Roadrunner F/A-18 with an in-flight refueling store mounted on its center fuselage station, had recovered, Maxwell was cleared to land the Black Star back aboard the *Reagan*.

Maxwell swept over the ramp, keeping his eyes riveted on the yellow ball. Still in the center.

Whump. On center line, on glide slope. He snagged a two wire—the target. His second carrier landing in the Black Star was better than the first. He was getting the hang of it.

After the short pullback to free the wire from the hook, he shoved the throttles up and powered the Black Star out of the landing area, to the number-one elevator on the forward deck. Within minutes, the stealth jet was chained to the deck. Maxwell and O'Toole climbed down the boarding ladder.

Maxwell saw the faces of the deck crewmen. They already knew about the Hawkeye. No grins, no high-fives, no bawdy jokes today. It was not a day for celebration.

CHAPTER 15

FACE OF THE ENEMY

The White House
0715 Sunday, 29 April

"It didn't happen," said the president of the United States.

As Benjamin expected, a stunned silence fell over his audience. On the video screen, he could see Boyce giving him that narrow-eyed, *I can't believe this shit* look.

Sitting beside the president were the chief of naval operations, the chairman of the Joint Chiefs, and the secretary of defense. Stationed on second row were the national security advisor and the president's chief of staff. On the other end of the link were Admirals Boyce and Hightree aboard *Reagan*, and Ambassador Joe Ferrone in Hanoi.

Boyce spoke up first. "Mr. President, with all due respect, it damned well *did* happen. The little bastards just murdered three of our people and took out some very high-value assets."

"Stand by, Red. You've known me long enough to know that I don't take the killing of our airmen lightly. What I'm saying is that the U.S. will not protest this incident publicly. Instead, we're going to come down hard on them in a way that will make them regret what they did."

"You mean we're going to kick some ass?"

"I couldn't put it better myself."

Boyce nodded his approval.

"Mr. President," said Joe Ferrone on the monitor screen, "has the PRC offered an explanation for the incident?"

"I put in an immediate call to the president of the People's Republic," said Benjamin. "He hasn't returned the call, but I know from experience what his response will be. He will deny any knowledge or culpability."

Ferrone said, "Has anyone considered the possibility that the PLA, or some unit commander, might have acted without a direct order from Beijing?"

Benjamin glanced over at the Joint Chiefs Chairman, General Matloff. Matloff cleared his throat and spoke up. "It's happened before. Remember when one of their fighter pilots went too far and collided with an EP-3 of ours? The EP-3 crew made an emergency landing at Lingshui, and the incident snowballed out of control. They held its crew captive for twelve days."

"And our response was to roll over and let them do it," said Boyce.

"There weren't any good options," said Matloff. "None short of going to war, which the Chinese were betting that we wouldn't do."

"And they're making the same bet this time," said Benjamin. He rubbed his chin for a moment, seeming to be deep in thought. Finally he said, "Red, are you convinced it was a stealth jet that shot down our two aircraft?"

"No doubt about it, sir. The classified details are in the after-action report that just went to you."

Benjamin nodded. "Without going into the details, can I assume we're no closer than before to detecting this stealth jet of theirs?"

"Yes, sir, I'm afraid that's true."

"What about, ah, our own similar assets?"

"The action report would indicate that it was also undetected."

"A standoff, you mean?"

"Yes, sir. So far."

Benjamin made a note on his yellow pad. He looked into the video cam again. "That's it, gentlemen. What you saw happen out there didn't happen because we're going to deal with it offstage. I can't tell you what our specific action will be, but I can assure that it will not be a speech by our ambassador to the United Nations. The Chinese are going to receive a wake-up call. Questions?"

There were none.

"Good. You can expect a tasking order in the next twenty-four hours."

The president rose from his seat. The screens went blank.

Lingshui Air Base, Hainan Island

"You incompetent idiots!" roared General Zhang.

He slammed the door of the chromatics laboratory so hard that one of the framed photographs fell from the wall. It was a portrait of the PLA commanding general.

Each of the six technicians froze in place. They stared with terror-filled eyes at the apparition before them. Zhang was still wearing his flight gear—laced-up anti-G suit, survival vest, and helmet with the hinged spectrum-sensing goggles still attached. From a shoulder holster jutted the grip of his Type 64, 7.62 semiautomatic pistol.

"You see this?" Zhang held up his helmet with the goggles dangling from their hinge. "Junk. These goggles are worthless."

Zhang hurled the helmet and goggles at the man nearest him, a research scientist named Fong. The object missed Fong's head and crashed into an LCD monitor on the table behind him. Hunks of glass and plastic exploded against the wall. The technicians crouched in a cowering position, waiting for the next missile.

"You have failed miserably," said Zhang. "The Americans have a stealth jet that is undetectable with these useless goggles."

The technicians looked at one another. None was sure what to say. Fong, who was the director of the lab, finally spoke for them. His voice quavered. "General, we are abjectly ashamed of the poor quality of the goggles. We offer a thousand apologies for our incompetence."

"Never mind your apologies. Your task was to develop sensing goggles that would detect the American stealth aircraft."

"It is a task we welcomed with great joy, General. But the specifications for the goggles were developed from our most current intelligence information about the American cloaking technology."

"Do not presume to tell me what I already know."

"I am sorry, General." Fong's voice was regaining some of its normal timbre. "I would only suggest that we obtain information about the most recent developments in the American cloaking technology."

Zhang continued to glower at Fong. The blundering fool was correct, of course. Zhang himself had been instrumental in placing the network of spies in the U.S. whose purpose was to acquire the secrets of the American Black Star. Since then, most of the network had been compromised. The flow of precious stealth data had nearly stopped.

But not all of it. Still in place in the U.S. were a dozen or so sources. Zhang had already placed an urgent request for new data on the American stealth program.

"Listen to me," said Zhang. "You have one more week to develop goggles that work. If you fail, you will finish your lives within the walls of a labor camp. Do you understand?"

They did. In unison they nodded their heads affirmatively. Zhang wheeled and left the laboratory. For emphasis he slammed the door behind him. He heard the satisfying tinkle of another photograph crashing to the floor.

USS Ronald Reagan

"What the hell's going on, Brick?"

Bullet Alexander was standing in the passageway outside the intel compartment. His arms were folded across his massive chest. His eyes blazed with anger.

"Bullet. What are you doing here?"

"Suppose you tell me what *you're* doing here." Alexander touched the sweat-dampened sleeve of Maxwell's flight suit. "You just came back from flying, right? Flying what? And don't give me any of that bullshit about bumming a seat in somebody's Hornet. I know better."

Maxwell just shrugged. When you were wearing a flight suit that smelled of fresh sweat and adrenaline, there was no point in saying you just came from the gym.

"Sorry. There are some things you don't need to know."

The answer ignited more anger in Alexander. "Go down to the ready room and try telling that to the Hawkeye crews. Tell 'em they don't need to know what just killed their squadron mates."

Over Alexander's shoulder, Maxwell saw someone coming out of the intel compartment. It was Boyce, giving them a curious look.

"I know how you feel," said Maxwell. "I wish I could tell you more, but I can't."

"Oh, yeah? Well, let me tell you what I *do* know, shipmate. There's something out there that we can't find with radar or IR, and it just killed Deb Abruzzo and Pete Schlemmer and their skipper, Herb Dooley. It was the same thing that killed my wingman, Hozer Miller. You know what it is, don't you?"

"You know the answer. No comment."

"And now you're flying something that looks like a goddamn Frisbee on steroids. How do I know? Because every seaman no-class on this boat knows it and they're talking like magpies about it."

"If you know so much, then why are you bugging me?"

"Because I want to know what you were doing out there while a ChiCom stealth pilot was killing our guys."

"Leave it alone, Bullet."

Alexander locked gazes with Maxwell. "Fuck you, Brick. You used to be a good guy until that blockhead Boyce hired you to do this black-ops shit. Now you've turned into a—"

"That's enough out of you, Commander Alexander."

Alexander flinched at the sound of the voice behind him. He turned to see Red Boyce, cigar in his teeth, glowering like a grizzly bear.

"Ah, sorry, Admiral. I didn't know you were standing there."

"What were you just saying? Something about that blockhead Boyce hiring someone to do what? Black-ops shit?"

Alexander's eyes widened. He looked like a condemned man meeting his executioner. "Well, sir, what I meant was—"

Boyce broke into a belly laugh. His laughter seemed to feed on itself, forcing him to remove his cigar and lean against the bulkhead. It was contagious, spreading to Maxwell, who couldn't help laughing with him.

Alexander stared at them. "Sir, may I offer an apology?"

"No."

"I was venting some anger, Admiral. I was out of line, and I—"

"Bullshit."

"Sir?"

"I know what you meant to say."

"Well, I take back the part about the—"

"Blockhead? Hell, I've said a lot worse about the blockheads I've worked for. Tell you what, Skipper Alexander. Come with me and Brick to the intel vault. I'm gonna make an exception and add your name to an eyes-only need-to-know list. Then you won't have to keep making an ass of yourself in the presence of senior officers."

Alexander exchanged a quick glance with Maxwell. "Ah, thank you, sir. That would be a good thing."

Alexander's eyes widened. "And the ChiComs have those things too?"

"Something very close," said Boyce.

Maxwell watched in silence while Boyce showed Alexander the images of the Black Star. They were in the intel compartment, seated at the steel briefing table. Boyce was working the bulkhead-mounted screen with a remote controller.

"How'd they get them?" asked Alexander.

"Same way they got most of their technology. They bought it, or stole it."

Maxwell noticed that Boyce was omitting most of the sensitive details—the Black Star's performance, the weapons load, the fact that they couldn't penetrate the *Dong-jin*'s skin cloaking sheath.

Alexander said, "And that's what they used to get Hozer Miller? And the Hawkeye?"

"That's it," said Boyce. "Now, do you want to see the guy who did it?"

Maxwell sat upright. He saw Boyce watching him. Boyce was up to his old tricks again.

A face flashed onto the screen. It was of a Chinese man. He wore the uniform of a colonel in the PLA Air Force. It was a handsome face, but the nostrils were flared as if he were in a seething rage. The corners of his mouth turned down, and the eyes blazed with some kind of inner fire.

"Who's that?" said Maxwell.

"Colonel Zhang Yu," said Boyce. "Recognize him?"

An electric jolt ran through Maxwell. "I remember that name."

"You should," said Boyce. "Zhang was in command of

the *Dong-jin* program when it was being developed. During the war with Taiwan, he was credited with at least eleven aerial kills and a slew of ships sunk."

Maxwell stared at the image. It was all coming back. He had never met Zhang face-to-face, but he had come within a few yards of him, once on the ground during the raid at Chouzhou, once in the sky over the Taiwan Strait. And that had been the end of Colonel Zhang.

"He's dead," said Maxwell.

"Oh?" Boyce was enjoying himself. "How can you be sure of that?"

"Because I killed him. We had good intel that it was Zhang flying the *Dong-jin* that I engaged over the strait. I saw the jet explode."

"Maybe you did, maybe you didn't. Take a look at this."

Alexander was switching his gaze from Boyce to Maxwell and back. He looked more confused than ever.

The face on the screen vanished, replaced by another image. It was almost unrecognizable as a face.

Maxwell recoiled at the sight. He heard Alexander suck in his breath.

"Not a pretty sight," said Boyce. "The face belongs to the same gentleman. Meet *General* Zhang, the most decorated hero in the PLA Air Force. Zhang survived his shoot-down in the Taiwan Strait, but not without a few injuries. His disfigurement is his ticket to fame. He's the rock star of the Chinese military and, according to reports, a favorite of the president himself. He's also a heavy in the *Te-Wu*—the secret police that purges the PLA of suspected dissidents."

Maxwell felt a chill run through him. He knew what Boyce was going to say next.

"Zhang still flies the *Dong-jin*. He heads up the Hainan military district, and he also commands the PLA Air Force's elite stealth squadron at Lingshui. Even though he's a general officer, he flies combat missions in the *Dong-jin*. We have good information that he's been active in the most recent operations in the South China Sea."

"Let me guess," said Alexander. "He's the guy who's been killing our people."

"CIA gives it a ninety percent probability it was Zhang who whacked the Viet transport and two fighters. They've got confirmation that he ran the mission against the Global Hawk and the Hawkeye."

"What about Hozer Miller?" said Maxwell. "Was it Zhang?"

Boyce nodded. "It fits his profile. He's reputed to be a scalp collector. Zhang wants to rack up the biggest kill score possible so he can make himself a legend."

"A real sweetheart," said Alexander. "Are we gonna get him?"

Boyce didn't answer. He looked at Maxwell.

Maxwell just nodded. He couldn't take his eyes off the face in the screen. The blazing brown eyes stared back at him.

CHAPTER 16

SENSORS

Shahezhen Capital Air Base, Beijing
People's Republic of China
1825 Sunday, 29 April

General Han Jianli tried to contain his anger, but he was unable. *Damn him. Damn Zhang and his impudence.*

Han took a deep breath and spoke again into the microphone mounted on his desk. "Are you aware that you may have triggered a war with the United States?"

"Please don't insult my intelligence, General Han. We both know the Americans will not go to war over the loss of two aircraft that were spying on our territory."

"President Xiang has demanded a full explanation of the affair."

"And correctly so. Do you wish for me to fly immediately to Beijing to brief the president?"

"It is my duty to brief the president, not yours." He let this sink in for a moment, then added, "He will want to know the disposition of the commander who conducted the attack on the American airplanes. What do you think I should tell him?"

"Tell him whatever you wish. It is of no interest to me."

Han could scarcely believe the insolence in Zhang's voice. How could a low-ranking general officer in the PLA Air Force presume to speak with his commanding general in such a tone?

He knew the answer. Because Zhang was untouchable.

Han's initial reaction upon hearing about the shoot-down of the American E-2C was to order Zhang's immediate arrest and removal from command. But that was before his meeting with the president. To Han's astonishment, President Xiang Fan-lo was ecstatic about Zhang's exploit. Zhang, he declared, was a modern Chinese military hero. Han himself was to be congratulated for having the brilliance to assign a warrior like Zhang to today's mission.

Han had nodded his agreement and accepted the president's congratulations for having ordered such a brilliant operation. He left the president's office both shocked and somewhat pleased. Zhang's insubordinate actions had brought them both an unexpected bounty.

He would have to go through the motions of chastising Zhang, of course. Untouchable or not, Zhang was still an officer under Han's command.

"You will submit a full report of this disastrous action today," Han said into the speakerphone. "Including the reasons for your unauthorized engagement of the U.S. E-2C."

He thought he heard a derisive snort from Zhang's end of the line. "Of course, General Han. Whatever you say."

USS Ronald Reagan

Ratta-tatta-tatta-tatta.

Maxwell had the rhythm going. He was working the gloves like a musical instrument, rotating his fists with each stroke. *Ratta-tatta-tatta-tatta.*

It was mindless exercise, but demanding of concentration. Like formation flying, he thought. The trick was to not focus on the task but to let it happen on a subliminal level.

He'd been at for ten minutes, the sweat flowing, enjoying the smooth beat of the speed bag, not thinking about stealth jets or Swallow Reef or the fuzzy rationale for going to war in the Spratly Islands.

"That's not the way to do it."

The voice came from behind him. He missed the bag with the next flick of his fist. It took a couple of beats before he could resume the rhythm.

"You probably think that sounds cool, that beat you've got, but trust me, you're doing it all wrong."

He gave the bag one last *whap*. He turned to face Dana Boudroux. She was wearing a blue warm-up suit and a white headband. The warm-up suit was damp with sweat. Beads of perspiration stood out on her cheeks.

"Doing *what* wrong?"

"Hitting the bag. You're playing with it like it was a percussion instrument, making that drumbeat sound. You shouldn't turn your wrists over so much."

"Pardon the sexist comment, but I've never met a woman who knew shit about boxing."

"You've never met a woman like me."

Thank God, he thought. "How do you happen to know so much about training on a speed bag?"

"My boyfriend in college was an Olympic boxer. I was his trainer. Trust me, I know boxing."

"Is there anything in the world you don't know more about than I do?"

"No, but don't take it personally. You're just not as smart as I am."

He turned back to the speed bag. "Guess I'll have to work on not feeling inadequate."

He was just getting the rhythm again when she said, "Don't you want to know why I came here?"

"I already know." He kept his fists moving. "To tell me how to punch this bag."

"Not just that. I wanted to tell you that I know how to shoot down the *Dong-jin*."

He took three more hits on the bag. He turned to look at her again.

"You're serious, right?"

"I'm always serious."

USS Daytona Beach

"Message from OPNAV, Skipper."

Commander Al Sprague looked up from his station in the control room. "OPNAV? Holy shit."

"Yes, sir," said the signalman. "That's what I said when it came in."

OPNAV was the office of the Chief of Naval Operations. Almost never did CNO send a direct communication to the skipper of a submarine. Not unless it was something too urgent to go through the usual channels. Or unless it was very bad news.

It was both, Sprague realized as he read the message.

USS Daytona Beach *SSN 776 will discontinue tracking of* Yuanzheng 67 *and proceed to* 08 38.24 N, 111 55.96 E *to intercept PRC vessels* Hoi Wan *and* Hoi Lin, *presently en route to PRC base Northeast Cay. After confirmation of vessels' identities, you will sink each by most expeditious means. Imperative that* Daytona Beach *remain undetected.*

Sprague shook his head when he read the last sentence. *Remain undetected?* What utter bullshit. It was obvious that the CNO—or whoever the nonsubmariner staff puke was who drafted the message—had no clue why they called this branch of the Navy the silent service.

He glanced again at the tactical display on his console. The Kilo was moving at nineteen knots, still unaware that he was being shadowed. Or else he was faking it, which Sprague doubted. This guy showed every sign of being a cocky sonofabitch, full of himself after sinking a defenseless ship full of civilians.

Sprague's mood darkened. *Now it's my turn, except that I get to hose two of them.*

Well, they started it, he reminded himself. The bastards had been taking out both Vietnamese and American assets, killing people like flies. Payback time.

But he hated breaking contact with the Kilo sub. It meant the Chinese sub had gotten a reprieve. If ever someone needed a torpedo up his ass, it was the skipper of *Yuanzheng 67*.

Sprague toggled the view in his tactical display to the wide-area chart. At a rough glance he estimated the position of the two Chinese ships to be no farther than a hundred miles from *Daytona Beach,* headed for the northwestern sector of the Spratlys. In fact, it even looked as if *Yuanzheng 67* might be headed in the same general direction.

This was going to be interesting.

USS Ronald Reagan

"It's all there on the tape," said Dana Boudroux.

They were in the tiny lab that had been set up for her in the ship's SCIF—Special Compartmentalized Intelligence Facility—located deep belowdecks in the ship's Surface Plot spaces. She was still wearing the blue jumpsuit. Maxwell had pulled his gray sweats over the workout trunks.

Leaning over her shoulder, looking into the LCD monitor, he inhaled a mixture of perfume and perspiration. Her hair was wet at the back of her neck.

"See? There it is." She was playing the HUD tape from Maxwell's last mission in the Black Star. On the digital read-out were the images from each of the four multifunction displays. "There's the IR trace you picked up on the *Dong-jin,* that little wavy red mark. And now it's gone again. What does that mean to you?"

"It means we couldn't nail him. Not visually, not with radar, and obviously not with an IR scan."

"You're missing the point. What it means is that the *Dong-jin* is *not* emission-free. Not a hundred percent, maybe not ninety-five percent. There's enough heat source leak that your primary onboard sensor was picking it up."

"But not enough to get a lock with the AIM-9 missiles."

"But one of the missiles *did* track the *Dong-jin*, even if it was very briefly."

Maxwell watched the slo-mo replay of the HUD tape. He felt again the frustration of seeing the squiggly trace of the *Dong-jin* blur in and out of view. Now you see it, now you don't.

"Okay," he said, "that's nice to know. What good does it do if the sensors won't lock on it long enough to provide a targeting solution? Or if the missile seeker head acquires a target, then loses it?"

She shook her head. "Now I know why they call you Brick. Are you sure you graduated from a real engineering school?"

"Yeah, but I didn't major in game-playing like you did. Why don't you just tell me what you're trying to tell me?"

"I'm trying to get you to think like a tactician. When you detect a weakness in your enemy's defenses, what do you do?"

He thought for a second. "A swift kick in the crotch."

"Figuratively, maybe. There's a more vulnerable place on the *Dong-jin*."

Maxwell nodded. "The source of heat emission."

"Brilliant, Commander. Keep this up and you could win a sixth-grade science prize."

He almost laughed. Beneath the woman's sarcasm there might actually be a sense of humor. "Okay, that's really cool. Now you're going to tell me you know how to track the *Dong-jin*'s heat leak."

"We already know how to do that. It's just a question of

getting the sensor heads to *keep* tracking after they've picked up the trace." She turned to a long plastic-sheeted table on which an array of electronic components was laid out. "Look at this. This is the Black Star's primary onboard IR sensor. This is the one that picked up the *Dong-jin*'s initial heat trace. I've been working on it, making some adjustments. I also added two silicon phototransistors, which ought to expand its sensitivity envelope by about thirty percent."

"Okay, but what about the AIM-9 air-to-air missile? Even if the onboard sensor tracks the *Dong-jin*, the missile still has to lock on."

"That's a tougher problem," she said. "The AIM-9 seeker head doesn't have multiple phototransistors like the primary sensor built into the airframe of the Black Star. But there is a way to crank up the sensitivity of the basic unit. The downside risk is that it will be inclined to track all sorts of spurious traces—sunspots, reflections, thermal anomalies in the atmosphere—and, of course, friendly aircraft. But if you launch at short range, it should work just fine."

Maxwell stared at the pieces on the table. He couldn't help but be impressed. "Sounds good. How do we know it works?"

"We don't. Not until you've tested it tomorrow against a real *Dong-jin*. In the meantime, let's celebrate by getting some coffee in the wardroom."

Maxwell led Dana into the dirty-shirt wardroom. A dozen or so officers, some in flight suits, some in working khakis, were seated at the tables. They all looked up, then looked again, each man fixing his eyes on the tall, red-haired woman in the blue jumpsuit.

"How does it feel being the object of their fantasies?" asked Maxwell.

"Normal. I'm used to being the only woman in a room full of horny guys."

Breakfast was finished, and a steward was putting out a

tray of glazed doughnuts. They went to the big silver coffee
urn. Maxwell poured coffee for them both.

"Sugar?" he asked.

"No sugar, no cream. And no doughnuts, thank you."

He shrugged and helped himself to a doughnut. No surprise. Sugar and doughnuts were definitely not Dana
Boudroux's fare. Following her to the table, he saw that her
hair was still damp at the back of her neck. Again he sensed
the subtle fragrance of perspiration and perfume. He was
stealing an appraising glance at the lithe figure when she
turned and caught him.

"I, ah, was just noticing that you look good in jeans."

She nodded. "Thank you, Commander."

"Brick."

She wasn't wearing the tortoiseshell glasses. For a long
moment she regarded him with her large hazel eyes. "Okay,"
she said. "Brick."

Well, he thought, that was progress. The Ice Queen might
not be thawed out, but she was melting a little.

Not until he was sitting did he notice the dark-featured
man in BDUs at the adjoining table. Lieutenant Commander
Wedge Flores was sitting alone, reading a magazine.

"Hey, Wedge, is that you? What brings you out to the
Reagan?"

The SEAL officer glanced up, not changing expression.
"Routine business." He didn't smile or offer to shake hands.
"Nothing that Airedales need to know about."

Maxwell nodded. You had to give Flores credit for remaining in character, he thought. Still an asshole. "Maybe
you didn't notice, but you're on an aircraft carrier. This is
Airedale country, pal."

Something resembling a smile flashed across Flores's
face, then vanished. He went back to his magazine. "That's
your problem, not mine."

Maxwell turned his attention to his coffee. Later, he reminded himself, he would give Wedge Flores a short lesson in the protocol of addressing senior officers.

Dana leaned close to him. "Isn't that the man we met at the bar back in Nevada?"

"I'm afraid so."

"He doesn't seem to like you."

"It's just a facade. Wedge and I are bosom buddies."

"I don't think so. What did you do to annoy him?"

"Become an Airedale. He can't seem to get over it."

"Are you sure he's on the same team you are?"

Maxwell glanced over at Flores, who was studiously ignoring them. Good question, he thought. He'd begun to wonder the same thing.

USS Daytona Beach

"Positive ID on the contacts," announced the radio officer. "SUBPAC confirms the *Hoi Wan* and *Hoi Lin*. The coordinates match our own displays."

Commander Al Sprague nodded. *Daytona Beach*'s onboard BSY-1 combat system array had already determined the identity of the two contacts—Chinese freighters of the size and screw signature of *Hoi Wan* and *Hoi Lin*—but Sprague wanted proof positive. Getting a visual by periscope was not an option, not with the screen of destroyers working the area. Another possible threat was their old friend *Yuanzheng 67*, still out there but no longer on *Daytona Beach*'s sonar.

The confirmation from SUBPAC, he presumed, was based on satellite surveillance and possibly even human intelligence. In any case, it removed any last nagging doubt he might have had before committing *Daytona Beach* to a torpedo attack.

Sprague could sense the tension in his crew. None, including himself, had ever fired a shot in anger. The cumulative years of training invested in the officers and men of *Daytona Beach* were now about to pay off.

The Chinese freighters were still plowing southeastward toward their anchorage in the Spratlys. *Daytona Beach*'s passive sonar had picked up at least two escorts—Type 051 Luda Class destroyers. Old warships, but fast enough to be deadly at close range.

Fewer than twelve hours had elapsed since the *Yuanzheng 67* had sent the Vietnamese freighter, *Ha Long*, to the bottom. Though the Chinese had surely prepared for retaliation from Vietnam, it was possible that they weren't expecting a response from a U.S. submarine.

Possible, Sprague told himself, but he sure as hell wasn't betting on it. He would play this one as if the entire PLA Navy was waiting for him, teeth bared and ready to fight.

After locating the freighters, Sprague had let them pass, then slid *Daytona Beach* into the acoustic shadow of their wakes. A broadside shot would have been easier—but riskier. Launching from beneath the wake turbulence gave Sprague more time to make his escape. Shoot and scoot, the tactic was called.

"Right standard rudder, steer one-four-five, make your depth seventy-two feet."

"Aye, coming to one-four-five. Depth seventy-two."

"Stand by tubes one and two," Sprague ordered. "I'll hold this track for two minutes for the tracking solution."

"Aye, Captain. Steady on one-four-five heading."

The noisy activities—readying the tubes, sealing the breach doors—had already been accomplished. Not until the torpedoes were forcibly ejected by compressed air from the tubes at six times the force of gravity would any further acoustic alarm be sent. Soon enough, God willing, *Daytona Beach* would be racing for the safety of the deep.

The control room was quiet, the crewmen speaking in hushed voices, exchanging only the most essential dialogue. Every face wore a sober expression.

"Captain, Sonar. Tracks 1102 and 1302 bearing 009 and 011. Range twenty-eight thousand yards. We have a good solution."

Sprague forced himself to take his time. Once launched, the MK 48 ADCAPs—advanced capability—wire-guided torpedoes would do all the work. The two torpedoes were programmed to run at speeds that would put each on its target at the same time. The first MK 48 would pass almost directly beneath the trailing freighter before detonating under the hull of the leading ship. A few years ago, such a trick would have been unthinkable. The MK 48 ADCAP was the smartest undersea weapon ever deployed on a submarine.

Of course, torpedoes didn't always perform as advertised, as Sprague well knew. In his own career he'd witnessed inexplicable failures of sophisticated weapons. He had also learned that when a meticulously planned operation turned to shit, you'd better have a back door.

His back door was the deep ocean. Shoot and scoot. If that didn't work, he had four more MK 48s ready to fire. Just in case.

"Match bearings," said Sprague. He took a deep breath and said, "Shoot one. Shoot two."

The weapons officer at the BSY-1 panel pressed the firing button. "Shoot one, shoot two."

A rumble passed through the hull of the *Daytona Beach* as the wire-guided MK 48 leaped from its tube.

"Tube one fired."

Seconds later, another rumble. "Tube two fired."

"Both weapons tracking under guidance."

"Stand by to clear the launch area," Sprague ordered. That was another bonus of the MK 48, and it was a big one. Each torpedo had ten miles of guidance wire packed in its aft section, and another ten miles was stowed on a reel inside the submarine. The *Daytona Beach* could make its escape while the torpedoes were still receiving guidance via their wires. If the wire snapped, or if Sprague found it necessary to close the outer door, the torpedo could be switched to its own active homing.

"Weapon one, ten thousand yards."

Sprague acknowledged with a nod.

"Weapon two, fourteen thousand yards."

Sprague found himself holding his breath.

"Weapon one switching to active homing."

A few seconds later, "Weapon two now active homing."

The MK 48s had acquired their respective targets, tracking with their own seeker heads. The guidance wires were no longer necessary. The torpedoes were on their own.

The submarine was halfway through its course reversal, bow tilting toward the depths. The sonarman called out, "Detonation on Track 1102." And then, in the next breath, "Detonation on Track 1302. Both weapons detonated, sir."

As programmed, the torpedoes had struck their respective targets almost simultaneously. No alerts, no warnings. Already *Daytona Beach*'s sonar was receiving the agonizing sounds of the Chinese ships in their death throes—tearing metal, tinkling glass, imploding compartments, screams of panicked seamen.

Sprague could visualize the chaos aboard *Hoi Wan* and *Hoi Lin*. The MK 48 ADCAPs had detonated directly beneath the freighters. The explosions tore through each hull like a blunt cleaver. The unlucky souls belowdecks, those in the engine rooms and lower deck working spaces, were already dead. As the freighter's hulls collapsed upon themselves, deck crewmen were being swept like ants into the sea. The fast-sinking hulks were sucking them along on a mile-and-a-half descent to the floor of the ocean.

Sprague put it out of his mind. He had more urgent business at hand. *Daytona Beach* could outrun the Chinese frigates escorting the freighters, but not their torpedoes. Nor could he outdistance their antisubmarine helicopters. He had to dive, stay passive, go quiet.

And listen.

Five minutes passed. Sounds of chaos still came from where *Hoi Wan* and *Hoi Lin* had gone down. There were engine noises, small craft, the beat of rotor-winged aircraft. But nothing seemed to be tracking *Daytona Beach*. Most of the surface activity was from the rescue of survivors. Sprague guessed that confusion and panic was running rampant through the convoy.

Maybe he had gotten away with it. He wouldn't be sure for another half an hour.

Sprague glanced around the control room. The faces of his young crewmen were taut, each expression sober and thoughtful. No cheering, no high-fives, no smart-ass remarks.

As it should be, he thought. The deaths of Chinese seamen were not a cause for celebration.

There was nothing personal about it, Sprague reminded himself. Submarine warfare hadn't changed since the first torpedo killed its unsuspecting prey. It was a messy, homicidal business. If you dwelled too long on the finer moral issues, you became a drunk or a suicide.

Sprague promised himself that when *Daytona Beach* was out of danger and the adrenaline of combat had subsided, he would address his crew. He would remind them that they were submariners—U.S. Navy submariners—and warriors. It was their duty to carry out the orders of their Commander-in-Chief. They had performed that duty with honor and skill. He was proud of them.

Yeah, that's what he'd tell them. But not yet. Not until they'd lived through the next thirty minutes.

CHAPTER 17

FIGMO

"Good morning, boys and girls," said Boyce.

He held up a sheaf of paper. "Here's what we've been waiting for."

The overhead fluorescent lights in the flag intel compartment glistened off his shiny pate. He stood at the podium and gazed out at his audience. As usual, Admiral Hightree was in the first row, with Captain Piles Poindexter positioned like a fixture at his elbow. All three of the Black Star crews were there, sprawled in the last two rows, wearing the same drab flight suits, no patches. Harvey Wentz, looking slightly bored, stood at the control panel for the plasma screen on the bulkhead.

Boyce noticed that Dana Boudroux didn't take her usual perch on the corner of the desk in the back. Today she arrived with Maxwell and dropped into the padded leather seat beside him. *Is the Ice Queen warming up?*

Boyce gave Maxwell a questioning look. He got a blank stare back.

"The tasking order is arriving in installments," said Boyce. "It keeps changing because the Spratly Island situation is very fluid. Little by little, the action seems to be zeroing in on Swallow Reef."

Boyce nodded to Wentz, and the lights dimmed in the compartment. A map of the South China Sea flashed onto the plasma screen. Boyce turned to the screen and aimed his laser pointer at one of the islands in the northwest portion of the Spratly archipelago.

"The Chinese appear to be using the Swallow Reef base as the hinge point of their effort to grab the Spratly oil deposits. They've moved a squadron of Flankers from Lingshui to the airfield at Swallow, and for the last two days they've been keeping a full-time CAP over the region. They're controlling the fighters with their new IL-76 AWACS-type aircraft, which stays in an orbit off the eastern shore of Hainan."

Another image flashed onto the screen. It was a heavy four-engine jet transport with a top-mounted, saucer-shaped radome. "They've just deployed this bird, and it's their pride and joy. See that radome on the roof? It doesn't rotate like ours, but its got a three-module antenna inside that gives it 360-degree coverage. It's a high-value asset. They're gonna keep it protected at all times with their Flanker fighters."

"Just like we protected our Hawkeye," muttered a voice on the back row.

Boyce shot him a scowl. "For your information, we haven't forgotten. And eye for an eye, bird for a bird. The Chinese are going to feel a little pain."

Boyce told them how some of the pain was going to be inflicted. They were going to engage the SU-27s in the air and maybe on the ground. They were going to target the PLA's new IL-76 AWACS ship, which they had just purchased from the Russians and which, according to intel reports, contained advanced radar capability copied from Israeli technology. An AWACS for an AWACS. It was only right.

He aimed the red laser pointer at the Chinese-held island. "Swallow Reef is going to be cordoned off by sea and by air. No resupply, no reinforcement of the PLA garrison on the island, no air support from Hainan or the mainland."

"Does that mean we're going to take the island back from them?" This time it was Gypsy Palmer asking the question.

"Not 'we,' Captain. Our Rules of Engagement prohibit any overt use of U.S. forces. We expect the island to be re-occupied by its previous owners."

She nodded. "The Vietnamese. But how—"

"You don't want to know how. If any of you, God forbid, are captured by the ChiComs, all they're going to extract from you is your own little piece of the big puzzle. Nothing more."

The truth was, Boyce didn't know the details about the Vietnamese landing either. He knew only that a sufficient force of Vietnamese troops would somehow be landed on Swallow Reef to overwhelm the thousand-strong PLA garrison already on the island. By air? No way, he thought. The Vietnamese Air Force's obsolete Russian-built transport aircraft would have no chance against PLA Air Force fighters, especially if the Chinese deployed the *Dong-jin*. The picture would be even uglier if the Viets attempted a seaborne assault using ships from their rusty old merchant fleet. They would be creamed by the PLA Navy and Air Force. The Rules of Engagement mandated by Washington forbade any *visible* support from U.S. ships or aircraft to the Vietnamese.

Which left only one means of inserting troops onto Swallow Reef. By submarine.

It was a gutsy play, Boyce reflected. He hoped that the tacticians who planned the operation knew what the hell they were doing. He could think of several spectacular disasters in which U.S. forces had backed an outgunned ally— the Bay of Pigs, the Iran hostage debacle, Beirut, Somalia.

He finished the briefing, then turned to the matter of the

Black Stars. "Have the IR sensors on the aircraft and the Sidewinders been modified, Dr. Boudroux?"

"Not all," said Dana Boudroux. "On two aircraft so far, and only the primary sensor. We decided to keep one of the Black Stars in its original sensor configuration until we've had empirical results to support the change."

This was news to Boyce. He frowned and said, "We?"

"Commander Maxwell and I. We also decided to modify just two Sidewinder seeker heads out of the four mounted on each jet."

Boyce nodded at this fresh snippet of news. *Commander Maxwell and I?* Boyce could feel his anger bubbling to the surface. He glowered at Boudroux for a moment, then at Maxwell. He had an overwhelming urge to tear off both their heads right here in front of the group.

"Okay, folks, that's the overview," said Boyce. "The final intel briefing is an hour from now. T-time at 1430, subject to update. Everyone is dismissed. Everyone except Dr. Boudroux and Commander Maxwell."

Maxwell had seen that look on Boyce's face before. He knew what was coming.

The admiral slowly removed the cigar from between his teeth. He fixed his gaze on Maxwell and Boudroux. "Do either of you free-thinkers happen to know the difference between a military unit and a civilian research lab?"

Maxwell saw that Dana was about to answer. He headed her off. "It was my mistake," said Maxwell. "I should have—"

"It was a scientific matter," said Dana Boudroux, "not a military one."

Boyce's face darkened. "Excuse me?"

"With all respect, Admiral, I'm a scientist and you are not. I'm the one who knows best how to configure the sensing spectrum of infrared sensors."

Boyce's eyeballs bulged like he'd been walloped from behind. "Dr. Boudroux, if I didn't know better, I'd think that you were deliberately trying to get yourself kicked off this team."

"Not at all. It just seems to me that you're being a bit autocratic about—"

"What Dana means," said Maxwell, "is that we should have consulted with you before making any configuration changes to the Black Star sensors."

She turned to him. "That's not what I—"

"For which we apologize," said Maxwell, keeping his eyes riveted on Dana. *Shut up, damn it.* "You can be sure that we'll run everything by you from now on. Isn't that right, Dr. Boudroux?"

She was staring at him as if he had just landed from Pluto. He prompted her with his knee.

"Yes," she muttered. "I suppose."

Boyce didn't look mollified. He kept his eyes fixed on Dana. "Let me explain something, Doctor. Despite what you would like to believe, the U.S. Navy is not a democracy. I'm the only one here who gets a vote. Your services are valuable, but no one is indispensable. Not me, not Commander Maxwell, and definitely not you. If I sense any further lack of cooperation from you, I will arrange a bucket seat on the next cargo flight to the U.S. Is there any part of what I just said that you do not understand?"

Maxwell could see the redness spreading over her face and neck. He nudged her again.

"I understand." Her voice was barely audible.

"Wonderful," said Boyce. He jammed the cigar back in his teeth, and headed for the door. "Now let's get this mission in the air."

Dana Boudroux was staring at the door that Boyce had just slammed behind him. "Did I blow it?"

"If you mean did you make any points with Boyce," said Maxwell, "I'd score it something less than zero."

She looked as if she might cry. That was a first. He didn't think Dana Boudroux knew how to cry.

"I don't know why I do it," she said. "I hate that in myself."

"What? Telling flag officers that you're smarter than they are?"

"I *am* smart. But I'm so goddamn stupid. I keep telling people that I know more than they do."

"I can confirm that."

"Not just you. People like Admiral Boyce whom I *really* shouldn't say that to."

"At least you're nondiscriminatory. You piss off admirals the same as us lower ranks."

She chewed on her lower lip. "I've had good jobs. I was hired to direct the phototonic department in the DARPA lab at Los Alamos."

Maxwell nodded. DARPA—Defense Advanced Research Projects Agency—was the U.S. military's most exotic research branch. "What happened?"

"I got fired. Or, to be accurate, I was reassigned."

"Because?"

"I told the lab director that he was an undereducated shoe clerk."

"Was he?"

"Sure. It didn't matter. He's still there, I'm gone."

"I think I see a pattern here."

"The awful thing is, I respect Admiral Boyce. Now he's going to get rid of me."

Maxwell didn't answer. He knew Boyce. Boyce would get over being furious at her, especially if it turned out that she *had* tweaked the Black Star so that it could kill Chinese stealth jets. But she didn't need to know that.

"Maybe," he said. "Or maybe he'll wait to see if you got the message."

She clutched her arms around her and stared morosely at the closed door. "What message?"

"That we've got a mission to fly. What do you say we get back to work?"

The final intel briefing was mercifully short.

Maxwell and O'Toole finished suiting up. They walked down the passageway toward the ladder to the hangar deck.

"You okay, Sharp?"

"What do you mean?"

"You're not running your mouth like a magpie. Something wrong?"

O'Toole looked uncharacteristically sheepish. A grin spread over his face.

"Nothing wrong," said O'Toole. "In fact, things have never been so good."

They turned the corner and followed the amidships passageway. Beneath the weight of flying gear and survival equipment, their boots made a clunking noise on the steel deck.

"How so?" said Maxwell. "Your love life take a turn for the better?"

"Yeah, actually it has. But that's not the big story. The real news is that I'm outta here."

They came to the ladder that descended to the hangar deck. Maxwell stopped at the top of the ladder. "Out of here?"

"I've been meaning to tell you. As soon as we're done with Dragon Flight, I'm FIGMO."

Maxwell looked at him quizzically. "FIGMO" was a time-honored military acronym meaning "Fuck it, I got my orders."

"Okay, cut the suspense. Orders to where?"

"You're not gonna believe this, Boss. I'm going into space."

Maxwell still didn't get it. Then he remembered: O'Toole had applied for astronaut training. "NASA? No kidding?"

"Just like you. Or almost like you. Mission specialist, next shuttle class at the Johnson Space Center."

"When did you learn about this?"

"Last night. I was gonna tell you, but not until we'd done the mission. Man, I'm still hyped. You and Gypsy are the only ones who know."

"Gypsy? What's she got to do with—" And then he caught himself.

"Yeah, Gypsy." A sly smile came over O'Toole's face. "Another little secret. She and I are gonna tie the knot when we get back to Nevada."

Maxwell had to shake his head. He should have known. It was right there under everyone's nose.

He turned and started down the ladder. O'Toole was right behind him.

"Congratulations, Sharp. You're buying the drinks for this whole outfit when we get back to Nevada."

"Drinks?" said the marine. "Gypsy and I are gonna throw the biggest bash you guys have ever seen."

The rumble of the two GE engines shook the airframe. Out the right side of his cockpit, Maxwell saw the catapult officer giving him the power-up signal.

The launch had been rolled back twice. The reason for the delay, according to the final intel brief, was to synchronize the Black Star sweep with the rotation of the SU-27s covering the Chinese AWACS. Maxwell guessed that there was more to it than that. They were synchronizing the attacks with action on the surface. And, he guessed, below the surface.

He gave the stick a full sweep, making sure the controls were free. His eyes scanned the cockpit one last time. No warnings, no cautions on the annunciator panel.

He snapped a salute to the shooter, then shoved his helmet against the headrest. He wrapped his left hand around the catapult grip to ensure that he wouldn't snatch the throttles back during the catapult stroke. In his peripheral vision he saw the shooter leaning into the wind, going through the traditional catapult officer's ballet act, arcing his right arm over his head to touch the deck. The signal to fire the catapult.

One and a half seconds later, Maxwell felt the jet lunge down the catapult track. His vision blurred. The deck of the USS *Reagan* swept beneath him.

The hard push of the catapult abruptly stopped. Ahead sprawled the hazy blue surface of the South China Sea. Maxwell retracted the gear and flaps, keeping the jet's attitude shallow until they'd accelerated to climb speed. He rolled into a right bank, swinging the nose to the northeast. Toward the Spratly Islands.

"Black Stars!" called the duty officer at the air defense command post. "Airborne from their carrier. More than one, according to the surveillance aircraft. Possibly three. They launched five minutes ago."

It was all Zhang needed to hear. He hung up the phone, a direct line from the air defense command bunker at Lingshui. He reached across his desk and shoved the mushroom-shaped alert button for the *Dong-jin* crew room. In the adjoining hangar, his two other ready crews were already briefed and prepared for the mission to Swallow Reef.

It was even sweeter than he had hoped. He had been skeptical of the capability of the new Ilyushin 76 early-warning aircraft, of the type the Americans called AWACS. The Ilyushin was on station over the South China Sea, monitoring the U.S. strike group led by the *Reagan*. Two of the ponderous four-engine jets had cost as much as a squadron of SU-27s.

The Ilyushin was paying for itself.

The controllers on the Ilyushin had reported indications of a peculiar activity aboard the American aircraft carrier *Reagan*. After a normal launch of several flights of F/A-18 and E-2C warplanes, which were easily detectable on the

AWACS radar, there was *another* launch. The sensitive AWACS radar array had tracked the carrier again turning into the wind, plane guard helicopters and escort destroyers again taking their stations, then the indications of catapults firing.

It could only be stealth jets.

The unexpected usefulness of the Ilyushin AWACS ship coincided with the even better news from the *Dong-jin* research laboratory. Fong and his team had succeeded in fabricating an enhanced version of the spectrum-sensing goggles. The new goggles were based on data extracted from the U.S. research labs where the Black Star's cloaking technology was produced. Now each of his *Dong-jins* was equipped with the new goggles.

While he watched his image in the wall mirror, Zhang put on his flight suit. It was the new fire-resistant model, the kind he wasn't wearing when he was shot down by the American. Perhaps it wouldn't have saved his face, but it would have spared him the agony of the third-degree body burns.

He retrieved the Type 64 semiautomatic from his desk, checked the magazine, then shoved the pistol into the holster sewn into his harness. He could feel the familiar buzzing in his brain—the hyperalertness he always experienced before flying into combat. Never before had he felt such confidence going against the Americans. The Black Star pilots had already demonstrated that they were unable to penetrate the *Dong-jin*'s cloaking.

Now Zhang had the improved goggles. He could see, they couldn't.

With that thought, he returned to his desk and pulled out the sliding wooden tray beneath the desktop. On it was taped the magazine page with the color photograph. Zhang lowered himself into his desk chair while stared at the photograph.

Maxwell. The man in the photograph seemed to be looking back at him.

Zhang Yu was a man who believed in destiny. He knew with an intuitive certainty that Maxwell would be out there today, and it would be Maxwell's style to assign himself the target of highest value.

Maxwell would attack the Ilyushin AWACS ship. And Zhang would be waiting for him.

CHAPTER 18

RED AND FREE

12,000 feet
South China Sea
1605 Monday, 30 April

It was hard for Maxwell to believe that this cluster of atolls was worth fighting over. On the display they looked like bird droppings in a parking lot.

They were climbing through a scattered cumulus deck. Fifty miles ahead lay the first of the specks in the ocean that were the Spratly Islands.

"Dragon One-one, Sea Lord. Your bogeys twelve o'clock, forty miles, high and low. Confirm Dolly."

Maxwell didn't answer. He was still maintaining EMCON—emissions control, meaning no radio transmissions unless they were critically urgent. Instead, he thumbed a button marked ACK on his radio console, which sent a silent, data-linked acknowledgment.

Sea Lord was the E-2C Hawkeye. Maxwell was confirming that the bogey information—the multiple contacts at twelve o'clock—was being data-linked to his onboard situational display. The Hawkeye was monitoring enemy movements, controlling fighters, and relaying "Dolly"—data-linked real-time information—not only from their own powerful radar array but also from satellite and shore-based assets.

Maxwell admired the guts of the Hawkeye crews. He'd seen their faces before the launch. No one could forget what happened to their squadron mates.

The slow-moving turbo-prop early-warning aircraft was just as vulnerable as before—with one difference. In addition to the BARCAP—barrier combat air patrol—of four F/A-18s from the Roadrunners, the Hawkeye had an invisible defender: Dragon Three-one, the Black Star flown by Crud Carruthers and Gypsy Palmer.

"Dragon One-one, Sea Lord. Your contact bears 025, thirty-two miles, twenty-eight thousand feet. Four more bogeys."

Maxwell pushed the ACK button.

There was a pause on the scrambled tactical frequency. Maxwell guessed that the controller in the Hawkeye was communicating with the air warfare commander on the *Reagan*. He could also guess what they were talking about.

He was right. Ten seconds later he heard "Bravo Golf clears Dragon One-one red and free."

Again Maxwell hit the ACK button. Then he flipped his master armament switch to the hot position. Cleared to engage, cleared to fire.

USS Daytona Beach

A classic ambush, thought Commander Al Sprague.

He studied the plot on his display. The PLA Navy convoy had cleared the jutting landmass at Macau. It was heading southwestward at nine knots toward the Spratly Islands. Sprague counted four large ships, freighters for sure, and six smaller vessels. Four of the smaller ships were darting back and forth like leashed watchdogs on either side of the convoy. The other two vessels Sprague's sonar officer had already tagged as frigates. One led the convoy while the other steamed in trail.

A well-protected convoy, reflected Sprague.

"Sovremennys," said Dale Schirmer, his XO. Schirmer was standing beside him in the control room.

Sprague nodded. The small, fast ships were Russian-built *Sovremenny* class destroyers, the cream of the PLA Navy. They carried an arsenal of missiles and torpedoes that could eliminate anything in its theater—surface, air, or submerged.

Sprague wasn't surprised to see the *Sovremennys*. Nor was he surprised at the antisubmarine helicopters working the sea around the convoy. If the intel reports were correct, the freighters carried at least a thousand Chinese amphibious troops and all their armament. The PLA intended to reinforce its garrison on Swallow Reef.

What did surprise Sprague was that they were making so much noise. Not just the freighters, which was normal, nor the pair of frigates, but even the swift and normally quiet-running *Sovremenny* destroyers. They were roiling the water like paddleboats in a creek.

Why?

Sprague could think of only two good possibilities. Either the convoy commander was stupidly incautious, so sure of his invincibility that he didn't have to worry about the excessive noise cancelling out the convoy's ability to obtain good sonar returns on submerged threats.

Or else they were screening something.

The thought caused Sprague to frown. Throwing up an acoustic wall was a primitive but effective way to hide assets. The more Sprague thought about it, the more sure he was that something else was out there. A PLA Navy submarine was escorting the convoy.

Nothing was showing on *Daytona Beach*'s four BSY-1 sonar consoles except the PLA Navy surface vessels. But that was not surprising: No passive sonar array would detect a nearly motionless Kilo class submarine.

Sprague had taken *Daytona Beach* to this station twenty minutes ago. On the opposite side of the convoy was USS *Melbourne*, another Los Angeles class SSN. On Sprague's console desk lay the printout from the COMSUBPAC order.

> Daytona Beach *and* Melbourne *to execute simultaneous intercept of PLA Navy convoy at approximate position N24° 23' E112° 13'. If convoy alters course to return to Guangzhou, Rules of Engagement preclude any further attacks on PLAN vessels except as commander deems necessary for defense and withdrawal.*

The order and the details of the ROE—Rules of Engagement—continued for a page and a half. Sprague had read it enough times to know it by heart. Each submarine was assigned geographic sectors of responsibility. *Daytona Beach* would operate on the convoy's starboard side, while *Melbourne* would remain on the port. *Daytona* would target the lead freighter and *Melbourne* the last. Each submarine would take out one escorting warship each, their choice. To Sprague, the obvious choice was a *Sovremenny*—the most dangerous of the surface escorts.

Unless I find a Kilo submarine. Sprague had already promised himself he would torpedo any PLA Navy submarine he could locate in the vicinity of the convoy.

He was still thinking about this when he heard "Captain, sonar. Track 1013 and 1016, bearing 275 and 314 respectively. Range 15,400 and 13, 800."

Sprague took a deep breath. Those were the designated targets—the lead freighter and the fast-moving *Sovremenny* off its starboard flank. The torpedomen were ready, the one and two tubes already flooded, each MK 48 ADCAP torpedo preset for its target. The firing solutions had been de-

rived by the TMA—target motion analysis—specialist and
verified by the manual plotting team using their own com-
puters to obtain a separate solution. *Daytona Beach* and
Melbourne were supposed to initiate their coordinated attacks at 0145Z.

Twenty seconds to go. Sprague watched his timer, letting
the seconds click by.

"Stand by one and two."

"Aye, one and two ready," acknowledged the weapons
control officer.

"Last bearing check."

"Bearing 276 . . . SET."

Sprague watched the timer count down. Four . . .
three . . . two . . .

"SHOOT. Stand by two."

A tremor ran through the ship.

"Track 1016, bearing 316 . . . SET."

"SHOOT."

Another tremor as the second torpedo cleared its tube.
And then silence.

South China Sea

"Dragon One-one, Sea Lord."

The voice of the Hawkeye controller broke through Maxwell's concentration. He was peering into the right MFD,
sorting out the multiple contacts in the screen. The Black
Star was still climbing, passing through 25,000 feet.

The controller said, "Purple Net reports two, possibly three
Stogies off Lingshui ten minutes ago. No further contact."

Three stogies. "Stogie" was the brevity code for the Chinese *Dong-jin* stealth fighter. Purple Net was a real-time
feed from Navy EP-3, Air Force Rivet Joint intelligence-
gathering aircraft, and current national asset data. At least
one of those national assets, Maxwell knew, was a surveillance satellite positioned to observed Hainan Island and

Lingshui Air Base. The satellite's electro-optic system couldn't see a *Dong-jin*, but if it were one of the advanced KH13 IMINT—image intelligence—satellites, it would have IR-detecting capability. The satellite's receptors had picked up enough heat emission from the Lingshui runway to indicate the launch of stealth fighters.

Maxwell was getting a bad feeling about this. If the *Dong-jins* had entered the game, it meant they had sufficiently good intel to alert them to the presence of the Black Stars. Their own satellite? Their AWACS? Or surveillance from the PLA submarine that had been snooping around the strike group?

He pushed the ACK button.

USS Daytona Beach

Watching the torpedoes on the display, Sprague felt like a witness to an impending train wreck. The wire-guided MK 48s were running at speeds precalculated to put them on their targets simultaneously.

"Both weapons under guidance, Captain."

Sprague acknowledged. The torpedoes were responding to the commands issued by the controllers aboard *Daytona Beach*. It was the quietest and most efficient way to move the weapons to a close range on their targets. When they were close enough that evasion was impossible, he would order them released to their own active sonar guidance.

"Two more torpedoes in the water," announced sonar. "MK 48s," he added.

Sprague felt like cheering. *Melbourne* had fired its own weapons. The torpedoes from *Daytona Beach* and *Melbourne* would not strike at exactly the same moment, but they would be close enough together that—

"Detonation bearing 207," called out the sonarman. "Second detonation bearing 223. The last freighter and a destroyer."

Melbourne's torpedoes had struck first. They'd fired at a closer range than *Daytona Beach.*

Sprague felt the tension mount in the control room. The danger level had just ratcheted up to the top of the scale. The Chinese convoy would be going to maximum search-and-destroy mode.

He waited. More seconds ticked past.

Finally, "Both weapons switching to active homing."

Sprague said, "Release both weapons."

"Weapons released on contacts 1013 and 1016, sir."

The sounds of the detonations, two seconds apart, were received at 0146Z. The lead freighter took the torpedo sixty feet aft of her bow, just below the waterline. The second torpedo caught the escorting *Sovremenny* as it was in a hard starboard turn, ripping its hull in half beneath the surface.

Now we earn our pay, thought Sprague. The Chinese would be launching every antisubmarine device at their disposal, or they would turn tail and run. He was fairly confident that *Daytona Beach* could egress the area without being detected. The two surviving *Sovremennys* were racing around like dogs in a junkyard. They wanted to kill something—but they didn't know what. If either became a threat, Sprague would exercise his discretion and put another MK 48 in them.

"Torpedo in the water!" called out sonar.

Sprague felt a chill run through him. His eyes snapped to the display.

He saw the trace, and at first it didn't make sense. The torpedo was definitely not a MK 48 or anything that resembled an American weapon. And it wasn't tracking toward *Daytona Beach.* It had originated from an empty space in the sea to the north. It was steering toward another empty space on the port flank of the convoy.

In a flash of clarity, it came to him. *Oh, sweet Jesus.* There *was* a Chinese submarine out there. It had been out there all along, and it was firing at a contact in its own vicinity. The sonofabitch had just fired a torpedo at the USS *Melbourne*.

But not an ordinary torpedo. This thing was moving at high speed. *Extremely* high speed. On the BSY-1 console screen, it appeared to moving at something over a hundred miles per hour.

A moment later, the sonarman confirmed it. "It's gotta be a *Shkval*. A *Shkval* in the water, Captain."

A feeling of helplessness passed over Sprague. The *Shkval*—squall in Russian—was a supercavitating, rocket-propelled weapon that moved through the water at two hundred mph. It had long been rumored that the PLA Navy was buying the supertorpedoes from the Russians.

The *Melbourne* had reached the same conclusion. Through the acoustic clutter of four sinking ships and the *Sovremennys* racing churning the water, Sprague discerned the elements of a deadly duel. *Melbourne* was deploying decoys, accelerating, going into an evasive maneuver to throw off the Chinese torpedo.

For a fleeting moment Sprague considered firing on the Chinese sub. He dismissed the idea. He would be as likely to hit the *Melbourne* as the enemy boat. In any case, it was too late. The fight between *Melbourne* and the Chinese sub would be over before he could get a torpedo into the game.

"Active homing!" called out sonar. "The torpedo's locked on."

USS Ronald Reagan

It was too good to be true, thought Boyce.

The formations of Chinese airplanes looked like gaggles of geese converging on Swallow Reef, halfway down the Spratly archipelago. Boyce knew that a convoy of surface ships was en route to the reef. The PLA was reinforcing its new base.

What are these guys thinking? Boyce wondered. It was as if they were practically begging to be shotgunned.

He was sitting at his console in the red-lighted *Reagan* CIC—Combat Information Center. The CIC compartment was the battle control nerve center of the ship. The red-lighted space had rows of terminal stations where controllers and special warfare officers peered into their screens.

Boyce glanced over his shoulder. Dana Boudroux smiled back at him from the elevated platform against the bulkhead. She had her arms wrapped around her, protecting herself from the frigid temperature of the compartment.

She was there at her own request. She'd been waiting in the passageway when he arrived at the door of the CIC. She wanted to observe the mission.

Boyce had almost said no. "Sorry, Doctor. I don't need your advice on how to run a combat operation."

"I apologize for what I said earlier, Admiral. It was stupid of me. If I promise to shut up, will you let me observe?"

He considered for a moment. She appeared to be sincere. None of that in-your-face, I'm-smarter-than-all-of-you research scientist attitude.

Technically, of course, she wasn't supposed to be there. Even though she had the security clearance, she didn't have the need-to-know requirement to be in CIC during a combat operation.

But what the hell. He was the air warfare commander, and it was his call. She might even be useful.

"Remember what I said about the bucket seat back to Nevada?"

She nodded.

"The seat's still open. Remember that, and you can be my guest in here today."

"I'll remember."

So far she was keeping her word. The scientist was sitting

in her padded seat, watching the screen over Boyce's shoulder. Her arms were still wrapped around her.

"Sorry about the Klondike temperature," said Boyce. "The electronics geeks like to keep it freezing in here to protect their fancy equipment."

"I'm okay."

In his plasma display Boyce could see the two formations of PLA Air Force fighters, each accompanying an in-flight refueling ship. Like mother hens, the tankers were leading the fighters from Hainan to their new base at Swallow Reef, topping them off with fuel before they landed. The fighters were flying high and low combat air patrol for the big, swept-wing H-6s. The H-6 was a knockoff of the Russian aircraft TU-16 Badger bomber, converted to a tanker.

On the eastern side of the display was the AWACS—the Ilyushin IL-76—also accompanied by fighters. Unlike the other PLA Air Force jets, the Ilyushin was not a knockoff. It had been purchased in hard cash from Russia, complete with cutting-edge phased array, wide-area radar.

The Ilyushin was in an elongated north-south orbit. The southern end of the orbit was nearly over the topmost islands of the Spratly group.

Which was peculiar, thought Boyce. Even with the four Flankers covering it, the AWACS was too valuable to risk being that close to a combat zone. Even more peculiar was the converging paths of the two flights of aircraft. As the tankers and fighters neared the Spratlys, they would fly within fifty miles of the Ilyushin's orbit.

Boyce tried to imagine what they were thinking. Chinese commanders behaved in ways that defied Western logic, but they weren't stupid. They wouldn't put their AWACS or the tankers at risk, even when defended by SU-27s.

Boyce thought about this while he unwrapped a Cohiba. He was wearing his battered G-1 leather jacket with the patches of a dozen different squadrons and ships. Not only was the jacket a talisman—he had worn it during every combat event of his career—it was his defense against the numbing cold.

On his display were three little yellow triangles—the data-linked images of the Black Stars. One was close by, in the same orbit as Sea Lord, the E-2C Hawkeye early-warning ship orbiting a hundred miles west of the *Reagan*. Dragon One-three, flown by Crud Carruthers and Gypsy Palmer, would back up the four Super Hornets flying CAP for the Hawkeye.

Two more triangles—Dragon One-one and One-two— were on divergent northwest tracks to intercept the separate gaggles of Chinese warplanes. Maxwell and O'Toole had been assigned to target the AWACS. Wayne and Heilbrunner would go after the tankers.

The Ilyushin was turning to the outer leg of its orbit. In a few more minutes, the two groups would be only fifty miles apart.

He keyed his microphone and called the controller in the Hawkeye. "Sea Lord, Battle-ax. Your signal is Night Train."

"Roger, Battle-ax," answered the controller. "Sea Lord copies Night Train."

"Night Train" was the code that signaled they were cleared to conduct the intercepts.

Boyce tilted back in his padded chair. The operation was now in the hands of the Hawkeye controller and the Black Star crews. All Boyce could do was watch.

And worry. "Where the hell are the *Dong-jins*?" he muttered.

CHAPTER 19

HEAT SEEKERS

USS Daytona Beach
South China Sea
1625 Monday, 30 April

Sprague clenched the arm rail of his seat.

He had to make an effort not to betray his emotions. Sprague knew *Melbourne*'s skipper, a feisty little guy named Mike Duffy. Duffy and Sprague had been rivals and contemporaries since their academy days.

"Second torpedo in the water," called sonar. A few seconds later, "It's an ADCAP."

Sprague nodded. *Melbourne* was countering the Chinese torpedo with a shot of its own. Sprague knew what Duffy was doing—shooting his MK 48 torpedo up the bearing line of the incoming torpedo. That would be Duffy's style—throw the attacker onto the defensive. But it was a desperation move.

And it didn't work.

"Detonation bearing 233," said the sonarman. "Torpedo impact," he added in toneless voice.

Sprague stared at the display. Despite what he wanted to believe, there was no mistaking the evidence on the screen.

Duffy's MK 48 was still running, but without guidance. The wire connecting it to the mother ship had been snapped.

The *Shkval* had struck *Melbourne*.

"Sir, it looks like *Melbourne*—"

"I see it," snapped Sprague.

A torrent of emotions roared through his head. He had an overwhelming desire to accelerate his own boat toward the enemy sub—it *had* to be a Kilo—and blow it to hell at close range.

It would be the wrong move. The reality was that *Daytona Beach* was in deadly peril of its own. At this moment they could very well be the target of another *Shkval*. And any overt action—accelerating its forward motion, launching more weapons, active pinging with his sonar—would make him an identifiable target.

Through the sonar came the terrible noises of pressure hulls rupturing, the rending of metal, the tinkling of glass. Some of this emanated from the four Chinese vessels already on their way to the bottom.

Their death throes had been joined by a new sound. *Melbourne* was dying with them.

Sprague felt nauseous. For nearly a minute the sonar carried the lonely sounds of the shattered *Melbourne* being dragged to the bottom. Mike Duffy and his crew of 130 had just been crushed in an avalanche of water and steel.

Searching for survivors was out of the question. The odds were immense against anyone escaping the destruction of the *Melbourne*. If any did, the Chinese would pick them up, along with the survivors of their own sunken vessels.

"Convoy's changing course, Captain. Turning northeast."

Sprague nodded. It was what they expected. With half their freighters sunk, they were cutting their losses and returning to Guangzhou. The frigates had slowed, apparently to rescue survivors. The *Sovremennys* were scurrying around like crazed terriers, still undecided whether to run or fight. A dozen active sonars were pinging the water—helicopters,

frigates, *Sovremennys*. Searching for the other American submarine. The pinging was not focused. There was no indication yet that they had a fix on *Daytona Beach*.

Sprague knew what his next move must be, and he
hated it.

"Left half standard rudder, steer 265. Make my depth
350."

The helmsman acknowledged, and the *Daytona Beach*
commenced its gradual exit from the area and away from the
convoy. The maneuver was slow and tedious, while the
pinging of the Chinese submarine hunters continued to play
like underwater cymbals. With each passing minute, *Daytona Beach*'s margin of safety increased.

Not until they were several miles removed from where
they had engaged the convoy did Sprague let himself relax.
They had accomplished their mission. But he could see
by the sober, grim expressions that no one in the control
room of *Daytona Beach* was thinking about that. They were
thinking about the *Melbourne*, entombed forever in the
South China Sea.

South China Sea

Get over it, Maxwell told himself.

In his primary IR scan display, the heat emission from the
big four-engine Ilyushin looked like a thermal eruption on
the sun. By contrast, the emissions from the four SU-27
Flankers covering the Ilyushin AWACS ship were like subdued background lights.

There was something distasteful about shooting an unsuspecting target. He was a fighter pilot, not an assassin. But
that was the nature of warfare. If it wasn't unsuspecting, it
would be shooting back. In any case, the Ilyushin was not
undefended. It had Flankers on each side.

And, probably, a *Dong-jin*.

The thought prompted Maxwell to peer again into the

screen, then toggle through the secondary sensor displays. Still nothing. No squiggly little red trace to indicate the presence of an invisible jet.

He's out there. I know he is.

When the op order came in that morning, Maxwell and Boyce had analyzed the probable targets—a pair of elderly H-6 refueling tankers, an assortment of SU-27 and J-8 fighters, and the Ilyushin AWACS ship. Maxwell made the Black Star crew assignments.

"Hey," O'Toole had said. "The Ilyushin? Why us?"

"Why not?"

"The real action is going be with those Flankers heading to Swallow Reef."

"The real action," said Maxwell, "is going to be where the *Dong-jins* are."

O'Toole still looked dubious. "You think they'll use the *Dong-jins* to—"

"To protect their shiny new AWACS ship? Wouldn't you?"

"They've got more than one *Dong-jin*. They'll protect the tankers too."

Maxwell had just nodded. O'Toole was right, but there was more to it. It wasn't just the *Dong-jin* that Maxwell was after.

He remembered the face in the plasma screen during the intel briefing. He could still feel the hate-filled eyes of General Zhang Yu gazing back at him.

From the file they had compiled on Zhang, Maxwell had constructed his own impression of the Chinese general. Zhang was an ambitious, ruthless officer of both the PLA and the secret police. It was Zhang who killed the Hawkeye crew. It was Zhang who shot down Hozer Miller.

Where was Zhang most likely to show up next?

Maxwell assigned himself and O'Toole to the Ilyushin because he had a gut feeling. His years as a test pilot had taught him to trust his gut feelings. The Ilyushin was too tempting a target. It had Zhang's signature on it.

Maxwell heard the seeker head of his AIM-9 Sidewinder missile emitting its familiar growling sound. It had a good lock on the target, which was now flying almost directly toward them.

The SHOOT cue was flashing in his HUD. Maxwell waited five more seconds, letting the range decrease to twelve miles. Then he squeezed the trigger.

The *Dong-jin* was high, slightly in trail, flying at the same speed as the Ilyushin AWACS ship.

"Where is the Black Star?" Zhang said on the intercom. He already knew Po's answer.

"I don't know, General."

Of course he didn't know. Zhang felt a mounting anger. Either the skimpy intelligence report about the American stealth jets launching from the carrier was wrong, or Zhang himself had been wrong about where they might appear.

Or else the new spectrum-sensing goggles didn't work.

Zhang hated the goggles. It was difficult swinging his helmet from side to side with the heavy, ill-fitting spectrum-sensing goggles attached. They were not only heavier than the old model, the view was worse. He felt as if he were peering through a murk of shimmering green soup.

Zhang scanned the sky for twenty kilometers behind the Ilyushin. He saw nothing. Only empty sky and the pair of SU-27s flying cover for the Ilyushin.

That thought caused Zhang even more anger. If it turned out to be the case, he knew exactly what he would do when he landed back at Lingshui. In the presence of the entire staff of bumbling technicians, he would put the muzzle of his pistol to the head of that simpering idiot Fong and splatter his brains on the wall of his laboratory.

Zhang returned his attention to the sky behind the AWACS. He saw the same greenish shadows and waves of shimmering soup. Nothing else. Nothing that suggested the presence of a—

"Missile!" screamed a hysterical voice on the radio. "Missile in the air. Coming toward us."

Zhang recognized the voice. It was the controller in the Ilyushin.

"Where?" Zhang demanded. "Say the bearing and range. Where is the missile?"

It was the first radio communication he had exchanged with the Ilyushin. Their tactical radio channels were supposedly secure. Still, they couldn't be sure that the Americans weren't intercepting and unscrambling their transmissions. But this was not a time to be concerned with intercepted communications.

"Two o'clock!" blurted the controller. "No, no, ten o'clock. High, ten kilometers."

Ten o'clock? Two o'clock? Zhang cursed to himself. It didn't matter. The reason he hadn't been able to detect the American stealth jet in the sky behind the AWACS was because he wasn't there. Zhang had made the fatal error of assuming the Americans would take the easy and traditional shot from the rear quarter of the AWACS.

He was attacking from the *forward* quarter. A more difficult attack, particularly for a short-ranged heat-seeking missile. But the American AIM-9 was perfectly capable of obtaining a lock on a target's frontal area, even though it emitted a far smaller heat signal. The big four-engine Ilyushin was an easy target from all angles.

Zhang shoved his throttles forward and swung the nose of the *Dong-jin* hard to the right, in the direction of the threat. Through the gloom of the spectrum-sensing goggles he saw the Ilyushin rolling into a severe evasive turn to the left. Flares were spewing from the big jet's tail.

Useless, thought Zhang. A missile coming at your nose wasn't distracted by flares pouring out your tail. The AWACS' only hope was the SU-27s, and Zhang saw that they were already moving. Both the twin-finned fighters were accelerating, plumes of flame torching from their afterburners. If they were lucky—and incredibly brave—one of them might be able to sacrifice himself to the oncoming missile and spare the more valuable AWACS.

Zhang was four kilometers behind the AWACS, which was still plowing through its hard left turn. The trail of flares looked like the tail of a comet. The SU-27s, one high, one low, were crossing in front of the AWACS.

And then Zhang spotted something, several kilometers ahead of the SU-27s. A dark shape in the greenish field of the spectrum-sensing goggles. It was pulsing in and out of view like a fish in a cloudy sea.

The Black Star. Zhang could see it.

In the next instant, the missile detonated.

Sixty miles away, Plug Heilbrunner had the lead H-6 tanker in his targeting display.

It would be a high-energy, descending aft quarter shot. A classic training command setup, thought Heilbrunner. You rolled in on the towed target and locked it up with your Sidewinder seeker head, shot it from behind. A piece of cake. A big fat target floating there in the front windshield, begging you to shoot it.

Just like this big H-6 tanker.

"Target twelve o'clock," Heilbrunner called from the backseat. "We shoot the tanker, then the two fighters on his starboard side."

"That checks," said Wayne.

Heilbrunner had all three AIM-9 Sidewinder missile stations armed and ready to shoot. His eyes went back to the left console, which had a repeater display of Duke Wayne's HUD in the front cockpit. He could see the Sidewinder seeker circle superimposed over the shape of the H-6. Off the right wing of the tanker were the two SU-27 Flankers.

In his earphones, Heilbrunner heard the squall from the

Sidewinder's seeker head. It was signaling that it had acquired a heat signal from the target.

Twelve miles. Close enough to shoot, but he knew Wayne wanted to get closer.

Heilbrunner wished they weren't shooting Sidewinders. The AIM-9 Sidewinder was a fine close-in weapon, good in a turning fight with a high-performance fighter that knew you were after him. What they should be shooting was the AIM-120 AMRAAM—advanced medium-range air-to-air missile. You could shoot the radar-guided AMRAAM from beyond visual range—a good thirty miles away—and forget it. The missile went on its own seek-and-destroy mission and took out your target while you made your egress.

The Rules of Engagement were explicit. No AMRAAMs. Someone with a brain the size of a walnut had decided that radar-guided missiles, being controlled initially by the fighter's acquisition radar and then by the missile's onboard tracker, were too overt. They didn't meet the requirements of a stealth war. Dragon Flight would only fire passively guided weapons.

"Ten miles, Duke."

"I know."

Heilbrunner didn't like this. They could fire from this range and still get a kill. The trouble was, once the first missile was in the air, all bets were off. The chickens would know the fox was there.

Then he saw it. On the right console display, the one showing the IR scans from the sensor array. It was close, maybe only three miles abeam.

A squiggly red trace.

"Oh, shit," said Heilbrunner. "We've got a *Dong-jin* out there."

Maxwell recognized Heilbrunner's voice.

"Sea Lord, Dragon Two-one is engaged, defensive!"

At almost the same instant Maxwell saw the Sidewinder he had just fired strike a target. But it wasn't the Ilyushin.

Damn. The missile had locked on to one of the Flankers. In his IR display he saw the big Ilyushin in a hard turn, streaming flares.

He was toggling his weapons page, setting up another Sidewinder shot, when he saw something new in his IR display—a squiggly red trace.

Something out there behind the Ilyushin. A *Dong-jin*?

The trace vanished. The fireball of the destroyed Flanker was flooding the screen, erasing all other traces.

The voice of the controller in the Hawkeye burst through the silence on the frequency. "Dragon One-one, snap vector, tactical, two-two-zero, thirty-five miles. Buster."

A snap vector was an immediate turn to a hot contact. Buster was the signal for maximum speed. It meant that Wayne and Heilbrunner were engaged with a bogey.

It had to be a *Dong-jin*.

He hesitated a moment. He could still shoot the Ilyushin. And the squiggly red trace he had seen—what was it? Another *Dong-jin*? It meant that at least two were out there.

Was Zhang flying one of them?

It didn't matter at the moment. Dragon Two-one was in trouble.

He rolled the Black Star inverted and pulled hard, grunting against the sudden G load.

"Dragon One-one is on the way."

Zhang watched the shattered pieces of the SU-27 whirl through space.

He didn't see a chute, and he was not surprised. When a supersonic fighter took an oncoming missile straight down the intake, it was like a collision of asteroids. There were seldom any survivors.

What was the pilot's name? Zhang didn't know, nor did he care. The enemy missile had been intended for the Ilyushin, which was still intact and in a hard turn back toward the Hainan. The suicidally brave SU-27 pilot had flown into the course of the oncoming missile.

Where was the Black Star?

Zhang's spectrum-sensing goggles had been blurred by the glare of the exploding SU-27. When his vision returned, the enemy stealth jet was gone.

Where? Still pursuing the AWACS?

Zhang maneuvered in a swooping, crisscross pattern above and behind the big Ilyushin. He swept the area—high, low, ahead and behind the AWACS—with the spectrum-sensing goggles.

And then Zhang heard the voice of Major Tsan, flying the *Dong-jin* covering the refueling tankers a hundred kilometers to the southeast. Tsan declared that he was engaged with an enemy stealth jet. A Black Star.

It was suddenly clear to Zhang. The enemy jet that had just killed the SU-27 had broken off to join the other engagement.

Zhang didn't hesitate another second. He rolled his jet into a hard turn to the southeast.

CHAPTER 20

GUN KILL

17,000 feet
South China Sea
1650 Monday, 30 April

The enhanced infrared sensors on Black Star were working.

"I've got him!" yelled Heilbrunner. "He's in our display, four o'clock, a quarter mile."

"So why hasn't he taken a shot?" said Duke Wayne. "He could have popped us already with a missile."

Heilbrunner didn't have a good answer for that one. He only knew that they were in trouble. Maxwell was on his way to help. It might not be soon enough.

He stared at the display, watching the red trace. It wasn't squiggly now, more of a solid pulsing triangle. He saw the arcing pursuit curve, the *Dong-jin* trying to get his nose inside their flight path. As if he were leading them.

It came to him.

"Guns," said Heilbrunner. "He's engaging us with guns."

"Guns? Why?"

"He can't get a missile lock, but somehow he has a visual on us. He's trying to get close enough to use his gun."

"Suits me," said Wayne. "If he wants a gunfight, he's

come to the right party. We'll drag him in close, then break to the right."

The *Dong-jin* had an overtake speed of thirty or forty knots, coming from the aft starboard quarter. They could see the Chinese jet pulling its nose ahead of the Black Star's. A classic pursuit curve.

"He's close," said Heilbrunner. "Wait, wait till he's—*oh, shit!*"

The trail of cannon fire was coming for them. It looked like a string of glowing golf balls arcing toward them.

Wayne hauled the Black Star into a violent right turn. Heilbrunner's head almost went into his lap under the weight of the seven Gs.

"Where is he?" called Wayne. "You got him?"

"He's outside our turn. He couldn't match our break and he overshot."

"Sweet. Stay on the display and call the reversal."

"Roger that."

This was an unbelievably shitty way to run a dogfight, thought Heilbrunner. Why didn't the intel pukes back on the *Reagan* tell them the ChiComs could *see* the Black Stars? It was like going blindfolded against a guy who already had you in his gun sight.

But they had the display. Whatever that lady scientist had done to the Black Star's IR sensors, it worked. There was the little red image of the *Dong-jin*, wiggling like a glow-worm on the screen.

And sliding outside their turn radius. The Chinese pilot had thought he had a sure kill and overshot the turn.

"Break left . . . *now!*" Heilbrunner called.

Again he felt himself slammed down in the seat. With his head leaned to the left side of the canopy, the weight of the helmet was almost too much for his neck.

The hard reversal brought them nose to nose with the *Dong-jin*. Heilbrunner peered out into the hazy sky. He saw something, a gray wavering object, swimming in and out of his vision.

The *Dong-jin* was coming at them.

Zhang saw him.

At least, he *thought* he saw him. He couldn't be sure, peering through the soup-green murk of the goggles. But the longer he stared through the device, the more sure he became. That batlike shape—it had to be the Black Star.

He was only fifteen kilometers ahead, perhaps a thousand meters lower in altitude. The American jet was in a shallow descent, accelerating.

Zhang had been right. This Black Star was on his way to join the fight between Tsan and the other Black Star.

Zhang estimated that he and the Black Star were at the same speed. The American jet would reach the location of the other Black Star and the *Dong-jin* before Zhang could catch him.

Zhang shoved the nose of the *Dong-jin* down. The only way to close the gap was to trade altitude for airspeed. He would dive the *Dong-jin* to an altitude beneath the Black Star, using the energy to overtake him, then zoom upward to a firing position. And if the Black Star turned in either direction, all the better, because Zhang could cut him off.

A disturbing thought flashed through Zhang's mind. *How had the Black Star pilot who was fighting Major Tsan managed to see him?* Had the Americans also developed goggles that would penetrate the cloaking of the *Dong-jin*? Or was it something else?

It didn't matter, he decided. All he had to do was stay in trail of the American jet, keep him in sight, and wait. When he maneuvered to insert himself into the fight ahead, Zhang would pounce on him like a cat.

"Dragon One-one, Dragon Two-one and the bandit are at twelve o'clock, ten miles, angels fifteen."

"Dragon One-one has both contacts."

Maxwell had the symbol of Dragon Two-one data linked in his display. On the IR scan he was getting the familiar red squiggle of the *Dong-jin*. The two jets were turning toward each other—entering a classic scissors duel.

They were six thousand feet beneath Maxwell's altitude. He would position his own jet above the fight, wait until the *Dong-jin* had crossed noses with Dragon Two-one, then set up an aft-quarter Sidewinder shot.

"Plug is gonna scream like a raped ape," said O'Toole.

"About what?"

"About us killing *his* bandit."

"Tough. He and Duke had their chance. Now we're gonna bail 'em out."

Maxwell saw in the display that the two jets were on a head-on pass, both in a high-G turn toward each other. Through the CFD goggles he had a visual ID on Dragon Two-one. He couldn't see the *Dong-jin* through the goggles, but he saw a clear image on the IR scan screen. They were only five miles away. Well within Sidewinder range.

Maxwell selected AIM-9 on the weapons page of his multifunction display. He heard the low growl of the Sidewinder seeker head coming alive.

"Hey, I see him!" said O'Toole.

"See who?"

"The *Dong-jin*. To the left of Dragon Two-one's nose, that fuzzy gray blob."

Maxwell looked, saw nothing, blinked his eyes. And saw it. It was barely visible, like a shape emerging from the fog.

He kept his eyes locked on the apparition. He corrected his own flight path to set up a targeting solution on the *Dong-jin* as soon as it had crossed noses with Dragon Two-one.

He lost sight of the *Dong-jin*, then it swam back into view. Then out of view. Maxwell knew where it was—on a nose-on course toward Dragon Two-one. He refocused his eyes on the shimmering Black Star, watching for—

It exploded.

Maxwell stared, too stunned to believe what he saw.

The Black Star was gone. In its place was a roiling fireball. Tentacles of flame were shooting in opposite directions from the core of the explosion. Fragments of airframe and engine were hurtling through space like pieces of shrapnel.

It took several seconds for the thump of the explosion to reach Maxwell's cockpit. He imagined he could smell the stench of flaming jet fuel, the cordite smell of detonated ammunition.

"Oh, man," said O'Toole in a hoarse voice. "I can't believe this shit."

Maxwell said nothing. They were directly above the spreading cloud of debris. He kept staring at the carnage, trying to make sense of what happened.

He became aware of the persistent voice in his earphones.

"Dragon One-one, Sea Lord. Answer up, Dragon."

He keyed the mike. "Dragon One-one here."

"We've been calling you, Dragon One-one," said the controller in the Hawkeye. "We lost the link on Two-one, and we don't see the trace on the bandit. Do you have a visual on them?"

"Dragon Two-one's down," said Maxwell. "Looks like a midair with the bandit."

There was a heavy silence. "Uh, Dragon One-one, say again. It sounded like you—"

"Dragon Two-one collided with the bandit. They're both down."

"Ah, hell." The controller's voice sounded dry and croaky. "Do you see chutes?"

"Negative." *And we won't see any,* thought Maxwell. No way did anyone survive a head-on collision at a combined speed of eight hundred knots.

Another silence of several seconds. Maxwell knew that

the controller was having a one-sided dialogue with the air warfare commander aboard *Reagan*. Maxwell wondered if they were going to scramble a search-and-rescue helo with armed escorts. Would the ChiComs do the same? If so, there would be another fight when they met over the crash site.

Let someone else deal with it, thought Maxwell. He had work to do.

Zhang stared at the fireball.

It was a few kilometers beyond where he'd last seen the Black Star. Zhang had dived below the Black Star's altitude, closing the distance between them. He had been almost close enough to engage with his gun when the explosion occurred directly in front of him.

The wavering green image of the Black Star was gone, obscured in the spectrum-sensing goggles by the brilliant flash of the fireball.

What happened? As Zhang watched, the explosion seemed to swell in size. He could see large pieces of airframe whirling in opposing directions through the sky. Secondary explosions were igniting inside the mushroom cloud.

Stunned, Zhang continued to stare at the roiling bank of smoke and flame. Did the Black Star shoot Tsan's *Dong-jin*? Or did Tsan kill the enemy jet? Zhang had seen plenty of air-to-air missile strikes, and this was different.

As he drew nearer to the billowing cloud, Zhang began to assemble the pieces of the puzzle. Tsan was gone. So was the Black Star Tsan had engaged.

"What happened, General?" asked Po from the backseat.

"A collision," said Zhang. "Tsan and the *gwai-lo* jet came together."

Zhang felt a wave of bitterness sweep over him. Major Tsan and his systems officer, Lieutenant Chiu, were his most experienced *Dong-jin* crew, next to himself and Po.

But they were expendable. The precious *Dong-jin* was not. Zhang's squadron—the only stealth jet unit in the PLA

Air Force—had four operational *Dong-jins*, and he had just lost a fourth of his inventory.

He shoved his anger aside. The brilliant orange fireball was subsiding into a blanket of black smoke. Somewhere out there was the Black Star he had been pursuing. He resumed scanning through the goggles. More than ever, Zhang wanted to kill him.

He was still scanning when Lieutenant Po surprised him. "I see him," said Po.

O'Toole saw them first. A trail of glowing balls, evenly spaced, coming up from below, past the left wingtip.

"Oh, shit! Tracers!"

Maxwell yanked the Black Star into a violent left break. He heard O'Toole groaning against the high G load.

In the next moment he felt it. *Thunk. Thunk. Thunk. .Thunk.* Like a sledgehammer pounding on the jet's skin.

"We're hit," said O'Toole. "Who the hell's shooting at us?"

"Who do you think? It's another *Dong-jin.*"

And he knew which one. It had to be the one he'd gotten the trace on before they disengaged with the Ilyushin.

"Okay, I've got him in the display," said O'Toole. "He's close. Only about a thousand yards."

Welcome to stealth warfare, Maxwell thought. Even with Dana Boudroux's enhanced IR sensors, the system only worked when it was looking straight ahead. It was marginally okay on the beam, worthless in the rearward view. They were being hosed by an enemy they couldn't see.

Thunk. Thunk. Thunk. More sledgehammer blows. They came from the belly and right wing. Despite the five-G turn, the *Dong-jin* pilot was tracking them well enough to get hits with his cannon.

Maxwell felt a stab of fear. He remembered why he had assigned himself the AWACS. It was because of who he thought would be covering the AWACS.

Zhang. He was there. And he had followed them.

*   *   *

Zhang squeezed the trigger again, holding it for less than a second. The GSh-301 cannon made a satisfying *brrrraaaap,* spitting thirty-millimeter shells at a rate of eighteen hundred rounds per minute.

There was nothing like a gun kill. Missiles were cold-blooded and efficient killers. You could fire them from great distances—beyond visual range—and kill your adversary without ever seeing him. But for a warrior like Zhang Yu, nothing matched the visceral feeling of the automatic cannon.

The *Dong-jin* magazine carried only four hundred rounds. Zhang was forced to shoot in tiny bursts, watching the tracers, working them like an artist's brush across the target.

He knew he'd gotten two solid hits on the Black Star. He'd followed the tracers, seen pieces fly off the skin of the American jet.

But the Black Star was still flying, still in a hard turn that Zhang was finding hard to match. His last burst had gone wide of the target, arcing off his right wing. The American pilot, even though he had been caught from below and behind, was countering Zhang's attack with great skill.

Was it Maxwell?

His finger closed on the trigger again.

Thunk, thunk, thunk.

This time the hammer blows were outboard on the right wing. The *Dong-jin* was matching their turn, carving inside enough to pull lead and get hits with his cannon.

Lights were illuminating in the annunciator panel. Two yellow caution lights—one said HYD for the failing hydraulic system, the other FUEL—told them something was not good in the Black Star's fuel system.

And then another light, this one red: FIRE.

"We've got a problem," said Maxwell.

"No shit." O'Toole's voice sounded squeezed under the weight of the five Gs. "This guy's shredding us."

Maxwell pushed the glowing red warning light, which dimmed the light and automatically pumped flame retardant into the right main fuel tank and the supply lines. It was supposed to extinguish the fire.

"Uh-oh," said O'Toole. "Check our right wing."

Maxwell looked. The fire wasn't extinguished. The outer half of the Black Star's black triangular wing was engulfed in a sheet of flame.

"We're out of here, Sharp."

"I'm with you, Boss."

Only once before had Maxwell ejected from a damaged jet. All he learned from the experience was that using an ejection seat was a lousy way to leave an airplane.

He relaxed the pressure on the stick, removing the five-G load from the jet. The ejection command switch was set to BOTH. O'Toole's seat would fire an instant before Maxwell's. The ejection rail of each cockpit was tilted a few degrees from the other to prevent the two rocket-propelled seats from colliding in the air.

Maxwell grasped the handle on the seat between his legs. He slammed his head back against the headrest, drew his elbows in close to his body, and yanked the handle.

He was vaguely aware of the canopy leaving the aircraft. A freight-train roar of slipstream noise filled the open cockpit. He heard a *bang* from the cockpit behind him.

O'Toole was gone.

Another *bang*. Maxwell's seat fired.

The three-hundred-knot wall of air hit him. The force of the blast slammed the breath from his lungs. Dimly he sensed the drogue chute deploying, stabilizing the seat while it decelerated in a long downward arc.

The automatic sequence of the SJU/5A Martin-Baker seat occurred precisely on schedule. The drogue chute released from the seat. Another small rocket fired from the top of the seat, extracting the main parachute. With a violent jolt, the main chute popped open, snatching Maxwell like a rag doll out of the seat.

He swung beneath the sprawling canopy of the parachute. Gone was the roaring freight-train noise. He heard only the rustle of wind over nylon.

For several seconds Maxwell hung limp in the harness, too stunned to think. He tried moving his arms, then his legs. Everything worked. He released his oxygen mask and looked around.

He guessed that he was passing through about eight thousand feet. A couple of miles away he saw a black-and-orange cloud. The exploded carcass of the Black Star was falling to the sea. He'd made the decision to eject just in time.

About a mile away was an island. Swallow Reef? No, not large enough. Wrong shape. It was one of the atolls in the northern group. One the Chinese occupied? He'd soon find out.

And then he remembered O'Toole. *Oh, hell, what happened to—*

There he was. O'Toole was at a lower altitude, about a quarter mile away. He had a good chute, and Maxwell could see him waving his arms. They would be able to communicate with their emergency radios.

Maxwell was groping in the pocket of his SV-2 survival vest for the radio when he heard it. A new sound.

The whine of a jet engine.

He swung himself around in the harness. He saw only empty sky.

The whine of the jet swelled. Coming closer.

CHAPTER 21

MUZZLE FLASH

8,000 feet
South China Sea
1705 Monday, 30 April

"We are approaching minimum fuel state," announced
Lieutenant Po.

"Five minutes," said Zhang. "Then we return to Lingshui."

Zhang pulled the throttles back to idle thrust. Slowing the
Dong-jin to four hundred kilometers per hour—216 miles
per hour—would conserve fuel. He didn't want extra speed.
What he wanted was the maximum time to strafe. He had
expended most of the GSh-301 automatic cannon's ammunition. With only about fifty rounds left, he had to make
every shell count.

Zhang was still filled with the elation of victory. Of his
nearly two dozen kills, none had been as glorious as the
downing of the Black Star. The only thing that would have
made it more glorious was if the jet had exploded *before* the
crew ejected. But then, of course, he would not have had this
opportunity.

Two parachutes. They were descending toward Northeast

Cay, which was occupied by PLA troops. Before the igno-
rant ground troops used the captured *gwai-los* for target
practice, Zhang would shred them like paper dolls.

There wasn't much time, a few minutes at the most.
Zhang could see that the chutes would land on the shore of
the atoll or in the surf along the shoreline.

He swung the nose of the *Dong-jin* toward the parachutes.
The airspeed was back to just under four hundred kilometers
per hour. A good strafing speed.

Which one is Maxwell?

The pilot-in-command's chute, at least in theory, would be
the higher. In tandem-place jets, the front seat was the last to
eject so that the backseater wouldn't be injured by the blast
of the rocket in front of him. But there were other factors—
rate of descent during ejection, body weights, timing of the
seat separation and chute deployment.

There was one way to be sure: Kill them both.

The higher of the two chutes was positioned in Zhang's
head-up display, encircled by the reticules of his gun sight.
The dangling man looked like a puppet suspended by its
strings.

Zhang took a deep breath, held it, forcing himself to hold
his fire. *Wait. Wait until you see his face.*

Maxwell heard it coming.

It was a low whine, not the full-throated roar of a jet at high
thrust. He hauled down hard on the right-hand riser—one of
the long straps connecting his harness to the parachute—
swinging the chute around so that he was facing the oncoming sound.

The jet was at slow speed.

The whine of the turbine engine swelled in volume.
Maxwell peered into the haze. He saw nothing, but he knew
without a doubt what it was. And who.

Zhang. Zhang would come back to strafe the crew.

He saw the yellow blinking light first. A gun muzzle. No

sound, no chatter of an automatic weapon, just that yellow blinking light. He knew the sound came later.

Whap, whap, whap. It sounded like hailstones. Bullets ripping through his parachute. He felt a sickening lurch as one of the risers separated.

Brraap. Brraap. The sound of the cannon caught up with the bullets.

Maxwell raised his arms, instinctively protecting his body. He kept his eyes on the yellow blinking light. It flickered, extinguished, flickered, extinguished again. He knew what the pilot was doing. Firing short, selective bursts, like someone playing with a flashlight.

He saw the *Dong-jin.* It was close, close enough that he could see the wavy, wispy shape of the jet. It had the amorphous look of a jellyfish, coming directly at him.

The little yellow light again. The wispy shape was wrapped like a shroud around the light. Maxwell stared at the muzzle of the cannon.

He knew it was coming. He felt a dull *smack*, then nothing.

O'Toole lost sight of the *Dong-jin.*

He had glimpsed it for only a moment—a shimmering silhouette, moving at a surprisingly low speed. Then he heard that awful growling noise, like the sound of a concrete drill. The gun. The noise sent a wave of raw fear surging through his nervous system.

The roar of the jet engine faded. O'Toole tried to follow the sound. It seemed to be arcing around him, moving back to where he had first heard it.

Circling for another pass.

O'Toole could see Maxwell's parachute. Ribbons of nylon were streaming from the canopy. Something was torn, flapping like a loose shoestring. He could see Maxwell hanging slumped in his harness, head flopped over on his shoulder. Both arms dangled at his sides. The rips in the chute were causing it to descend faster than O'Toole's.

A feeling of hopelessness swept over O'Toole. He guessed this was how a swimmer felt when he saw a shark coming. That murdering sonofabitch strafed Maxwell while he was hanging in the straps. Now he was coming for O'Toole.

This wasn't the way a fighting man was supposed to go out, he thought. Letting some gomer shoot at you while you were a defenseless target.

He corrected himself. *Defenseless my ass.* He was a Marine, goddamn it. Marines were never defenseless.

He pulled his sidearm from its web holster. The butt of the pistol—a Colt .45 semiautomatic—had a nylon lanyard that kept it connected to the holster.

He heard the distant roar of the jet changing pitch. Coming closer. He swung himself around in the chute to face the oncoming sound.

He saw the muzzle flash. A second later he made out the shape of the stealth jet itself. It was coming directly at him, wavy and ghostly-looking in the afternoon haze.

O'Toole superimposed the sight of the pistol over the gray shape. He squeezed off a round, feeling the recoil of the big pistol. It felt good. Crazy as hell, but good.

He fired again. And kept firing.

"Minimum fuel, General. We must leave immediately."

Zhang heard the urgency in Po's voice. He had no doubt that the dutiful systems officer would remain with the *Dongjin* until it ran out of fuel—if Zhang so ordered. But Po knew that a worse fate would befall him if he didn't warn Zhang about the impending fuel problem.

"I know," said Zhang. He had already turned the *Dongjin*'s nose in the direction of Hainan Island and their base at Lingshui. He had used up his remaining thirty millimeter ammunition and most of his fuel. They had barely enough for the flight back to Lingshui. The flight management computer was showing that they could expect to touch down with two hundred kilos of fuel—less than fifteen minutes flying time.

Too close for normal operations. Today, of course, had not been a normal operation.

The *Dong-jin* had prevailed over the Americans. Two Black Stars destroyed, both crews annihilated. The PLA Air Force had lost one *Dong-jin*, one SU-27. Such losses were regrettable, particularly the *Dong-jin*, but acceptable.

It was the most glorious day of Zhang's career. The war in the South China Sea would soon be over. When the history of the campaign was made public, General Zhang Yu would be recognized as the greatest military hero in the People's Republic of China.

He pushed the throttles up. He would climb to a higher altitude where the *Dong-jin* would obtain the longest range for its meager remaining fuel.

Zhang took one last glance over his shoulder. He saw the curving shoreline of the atoll where the two chutes had descended. One was landing about a hundred meters inland, the other hadn't reached the island.

It was fitting, thought Zhang. Let the sharks dispose of the remains.

Borne on the fifteen-knot breeze, the inert body dropped into the sea. He plunged beneath the surface, bobbed up, and was dragged across the waves by the wind-filled parachute canopy. After fifty yards, the chute collapsed onto itself and spread like a mat across the surface.

The man was still attached to the chute by the harness fittings. The canopy settled in the water like a sea anchor. The man slowly sank beneath the waves. Seawater filled his mouth and nostrils.

His eyes opened.

Darkness was enclosing him like a coffin. He tried to breathe and sucked water into his lungs.

He was drowning.

Panic overtook him, and he clawed wildly for the surface, flailing with his arms and legs.

His foot struck something. He kicked again and felt his boot dig into a soft, yielding surface.

Sand. The water was shallow. He kicked against the bottom and propelled himself upward, thrusting his head above the surface. He coughed, gasped, then sank back under the water. Again he kicked off the bottom. He expelled water, trying to suck in air. Trying not to let his panic kill him.

He made two more round-trips to the bottom, kicking back to the surface. He gasped for oxygen, fighting the panic that had seized him like a wild animal.

In a series of tiny flashes, his brain was returning to life. Then he remembered. He had a life preserver attached to his SV-2 survival vest.

He found the toggles and yanked them. The flotation device swelled around him and he popped like a cork to the surface. Between fits of coughing, he regurgitated what seemed like gallons of seawater.

Finally he thought about the Koch fittings—the attachments that fastened him to the parachute. One at a time, he released the fittings. He disentangled himself from the shroud lines and let the parachute sink beneath the surface.

His vision was clearing. He saw that he was only about fifty yards from the shore. He paddled and kicked toward the shore until he felt his boots again scraping the bottom. He reached a depth where he could stagger through the two-foot surf onto the shore.

On the rocky beach he collapsed to his knees. For several minutes he heaved his insides out, purging himself of the warm, salty water. His head throbbed. Waves of nausea kept sweeping over him.

He pulled his helmet and scalp liner off and dropped them on the sand. Between sessions of retching he looked at the helmet. There was something peculiar about it.

The left side of the helmet had a groove through it, as if it had been struck by a thin round object. He continued to stare at the helmet. *What happened to it? What made that groove?*

It came to him. The yellow winking light—the *Dong-jin*'s automatic cannon. Strafing him while he descended in the chute. He recalled the *whap* of the shells tearing through the nylon of the parachute. Then a blow on the head.

He could see it now, a thirty-millimeter-sized groove through the composite shell of the helmet. The bullet missed his scalp but walloped him hard enough to knock him senseless.

He gave himself an inspection for other damage. No other bullet wounds. Nothing broken or badly sprained. There was only this throbbing headache from the bullet slap, and the nausea from a bellyful of seawater.

His brain was idling at one-tenth its normal power. He felt like a sleepwalker who had awakened to find himself in a strange land. He sat on the rocky beach, fighting back the nausea, and assessed his situation.

I was shot down. I ejected. The sonofabitch strafed me in the parachute. He missed, except for the round that whacked my helmet, and then I nearly drowned, but I didn't, and now I'm on this damn island.

What damn island?

I was with . . . He had to think for a moment. O'Toole.

Maxwell forced himself to his feet. A wave of dizziness swept over him, and he nearly toppled over.

The island rose inland to an elevation of no more than ten or fifteen feet. The surface appeared to be a porous rocky substance, probably of volcanic origin. Pale green scrub brush, three to four feet high, covered most of the terrain as far as he could see. There was no sign of habitation, no movement anywhere, no sound except the low rumble of the surf.

He remembered the radio. In its Velcroed pouch on his torso harness was the CSEL—Combat Survivor Evader Locator. With it he could talk to the SAR units and Sandy—the search-and-rescue unit and their gunship escorts.

And he could talk to O'Toole, wherever he was.

Wobbling on his feet, Maxwell pulled the radio from its pouch. He was still fumbling with the ON switch when he glimpsed something over the nearest brush-covered ridge. Something white, ruffling in the breeze like a laundry on a line. It was just visible over the tops of the scrub brush.

The canopy of a parachute.

Maxwell lurched across the beach. His legs tried to buckle beneath him. The toe of a boot caught a loose rock and he pitched onto his hands and knees. Shaking his head, he rose and continued toward the low ridge.

He staggered up the shallow incline, stumbling over rocks, pushing with his knees through the clinging scrub brush. At the crest of the ridge he could see for nearly a mile across the interior of the island.

He saw the ruffling white parachute canopy, snagged on an outcropping of rock. It was still attached to the figure lying motionless against the ridge.

Despite his dizziness, Maxwell broke into a trot. As he trotted, he heard a disembodied, crackling voice.

"Dragon One-one, this is Battle-ax."

The CSEL emergency radio. He had already forgotten that he'd turned it on.

"Answer up, Dragon One-one. We need a comm check."

Maxwell didn't answer. He kept running toward the figure on the ground.

"How much fuel?" Zhang asked.

The stealth jet was parked inside the fortified hangar. The big bifold door had already sealed it off from the rest of the base at Lingshui.

"Slightly less than two hundred kilos," said Po.

Zhang nodded. Ten minutes flying time, perhaps less. Closer than he had expected, but such risks were sometimes necessary.

Po was waiting beneath the *Dong-jin*'s nose. Zhang dismissed him with a wave of his hand.

He waited until the young officer had gone inside the operations office. Then he began his inspection.

First he examined the pointed nose of the jet. He walked along the leading edge of the right wing. The dull gray surface always reminded Zhang of the skin of a shark. Hard, dark, smooth. He studied every millimeter of the radar-absorbent surface, sliding his hand over it.

Two meters from the tip of the left wing, he found what he was looking for. He focused the beam of his pencil light on the small hole in the leading edge. He put his finger in the indentation, guessing at the caliber. A heavy blunt round, ten or twelve millimeter.

Zhang had to laugh. It was so stupid. Stupid and audacious. But he was a soldier, and he could almost admire the audacity of the man who made this hole in the *Dong-jin*.

The bullet had come from the second of the two parachutes. Zhang had already killed the man in the first. He was certain because he had seen the man's body slump after the barrage of cannon fire. He was almost out of ammunition, and for the second target Zhang forced himself to wait. He was flying the *Dong-jin* at a slow speed, giving himself the easiest shot.

He waited until he was close enough that he could see the man's face. The figure in the parachute was aiming a weapon. Firing at him.

That was when he felt it—a tiny *plink*—somewhere in the airframe of the *Dong-jin*. Zhang didn't believe it. No one could hit an onrushing jet fighter—an *invisible* jet fighter—with a handgun.

He had squeezed his trigger again, only for a second. The rattle of the cannon abruptly ceased. He had spent the last of his ammunition, but it didn't matter. He could see that the last burst had been on target.

CHAPTER 22

HELLFIRE

Northeast Cay, Spratly Islands
South China Sea
1745 Monday, 30 April

Maxwell stopped trotting. There was no reason to hurry. Slowly he walked through the scrub brush. The parachute was flapping in the light breeze.

O'Toole was lying facedown. A pool of blood had accumulated beneath him.

Maxwell knelt beside him. He knew what he'd find. O'Toole's upper body had been hit by at least two thirty-millimeter rounds.

Gently, Maxwell rolled him over. He released the Koch fittings that still attached O'Toole's body to the chute. He detached the oxygen mask, then removed the helmet. He closed O'Toole's eyes.

A dull, metallic object caught his attention. It lay in the dirt beside O'Toole, still connected by its lanyard to the web holster. Maxwell picked up the Colt .45 and looked at it. The slide was open, and the extended ten-round magazine was empty.

A voice crackled again from the emergency radio. "Dragon One-one, this is Battle-ax. Speak to me, Dragon."

Maxwell felt a great weariness come over him. He sat on the ground beside O'Toole's shattered body. He pulled out the emergency radio and stared at it for a while.

"Damn it, Dragon One-one," said the voice, "answer up."

Maxwell keyed the transmitter. "Dragon One-one hears you, Battle-ax."

"About time, Dragon. Authenticate, please."

Maxwell had to think. What the hell was the authentication code for the mission? His head throbbed. A deep fatigue had settled over him.

Finally it came to him. "Golf Bravo forty-five."

"Say the status of you and Dragon One-two."

Maxwell turned to look at the body of Sharp O'Toole. His eyes were closed, and he looked as if he were asleep.

"Dragon One-one Alpha is okay. Dragon One-one Bravo is dead."

A silence of several seconds passed. Maxwell thought he heard Boyce sigh over the frequency. "Copy that," said Boyce. "Listen to me now, Dragon. I want you to move to the east end of the island as fast as you can. You've got ground contacts moving your way from the west."

Ground contacts? Maxwell's brain was still not up to speed. How did Boyce know where he was? How did he know about ground contacts?

He stared at the CSEL emergency radio—and then it came to him. It was automatically transmitting Maxwell's encrypted longitude and latitude. But how did Boyce know about the ground contacts? Did they have a surveillance drone in the area?

"Move, Dragon," said Boyce. "Get out of there."

"What about Dragon One-one Bravo?"

"We'll do our best to recover him, and that's a promise. Take his radio and sidearm with you. Use your handheld GPS to find the eastern tip of the island."

Maxwell had forgotten about the GPS—the Global Positioning Satellite receiver—in the vest pocket of his flight suit. It was the size of a pack of cigarettes, battery-powered, and had a tiny backlit screen. He pushed the ON button, then stuffed it back in his pocket without waiting for it to boot up.

He looked again at O'Toole's body. *I let the* Dong-jin *shoot us down. O'Toole would be alive if—*

Something caught his eye. Over the ridge a hundred yards to the west. Silhouettes against the sky.

Troops coming his way. A column of them, jogging along as if they knew exactly where they were going. And something more ominous. The *whop whop* of rotor blades.

Ours or theirs?

Boyce's voice came over the radio again. "Dragon One-one, move, damn it! You've got ChiComs inbound."

He knelt over O'Toole's body. He removed the emergency radio, the .45 pistol, and the extra magazine of ammo. He wobbled to his feet and took one last look at the Marine's body. *Sorry, Sharp. It was my fault.*

Then he keyed the mike on the CSEL. "I hear you, Battleax. Dragon One-one's moving out."

Running made him want to puke again. His boots pounded on the loose rocks. His head throbbed, and the seawater that remained in his stomach kept gurgling to the surface. The scrub brush grabbed his legs, slowing him, making him want to stop and walk. Fatigue was seeping through his bones.

Little geysers of dirt erupted six feet behind him. A minisecond later came the crackle of gunfire. He glanced over his shoulder and saw the dark-clad troops one ridge to the west.

The bastards were shooting at him.

No more time for puking. With renewed energy he scrambled over the next low ridge. He ran like a sprinter through more rocks and scrub brush.

The *whop whop* of the rotor blades was becoming louder. And in the background Maxwell picked up another noise—a distant buzzing that sounded like a lawnmower.

He took another glance over his shoulder. *Oh, hell.* There it was, coming over the ridge—the dark shape of a helicopter. And he no longer had any doubt whose it was. He recognized the camo-painted, slope-nosed shape of a Z-9, the Chinese knockoff of the French Dauphin. This one was configured as an assault ship with weapons pylons on either side of the fuselage.

His breath was coming in hard rasps. His legs felt heavy and clumsy. The weight of the SV-2 survival vest was slowing him down. He stopped long enough to unclasp the vest. He threw it into the brush and resumed running.

The sound of the rotor blades was close now. Very damn close. No way could he outrun a helicopter. *Now what, smart guy?*

Another ridge lay directly ahead. Maxwell scrambled over the brush-covered incline, then ducked behind an outcropping of igneous rock. He pulled the .45 from the leg pocket of his flight suit. He'd follow O'Toole's example, keep firing at the bastards until they killed him.

He peered over the edge of the rocks. The Z-9 pilot knew where he was. The helicopter was bearing down on him.

Maxwell waited. The helicopter was close enough now to open up with its automatic guns. Maxwell could see the faces through the glass of the cockpit. The barrel of the gun mounted on the right pylon was aimed at him.

It still wasn't firing.

As the helicopter swept directly over him, Maxwell fired two rounds from the .45. Useless, he knew, but satisfying. The helicopter pulled up into an abrupt climbing turn, then started back toward him. It seemed to be slowing, its nose tilting up. A tornado of sand and brush kicked up under the chopper. Maxwell wondered what was going on. The gomers could have fired the automatic weapon and shredded him, but they didn't.

He knew. They wanted him alive.

He glanced behind him. The column of troops was only about seventy-five yards away. Inside the Z-9 were probably six or eight more armed troops. They had him sandwiched.

Maxwell pulled a fresh magazine of ammunition from his pocket, ready to ram into the grip of the .45. He would fire until the first magazine was gone, then he'd—

What was that?

His eyes were fixed on the Z-9, but something else came into his peripheral vision. A blurry object, zigzagging like a bat behind the helicopter. And in the distance another object—an airplane?—higher, barely visible in the waning light. There was something familiar about the odd, inverted-V tail. And the buzzing lawnmower noise.

The blurry object made a final erratic course change, then it flew into the right turbine exhaust of the helicopter.

The helicopter's aft section folded upward, blown from the main body of the fuselage. The mortally wounded aircraft plunged to the ground and exploded with a dull *whump*. Maxwell ducked as shrapnel from the disintegrated machine whirred through the air.

Slowly he raised his head. A dozen small brush fires blazed around the wreckage of the Z-9. The broken rotor blades were folded over the burning carcass like black tentacles. He could see two figures still in the cockpit, slumped over the controls.

He peered to the west, where he'd last seen the column of troops. They had ducked for cover too. Now they were rising to their feet. One was pointing upward, toward the northwest. In the direction of the buzzing noise.

Maxwell looked upward also. He knew what he'd see.

It looked like an airborne praying mantis. The Predator UAV—unmanned aerial vehicle—had an inverted-V tail and an array of video and infrared cameras mounted in its long, bulbous nose. The buzzing noise came from its four-cylinder Rotax engine, the same power plant used on ultra-light airplanes. It was remotely piloted by a controller who interfaced with the vehicle via a Ku-band satellite data link.

The Predator could be configured to carry AGM-114 Hellfire missiles, which were designed to be used against slow-moving vehicles. Maxwell had just witnessed a demonstration.

He rose, crouching behind the rocks, and peered at the next ridge. The troops were moving again. Coming in his direction.

Run.
Each footstep made a crunching sound in the soft gravel surface. It was impossible to run quietly in the clunky, steel-toed flight boots. His breath was coming in labored gasps.

He wanted to puke again. He had caught his boot on the root of a low bush and tumbled butt-over-shoulder on the hard ground.

Still running, he pulled out the handheld GPS unit. In the tiny screen he could see the outline of the island. There were no terrain features, no references, just the shape of the island. There was a tiny pulsing datum circle that showed his location. He was about a mile from the eastern tip of the island.

He looked around. The sky to the east was a horizonless blue-black. Over the noise of his own running, he heard something else. Scuffing noises ahead and to the right. Boots crunching on loose stones. He stuffed the GPS back in his pocket.

"Turn left, Dragon!" said Boyce on the CSEL. His voice sounded more urgent than before. "They're on your right flank, trying to cut you off."

Maxwell turned to confront them. They were bounding over the ridge to his right, twenty yards away. They wore camos and Fritz helmets similar to the ones worn by U.S.

troops. There were three of them, running at full tilt, carbines held in front of them.

They spotted Maxwell just as he got off his first shot. The .45 kicked back in his hands. The first soldier's legs were still kicking as he pitched headlong down the incline. The other two skittered and hopped sideways, swinging their carbines toward Maxwell.

Maxwell fired at the one on the left, hitting him in the shoulder, spinning him around. He glimpsed the one on the right aiming his carbine.

Maxwell pumped off a shot, lunging to the left. He knew he'd missed. He felt the 7.62 round from the Chinese carbine zing past his ear.

He hit the ground and kept rolling. Another round thudded into the ground beside him. He rolled again, came up with the pistol in both hands. He pointed and fired, then fired again.

The second shot caught the soldier in the throat. He staggered backward, firing off a wild, high burst. He dropped the carbine and toppled to the ground.

Maxwell whirled back to the second soldier, the one he'd wounded. He was raising his carbine with one arm. Maxwell fired a bullet into the man's midsection. The soldier grunted, then dropped backward.

God bless Mr. Colt and his Model 1911, thought Maxwell. The clunky pistol was short-ranged and heavier than the service-issue Beretta nine-millimeter, but the big .45 slug stopped whatever it hit.

"Good job, Dragon," said Boyce on the CSEL. "Now get out of there. Keep running until you get to the beach on the east end."

Maxwell needed no more urging. He ran down the shallow ravine between ridges. As he jogged, trying not to stumble in the gathering darkness, he wondered again how Boyce knew so precisely what was going on.

Then it came to him. That buzzing lawnmower noise. It

was coming from the darkened sky above and in front of him. The Predator was still out there. It was relaying video images to Boyce's console aboard *Reagan* more than a hundred miles away. And it was armed with more Hellfire missiles, he hoped.

Maxwell pulled the emergency radio out of its pouch. He keyed the transmitter. "Battle-ax, Dragon. How many are out there?"

"Twenty, maybe twenty-five. PLA spec-ops troops, judging by their equipment. They landed on the west end in a couple of fast hovercraft right after your shoot-down. Looks like you're the object of their interest."

"What am I supposed to do when I get the east end of the island?"

"Keep your head down and wait. Don't get in any more shoot-outs. You'll be outgunned."

"Thanks for the advice. What if—uh-oh."

He saw something over his right shoulder. It looked like a Roman candle, arcing into the sky.

Something going after the Predator.

Maxwell slowed his pace, keeping his eye on the object. It flew a serpentine path, quickly overtaking the slow-flying Predator. A bright flash illuminated the dark sky. A brief, eerie glow illuminated the brush-covered landscape. The carcass of the destroyed UCAV went down like a shotgunned pigeon. It hit the earth a hundred yards from Maxwell.

"What the hell?" called Boyce. "We've lost our video link."

"The Predator got flamed," said Maxwell.

"Shit," said Boyce. "What happened?"

"They brought MANPADS. Looked like an SA-16." MANPADS—man portable air defense missiles—were mobile, shoulder-launched weapons. The Russian-built SA-16 MANPAD was deadly against low-flying targets like the Predator.

"That's bad news," said Boyce. "You're on your own, Dragon."

Maxwell had already figured that out. He was on the move.

"Keep going," said Boyce. "Keep moving to the east."

Maxwell wanted to ask what would happen when he ran out of island. Before he could ask the question, he heard sounds nearby. Boots on gravel. They were close, just over the ridge to his left.

He turned and ran.

CHAPTER 23

ASDS

Northeast Cay, Spratly Islands
South China Sea
1830 Monday, 30 April

Hurry, darkness.

The shadows spreading over the terrain made it harder for the PLA troops to find him. It also made it impossible to run without stumbling over the nearly invisible bushes. It was taking all Maxwell's energy to keep his feet beneath him.

He wished he had his air-soled running shoes. If the gomers wanted to track him, all they had to do was listen. The clunky flight boots sounded like the hoofbeats of a Clydesdale.

In his premission planning, he had not given serious thought to the possibility of being captured. Of all the scenarios, that one was far down the list. If he was shot down, he'd be in the water. If he were still alive, the mighty hand of the U.S. military would reach for him.

So much for the mighty hand. He was being chased like a rat over this miserable sliver of rock. The Chinese wanted him alive. He remembered Boyce's words in the intel brief: *If one of you, God forbid, is captured by the ChiComs, all*

*they're going to extract from you is your own little piece of
the puzzle. Nothing more.*

But Maxwell's piece of the puzzle was large. He'd been a
test pilot and an astronaut. He knew as much about the
Black Star and stealth technology as anyone on active duty.
The Chinese would employ every means—none pleasant—
to extract information. Every man had a limit to how much
he could endure.

With that thought, his hand went to the .45. It had a full
magazine. In the pocket of his flight suit was O'Toole's pistol,
also full up. In his pocket he had another loaded magazine.

He would not be a prisoner.

He came to another ridge. Instead of crossing it and sil-
houetting himself on the skyline, he turned left, staying in
the shadow between ridges. He and Boyce hadn't exchanged
communication since the shoot-down of the Predator. This
was not the time or place for voice dialogue. Anyway, the
CSEL was automatically transmitting his coordinates.

Maxwell stopped. He listened to the sounds around him.
There was only the rustle of wind, the chirp of insects. The
crunch of boots had faded.

Then he picked up another sound, faint and lilting. It took
him a moment to recognize it. *The ocean.* He pulled out the
handheld GPS, shielding it in his palm so that the backlit
screen didn't flash in the darkness. He was near the beach,
only about thirty yards. The little pulsing cross that marked
his location marker showed him to be a quarter mile from
the easternmost tip of the island.

He moved up to the last ridge and peered through the topmost bushes. The rocky beach was about twenty yards wide.
He could see a white ribbon of surf, darkness beyond. He
peered in each direction down the beach. No sign of life.

He was tempted to follow the beach. He wouldn't have to
deal with the entangling shrubs and rocky outcroppings. But
he'd be easy to spot. He put the GPS away and headed inland again.

After ten more minutes of picking his way over the rough terrain, he heard the soft rustling noise of the surf again. He was nearly to the eastern end of the island. Boyce had said to stay low and wait. Wait for what? He'd have to ask.

Maxwell dropped to one knee. He was pulling out the CSEL radio when he heard boots again. Several of them, coming from somewhere behind him. He shoved the radio back in its pouch and scrambled to his feet.

He was less than a hundred yards from the beach. Running in a low crouch, parallel to the last low ridge, he tried to keep his body beneath the skyline. At the end of the ridge was a rocky promontory covered with scraggly brush. Running with his head lowered, Maxwell rounded the end of the ridge. He could feel a damp sea breeze from the open beach.

He slammed headlong into a running figure. Maxwell heard the man grunt as they went down.

Even in the darkness he recognized the camo color and the helmet. The soldier already had a grip on his collar. The Chinese soldier was smaller and lighter than Maxwell, but he was surprisingly strong. He planted a foot in Maxwell's stomach and kicked. Maxwell went over the top, hitting the ground on his shoulder. He rolled to his feet. The soldier lunged at him.

Maxwell feinted backward, then stepped into him, driving a straight left jab into his face. The soldier recoiled, his knees sagging.

Maxwell threw an arm around his neck, giving the man's head a single violent twist. He heard a *crack,* like the snapping of a limb. The soldier slumped to the ground, his legs twitching spasmodically.

Maxwell heard more boots on the gravelly soil. More soldiers appeared, coming from the right. He whirled to face them. He had his fingers on the grip of the .45 when something rammed him from behind.

He hit the ground face-first. Before he could move, a pair

of knees rammed into his back. His right arm was under his body, his hand still clutching the grip of the pistol.

He rolled to his side, flinging the man from his back. He heard someone shout in Chinese. A blurred object was swinging toward his head. He ducked, raising his arm to deflect the barrel of the carbine the soldier was swinging at him. The hard steel of the carbine caught the barrel of Maxwell's .45, tearing the pistol loose from his grip.

Maxwell was trying to retrieve the pistol when they grabbed him. They yanked him upright, both arms firmly held by soldiers who had come from behind him.

One of them—Maxwell guessed it was the officer in charge—stood facing him. He was a foot shorter than Maxwell. Even in the darkness Maxwell could see the hard, angry look on the officer's face.

Maxwell's pistol was dangling at the end of its lanyard next to his right boot. He saw a PLA soldier stooping to retrieve it. As the man's head went down, Maxwell lashed out with his foot. The man screamed and fell back on his haunches, blood spurting from his smashed nose.

The officer facing Maxwell yelled in Chinese. The soldiers holding Maxwell tightened their grip on his arms. The officer pulled something from his belt. In the thin light Maxwell saw a metallic glint from the blade of the assault knife.

Maxwell saw the dark eyes fixed on him, filled with hate. *Now you've done it. Why did you smash the guy's face?* They might also be unhappy about his having killed four other PLA soldiers. Instead of taking him prisoner, they were going to slice up him like a game trophy.

The officer brought the blade up to Maxwell's face. Maxwell stared at the shiny tip of the long, slender blade. As he watched, the officer slowly brought the tip of the blade toward Maxwell's face.

Toward his left eye.

Maxwell felt panic surging through him. He lashed out

again with his boot, but the officer easily stepped aside. He kept the point of the blade moving toward Maxwell's eye.

Six inches.

Maxwell struggled against the grip of the soldiers holding him. There were at least three of them. He couldn't shake them.

He bit his lip, preparing for the inevitable agony. *Don't scream. Make the bastards kill you.*

Three inches.

Maxwell struggled again. He couldn't move. His heart was thumping like a jackhammer.

The officer's face was close enough that Maxwell could see his eyes. They were dark brown, cold as ice. The eyes of a killer.

Maxwell no longer had any doubt about what would happen next. The point of the blade was about to pierce his eye.

He heard a noise—*pphhhutt.* It sounded like a wine bottle being uncorked.

The point of the knife veered toward Maxwell's eye, then flicked through his eyebrow. The knife disappeared from his view.

Maxwell saw the officer's face. Between the dark, hate-filled eyes was a purplish cavity. The eyes were frozen, all life gone from them.

The officer toppled over backward.

Maxwell felt the grip on his arms release. He saw silhouettes in the thin light—PLA soldiers running, falling, kneeling to fire their carbines. Between the distinctive three-round bursts from the Chinese assault rifles Maxwell heard other sounds. The staccato chatter of an automatic weapon.

More muffled *pphhhutts.* More uncorked wine bottles.

Dark-clad figures were moving like ghosts in the darkness. Maxwell was having trouble seeing, then realized that blood was flowing into his left eye from his slashed eyebrow. He swiped at the wound with his sleeve, wiping blood from his eye. From the leg pocket of his flight suit he yanked out O'Toole's .45.

A figure in camos and helmet stopped in front of him. He was aiming his carbine at something in the darkness. Maxwell raised the .45 with both hands, took aim and—

He heard another *pphhhutt*. The PLA soldier dropped to his knees, then pitched over on his face.

A large, dark figure materialized out of the gloom next to Maxwell.

"Put that thing away before you hurt yourself." He pushed the barrel of Maxwell's .45 down.

"Who the hell are you?" said Maxwell.

"The guy they sent to get your silly ass out of here."

The voice sounded familiar. He looked like an apparition from hell. He had a long, menacing snout, which Maxwell realized was an NVG unit—night-vision goggles. He was clad in some kind of slick, skintight outfit.

The sounds of gunfire ceased. Maxwell swiped again at the cut over his eye to clear his vision. He saw bodies on the ground, several of them, and they wore PLA camos and helmets.

More slick-suited figures were appearing from the gloom. Maxwell counted at least six of them.

He looked again at the large man he had seen first. He had the physique of a gorilla.

"Is that you, Wedge?"

The long-snouted figure didn't answer. He reached into the kit strapped to his waist and pulled out a compress. "Here. Stick that over your eye. I hate the sight of blood."

Maxwell took the compress. "Thanks for bailing me out."

"Don't get mushy on me, Airedale. How about if you shut the fuck up so we can get off this island?"

Good old Wedge Flores, Maxwell thought. Congenial as ever.

They dragged the inflatable boat into the waist-deep surf. Maxwell climbed in behind Flores.

"What about my wizzo?"

"What about him?" said Flores.

"His body is back there. I want him recovered."

"Not my job."

"Whose job is it?"

"Who the hell knows? Take it up with your boss."

Maxwell started to argue, but the boat was already underway. He was surprised at its speed—something over twenty knots. He couldn't tell whether the motor was electric or internal combustion. It barely made a sound.

There were seven altogether—Maxwell plus Wedge Flores's SEAL squad—hunched down behind the flat spray screen in the bow. Maxwell had extracted enough information from Flores to determine that the SEALs had arrived on the eastern end of the island at about the same time the PLA spec-ops troops landed on the western tip.

They'd only gone about a mile when Maxwell felt the boat slow. He peered into the darkness ahead. He saw a long, tubular object barely awash in the three-foot waves. As they drew closer, he saw that it looked like a very large torpedo—or a miniature submarine. It had no sail or conning tower. An antenna protruded from either side amidships.

"What the hell is that?"

"An ASDS," said Flores.

"Which stands for?"

"Advanced SEAL Delivery System."

By Flores's tone, Maxwell could tell that that was all he was going to learn. Actually, he had heard of an ASDS, but he'd never expected to be a passenger on one. It was a new class of submersible vehicle, about sixty-five feet long. It could be mated to the top of an attack or cruise-missile submarine and was intended for the insertion of SEAL units.

As the raft approached the ASDS, Maxwell saw a hatch open atop the hull. A wet-suited crewman appeared, standing waist-high in the open hatch. A SEAL in the forward compartment of the raft tossed a line to him.

"We're doing this because of you," said Flores.

"Doing what because of me?"

"Boarding the vehicle on the surface. Dangerous as hell right now with the ChiComs swarming all over the place. Normally we'd go aboard the same way we left—submerged. But we've got to drag you along. You'd drown if we hauled you underwater."

"That's really thoughtful of you, Wedge."

"Up yours, Airedale."

Maxwell wanted to ask what they were going to do with the inflatable boat after they'd boarded the submersible, but he could tell Flores was in no mood for more explanations. The SEALs were already climbing over the gunwales and boarding the submersible. Maxwell allowed himself to be hoisted by two SEALs onto the slippery hull of the ASDS, where the crewman in the hatch hauled him headfirst into the vehicle.

He took a seat at the end of one of the two long benches inside the main compartment. As soon as the last SEAL had boarded, they closed the hatch of the ASDS and submerged.

Maxwell sat by himself, listening to the low thrum of the vehicle's engine. He couldn't see the crew of the ASDS, who were in the forward compartment on the other side of a watertight bulkhead. Like most airmen, Maxwell felt a nagging claustrophobia in the windowless, steel-enclosed confines of a submarine. He had no idea how fast or how deep they were going. Asking Flores any more questions wasn't worth the effort.

For the first time Maxwell noticed that one of the SEALs, a short, stocky young man with a black brush cut, had a gunshot wound in his thigh. Flores was busy dressing the man's wound, talking to his team in a voice too low for Maxwell to hear over the ambient sound in the compartment. Bitching about Airedales again, probably.

But he couldn't help noticing something else about Flores. The other SEALs—all petty officers—treated him in an almost reverential manner. Flores looked older than any of them. Maxwell guessed that he was a mustang—a former senior enlisted man who had received an officer's commission. Mustangs were a special breed in the Navy, particularly in the SEALs, where much of the leadership came from within the ranks.

Maxwell closed his eyes. The low hum and vibration from the vehicle was lulling him into a stupor. The headache from the cannon shell that struck his helmet was gone, and so was the nausea from ingesting the seawater. He felt a deep fatigue, the product of adrenaline overload and the exertion of running like a chased animal.

He didn't know how long he was asleep. Someone—it had to be Flores—was shaking his arm.

"Hey, time to get your ass moving."

Maxwell sat up and tried to focus his eyes. "Where are we going now?"

"Not we, Airedale. You. You're taking a chopper ride."

CHAPTER 24

GOOD TO GO

Swallow Reef, Spratly Islands
South China Sea
2045 Monday, 30 April

Colonel Minh listened to the sounds of battle. The Vietnamese recapture of Swallow Reef had been underway for eight hours.

It was eerie, he thought. The gunfire was coming in intermittent bursts. Instead of the steady din of grenades and mortars and the cacophony of automatic weapons, there were periods of utter stillness. The lull in the gunfire meant either that the PLA forces were in retreat or the Vietnamese had lost their advantage.

Minh squatted in the darkness beneath the ridge that ran like a spine down the length of Swallow Reef. With him were his radioman, two runners, and a squad of commandos who had taken defensive positions along the ridge.

Since their landing just after nightfall, Minh's commandos had fought for the narrow little island. The PLA troops had recovered more quickly from the shock of the Vietnamese landing than Minh would have guessed. During the critical first hour of fighting, the only thing that saved

Minh's tiny force was the specter from the sky—the *invisible* specter—that somehow destroyed the PLA warplanes based on the airfield. Without their attack helicopters and close-air-support jets, the PLA troops were forced to fight a defensive battle.

Meter by meter, hummock by hummock, Minh's commandos had advanced along Swallow Reef. Two hours into the battle, they took the airfield. From there his force divided into platoon-sized units and fanned out on divergent tracks in the darkness.

The fact that they were outnumbered four to one by the reinforced Chinese garrison did not trouble Minh. Such a ratio was normal. For a thousand years the Vietnamese had waged war against the lumbering giant, China. They were always outnumbered.

The radioman was motioning for Minh.

"What is it?"

"Captain Lieu," said the radioman. "He reports that they have captured the prison facility. His platoon has freed nearly three hundred of our captured troops."

Colonel Minh nodded his approval. Captain Lieu was an aggressive young officer whom he had chosen to command the lead platoon of the commando force. Lieu made no secret of his intention to be the first to storm the headquarters complex of the PLA garrison where the Vietnamese soldiers were interned. Lieu's platoon had advanced even faster than Minh had hoped.

It was purely a symbolic gesture, of course. The released prisoners would be of little use in the battle for the island, but freeing them transmitted a powerful message to both sides. The PLA troops were in full retreat. The Vietnamese prisoners would be replaced with Chinese prisoners. The battle for Swallow Reef—the latest battle—was nearly over.

And not too soon, he thought. The eastern sky was turning pale. Minh couldn't help wondering what the new day would bring. With the coming of daylight, the attacker's advantage would be gone.

Tonight's battle would mark the third change in ownership of the island since Vietnam planted its flag on Swallow Reef two years ago. Colonel Minh had no illusions about his ability to retain possession of the reef. Without the covert but palpable support of the United States, the PLA would obliterate not only Minh's little force but every military asset owned by Vietnam.

Minh's landing force had arrived in the vicinity of Swallow Reef aboard three American submarines. Soon after nightfall, the submarines had surfaced. Minh's troops clambered into inflatable boats and motored the last few kilometers toward their beachhead on the western shore of the reef. Precisely timed with their arrival on the beach came a barrage of Tomahawk missiles targeting each gun emplacement and shore defense battery set up by the PLA. It was then, while he was still sprinting across the narrow beach, that Minh became aware of the invisible specter that was systematically destroying every PLA aircraft on the airfield.

Amazing, thought Minh. Without the Americans—the other lumbering giant with whom they'd been at war—they would have no chance against the PLA. But there was some kind of protocol to which Minh was not privy. Neither the U.S. nor China was using their heavy, visible weapons. An entire U.S. Navy carrier strike group was somewhere in the South China Sea, watching but not joining the battle. And the PLA's massive offensive forces were staying mostly out of sight, deploying submarines and their own species of invisible jets. After losing a number of strike fighters on the ground and in the sky around Swallow Reef, they seemed to be staying low.

For how long? Minh had a bad feeling about the Spratly Island war. The fate of his tiny garrison—and of the Vietnamese claim to the Spratlys—depended on the ability and the will of the Americans to fight the Chinese.

The radioman was motioning again to Minh.

"What?"

"Captain Lieu reports that the PLA forces have retreated to the far end of the island. They have ceased firing and he sees a white flag being hoisted."

Minh nodded and rose to his feet. Just in time, he reflected, looking over his shoulder at the glow on the eastern horizon. He would accept the surrender of the Chinese commander—the same commander who had accepted the Vietnamese surrender only a few days earlier.

Minh wondered if he was next in line.

"Tell Captain Lieu I'm on my way."

USS Ronald Reagan

Boyce watched the Seahawk settle onto the flight deck.

It was nearly midnight. A round splash of light illuminated the deck directly beneath the boarding door of the helicopter. Two helo crewmen exited first, followed by the lone passenger. Like all fighter pilots forced to ride in rotor-wing aircraft, the passenger ducked as he moved beneath the still-whirling blades. Hunched over, he followed the waiting yellow-jerseyed crewman across the deck to the door in the island where Boyce stood.

Boyce waited until they had stepped inside and Maxwell removed his cranial protector. It was as Boyce expected. Maxwell looked as though he'd been through a meat grinder.

"Congratulations," said Boyce. "You look like shit."

Maxwell forced a grin. "Thanks, Admiral."

"What the hell happened to your eyebrow? Looks like you were whacked with a cleaver."

"You're close."

Boyce already knew. He'd been briefed by Wedge Flores on Maxwell's encounter with the knife-wielding PLA soldier. He also knew about the extraction by the SEAL team, the transfer to the ASDS submersible, then the pickup by the Seahawk.

There were big parts of the story that Boyce hadn't been told. Where did the ASDS submersible come from? A submarine? Did it return to the same submarine after off-loading Maxwell? Flores had taken an obvious pleasure in telling a rear admiral that he didn't need to know such things.

Boyce was looking at Maxwell's flight suit. "Do everyone a favor and trash that flight suit, okay? Looks like somebody puked on it."

Maxwell shrugged. "Somebody did."

Boyce led them down the passageway, around a corner, then down a ladder.

"Where are we going?"

"Sick bay. They're going to check you out, dress that wound, see if you've got any serious damage."

"I'm fine."

"Yeah, right. Try looking in a mirror. After the quack is finished with you, we go to flag intel. And don't worry, I'm not going to let them grill you tonight. We need a firsthand account of what happened to Wayne and Heilbrunner. And we want to know about your furball with the *Dong-jin* while it's fresh in your mind."

"The furball I lost, you mean."

"The one we *all* lost. Nobody expected that the *Dong-jins* could penetrate our cloaking."

"I shouldn't have let Zhang get in my six o'clock."

Boyce stopped in the passageway and looked at Maxwell. "Why do you think it was Zhang?"

"I knew it from the moment he jumped us. He confirmed it when he came back to strafe us in the chutes. Had to be Zhang."

Boyce caught the hard edge in Maxwell's voice. "How did he happen to miss when he strafed you?"

"He probably thought he killed me. A shell smacked the

side of my helmet and knocked me out. Then he went after Sharp."

Boyce nodded, then continued down the passageway to the ship's sick bay. Waiting inside was Knuckles Ball, the airwing flight surgeon, and two medical corpsmen.

Maxwell endured the flight surgeon's probing and testing, then let one of the corpsmen clean and dress the cut over his eye. The doctor gave it four stitches, applied a bandage, and declared him physically okay. Nothing broken, a minor concussion, some scrapes from the rocky surface of Northeast Cay. What Maxwell needed was sleep and rehydration and a break to get his mind off what had happened. He ought to take some leave, go lie on a beach somewhere, drink a few mai tais.

Boyce and Maxwell both nodded, neither changing expression. Boyce thanked the flight surgeon and steered Maxwell out of the sick bay.

"Knuckles means well," said Boyce.

"I liked the part about lying on a beach and drinking mai tais. When do I start?"

"In your next life. This one ain't over yet."

Maxwell shrugged.

After stopping at Maxwell's stateroom long enough for him to change into clean khakis, they continued to the flag intel compartment. Boyce stepped inside the harshly lit compartment, blinked, then saw the figure sitting at the end of the briefing table.

"Uh-oh," he said in a low voice.

Gypsy Palmer was still wearing her flight suit. Her face looked haggard, her eyes red. Beside her sat Dana Boudroux, wearing the trademark blue jumpsuit, no makeup, hair pulled back in a ponytail. She nodded to Boyce and Maxwell as they entered.

Crud Carruthers was standing in the front talking to Harvey Wentz. Wentz was pointing at something on the illuminated chart of the South China Sea. They stopped talking and looked at Boyce.

Maxwell went to Gypsy. "I'm sorry, Gypsy."

She looked at him through red-rimmed eyes. "Did Sharp tell you?"

Maxwell hesitated, looking over at Boyce. Boyce gave him a nod. Before their deployment aboard *Reagan*, Boyce had learned about the romance between O'Toole and Palmer. They promised him they would keep it out of sight until Dragon Flight was over.

"He told me," said Maxwell. "Sharp was very excited that you two were going to be married. He was as happy about that as he was that he'd been selected for astronaut training."

She chewed on her lower lip for a moment. "You were his hero, Brick. He was so proud that he was following in your footsteps."

Maxwell closed his eyes for a moment, then lowered himself into the seat next to Gypsy. "Listen, Gypsy. What happened to Sharp was my fault. He did his job exactly right. If I had been doing my job, we would have—"

"That's enough," snapped Boyce. He walked over to the table. "We're not going to hear any of that crap about who's to blame. This is war, and we're professional warriors. We have to accept the fact that the results of battle don't always match our expectations."

He paused and looked around the room. They all wore fatigue-filled, cynical expressions. Gypsy was staring at him with her grief-stricken face. Maxwell was giving him that old narrow-eyed look that Boyce had seen enough to know what it meant: *Say whatever you want, but I'll believe what I want to believe.*

Boyce sighed. He hadn't planned to give a speech tonight. Not while nerves and feelings were still raw. But he could sense the morale of the Dragon Flight team eroding like a castle in the sand.

He walked up to the front of the compartment. Harvey

Wentz took one look at his face and moved aside. Boyce pulled out a half-gnawed Cohiba and rolled it around in his fingers.

"I know what you're feeling. We lost three terrific guys today. They were like my own kids, and I grieve for them as much as any of you. But we're not gonna waste our emotional energy beating up on ourselves about it. Duke and Plug got killed fighting a determined and probably suicidal enemy. Sharp is dead because some murderous ChiCom pilot—and we have an idea who it was—shot him while he was hanging in his chute. Here's the bottom line, folks. We're going to mourn our lost brothers. But we're going to dry our tears and go back out there and make the sons of bitches sorry they ever went to war with us."

A moment of silence passed, then someone—it sounded like Crud Carruthers—said, "Amen."

Boyce studied his cigar for a moment. "The news is bad, but it's not all bad. Our covert efforts both in the air and under the sea have turned back the Chinese. I've just been informed that Vietnamese troops have recaptured Swallow Reef, thanks to your efforts. The convoy that was coming to resupply and reinforce the ChiCom garrison lost a couple ships and has turned back to its port in Guangzhou."

"What about Otis and Foxy?" asked Carruthers. Otis McCollister and his wizzo, Foxy Wolfe, were in the sole remaining Black Star. They were on their second consecutive sortie covering the landing on Swallow Reef.

"They splashed two SU-27s about an hour ago. Since then no others have come out from Hainan to join the fun. The PLA aircraft on the field at Swallow Reef were taken out before they got airborne."

"What about the *Dong-jins*?" asked Maxwell. "Did Otis and Foxy engage any?"

"No contact," said Boyce. "It doesn't mean they're not out there, but if they are, they're staying out of the action. They probably haven't figured out that we're down to one stealth jet. For that matter, we don't know how many operational *Dong-jins* they have either."

Boyce could see the skeptical looks on their faces. He knew what they were thinking. Just because the People's Republic of China lost a few jets and ships, they weren't about to abandon the Spratly Island oil reserves. Not without a fight.

"We've got two more Black Stars and two combat-ready crews coming from Groom Lake, via Guam." He pointedly looked at his watch. "Go get some rest, folks, and then be ready to fly. We're gonna be busy."

He watched Maxwell get up and follow Harvey Wentz into the enclosed debriefing cubicle. He looked beat-up, thought Boyce. But he'd seen Maxwell beat-up before. He always bounced back.

Well, reflected Boyce, he'd better bounce back again. This goddamn war was just beginning.

Gypsy Palmer was still there when Maxwell came out of the debriefing cubicle.

"You look tired, Brick."

"So do you."

She shrugged. "It's been one of those days. Are you flying tomorrow?"

He shrugged. "The doc says I'm good to go."

"I'm good to go too."

Maxwell looked at her red-rimmed eyes. "No way. Not for a while."

"I have to. It's important."

"You heard the admiral. We've got a replacement crew coming in."

Her face hardened. "Damn it, you don't need a replacement for me. I'm fine. I want to be in your cockpit."

"I know how you feel, but you've had an emotional trauma. I can't—"

"I'm the best wizzo in this unit. Sharp always said he was the best, but he really wasn't. I was, and I still am."

"You're obsessed right now, Gypsy. You want to go out there and flame the ass of that Chinese pilot who killed Sharp. Believe me, so do I. But revenge is a stupid motivator for a professional warrior."

"It's not about revenge; it's about doing my job. It's what Sharp would expect me to do."

"That's still not a reason to—"

"Please, Brick. I won't let you down. I promise."

Maxwell didn't answer. Her eyes were no longer filled with tears. Her voice had lost some of its quaver.

He shook his head. Hell, they were both basket cases. His wounds were physical, but Gypsy Palmer was an emotional wreck. It didn't make sense putting them in the same cockpit.

But nothing was making sense anymore. Sometimes you had to go with your instincts.

"Promise me, Gypsy."

"What?"

"That you won't do anything stupid."

"Does that mean I get the job?"

He nodded. "We'll give it a shot."

Her face brightened for the first time since he'd seen her tonight. She hoisted her right hand and hit him with a high-five. "I promise."

He saw Boyce on the far side of the compartment watching them with a worried look. He knew what the old man would say when he found out. He'd have one of his foot-stomping, nostril-flaring, red-in-the-face tantrums.

Tough shit, Maxwell decided. He'd remind Boyce that he was the one who always said the essence of leadership was to put good people in command of their units then get the hell out of their way. This was a great time for him to get the hell out of the way.

CHAPTER 25

BREAKTHROUGH

USS Ronald Reagan
South China Sea
0715 Tuesday, 1 May

He slept for six hours.

It wasn't enough, but he couldn't sleep any more. The events of yesterday kept replaying in a continuous loop. The yellow light of the *Dong-jin's* cannon kept winking in his mind. The taste of seawater was rising like bile in his throat. The headache was gone, but the cut over his eye was tender and raw. He felt creaky and sore in the joints.

He hauled himself out of the bunk and pulled on gray sweats and his running shoes. He needed coffee and a workout, in that order.

On his way out he noticed the answering machine. The red light was still flashing. He'd been too tired last night to bother with it. The only message he'd get in his stateroom was the kind he didn't want to hear before he slept.

There were two. Bullet Alexander asked him to stop by the Roadrunners' ready room. The second was from Dana Boudroux, who wanted him to call back. He looked at the machine for a moment, then deleted the messages.

The dirty-shirt wardroom was nearly empty. It was the informal officer's mess where flight crews and deck officers could get fast food without having to be in the uniform of the day. A steward was working behind the long stainless-steel serving counter. Two flight-suited Hornet pilots from VFA-34 waved to Maxwell from their table, then resumed their conversation. Maxwell helped himself to a black coffee from one of the three large urns. He sipped his coffee standing, not bothering with the serving line where breakfast was still available. He'd run, then do breakfast later.

It took two circuits of the hangar deck, dodging a pair of Super Hornets under tow, before he had the kinks out. Running on an aircraft carrier took concentration. He had to be careful not to catch a shin on one of the ubiquitous tie-down chains that fastened aircraft to the deck.

By the third lap he'd picked up the pace to an eight-minute mile. Sweat trickled down his back. His breathing settled into an easy rhythm. He ran past the bay of the number-two elevator. Through the huge enclosure he could see directly out to the open sea. The horizon was fuzzy, with a haze over the South China Sea and a fleece of cumulus casting irregular shadows on the water.

He saw a figure jogging toward him from the opposite direction. Even before he saw her face, he knew who it was.

She slowed her pace, then turned to run along with him.

"Why didn't you return my call?" asked Dana Boudroux.

She looked good, he thought. She was wearing a pale blue warm-up suit and running shoes. A sheen of perspiration glistened on her forehead.

"I had to run first. Get my head straightened out."

"Is it straightened out now?"

"It will be after another lap and a shower."

They ran for a while in silence. Again he was aware of her smooth, fluid stride. Dana was a natural runner. He, on the other hand, would always be a deck-pounder.

"You should have let Admiral Boyce fire me," she said.

"Why?" Maxwell looked across at her. "Because you told him he didn't know jack about stealth technology?"

"Because I made everyone believe we'd be able to detect the *Dong-jins.*"

"Knock it off, Dana. You were at the debriefing. The scanners worked. We *did* pick up the IR trace on the *Dong-jins.*"

"It wasn't enough. Picking up a tiny IR trace isn't the same thing as *seeing* the enemy jets. And it seems pretty certain now that they're seeing through our cloaking."

"There's enough blame to go around. What happened to Sharp wasn't your fault, it was mine. And what happened to Duke and Plug was just plain bad luck. The fortunes of war."

"If they had been able to see the *Dong-jin,* they wouldn't have collided with it."

"Maybe. And if I had been there in time, we would have shot the *Dong-jin* down before it collided with Duke and Plug."

She kept running, saying nothing. They came to the aft end of the hangar deck. She followed Maxwell as he weaved between a parked Hawkeye and the nose of a Seahawk helicopter. The sight of the chopper brought fresh memories of being plucked from the open hatch of the ASDS submersible. He felt a flash of nausea, tasting again the seawater in his gut.

"That's what I called you about last night."

"To tell me that you're on a guilt trip."

"To tell you good-bye."

"Good-bye? Where are—"

"Back to the States. I told the admiral last night, after you left the intel space."

"You're quitting."

"It's called requesting reassignment."

"What did Boyce say?"

She ran for a while more. "You know Boyce. He gnawed on his cigar and gave me that laser-eyed look that the Navy must teach them before they let them be admirals. He said he was too busy. Come back and talk to him tomorrow."

"So have you?"

"Not yet. I wanted to—"

She was staring at a figure at the end of the hangar deck. He was wearing a leather flight jacket and a piss-cutter uniform cap with one star.

They slowed to a stop.

"Where the hell have you been?" said Boyce. He motioned for them to follow him. "I've got something to show you."

Maxwell stared at the pile of junk. It looked like the contents of an overturned Dumpster.

"Well?" said Boyce. "Recognize it?"

"No."

They were in the secured space off the port side of the hangar deck. It was adjacent to another large compartment where the maintenance facility had been set up for the Black Star, out of view from passersby on the hangar deck. Two Marine sentries were posted at the sliding door.

"I do," said Dana Boudroux.

She was kneeling, running her hand over the surface of the jagged metal. "It's what we've been praying for."

Maxwell continued to stare at the mess on the deck. There were scraps of honeycomb material, pieces of ripped metal, tubing, and bundled cable. Inside the pile were strands of wire and shiny hardware that looked like the parts of a jet engine.

Maxwell knew he was seeing the wreckage of an airplane. What airplane? The wrinkled skin had a grayish tint to it, unlike anything he remembered seeing.

Dana was smiling, picking up pieces and turning them over in her hands, caressing them almost lovingly. Her face glowed like that of a child opening a gift.

Maxwell kept staring at the junk—and it came to him. He *had* seen it before.

"The *Dong-jin.*"

"Took you long enough," she said.

Maxwell ignored her. "Where did they find it?"

"At the bottom of the South China Sea," said Boyce. "Close to where it collided with the Black Star. We're going to get that back too, but not yet. This was more important."

"Who found it?" said Maxwell.

"Who do you think?" said a voice from behind them.

Maxwell turned around. Wedge Flores was wearing creased BDUs and black, spit-polished boots. His face had the same unsmiling expression.

"That's not all they brought," said Boyce. "Wedge's SEALs recovered Sharp O'Toole's body."

Maxwell held eye contact with Flores. The SEAL officer gazed back at him.

"You said that wasn't your job," said Maxwell.

"It wasn't. Sometimes I moonlight."

Maxwell nodded. "I guess I should say thanks."

"For what?"

"For saving my butt back on the island. And for getting Sharp's body back. And now for pulling up the Chinese jet."

"Hey, Airedale, you're getting all mushy again. I can't stand tears."

"Sorry, Wedge. What I meant to say was you're still an asshole. But at least you're consistent. Good job."

Something close to a grin appeared on Flores's face. "Up yours, Airedale."

Keep walking.

That was the trick, Hollis Benjamin had learned. Smile, give them the occasional wave, pretend to be discussing some urgent matter with the staffer who was trying to keep up with you. Keep walking.

Twenty more yards to the side gate of the West Wing. The reporters were lined up on either side of the walkway.

"Mr. President, would you care to comment on the recent developments in the Far East?"

"Mr. President, is it true that we're engaged in combat operations against the People's Republic of China?"

Keep walking.

One of the reporters, a guy from the *Washington Post* named Leroy Womack, who, in Benjamin's opinion, was a card-carrying idiot, was flapping his arm to get Benjamin's attention. "Mr. President, are you concerned about Senator Wagstaff's remarks that you should be impeached?"

Benjamin smiled. He kept walking.

Ten yards.

"Mr. President, the Chinese press is reporting that American submarines have attacked unarmed merchant ships in the South China Sea. Can you confirm that report?"

He waved.

The occasion was a press conference in the Rose Garden. It had been scheduled several days before, and its purpose was to update the press on pending legislative matters including the new defense spending bill, which he had threatened to veto unless the sponsoring senators removed several hundred million dollars of their favorite pork.

The press corps didn't want to hear about the defense spending bill. They wanted him to comment on Senator Wagstaff's remarks this morning on *Face the Nation*. The Benjamin administration, Wagstaff said, was conducting a clandestine military operation in the Spratly Islands on behalf of the communist government of Vietnam.

After Benjamin's canned remarks at the press conference, he declined to take questions. The press corps, as he expected, wasn't having any of it. They pushed against the restraining ropes and shouted after him as he walked.

"Mr. President, can you confirm the rumor in *Aviation*

Week about a secret stealth jet that has been deployed to the South China Sea?"

"Mr. President, what do you have to say about—"

Benjamin reached the gate. It clanged shut behind him, and he kept walking. He could still hear the reporters babbling outside the fence, but he no longer understood what they were saying. He passed through the Oval Office without stopping and continued to his private study.

The president flopped down in the padded chair. Josh Watanabe, his assistant and chief of staff, was already there. Watanabe was wearing his trademark bow tie.

"I hate this fucking job," said Benjamin.

"This is nothing," said Watanabe. "Wait till they find out about the submarine we lost with a hundred and thirty men aboard."

Benjamin nodded. He had never been much of a drinker, but it occurred to him that this would be a good time to start. He was in a hell of a mess, and the worst part was that it was a mess he had made for himself. For the first time in his presidency, he was questioning his own judgment. Perhaps Wagstaff was right. Maybe he should be impeached.

Joyce Appleby, the baby-faced staff secretary, came through the door. At the same time, Benjamin noticed the flashing light on his telephone console.

"Beijing on the green line," said Appleby. "The office of the PRC president."

Benjamin stared at the console. He knew without asking that Appleby had already alerted the China desk over at the State Department. There would also be at least two China specialists from the National Security staff listening in. Benjamin made it a point never to go one-on-one with another head of state without plenty of backup.

He took a deep breath and pushed the button on the speakerphone. He listened to the translator in Beijing announce in singsong English that President Xiang Fan-lo wanted to speak to him personally.

"I'm honored to receive a personal call from the president." Benjamin saw Watanabe rolling his eyes. He waited while the translator relayed his greeting to Xiang.

Then he heard the nasal twang of the PRC president on the line. Without knowing a word of Mandarin, Benjamin could hear the agitated tone in Xiang's voice. The Chinese head of state ranted on for a solid minute, his voice rasping and cracking. He paused while the translator delivered the message in English, then he resumed ranting.

Benjamin listened, offering no comment. Xiang's monologue and the intermittent translations went on for five minutes.

Benjamin said, "I understand your position, Mr. President. I will take this matter under consultation with my advisors. You will be hearing back from me very soon."

He heard the translator passing his message, then a buzzing sound as the connection to China went dead.

Benjamin pushed the speaker button and the buzzing stopped. He stared at the silent telephone for a while. He felt Watanabe and Appleby watching him, wondering what he would do.

"What time is it in Hanoi?" Benjamin asked.

Appleby had to think for a moment. "Coming up ten o'clock in the evening."

"Good," said the president of the United States. "Get Joe Ferrone on the line."

Hanoi, Socialist Republic of Vietnam

"Did I catch you at a bad time, Skipper?"

"No, sir," said Ferrone. "A very good time. You rescued me from a boring reception here at the embassy."

"It's no wonder ambassadors love what they do. They don't do anything except take vacations and throw parties."

"It's a lousy job, but somebody's got to do it."

Ferrone heard the president chuckle on the phone. He had

no idea why Benjamin had called, but he knew it wasn't to chat about his social life.

Ferrone was in the private office just off the rotunda. The reception outside was winding down, most of the guests already gone and the others having drinks around the long rosewood bar. Half a dozen diplomats and several Vietnamese officials were still there, including the president of the Republic of Vietnam.

The truth was, Ferrone was enjoying himself. He was wearing his white dinner jacket and black tie, showing off Kim to the party guests. The president of the Republic of Vietnam, Van Duc Chien, was smitten by Ferrone's bride. He had attached himself like a fixture to her elbow.

Ferrone had been behind the bar mixing drinks while the white-coated bartender watched with a dubious expression. His deputy, Mike Medford, had signaled, holding one finger to his ear—sign language for a call from the White House. Ferrone excused himself and followed Medford into the private office off the rotunda.

The president of the United States chatted for another half minute on the phone before he got to the point.

"There's been a breakthrough out there," said Benjamin.

They were on a secure line, but no embassy phone line was considered secure enough for ultrasensitive communications.

Ferrone said, "Ah, have you heard something from Panda?" "Panda" was their code name for the leadership of the People's Republic of China.

"Affirmative. About half an hour ago. Panda is suddenly very worried about the escalation of hostilities with Vietnam."

"Imagine that. Something finally got Panda's attention." *Something like a show of force by submarines and stealth jets.*

"He seemed quite agitated. He rambled on for ten minutes about reckless interference and dangerous provocations. Then he surprised the hell out of me. Listen to this, Skipper. He proposed that each side back off and demonstrate good faith by taking no further offensive actions. No more provocations."

"Interesting, particularly since it was he who initiated the provocations. Do you trust him?"

"As much as I trust anything Panda tells us."

"Which means yes, we trust him, but we don't put down our weapons."

"You get the picture."

Ferrone's mind was racing. *No offensive actions.* It meant that the recent Vietnamese repossession of Swallow Reef would remain, at least for the time being, a fait accompli.

"Where do we go from here?" said Ferrone.

"To the table."

"Table? Where? Who will be the—"

"You. You're going to meet the PRC foreign minister in Hong Kong."

Ferrone felt something very much like panic ignite in him. "Ah, Mr. President, I'm very flattered by your confidence in me. But don't you think that a mission like this ought to be handled by the secretary of state? Or at least a very senior diplomat?"

"Negative, Skipper. No publicity, no announcements, no high-profile officials. Your mission will be carried out in absolute secrecy. Remember, we're not—and never were—involved in the Spratly Island dispute."

"What about the Vietnamese? They have to come to the table too."

"They do, and they will. You're going to persuade your new friend, the Vietnamese president, to accompany you and participate in the negotiations."

Ferrone was temporarily speechless. The president had just given him an assignment of enormous responsibility. There was no way he could decline. Anyway, he *was* the U.S. ambassador to Vietnam. This was his job. And beyond that, damn it, he was a retired vice admiral in the United States Navy who knew as much about the implications of war in the South China Sea as any man alive. Bringing an honorable end to the conflict would be the crowning achievement of his career.

"Yes, sir," said Ferrone. "I will carry out your instructions to the best of my ability."

"I know you will, Skipper. I'm counting on you."

Ferrone heard the familiar change in background noise as the satellite connection was severed. For several more minutes he remained in the empty office, thinking.

He went back out to the rotunda. The guests were still clustered around the bar. The bartender was making drinks again, pleased that he'd gotten his job back. Kim was still talking to Van Duc Chien, the Vietnamese president, who wore the same enchanted expression on his face.

"Ah, Joe is back," said the president, switching from Vietnamese to English. "No bad news, I hope."

Ferrone smiled. *Joe.* Since their initial meeting at the Presidential Palace, Ferrone and the president had become more than diplomatic acquaintances. They were on a first-name basis.

"Not at all. In fact, if you will come with me to my office, I have some very interesting news."

CHAPTER 26

REQUIEM

USS Ronald Reagan
South China Sea
1725 Thursday, 3 May

"It works," announced Dana Boudroux. She held the object up in her hands, displaying it like a trophy.

Maxwell recognized the device. It had the snoutlike appearance of night-vision goggles, and it worked on a similar principle of optical physics. But the CFD—chromatic frequency detecting—goggles, he also knew, were a thousand times more sensitive to tiny increments of light-wave variations.

Dana looked tired, but she wore a self-satisfied look. Her hair was pulled back in a ponytail. She had a smudge of what appeared to be grease on her cheek. She'd been working on the CFD device for nearly twenty-four hours straight.

She had summoned Maxwell and Boyce to her makeshift lab off the hangar deck. Adjacent to her lab was the maintenance space for the Black Stars, which numbered three again. During the night, the two replacement stealth jets had been delivered to the *Reagan*, after having been flown by C-5 to Cam Ranh Bay and loaded aboard a U.S. Navy freighter.

Also aboard *Reagan* were the two new Black Star crews, who had undergone an overnight carrier qual program—two quick field carrier landing practices and a blessing by the LSO—at Groom Lake. The replacement pilots and wizzos had accompanied the jets aboard the C-5, and all were now catching up on lost sleep.

"How do we know it works?" said Boyce.

"Because I was able to match the CFD sensor to the predicted wavelength of the *Dong-jin*'s skin cloaking."

"Predicted?" said Boyce. "How can you predict such a thing just from a pile of wreckage?"

Maxwell knew that tone in Boyce's voice. He was fishing. He wanted to see if she would give him another I-could-explain-but-you-wouldn't-understand answer. If she did, Boyce was going to cut her off at the knees.

"I determined that the plasma coating in the *Dong-jin*'s outer skin has a finite density, Admiral. And I was also able to reconstruct enough of the skin cloaking generator to establish within a few nanometers what the actual wavelength ought to be."

"I see," said Boyce, though his expression showed that he didn't.

She gave him a smile, like that of a schoolteacher helping a slow student. "If you want proof positive, of course, then we'll have to test it in combat against a real *Dong-jin*. The goggles may require a tiny bit more tweaking, but I'm confident that they will penetrate the *Dong-jin*'s cloaking."

Boyce pulled out a pair of reading glasses. He turned the goggles over in his hands, examining them closely. "Very impressive, Dr. Boudroux. Congratulations. You've performed a valuable service."

"Thank you, Admiral." Her voice sounded uncharacteristically modest.

She caught Maxwell watching her. She gave him a wink.

*   *   *

Gia Lam Airfield, Hanoi

"Stop the car," said Ferrone.

Trunh Bao looked over his shoulder in surprise, then motioned for the driver to stop. They were at the entrance to Gia Lam, the old airfield on the exterior of Hanoi.

"What's the matter?" said Kim. She was in the backseat with Ferrone.

"Nothing. I just want to have a look."

The driver stopped. For reasons of secrecy, it had been decided that Ferrone would depart from Gia Lam instead of the Noi Bai International Airport. For the same reason, they were in a plain brown Toyota instead of the official embassy limo.

Kim was watching him. "You were here before, weren't you?"

"Once."

Ferrone gazed around. The place had changed. No more gun emplacements, no drab paint or camouflage nets. Gia Lam had been on the off-limits list until Operation Linebacker. Then it got bombed just like the rest of North Vietnam.

He remembered the day he last saw Gia Lam. It was chilly, the sky overcast, but none of the 112 prisoners marching across the ramp cared. Waiting on the ramp at Gia Lam was a U.S. Air Force C-141. There was a brief ceremony. When Joe Ferrone's name was read, he saluted the American officers and then boarded the big transport. It was 12 February, 1973, and it was his last day as a prisoner.

Ferrone signaled the driver to go on. The green-uniformed sentries were expecting them. After an ID check and a brief chat with the driver, they waved the Toyota through the gate. An Airbus A319 in the livery of Vietnam Airlines was parked on the ramp.

Kim squeezed Ferrone's arm. "Have I told you how proud I am of you?"

"Proud of me? For what?"

"For being who you are. You've shown everyone in Hanoi that Americans and Vietnamese can put the past behind us. You, of all people. Even the president thinks you're a hero."

Ferrone just nodded. It was a paradox. As the U.S. ambassador to Vietnam, he was more popular in Hanoi than he was in Washington. The Vietnamese newspapers ran glowing articles about him, celebrating his transformation from prisoner of war to diplomat, making special note of his marriage to a Vietnamese beauty. Meanwhile, conservative columnists in the U.S. were reviling him as a betrayer of his wartime comrades-in-arms. His old colleague, Thad Wagstaff, had taken to calling him "Hanoi Joe" on the floor of the Senate.

The Toyota stopped on the ramp. An honor guard of Vietnamese soldiers was waiting to escort him to the boarding ladder of the Airbus. Another paradox, he thought. Those were the same green uniforms and red hatbands that they wore on that day in 1973.

Trunh was out of the car, holding the door open for Ferrone.

"Will you call me from wherever you are?" said Kim.

"Sure." In truth, he had no idea whether he could call or not. It depended on the outcome. If the negotiations failed, no one would know they ever took place.

Kim didn't know that the president of Vietnam was already aboard the Airbus. Van Duc Chien had come to the airport in his own plain automobile, no escort, no fanfare. They would arrive the same way at the Hong Kong airport, bypassing the immigration and customs gates.

He leaned over and kissed her, then held it for an extra twenty seconds. They were still newlyweds. This would be the first time they'd been apart.

It occurred to Ferrone that he had spent most of his adult life saying good-bye and scurrying off on urgent missions. It had never bothered him. He was a loyal servant of his country, and that's what he did.

Now it bothered him. Since he'd met Kim, there was a good reason to stay home. The thought had even slipped into his consciousness that someday he might just stay home for good. To hell with urgent missions. Let someone else have the glory.

But not yet. Not until the Spratly Island dispute was put to bed.

He opened the door. Trunh Bao was waiting outside. Trunh was Ferrone's translator and aide. He would be the only staff Ferrone would take to the talks in Hong Kong.

"Watch out for him, Trunh," said Kim.

"Not to worry, Mrs. Ferrone," said Trunh, flashing a smile. "I'll take care of him."

USS Ronald Reagan

". . . and so we commend the souls of Major Michael O'Toole, Lieutenant Commander Elwood Wayne, and Captain Carl Heilbrunner to the bosom of the Almighty, in whom we place . . ."

Maxwell tuned out the rest. Over the years he'd attended too many memorial services, heard too many eulogies. This one was being delivered by Cmdr. Preacher Peebles, the *Reagan*'s chaplain. Only a week ago Peebles had conducted the service for the crew lost on the E-2C Hawkeye.

A warm breeze wafted through the open hangar deck. Maxwell let his mind wander. Monsoon season was coming. The weather in the South China Sea would turn rainy and overcast. A lousy time for war.

A hundred or so mourners had turned out to say good-bye to the three airmen. They stood at the number-three elevator bay, which was now open to the sea. On an inclined ramp lay O'Toole's casket, covered with an American flag.

Maxwell glanced around. With the exception of the

Dragon Flight team and a few senior officers, none of the men and women there had known O'Toole or Wayne or Heilbrunner. The deaths were reported on the ship's closed-circuit television in the vaguest terms—that they had died in "an operational accident."

Maxwell spotted Boyce across the compartment. He was standing next to his fellow admiral, Jack Hightree. Bullet Alexander had shown up, wearing service whites. Captain Sticks Stickney, the *Reagan*'s captain, was there, a head taller than most of those around him.

Dana Boudroux was at Maxwell's left. Gypsy Palmer stood on his other side, clutching his arm. He heard Gypsy suck in a deep breath, then stifle a sob. That morning Maxwell and Gypsy had sifted through Sharp's few personal effects in his stateroom. He hadn't brought much with him to the *Reagan*— a service dress Charlie uniform, a few paperbacks, the ubiquitous compact hi-fi and stack of CDs that every seagoing officer had in his quarters. There were framed photos of Sharp and Gypsy together on a beach, on a ski slope, grinning from the interior of his Corvette. And an eight-by-ten color shot of the space shuttle lifting from its pad.

"It was like the holy grail," Gypsy had said, holding the photo up. "The space shuttle was his dream."

Like most combat aviators, Sharp had left a will. Most of his possessions were to be divided between his parents, siblings, and his fiancée, Gypsy Palmer. He had been specific about the disposition of his remains. If something happened during this deployment, he wanted a burial at sea.

Preacher Peebles droned on for five more minutes, recounting a few details from the lives of the three men. Wayne and O'Toole were graduates of the Naval Academy. All three had graduate degrees and had been trained as test engineers. O'Toole had just been selected to be an astronaut.

Nothing was said about Groom Lake. No mention of the Black Star. No reference to aerial combat over the South China Sea.

On a linen-covered table was a collage of personal items—Sharp's Naval Flight Officer's wings, a brass Marine Corps emblem, Duke Wayne's officer's sword, Plug Heilbrunner's captain's bars. There was a framed photograph of each man. In his photo, Sharp O'Toole was flashing his toothy, trademark Irish grin.

"The Lord giveth and the Lord taketh away," intoned Peebles. He concluded the service with a prayer.

The Marine honor guard took over. A burly sergeant bellowed, "Firing party, pree-sent *arms!*"

Two rows of Marine casket bearers tilted the casket toward the deck edge. There was only one casket. The bodies of Wayne and Heilbrunner had not been recovered.

Sharp O'Toole's silver casket glided from beneath the flag and arced downward toward the sea. It disappeared from view beyond the deck edge.

"Ready . . . aim . . . fire!"

The carbines crackled once, twice, three times. Maxwell felt Gypsy flinch with each volley. The melancholy notes of Taps resonated through the steel bulkheads of the hangar deck. Each mournful note hovered in the air then seemed to melt away in the open sea.

The ceremony concluded. The Marine casket bearers folded the flag and handed it to Admiral Boyce, who walked across the deck and presented it to Gypsy Palmer.

The crowd dispersed. Dana nodded to Maxwell, then walked back across the hangar deck. Gypsy remained at the deck edge, clutching the folded flag, peering out at the shallow whitecaps where Sharp O'Toole's casket had disappeared. Maxwell stood with her, saying nothing. They were alone.

Finally she turned away from the sea. Her eyes were clear and dry. Her face had a calm, resolute look.

"It's over," she said. She looked at her watch. "I'm ready to fly."

*　　*　　*

Hong Kong, People's Republic of China

Ferrone was sick to death of Chinese tea.

They kept bringing the stuff by the pot. It was green, sticky, and sweet. Whenever his cup was half empty, a white-coated waiter would rush to refill it.

And dim sum. Chinese finger food, except that you were supposed to pluck out each morsel with your chopsticks. The waiters brought unending trays laden with dumplings and rolls and balls of rice with globs of fish and shrimp inside. Ferrone was sick to death of dim sum too.

The Chinese Foreign Ministry had chosen the top floor of the Bank of China building in the downtown area of Victoria Island for the meeting. No announcements were made, no members of the press invited. The conference room was vast, occupying the entire top floor. Thick carpets lay on a gleaming parquet floor. Chinese art and pottery were displayed on three walls, while the fourth contained a massive tinted window with a view of the harbor and the New Territories to the north.

Ferrone and Trunh arrived from the airport in an unmarked Lexus. Likewise, Van Duc Chien and his three staffers traveled from Chek Lap Kok Airport by private auto. All had escaped notice from the press or from curious government officials.

They were in the third hour of talk. And that was all it amounted to, thought Ferrone. Talk. An endless loop of recriminations about each other's ships and aircraft and oil-drilling facilities. Negotiating with the Chinese was like replaying old chess games. Each side knew the other's moves, but they still had to go through the motions.

The participants in the talks had arranged themselves around a long teak table. Van Duc Chien and his team were on one side, with the Chinese foreign minister and his staff of six facing them from the other side. Ferrone sat several feet distant from Van, befitting his role as mediator and noncombatant.

Except that the Chinese minister wasn't buying it. He was shaking his finger at Ferrone.

". . . and your submarines have torpedoed five unarmed vessels of the People's Republic," he said in a strident voice. "Is this not an act of war against our country?" It was the fourth time in the last hour the foreign minister had brought up the matter of submarines and lost ships. Each side was delicately avoiding the subject of stealth jets.

"Vessels and aircraft from each side in this conflict have been attacked," said Ferrone. "I suggest, Mr. Foreign Minister, that we move this discussion forward. Instead of dwelling on what has already occurred, we should seek a resolution to the dispute."

While he waited for the translator to convey his reply, he took another sip of green tea. He tried not to make a face. *Damn.* The stuff tasted like warm owl piss.

The Chinese minister said, "There will never be a resolution to the dispute until Vietnam admits its aggressive conduct and withdraws its illegal forces from the Spratly Islands."

At this, Van Duc Chien sat upright. "Vietnam's forces are the *only* legal forces in the Spratly Islands. Our ownership of the territory dates back over a quarter of a century."

"Planting your flag on a reef does not give you ownership of the entire archipelago."

"Attacking Vietnam's oil-drilling facilities with military force does not give you ownership of *our* islands."

"The occupation of Swallow Reef by Vietnamese forces—with the covert help of the U.S.—is a blatant act of war."

"So was the invasion of the reef by Chinese forces."

Back and forth. Ferrone followed the exchange as if he were watching a tennis match. An endless repetition. The Vietnamese president and the Chinese minister were sticking to their scripted lines.

Or were they?

Ferrone sensed a subtle change in the script. Something

else was going on. What had the Chinese minister said?
Something that seemed to diverge from the script. Ferrone
listened more closely.

And the minister said it again: "Vietnam is not entitled to
possession of the entire archipelago."

Ferrone nodded. Possession of *the entire archipelago*.
That was it. The minister was cracking the door open. Just a
crack, but there it was.

As if to confirm his meaning, the Chinese minister paused
and glanced at Ferrone. Van Duc Chien was gazing at him
too. They seemed to be waiting for him to speak.

It was the moment Ferrone had been waiting for since he
arrived at the meeting.

"Gentlemen," he said. "Allow me to offer a proposal that
may interest you."

CHAPTER 27

HANGFIRE

28,000 feet
South China Sea
1755 Friday, 4 May

"Bogeys twelve o'clock, thirty miles, angels twenty-two," said Gypsy Palmer on the intercom.

Maxwell could hear the excitement in her voice. Gypsy was hyped. She sounded like a hunter on opening day of the season.

"Flankers," said Maxwell. He was getting the EID—electronic—ID in his own display. They showed up as little horizontal bars, four of them, and they were definitely SU-27 Flankers.

"What are they doing?" asked Gypsy.

"Turning. They're defensive."

"How can you be sure?"

"They're on a CAP station. Probably covering an AWACS or a surface asset."

"Are we going to engage?"

"Negative."

"Why not? We've got them cold."

"You know the ROE," said Maxwell. He was beginning

to wonder if it was a mistake putting Gypsy Palmer back on flight status so soon. Her judgment was warped. She wanted to kill enemy airplanes—any airplanes. Flankers, freighters, *Dong-jins*. She wasn't fussy as long as they belonged to the PLA.

After a moment she said, "Yeah, I know the ROE."

He could hear the frustration in her voice. The Rules of Engagement came from somewhere higher than Boyce in the command structure. The ROE put conventional fighters like SU-27 Flankers off limits unless they displayed hostile intent. Since the Vietnamese reoccupation of Swallow Reef, the PLA had shown no interest in taking further losses in the South China Sea. Not unless a Chinese warplane was targeting friendly aircraft, ships, or surface assets could they be locked up and killed.

The only exception was the *Dong-jin*. Boyce's orders at the briefing were, "If it's a *Dong-jin*, he's fair game. I don't care if he's delivering milk to orphans. Kill it. If we're lucky, Zhang will be flying the sonofabitch."

But not Flankers. At least Flankers that were cruising along like fat geese, showing no hostile intent. These guys were subsonic, cruising in a spread-out formation of two separate elements. They showed no indication that they knew the Black Stars were in their space.

Or was it a setup?

Maxwell had an uneasy feeling. The PLA Air Force had already showed that they didn't mind sacrificing a few conventional fighters to draw out the Black Star. Did they have a *Dong-jin* covering the Flankers?

Let's find out. He reached up and pulled the CFD goggles down from his helmet visor. His view of the world outside turned to a soupy green. The goggles were the enhanced model that Dana Boudroux had produced.

"Fifteen miles," called out Gypsy Palmer.

The Flankers were still loafing along, turning their tails to them, unaware of any threat. Easy targets, thought Maxwell.

Too easy. He was glad the ROE put them off limits. Killing the Flankers wouldn't be an aerial victory, it would be an execution.

He peered out into empty space, in the direction of the Chinese Flankers. They were still too far away to acquire visually. Chances were, nothing was out there with them. They still wouldn't know whether the goggles worked or—

"IR contact!" called Gypsy.

"Yeah, four Flankers," said Maxwell. He wondered why she bothered telling him. Each of the Flankers was putting out enough infrared signature to light up a small city.

"Not the Flankers," said Gypsy. Her voice was excited. "Something else."

"Where?"

"It's on your display. Just above the lead element, crossing right to left."

Maxwell glanced at the display. Yeah, there it was. He peered back outside in the direction of the contact. He blinked, refocusing his eyes to infinity. The Black Star's onboard infrared sensor—the one Dana Boudroux had tweaked to increase its sensitivity—was picking up a heat signal.

Maxwell felt a stirring in his blood. A *Dong-jin*. Had to be.

But it wouldn't be a duck shoot. The Chinese had already demonstrated that they could get a visual on the Black Star. Zhang had seen him well enough to shoot him down with his cannon.

The thought stirred Maxwell's hopes. There was no way of knowing whether Zhang was flying this jet, but Maxwell wanted to believe that he could spot Zhang by the way he flew. Chinese fighters pilots were predictable and unimaginative. Zhang was different. He was skilled and full of surprises.

"Ten miles," said Gypsy.

Still no visual ID. The trace was still there, blurring in and out on the display. The Flankers were still turning, placing themselves in position for a potential starboard beam shot from the Black Star.

Maxwell peered through the green haze of the CFD goggles. He saw the wavy specks of the Flankers, still in two elements. He nudged the nose of the Black Star upward, gaining an altitude advantage.

He saw it.

And then he didn't.

Damn. He blinked, glanced back inside the cockpit to refocus his eyes at close range, then out again. Through the pea soup he saw little specks, the silhouettes of the Flankers, sunspots—

He saw it again.

"Got it," he called.

It was a thousand feet below them. It looked like a manta ray, wavy and gray, diamond-shaped. It was a *Dong-jin*, and by the Rules of Engagement it was fair game.

He could take a Sidewinder shot, but he didn't have any faith that the AIM-9 Sidewinder's heat-seeker head would stay locked on the *Dong-jin*'s faint IR emission. But that wasn't the real reason he wasn't shooting a Sidewinder. He wanted to kill this guy the same way Zhang killed Sharp O'Toole.

Without taking his eyes off the object, he reached forward and toggled the weapons select to GUN.

"Dragon One-one, Battle-ax."

Maxwell heard the call on the tactical frequency, but he was too busy to answer. He had the *Dong-jin* in sight. He rolled into a right turn, opening up some space behind the Chinese jet before he reversed and rolled back—

"Dragon One-one, Battle-ax. Answer up, Dragon."

The voice on the frequency was persistent. And familiar.

"Dragon One-one, do you read Battle-ax?"

"Stand by, Battle-ax. Dragon is engaged, neutral."

"Remain neutral and disengage, Dragon. Your signal is Hangfire. Acknowledge Hangfire."

Maxwell couldn't believe it. "Hangfire" was the signal for "abort the mission and return to base."

He kept his eyes on the wavy shape of the *Dong-jin*. Ten more seconds and he would reverse and roll in on the target. At five hundred yards he would open fire with the cannon.

"Acknowledge, Dragon. Confirm you copy Hangfire."

Maxwell knew that Boyce was following the engagement in his own data-linked monitor. He already knew that in forty seconds the *Dong-jin* would be converted to a flaming hunk of trash. *Why was he aborting the mission?*

"Don't acknowledge, Brick," said Gypsy. "Not yet."

Maxwell kept his eyes on the *Dong-jin*. Boyce knew something that they didn't. "Dragon One-one copies Hangfire." He removed his thumb from the mike button and said on the interphone, "Sorry, Gypsy."

No reply from the backseat. He could tell by the sound of Gypsy's breathing over the hot mike—rapid and forced—that she was furious. More than furious. At this moment Gypsy Palmer hated Maxwell and Boyce more than she hated Zhang.

He left the master armament switch hot, just in case. He rolled away from the *Dong-jin*, keeping his eye on the enemy jet. Turning your tail to an enemy fighter was a good way to get your butt flamed. But the *Dong-jin* appeared not to have spotted the Black Star. He was in a shallow bank, still covering the flight of Flankers.

Maxwell dropped the nose of the Black Star and nudged the throttles forward. He watched the airspeed swell as the altitude decreased. As the distance between the Black Star and the Chinese jets opened up, he began to relax. They were out of range of the *Dong-jin*'s missiles and its deadly cannon.

They flew back to the *Reagan* in silence. Gypsy sulked in the backseat, saying nothing.

Their Black Star was the only aircraft airborne from the *Reagan* except for a Hawkeye, still on station, a CAP flight of Super Hornets from the Roadrunner squadron, and the plane guard SH-60 hovering off the starboard side.

Maxwell landed the Black Star aboard. An okay pass to a two wire.

The deck crew chained the Black Star to the deck. While the elevator was still descending to the hangar deck, Gypsy climbed down from the cockpit. She didn't wait for Maxwell. When the elevator clunked to a stop, she was gone. Maxwell could hear the heels of her boots pounding the steel deck.

U.S. Consulate, Hong Kong

Ferrone paused to take another hit on his scotch. After all that owl-piss tea, he needed a real drink.

He looked back at the videoconferencing screen. "It's not a done deal, Mr. President."

"Sound like it's as good as done," said Hollis Benjamin.

"The president of the PRC still has to sign off on it. And you too, of course."

"No problem on this end, Skipper. And as far as President Xiang is concerned, he assures me he's on board."

Ferrone took another pull on the drink, a Dewar's on the rocks, and tilted back in the leather chair. He felt a mixture of elation and fatigue. The negotiating session with the Vietnamese and Chinese had dragged on for nearly eight hours. In the end, neither side had gotten as much as they wanted from the other. But each had agreed to cease hostilities. Ferrone's proposal to apportion the oil-drilling rights between the two countries was met by outright rejection, heated debate, and then a grudging acceptance. The matter of sovereignty over the islands was solved by their agreement to appoint an international commission to govern the area and to administer the oil rights pact.

All in all, thought Ferrone, an elegant solution to a messy problem.

From the Bank of China building he and Trunh had driven directly to the U.S. Consulate on Garden Road. There he availed himself of the consulate's excellent VIP lounge, made himself a drink, then used the secure videoconferencing to report the status of the negotiations to the president.

Beaver Benjamin was grinning at him from the screen.

"I knew I could count on you, Skipper. The accord you just negotiated will spare the world another war. It just might also spare my presidency."

"Thanks for the generous words, Mr. President. But you and I know who deserves the real credit. The guys who brought the players to the table."

"Don't worry, Skipper. I haven't forgotten them."

The consulate's videoconferencing net was not considered secure enough for highly classified discussions. They wouldn't discuss the role of U.S. Navy submarines or Black Star jets during the recent action in the South China Sea. But Ferrone had no doubt that without them, China would have rolled like a tsunami over the Vietnamese installations in the Spratly Islands.

"When do hostilities cease?" said Ferrone.

"I have already issued a stand-down order to Red Boyce's unit. Your friend the Vietnamese president has ordered his forces to stand down, and President Xiang has agreed to do the same."

"What are my orders now, Mr. President?"

"Go home. Give your bride a hug for me. Tell her that in a couple of weeks the two of you will be flying to Washington to have a Presidential Medal of Freedom awarded to you."

Ferrone shook his head. "I have enough medals, thank you."

"None that I had the honor of pinning on, Skipper. Hey, humor me. This is my treat, not yours."

Ferrone grinned tiredly at the screen. Beaver Benjamin. Pushy as ever. "Yes, sir," he said.

Benjamin congratulated him again and signed off. The screen went blank. Ferrone rose from the videoconferencing console and signaled the steward for another scotch.

A State Department C-20 Gulfstream was waiting at Chek Lap Kok Airport to fly him back to Hanoi. President Van Duc Chien and his staff had already departed aboard the chartered Vietnam Airlines Airbus. Ferrone's aide, Trunh Bao, would stay another day in Hong Kong.

Ferrone accepted a fresh drink from the smiling Chinese steward. It suited him to be alone now. He wanted to reflect on the day's events, make some notes, sip a couple more scotches, maybe take a nap. Then he would ride in the back of a plushly appointed executive jet as if he were somebody important.

CHAPTER 28

GIA LAM

Lingshui Air Base, Hainan Island
1910 Friday, 4 May

"Yes, of course I understand the order," said General Zhang. "Do you think I am an imbecile?"

Without waiting for a reply, Zhang slammed the phone down. He slammed it so hard that the black plastic receiver cracked in half.

For several minutes Zhang sat at his desk. He stared at the shattered telephone. His temples were pounding and his chest heaved. The fury coursed in his veins like molten lava.

The thought passed through his mind that an officer, even a general officer like himself, was not supposed to speak in such a manner to the commander of the PLA Air Force. Zhang didn't care. General Han Jianli was a spineless hack. But what was infinitely worse, so was Xiang Fan-lo, the president of the People's Republic of China. In Zhang's opinion, the president had just committed a heinous act of treason. He had entered into an agreement with the United States and its puppet state, Vietnam, to cease hostilities in the South China Sea.

Adding to Zhang's rage was the botched mission this

morning. One of his *Dong-jins* had just returned from a mission escorting a flight of SU-27s. The crew—Major Tsan and his weapons officer—had reported no contact with enemy aircraft. Zhang was furious with Tsan. He was sure that at least one U.S. Black Star had been airborne and probably in the area. An Ilyushin AWACS ship had reported the unmistakable signs of a catapult launch from the American carrier, *Reagan*, but no radar-identifiable aircraft departing the ship.

Could it have been Maxwell?

The possibility caused Zhang's scalp to tingle. He reached for the photograph that had been delivered to him this morning. It was a digital photo taken by the commander of the unit assigned to recover the crew members from the Black Star that Zhang had shot down.

They had failed. Instead of capturing the surviving crew member, they allowed him to escape. He was rescued by a U.S. special operations unit, which then returned to retrieve the body of the dead crew member.

Zhang held the photograph under the direct light of his desk lamp. The photo was of a dead man, an American whose body had been shattered by the shells of an automatic cannon. He had dark hair and he was clean-shaven. He appeared to be in his early thirties, and the emblems of rank on his flight suit identified him as a major or lieutenant commander.

It wasn't Maxwell.

Two PLA commandos who survived the battle with the American special operations units described the pilot who escaped. He was a tall man with a dark mustache, about forty years old.

Zhang shook his head. He could almost admire such a warrior if he didn't hate him with every fiber of his being. This man Maxwell possessed an uncanny ability to survive anything, even being strafed in a parachute. Until the telephone discussion a few minutes ago with the idiotic commander of the PLA Air Force, Zhang had fully expected to confront Maxwell in the sky again. One last time.

Now the cowardly president of the People's Republic of China had agreed to peace. Just when the PLA was poised to eradicate all the Vietnamese presence in the Spratly Islands. The American stealth jets had proven themselves to be ineffective. And although the U.S. submarines had caused serious disruption to the Chinese invasion schedule, it was only a matter of time before the PLA Navy neutralized the threat.

A red blinking light on his telephone console caught Zhang's eye. For a while he ignored it. He didn't want to talk to anyone.

Then he noticed on the console screen that the call was not from a PLA mainland switchboard. It came from Hong Kong, on the secure wireless net.

He didn't bother trying to use the smashed handset. He pressed the speaker button.

"Zhang."

The voice on the other end belonged to a *Te-Wu* agent. He had been present at the secret negotiations between the Vietnamese president, the U.S. ambassador to Vietnam, and the PRC foreign minister. Zhang listened while the agent described the talks, the strategies of each side, the behavior of the negotiators. Zhang didn't interrupt, even though he already knew the result. China had capitulated. The foreign minister, acting on the orders of the president, had surrendered China's future.

Zhang waited until the agent gave him the last critical item of information. It was all he needed to know.

He hung up. Yes, he thought, a great blunder had been made by the foreign minister and the president, but it wasn't final. If he acted boldly, he could still save China.

With that thought he punched the buzzer that alerted his *Dong-jin* ground crew.

"Yes, General?" said his crew chief, a sergeant named Siu.

"Ready the number one *Dong-jin*," said Zhang. "Full fuel, standard weapons load. Alert Lieutenant Po. We take off in one hour."

Kim clutched her bare arms around her. With the coming of darkness, the air had turned chilly. Off to the west, in the direction of the Hoang Lien Mountains, she could see tendrils of lightning. It hadn't begun to rain yet, but she could feel it in the air.

The ramp at Gia Lam Airfield was nearly deserted. She was alone except for the driver and the two green-uniformed Vietnamese Air Force officers who had escorted her out to the ramp. Joe had telephoned from Hong Kong. He was on his way to the airport, he said, and he would be landing at Gia Lam at about nine o'clock. He was being flown back to Hanoi in a U.S. State Department Gulfstream jet.

She still didn't know why he had flown to Hong Kong, or why it was supposed to be a secret. She guessed that it had something to do with the Spratly Island problem. Some kind of negotiation with the Chinese. She also guessed that it had gone well, judging by Joe's voice. He sounded tired but jubilant. She could tell he'd had a couple of drinks. He was in a celebratory mood.

The conflict in the South China Sea was the most troublesome problem in Vietnam. If Joe had negotiated a peace with China, he would be the most popular foreigner ever to reside in Vietnam.

And then what? Ambassadors didn't stay in their post forever. Would the president give him another assignment? A job in Washington? Or would they retire and settle down somewhere?

The thought made her smile. Joe Ferrone was not the kind who could putter in a yard or watch television or play golf. He was a man who had flown supersonic jets, commanded ships, counseled presidents. He was the most exciting man she had ever known. Marrying Joe Ferrone was the high point of her life.

"There," said one of the officers, a colonel. He looked young, thought Kim. Practically a teenager. But they all looked so young these days. The officer was pointing off to the west.

The landing lights had just descended from the overcast. They were shimmering like celestial objects against the dark cloud base. The Gulfstream was on final approach. She saw the ground crew across the ramp wheeling out mobile stairs. A truck with a flashing light headed out to the runway to greet the arriving jet.

Kim felt a happy glow inside her. She and Joe were still newlyweds. The twelve or so hours he'd been gone was the longest they'd been separated since they'd been married.

She kept her eyes on the approaching jet. She could make out its sleek silhouette now. Kim felt a flash of pride that the U.S. government thought highly enough of her husband that they would dispatch a private jet to—

What was that?

Something in the night sky behind the Gulfstream. It looked like a firefly. A tiny, zigzagging blur of yellow light. The Air Force officers saw it too. One was pointing, while the other, the young-looking colonel, was pulling a portable transceiver from his belt.

Kim didn't know what was happening, but her intuition told her that something was wrong. She kept her eyes on the zigzagging object. It was moving fast, very fast. Catching up with the Gulfstream.

She heard the colonel barking something into his radio in Vietnamese. Something about a warning, missile defense, unidentified threat. It was more than she could comprehend. She lost sight of the zigzagging yellow light. Her heart began to accelerate.

An explosion erupted in the tail of the Gulfstream.

Kim stared. *No. This isn't happening.*

The fireball blossomed in the tail of the jet, then engulfed the aft fuselage. Orange light reflected from the base of the cloud deck, illuminating the landscape below. Kim could see the white-and-blue markings of the Gulfstream. She saw the sleek pointed nose, the long graceful wings with the vertical winglets at the tips.

The Gulfstream folded in half. The wingtips rose like outstretched arms to join over the fuselage. The flaming hulk plunged to the ground. A brief fireball marked the place where the wreckage impacted the low hillside.

Kim stood transfixed. It took a full ten seconds for the metallic *whump* of the crash to roll across the open expanse. Her body jerked as the sound reached her. The orange glare was fading. There was only a faint glow against the blackness of the countryside.

The colonel was chattering in a high-pitched voice on the radio. She had no idea what he was saying. Trucks and utility vehicles were racing across the field, lights flashing, sirens warbling like demented parrots.

In the bedlam that descended on Gia Lam Airfield, no one seemed to notice Kim. She kept staring into the western sky. Both the Air Force officers had run inside the operations building. Ground crewmen were scurrying around the ramp like ants on a mound. A column of vehicles was heading across the field.

The mobile boarding stairs stood on the empty tarmac.

A string of unbidden thoughts rushed through Kim's mind. Maybe it wasn't Joe's airplane. Maybe he wasn't aboard. Maybe there were survivors. Maybe—

No. She turned away from the flashing lights and smoldering wreckage. She was Vietnamese. She had learned not to wish for the impossible.

CHAPTER 29

WILDCAT

The White House
1435 Friday, 4 May

"Are we certain it was the Chinese, Mr. President?"

Hollis Benjamin gave Greenstein, the secretary of defense, a withering look. Another inane goddamn lawyer question. "Who the hell do you think it was?"

He saw Greenstein's injured expression, and he regretted the caustic answer. "Sorry, Dick," he said. "What I meant was, yeah, we're as certain as we need to be."

"I understand your feelings, sir. I only meant to suggest that we need some evidence to identify the—"

"Enough evidence was collected on the crash site to confirm that it was a Chinese-built PL-8 heat-seeking missile."

"But that doesn't identify the source," said Greenstein. "Couldn't it have been deployed by some other entity than the PRC?"

Benjamin felt his frustration building up. Greenstein was a pedantic hairsplitter. It came from his years as a partner at the third-largest law firm in Philadelphia.

Benjamin knew that his own judgment at this moment was not objective. He still felt as if he'd been kicked in the gut. Losing Joe Ferrone was like losing a father. Worse, because Ferrone had been more of a parent than his own father. Ferrone was his mentor, counsel, confidante. Joe Ferrone was the kind of man Benjamin wished he could be.

The murdering little bastards.

He knew that presidents weren't supposed to let their emotions dictate policy. But there were plenty of instances in history where a little old-fashioned emotion—a commander-in-chief's righteous outrage—was the appropriate response. Sure, there were times when the leader of the most powerful country in the world was obliged to demonstrate restraint. There were other times when he was obliged to kick the shit out of a country like the People's Republic of China.

This was one of those times.

General Matloff, the Joint Chiefs chairman, spoke up. "In theory, the missile could have been deployed by anyone, but the fact that there was no apparent source *is* the evidence. It had to come from a stealth jet. One of NRO's satellites picked up an IR trace from the runway at Lingshui about an hour before the Gulfstream went down at Gia Lam, and they're sure it was a *Dong-jin.*"

"Have you confronted the Chinese over the matter?" asked Greenstein. He was being a lawyer again.

"An hour ago," said Benjamin. "Xiang denies any knowledge of it. He swears no PLA aircraft was ordered to attack our Gulfstream."

"Do you believe him?"

"Of course not. But we shouldn't totally discount it either. The China desk at the CIA is of the opinion that it was a wildcat mission by a unit on Hainan."

"It's possible," said Matloff. "The PLA has a culture that defies all Western rationale. Unit commanders sometimes thumb their noses at their superiors. They get rewarded for getting away with it, or else the PLA high command hands their head to them on a tray."

"This time we're going to save the high command the trouble," said Benjamin.

"Sir?" Matloff and Greenstein were looking at him with raised eyebrows.

"The wildcat unit on Hainan is going to learn the price of killing a U.S. ambassador," said Benjamin. He looked at Matloff. "Let's get busy on a tasking order, General. Get it off to the *Reagan* as soon as possible."

Lingshui Air Base, Hainan Island

Gen. Han Jianli felt the wheels of the three-engine TU-154M thump down on the runway. He peered out the cabin window at the sprawling ramp. He saw no extraordinary activity, no honor guard, no flags or pennants waving as they usually did when the commander of the PLA Air Force arrived at a base.

Which was good. It meant that word of his visit to Lingshui had not been leaked. Even the markings of the Tupolev transport were generic, just the drab color scheme of a PLA troop transport instead of the bright flag and insignia of General Han's personal executive jet. As far as the air traffic controllers and the Lingshui base staff were concerned, the Tupolev carried only supplies and replacement personnel for the squadrons.

With Han on the transport were two of his staff, both colonels, and a twelve-man squad of special military police. He didn't trust the military police at Lingshui to carry out the orders he intended to give.

The Tupolev reached its parking spot, and the engines whined down. Han's hand trembled as he reached for his attaché case. He was agitated, and for good reason. His twenty-nine-year ascent through the ranks of the PLA had nearly come to a spectacular end. This morning, the president of the People's Republic had accused him of sedition and treason. It had taken all of Han's powers of persuasion to convince Xiang that no unit of the PLA Air Force was connected with the mysterious loss of a U.S. ambassador's aircraft as it approached Hanoi.

A lie, of course. But it bought him time. He knew in the core of his being what had happened—and who was responsible.

The cabin door opened. A sergeant stood at the top of the boarding stairs. His expression froze when he saw General Han. Before the sergeant had time even to snap to attention, he was grabbed by two of the special military policemen. They hustled him down the ladder and across the ramp to the operations building. Minutes later they returned with a pair of utility vans.

Han deplaned and climbed into the second van. The rest of his entourage—the military policemen and the two colonels—joined him and they sped off across the ramp.

As they approached the command post of the Hainan military sector, Han reflected on his situation. He had already committed a grievous error. Despite all the warning signals—the insubordinate behavior, the flaunting of orders, the unauthorized combat actions—he had allowed Zhang Yu to remain in his post.

Why?

Han remembered the rationale. Zhang was a national hero. Zhang was a brilliant aerial tactician. Zhang's knowledge of the *Dong-jin* was critical to the country's security.

All irrelevant. There was only one compelling reason why Han had not removed Zhang from his post as commanding general of the Hainan military sector and the commander of the *Dong-jin* unit.

Han was terrified of Zhang.

The dreaded *Te-Wu* secret police—Zhang's patron organization—had the power to intimidate every officer in the PLA, even the commander of the Air Force. No one, including General Han Jianli, was willing to risk a direct confrontation with Zhang.

Until now. A line had been crossed. The scar-faced general was out of control. Killing the U.S. ambassador to Vietnam was an act of war against the most powerful adversary on the planet. Han had to act before he himself was held responsible for triggering a war with the Americans.

The van pulled up to the entrance to the headquarters. Two helmeted sentries with automatic weapons guarded the main gate. They moved to challenge the intruders, then stopped, confused by the sight of a four-star general striding toward them. Before they could decide what to do, each was disarmed and handcuffed by Han's policemen.

Behind the phalanx of police with their automatic weapons pointing straight ahead, Han stormed into the headquarters building. They marched across the tiled lobby, through a series of outer offices, past a row startled clerks, into General Zhang Yu's inner chambers.

A large mahogany door bore a placard that identified the next room as the private office of General Zhang Yu, Commander of the Hainan Military Sector of the People's Liberation Army.

Han didn't knock. He flung the door open and marched inside.

The light in the office was subdued. The walls were paneled in a dark veneer. A shadowy figure sat facing him across a massive desk.

"General Han," said the figure. "To what do I owe the pleasure of this visit?"

Even in the low light, Han had no trouble distinguishing the scarred visage. Zhang was wearing a green, tight-fitting flight suit. He had a yellow scarf tied at his throat.

"General Zhang, I have come to relieve you of all duties in the People's Liberation Army Air Force."

Zhang's eyes became slits in the scarred tissue. "Relieving me? On what grounds?"

"On grounds of sedition and treason. You are under arrest."

"That is preposterous. Explain yourself, please."

"I don't have to explain anything. For your treasonous

conduct, you can expect to be tried and summarily executed."

Zhang laughed. It was an insolent, scoffing laugh. It made Han furious.

"You find this amusing, General Zhang?"

"I find it ironic. It is not I who will be tried and executed."

"What do you mean?"

"I mean you. Your trial has just been conducted. You will now be sentenced."

Han felt a cold wave of fear rush over him. Zhang was a lunatic. It was time for the military policemen to conclude this business. He glanced behind him.

There were no military policemen. The door was closed. He heard a scuffle in the outer room. There was the muffled sound of barked orders, the clatter of weapons dropping to the floor.

He looked again at Zhang. Zhang was holding a pistol in his right hand. Han recognized it—a Type 64 semiautomatic pistol. It was pointed at Han.

"General Han Jianli," said Zhang. "For your many acts of cowardice and incompetence, I hereby sentence you to death."

Han saw the muzzle flash at almost the same instant he felt the bullet strike his chest. The crack of the gunshot reverberated on the paneled walls. He gazed down at the reddened hole in his tunic. He had the sense of drifting into a dream.

Another muzzle flash. This time the crack seemed to hang in the air. Time slowed to a standstill. Han knew without looking that the bullet had pierced his heart. He felt his knees buckle, and blackness overtook him.

* * *

USS Ronald Reagan

Clunk, clunk, clunk. It was the only sound in the passage-way—boots thumping on the steel deck. No chatter, no ban-ter, no exchange of insults.

It was like the replay of an old movie, thought Maxwell. He'd seen it enough times to know the script. Same old clunk of boots. The scratchy-eyed feeling from not enough sleep before a predawn strike. The weight of all the stuff dangling from your torso harness and SV-2 vest. Nerves twanging from the mix of black Navy coffee, burned toast, and adrenaline.

Maxwell looked behind him. They were in pairs, each crew staying together. The pilots and wizzos walked in si-lence to the ladder that led to the hangar deck where they'd man their jets. While the elevators were still lifting them topside to the flight deck, they'd start engines and be ready to taxi to the catapults.

Gypsy Palmer was clunking along two paces behind him. Her face looked grim and determined.

"You get enough sleep?" asked Maxwell.

"Yes."

"Any problems?"

"No."

It was a typical conversation with Gypsy. Maxwell still wasn't sure about her. She hadn't gotten over her fury at not being allowed to kill the *Dong-jin* on the last mission.

Even this new mission—the strike on the *Dong-jin* revet-ments at Lingshui—didn't seem to elevate her mood. She sat through the intel brief, nodding her head at the target data, showing no change in expression.

They descended the ladder to the hangar deck. Maxwell could see the ghostly shapes of the Black Stars profiled in the open elevator bays. In the distance, through the bays, there was only blackness, no horizon between the sea and the sky. The launch would be in the predawn darkness, putting them over Lingshui just as day was breaking.

He reached the bottom of the ladder and stepped onto the red-lighted hangar deck. He caught the silhouette of someone in the shadows by the bulkhead.

"Brick?"

He stopped and waited for the others coming down the ladder to pass. Gypsy Palmer gave him a glance, then kept walking toward their parked jet.

"What are you doing up at this hour, Dana?"

She moved out of the shadows. "I came to wish you luck."

"I thought scientists didn't believe in luck."

"Guess I'm not a real scientist."

She was wearing a white jumpsuit that accented her narrow waist. Her hair was pulled back in her standard ponytail. In the dim artificial light, her face looked young, almost childlike. Maxwell caught a scent of perfume.

"If this works today," he said, "we'll be going home."

"And then what?"

"You go back to your lab. I go back to Fallon."

"Fallon's not that far from Groom Lake. Do you think that . . ." She shuffled her feet, chewed for a moment on a thumbnail. "Do you think you and I could, you know, start over again?"

This was a different Dana Boudroux than the one he'd met at Groom Lake three weeks ago. This wasn't the Ice Queen. He liked this one better.

"Give it another shot?"

"Something like that."

"So you can show me how to punch a speed bag?"

"Punch it any way you want," she said. "Even if it's wrong."

He smiled. "Okay."

"Okay what?"

"Okay, let's give it a shot."

She stepped close. She raised herself on her toes and kissed him, her lips just brushing his. "Promise me one thing."

"What?"

"You'll come back alive."

"I promise," he said, and walked toward his jet.

CHAPTER 30

SNAKE NEST

USS Ronald Reagan
South China Sea
0525 Monday, 7 May

"Relax, Jack," said Boyce. "It's gonna be a walk in the park."

He could tell by Hightree's worried expression that he didn't believe it. "Easy for you to say," said Hightree.

They were on the *Reagan*'s flag bridge. It was still dark outside. All three jets were positioned on the catapults.

"Hell," said Boyce, "we might see some real action today. You can be a real strike group commander."

"Goddamn it, Boyce, I *am* a real strike group commander. Don't you forget it."

Boyce turned his face to the glass pane so Hightree couldn't see him grin. It was so easy to push Hightree's buttons.

Boyce and Hightree went back over twenty years in their careers. Hightree was already a rear admiral and a strike group commander when Boyce, still a captain, led the *Reagan*'s air wing. Now Boyce wore one star, and Hightree had just been selected for his third. In a couple of weeks he'd be headed for the Pentagon and a new job.

The two were opposites in style and temperament. Unlike Boyce, who had earned a legion of enemies by his flamboyant style, Hightree was a low-profile commander who hated taking risks. A black-ops mission like this was exactly the kind of operation he loathed.

Peering down at the flight deck, Boyce could make out the dim outlines of the Black Star jets. Not in his wildest dreams would he have imagined such a thing. Three unescorted jets going against one of the most heavily defended targets in Asia. The Black Stars were loaded with JSOWs—joint standoff weapons. Enough to take out the PLA Air Force's entire stock of *Dong-jin* stealth fighters at Lingshui, if the intel estimates were correct.

No other warplanes from the *Reagan* were airborne except a Hawkeye and four Super Hornets configured as refueling tankers. After the Black Stars launched, they would rendezvous with the tankers and top off before proceeding to the target.

Before the Black Stars arrived on target at Lingshui, the *Reagan* Strike Group would be at DEFCON One—the highest level of defense condition. A Barrier CAP of sixteen Super Hornets would be airborne, controlled by Navy Hawkeyes and an Air Force E-3B Sentry AWACS ship from Kadena. A complete SEAD package—antiradiation missile-armed Super Hornets, four F/A-18G Growler electronic jamming aircraft, and four U.S. Air Force KC-10 tankers on station.

Just in case. This Black Star raid could trigger the mother of all modern sea battles. *God help us,* thought Boyce.

Hightree was still glowering at Boyce when the intercom speaker on his console crackled. "Flag, air ops. The jets are up and ready. It's T minus five. Do we have a go for launch, sir?"

"You have a go," said Hightree. "Launch the strike package."

"Aye, aye, sir."

The minutes ticked past. The JBD—jet blast deflector—

raised from the deck behind the jet on the number-one catapult—the starboard bow catapult. Maxwell's jet would be
the first to launch.

Through the thick glass Boyce heard the rumble of the engines going to full thrust. The jet seemed to squat, its nose
strut compressing. An instant later the wedge-shaped aircraft hurtled down the catapult track. The jet swept over the
bow and vanished in the darkness. A trail of steam wafted
from the empty catapult track.

Seconds later, the jet on the port bow catapult squatted,
then lurched down the track. Then the waist catapult. Boyce
saw a blurry shadow race down the angled deck and disappear into the gloom off the port bow.

All three jets airborne. After refueling on the tankers,
they'd point their noses in the direction of Hainan Island. No
overt communications, no SAM suppression, no battle reports. The Black Stars were on their own.

A damned strange way to run a war, thought Boyce.

Hightree was looking at him again. "Well, Red. Let's
hope we're doing the right thing."

Boyce nodded. Hightree was being Hightree again. If the
decision to attack Lingshui had been left to him, it wouldn't
be happening. The op order had come through the traditional
chain of command, but Boyce knew who had made the decision. They were carrying out the orders of the president.

"No sweat, Jack," said Boyce. "A walk in the park."

Huangzhu Auxiliary Airfield, Hainan Island

"Has the *Dong-jin* been prepared for combat?" asked
Zhang.

"Yes, General," said Lieutenant Po. His young face bore
a troubled expression. "But this has been very troubling. I
would most respectfully ask, why must we—"

"Enough!" snapped Zhang. "I'll hear no more of your impertinent questions. Carry out your duties and wait for my orders."

Po hesitated. Then he saluted and did an about-face.

Zhang watched the weapons systems officer leave. Something would have to be done about Po. He had been behaving in this sullen manner since this morning, when they moved the *Dong-jin* to the auxiliary airfield at Huangzhu.

In normal circumstances, Zhang would have Po arrested and grilled by the *Te-Wu*. The impudent officer would receive a reeducation in protocol. Junior officers in the PLA were expendable.

But these were not normal circumstances. Zhang needed Po's services, at least for one final mission. Since he'd executed the commanding general of the PLA Air Force, Zhang knew that he was a general in name only. Without question, the PLA security police had already received the order to arrest him. For that reason he had secretly moved his *Dong-jin* to Huangzhu.

Zhang looked around his makeshift office. It was rudimentary—a single desk for him and a plain steel table for administrative staff. Several months ago he had secretly established this facility. The field had a concealed revetment for a *Dong-jin*, a basic maintenance shop, and a headquarters for him and his staff. With him at Huangzhu were two dozen loyal *Te-Wu* agents—the same ones who had neutralized General Han's staff when they arrived at Lingshui.

Zhang tilted back in the hard wooden chair and reflected on his situation. Executing General Han had been an audacious move, but so was the killing of Ferrone, the U.S. ambassador. According to Zhang's *Te-Wu* agent in Hanoi, this man Ferrone had been a former high-ranking naval officer. He had been a prisoner of the Vietnamese during their war with the U.S. The *Te-Wu* agent had also reported that Ferrone was a close confidante of the U.S. president, himself a former naval officer.

And then came the news that had set Zhang's emotions

aflame. Ferrone, the agent reported, was a family friend and colleague of Maxwell—the single human whom Zhang hated more than any other on the planet. Ferrone had served in the Navy with Maxwell's father. Ferrone had even hosted Maxwell in Hanoi not more than three weeks ago.

Killing Ferrone was a pleasure. It was also a brilliant tactical move, because it would undo the shameful armistice negotiated by Ferrone and the PRC foreign minister. Zhang understood the infantile nature of Americans.

The U.S. would retaliate. And Zhang was certain he knew where they would strike.

A rap on his door interrupted Zhang's thoughts.

Without waiting, Lieutenant Po rushed into the office. His face was flushed and his chest was heaving.

Zhang's hand went to the grip of his semiautomatic pistol.

"Sorry to interrupt, General," Po said, catching his breath. "The air defense net reports an attack. Enemy aircraft, stealth jets, precision weapons."

Zhang relaxed his grip on the pistol. "Where?" he asked, already knowing the answer.

"Lingshui."

USS Ronald Reagan

"Kilo class," said Hightree, pointing to the triangular symbol on the tactical display screen.

Hightree and Boyce watched the surface tactical display. The Chinese submarine was back.

"That symbol is twenty minutes old. The ASW commander says the surface ships have lost him, but one of the SSNs—*Daytona Beach*—is still hawking him."

"What do you want to bet it's the same guy we chased away last time with depth charges?" said Boyce. "Good old *Yuanzheng 67*."

Hightree frowned, still studying the symbol. "That was

before we lost *Melbourne*. Now we know the Chinese can shoot *Shkval* torpedoes."

"So what are you gonna do?"

Hightree kept watching the triangular symbol. "Watch him. If he shows any sign of hostile intent, we're going to blow him out of the water."

Boyce nodded. "Sounds good to me."

22,000 feet
Hainan Island

"Forty miles to release," Maxwell said on the intercom.

Gypsy didn't reply. She could see the release point on her own display. Maxwell was just trying to get her to talk. To hell with him.

She knew she was behaving like a snitty teenager, but there wasn't any rule that said a wizzo had to act all warm and fuzzy. Later, maybe. When Dragon Flight was a wrap and they were headed back to Groom Lake, she'd patch it up with Maxwell. He was an okay guy, just too much of a Boy Scout. He should have flamed that *Dong-jin* before they ac-knowledged the stand-down order from Boyce.

There was something in the display. Something off the southeast coast of Hainan.

"Contacts," she said in the hot mike. "Two o'clock, fif-teen miles, twenty thousand."

"Flankers," said Maxwell. "Looks like a CAP. Keep them tagged in case they acquire us."

The Flankers were no big deal. It would have been odd, Gypsy thought, if Chinese fighters *weren't* out there some-where. The Flankers were no problem unless they had been reconfigured with sensors to penetrate the Black Star's stealth cloaking. Not likely.

In the display she could see the other two Black Stars. Their positions were all data-linked via satellite. They had separated for deconfliction and mutual support. Now they were all on convergent courses toward Lingshui.

Each Black Star carried two two-thousand-pound GBU-27 bombs with hard-target-penetrator warheads. The bombs were guided by a computer-sorted mix of GPS commands, inertial guidance, and laser targeting. Each of the weapons was programmed to take out one of the concrete *Dong-jin* revetments at Lingshui.

It was like exterminating a nest of snakes, Gypsy thought. Easy unless one of the snakes came after you. If a *Dong-jin* got airborne unobserved, it could kill all of them. Which was why two Black Stars—Maxwell and Otis McCollister—were tasked to remain overhead after the attack to intercept any *Dong-jins* that might get airborne. The third Black Star, flown by Crud Carruthers, would sweep the target with its onboard surveillance cameras for bomb damage assessment.

"One minute," said Maxwell.

Another needless call. Gypsy didn't bother replying.

"Thirty seconds."

"Ten."

"Three, two, one—"

She heard the roar of the wind blast as the internal bay doors opened. The first bomb released with a *thunk*.

Two seconds later, the second bomb. The doors closed, and the wind blast abruptly ceased.

The bombs were on their way. Their movable guidance fins were obeying the satellite-delivered orders of the GPS navigation unit.

Maxwell hauled the nose of the Black Star around in a climbing turn to the right, then back to the left, opening up the distance from their descending bombs. Gypsy kept her eyes riveted on the elapsed timer. She had calculated that the GBU-27s would take something around forty seconds to impact.

She was close. Forty-two seconds from release the first bomb struck.

In the next few seconds, all the bombs from the Black Stars were impacting Lingshui. Penetrator warheads were detonating inside each revetment. Gypsy could see pillars of fire and smoke erupting like lava from the subsurface emplacements. Interior explosions were punching holes in the concrete surface of the base.

Nothing could survive those explosions, she thought. None of the *Dong-jins* could possibly have—

"Bogey on the runway," called someone on the tactical frequency. She recognized the voice of Otis McCollister. "A Bogey is rolling," called Otis. "Shit, he's airborne already."

Gypsy felt a jolt run through her. *Bogey? A Dong-jin?*

It was. She saw it through the greenish glare of the CFD goggles. A shimmering dark diamond. It was racing down the runway, just lifting off.

"Dragon Two has a lock," called Otis.

"We should take him," said Gypsy on the intercom.

"We'll stay high and check for spitters," said Maxwell. "Spitters" were unobserved entrants to the fight.

"But we're in better position. We can—"

"Cool it," snapped Maxwell. "Just do your job."

Gypsy fought back her anger. She saw the *Dong-jin* climbing from the runway. It was accelerating, shimmering like a mirage. Begging to be shot. From where they were, high and left, they could flame him in a matter of seconds.

But so could Otis. The Black Star was swooping from the right like a raptor after a sparrow. He had at least two hundred knots overtake speed on the *Dong-jin*.

She saw the squiggly white trail of the AIM-9 Sidewinder as it left the extended launcher rail on Otis's Black Star. It was flying a perfect curve, leaping out ahead of the flight path of the *Dong-jin*. Gypsy held her breath. It would be a classic missile kill. In another three seconds the proximity fuse of the warhead would—

"It missed," said Maxwell.

Gypsy stared. The missile had gone dumb. It was arcing ahead of the *Dong-jin*, not tracking anything.

So much for the new and improved seeker heads. The new sensors on the Black Star worked, and so did the goggles. Forget the missile seeker heads.

The Chinese pilot had awakened to his near-death experience. The *Dong-jin* was in a violent turn to the right, pulling vapor trails off each wingtip.

"Otis blew it," said Gypsy. "We've got a shot at this guy now."

"Negative," said Maxwell. "Otis still has him locked."

Gypsy seethed in the backseat. *Boy Scout.*

The panicked Chinese pilot's hard turn was taking him directly across Otis's nose. The Black Star still had a huge overtake speed on the *Dong-jin*. Gypsy saw the Black Star pull off to the left, crossing the trail of the *Dong-jin*, then back to the right, opening up the distance between him and the Chinese jet.

Gypsy saw tracers. She remembered the argument back aboard the ship about whether to load tracer rounds in the Black Star's Vulcan cannon. Tracers showed where your cannon bursts were going. They also revealed your position, which negated the value of the stealth cloaking.

Maxwell had cast the deciding vote. They were carrying tracers.

The tracers from Otis's cannon were arcing out in front of the *Dong-jin*. Gypsy saw Otis haul the nose of the Black Star tighter into the *Dong-jin*'s turn.

More tracers. Still in front.

Another burst, and this time Gypsy saw pieces coming off the *Dong-jin*. It looked like confetti streaming backwards. The wedge-shaped *Dong-jin* slewed into a skid, streaming smoke.

It exploded.

"Splash one *Dong-jin*," came the throaty voice of Otis McCollister. Technically, the call violated the radio silence order. No one was going to complain today. Shooting down a *Dong-jin* earned you a little slack.

Gypsy watched the hulk of the *Dong-jin* tumble like a shattered toy. It crashed into a cultivated field, sending up a geyser of dirt and black smoke.

There were no chutes. The *Dong-jin* crew had gone in with the jet.

Good, thought Gypsy Palmer. To hell with them.

CHAPTER 31

SCISSORS

USS Ronald Reagan
South China Sea
0640 Monday, 7 May

"What's the place called again?" Boyce said.

"Huangzhu," crackled the voice on the speaker. "A hundred kilometers north of Lingshui."

Boyce's eyes went to the map of Hainan on the bulkhead. It took him a few seconds, then his finger went to it. "Okay, got it. What's the probability it was a *Dong-jin?*"

"We give it eighty percent. The IR trace on the runway matches the confirmed ID signatures we have from Lingshui."

The voice on the speakerphone belonged to the Director of the National Reconnaissance Office in Chantilly, Virginia. Boyce had met him once. He was a civilian named Karstadt, a career spook who had come up through the CIA's electronic intelligence branch. The NRO managed all the U.S.'s space-based intelligence-gathering apparatus, and Boyce knew they had parked a KH-13 spy satellite over Hainan. He inferred from the other snippets Karstadt had told him that the KH-13 had electro-optical capability, allowing it to read the infrared reflections of jet engine exhaust on concrete—even when the jet was invisible.

Boyce glanced at the bulkhead clock. "That was four minutes ago. Where did he go?"

"We don't know," said the Director. "We only got the reflection from the runway. Then we lost him."

Boyce peered at the map. What the hell was a *Dong-jin* doing at an outlying, one-runway field like Huangzhu? Was it a coincidence that he launched just as the Black Stars were hitting Lingshui?

No way.

His eyes went to the situation display on his console. He could see the data-linked symbols of the three Black Stars over Hainan. Their bombs had all impacted on target. Maxwell and McCollister were sweeping for airborne *Dong-jins*. Carruthers was making his first damage assessment pass with the surveillance package.

He turned back to the speakerphone. "I appreciate your personally giving me this data, Mr. Karstadt. I know without asking that you'll pass us any updates."

"That's my job, Admiral." Karstadt hung up.

Across the flag bridge Boyce saw Hightree huddled with Piles Poindexter, the Air Wing Commander, and the flag ops officer, Captain Guido Vitale. Down on the flight deck, Super Hornets with various ordnance loads were spotted for contingency strike assignments. Tankers were already on station, and so were the CAP jets.

Boyce's responsibility ended with the Black Star raid on Lingshui. Hightree had the greater burden of protecting the entire *Reagan* strike group. An armed response from the Chinese was Hightree's biggest worry now.

He gnawed on his cigar while he thought about it. Was the *Dong-jin* that just left Huangzhu going after the Black Stars? Or something else? The answer kept buzzing at him, like an insect inside his hat.

He went to the console with the plasma situational display.

He picked up the electronic highlighting pen and tapped the spot on the display that denoted Huangzhu, where the *Dong-jin* departed. Then he tapped the symbol in the South China Sea that designated the position of the *Reagan*. He selected the DIST/BRG icon on the console. After a couple of seconds, the numbers *178°/335*—bearing and distance between the two points—flashed in the corner of the screen.

Boyce stared at the display. A scenario was forming in his mind. In six, now going on seven minutes, the *Dong-jin* would be about—he did a rough calculation—fifty some miles from Huangzhu.

Which put him relative to Maxwell's Black Star—he tweaked the display filter to show the symbols of the three Black Stars—*there*.

He peered at the display for several more seconds. Then he snatched up the headset and boom mike from his console. He keyed the microphone for the Dragon Flight tactical channel. He wouldn't violate the emissions control status of the mission unless it was something urgent. This was urgent.

"Dragon One, Battle-ax."

After a couple of seconds, he heard Maxwell's voice. "Dragon One. Go, Battle-ax."

"Snap vector, Dragon. Possible contact one-three-five degrees, twenty miles," called Boyce. Then he added, "Buster."

Speed.

Zhang wanted all he could get. The more the better. He held the nose of the *Dong-jin* down, letting the jet accelerate in a shallow climb. The patchwork of brown and green paddies blurred beneath him like an unfolding carpet.

Po spoke for the first time since takeoff. His voice had the same sullen tone. "General, may I ask why those troops tried to stop us?"

"They were part of a treasonous movement in the PLA. Don't worry. They have already been dealt with."

He could tell that Po wasn't convinced. It didn't matter. After this mission, he wouldn't need Po.

It had been a close thing. A contingent of PLA security forces had arrived at Huangzhu in a pair of troop-carrying helicopters. Only through the intervention of his loyal *Te-Wu* troops did Zhang manage to reach the *Dong-jin*. As he roared across the apron toward the runway, he had glimpsed the firefight between the two sides. The outgunned *Te-Wu* troops were falling like flies.

That was the nature of war, he thought. Sacrifices were made. Great victories were snatched from certain defeat by the narrowest of margins. Sometimes it came down to a matter of nerve and will.

"Give me the direct course and distance to the target," Zhang said in the intercom.

"I'm inserting the new coordinates in the navigation computer now," said Po.

A few seconds later, the course and distance appeared as a southeastward magenta line on Zhang's navigational display. The target lay at the *Dong-jin*'s maximum range, but it didn't matter. Zhang didn't plan to fly the entire distance. The last hundred kilometers would be covered at three times the speed of sound by the Kh-77 Krait ship-killer missiles stored in the internal bay.

The Krait was a murderously effective weapon. It skimmed the surface low enough to render it invisible to most air defense radars. Its speed made it all but invulnerable to conventional antimissile systems. The three missiles that Zhang had commandeered didn't have nuclear warheads, but their uranium-shelled tips could penetrate any armor. Even the thick double hull of the world's mightiest warship.

Maxwell rolled the Black Star into a hard right turn. He had heard the urgency in Boyce's call. "Buster" was code for maximum speed. It meant the contact was flying away from them.

The trouble was, this wasn't a real contact. No radar lock, no IR trace, no altitude report. Boyce was taking a wild guess about the location of the missing *Dong-jin*. He was guessing that the Chinese jet was headed into the South China Sea, in the direction of the *Reagan* Strike Group.

An ominous thought came to Maxwell's mind.

"Battle-ax, Dragon One. Is our bogey the guy with the bad face?"

He knew that the tactical frequency wasn't supposed to be used for such a question. But he needed to know.

"High probability, Dragon."

Maxwell nodded. *Zhang.* Boyce was still guessing, but it made sense.

Maxwell had the new CFD goggles down, peering at the world again through a pea-green haze. "Set the IR sensors to random scan," he said on the intercom.

"Already done, Boss," said Gypsy.

Maxwell caught the "Boss." It was the name Sharp O'Toole used for him. Now that they were hunting General Zhang, Gypsy's voice had shed some of its anger.

He watched the jet's airspeed increase with agonizing slowness. The Black Star had no afterburners. Even at full military power from both engines, it could barely reach .9 Mach—ninety percent of the speed of sound.

But the *Dong-jin* was no faster. It would be a dead heat.

"Nothing on the scan so far," said Gypsy.

In his display Maxwell could see the sensors sweeping the sky ahead, changing azimuth and elevation. He switched his gaze outside, peering through the goggles. It was awkward, adjusting his eyes to the soupy view outside, then refocusing on the displays in the cockpit.

They were seventy-five miles offshore. Their course would take them directly to the *Reagan*. He leveled the Black Star at twenty thousand feet. Not the best altitude for maximum speed or range, but it offered the best view above and below.

He tried to put himself in Zhang's position. What would he do if he were flying a single stealth jet against a U.S. Navy strike group? What kind of weapon? A cruise missile, maybe. Or an air-launched torpedo. Or a—

"Contact!" Gypsy's voice cut like a blade through his thoughts. "One o'clock, twelve miles. He's low, Boss."

A pair of fishing boats flashed beneath the nose of the *Dong-jin*.

From the cockpit, Zhang could see the crew hauling the nets. It amused him to imagine their reaction to hearing the blast of jet engines directly over their mast—and seeing nothing.

He was flying the *Dong-jin* at two hundred meters above the water. It was low enough to launch the missiles without their being instantly detected by enemy radar, but high enough to avoid the salt spray that fouled the *Dong-jin*'s windscreen and optical sensors.

"One hundred-ten kilometers," announced Po. The weapons systems officer's voice sounded strained. Zhang could tell that Po would be glad when this mission was finished.

Almost within launch range. The yellow in-range cue was already illuminated on his weapons display screen.

It was a pity, thought Zhang, that he would not observe at close range the effect of the Krait missiles. Each of the supersonic weapons would puncture the aircraft carrier's hull at a different spot beneath the waterline. The penetrating warheads were fitted with delayed fuses. Not until they'd plunged deep into the carrier's bowels would they explode like dynamite in a tin can. The nuclear reactor would burst apart, and the hull would split open to the sea.

It would be glorious.

The in-range cue was flashing green. Zhang wrapped his finger around the firing trigger.

"Aiiiiyeeee!"

The shriek came from the backseat. Before he could ask what was wrong, Zhang saw for himself.

Out the right side of his canopy. They looked like tiny meteorites passing below the wing, barely missing the airframe of the *Dong-jin*.

Tracers. In a flash of comprehension, Zhang knew where they were coming from. But he had one final task to complete.

He squeezed the trigger on the control stick.

The *Dong-jin*'s airframe buffeted as the weapons bay doors opened. One after the other, three long, finned Krait missiles were ejected from the belly of the *Dong-jin*. Each ram jet engine ignited, driving the weapon ahead like a yellow-tailed comet.

Zhang didn't wait to see if the missiles were tracking. He snatched the spectrum-sensing goggles down over his eyes and jammed both throttles to full thrust. He pulled on the stick, yanking the *Dong-jin*'s nose into a brutal, seven-G pitch-up. From the backseat came a gasping sound as the Gs slammed Po's body down hard into the seat.

Grunting against the G load, Zhang hauled the jet's nose through the vertical, back toward the horizon. He rotated his head and squinted over his shoulder.

It was there, just as he knew it would be. A shimmering gray shape silhouetted against the dark sea.

Gypsy transmitted the warning.

"Missiles in the air!" she called on the tactical frequency. "Three missiles inbound to mother, range sixty miles, weeds." She was alerting the *Reagan* Strike Group that they were targeted by low-flying missiles, a hundred kilometers out.

Helplessly, Maxwell watched the yellow torches erupt from the tails of the three cruise missiles. Already they were accelerating nearly out of sight.

Damn it. His first burst with the cannon had missed. He knew it was a long shot—over three thousand feet—but it was the only shot he had. He had no faith in the Sidewinder.

He wasn't gaining on the *Dong-jin*, and the Chinese jet was getting close enough to launch missiles.

Which it did. Three missiles were ripping through the air toward the Strike Group.

The voice of the tactical controller aboard the *Reagan* came over the frequency. "Say again, Dragon. Missiles in the air? Okay, we see 'em on the screen now. Are you engaged, Dragon?"

"Affirmative," said Gypsy. "Dragon One is engaged, neutral. Be advised that the incoming missiles appear to be Kraits."

"Copy that."

After launching the missiles, the *Dong-jin* had pitched up steeply, going for a vertical line. Maxwell waited, letting the Chinese jet spend some of its energy. Then he hauled the Black Star's nose up in a brutal seven-G pull, matching the *Dong-jin*'s line. He stopped on a vertical line and rolled the jet on its axis. He peered through the goggles.

Where was the *Dong-jin*?

There. Nearly parallel, arcing over the top of its own vertical line. The range at which Maxwell had opened fire on the *Dong-jin*—something over three thousand feet—had given the *Dong-jin* enough space to turn and counter Maxwell's attack.

"Shouldn't we take a Sidewinder shot, Boss?" called Gypsy.

"The Sidewinders won't track him. We have to use the gun."

Both jets were reaching the apogee of their climbs. The *Dong-jin* pilot—it *had* to be Zhang, Maxwell decided—was flying his jet to the maximum. He had just converted his situation from defensive to neutral.

Maxwell pulled the nose of the Black Star back toward the horizon. He saw the *Dong-jin* doing the same, matching his move. Their paths would cross when they pulled out on the bottom of the maneuver. The fight had evolved into a classic vertical scissors.

The cycle repeated itself. The jets pulled up again to the vertical. Neither jet had the brute thrust to continue the fight in a vertical plane. Soon it would degrade to an old-fashioned horizontal turning fight. And as their energy was depleted, they would descend to a lower and lower altitude. Only one of the jets would exit this fight.

CHAPTER 32

KRAIT

USS Ronald Reagan
South China Sea
0705 Monday, 7 May

Klaxons were blaring throughout the ship.

"Missiles inbound," said Captain Guido Vitale from the far console. He was wearing a headset, monitoring the tactical frequencies. "The Black Star engaging the *Dong-jin* just reported three missiles launched. They appear to be Kraits, inbound to the Strike Group."

Hightree shook his head. The Strike Group's Aegis air defense system was already tracking the missiles.

Hightree was studying the surface display. "Where's the Chinese Kilo?"

"On our perimeter. No sonar contact from the surface ships, but *Daytona Beach* has a contact."

Hightree nodded. "Order him to sink the Kilo."

Vitale blinked once. "Aye, aye, sir."

Standing to one side, Boyce watched the scene on the flag bridge. Hightree never stopped surprising him. There was a time when he worried that old cautious and conservative

Hightree might dither too long before making a decision. He was wrong. This was a new Jack Hightree.

7,000 feet, South China Sea

A sense of calm had settled over Zhang.

He was not worried about the Black Star. The fight was nearly over. It was only a matter of time and geometry. He was a better fighter pilot than this *gwai-lo*. All he had to do was wait for the American to make a mistake, as he inevitably would.

By then he would be rewarded with the sight of a pillar of smoke on the horizon. The devil ship—the aircraft carrier from which the Americans had sent their jets to destroy the Lingshui complex—would be sliding to the bottom of the South China Sea.

But Lieutenant Po was becoming panicky.

"Airspeed, General! We're too slow. We're too close to the water. We're—"

"Shut up!" Zhang wished he could eject Po from the jet. That wasn't an option. Unfortunately, he couldn't eject the backseater without also ejecting himself.

The fight had descended now through two thousand meters altitude—about 6,500 feet. And Po was right, their airspeed was slow. *Both* jets were clawing for the energy to remain airborne. Zhang knew that the Black Star was just as slow, close to a shuddering stall and spin.

But Zhang knew his airplane. He could *feel* the subtle buffet in the airframe that signaled an impending stall. He knew when to relax pressure on the controls, when to bite into the air and make the *Dong-jin* dance.

He saw the Black Star carving back toward him, at a slightly higher altitude. As the noses of the two jets crossed, Zhang rolled the *Dong-jin* into a reversal back in the other direction. He knew even before looking that the *gwai-lo* jet was doing the same thing—reversing his turn to come back around and again cross noses.

It was now a horizontal scissors fight. Each pilot was bending his jet back around in a minimum radius turn, trying to get on the tail of the other, trying to gain enough angle to use the cannon. They were in the third cross of the scissors fight, and neither pilot had yet gained an advantage on the other.

Soon, Zhang thought. He could feel the duel turning in his favor.

"It's *Yuanzheng 67*," said Lieutenant Commander Dale Schirmer, *Daytona Beach*'s executive officer. "I'd bet a month's pay on it."

Commander Al Sprague just nodded, keeping his eyes on the number four console of the BSY-1 combat system array. The computer had already told them the contact was a Kilo submarine. Their most recent intel update placed their old friend *Yuanzheng 67* in this sector of the South China Sea.

It had to be him. And the same intel report gave it an eighty percent likelihood that it was *Yuanzheng 67* that killed USS *Melbourne*.

Which meant that the next order issued by Al Sprague would be the most satisfying of his career.

"Fire one," said Sprague.

USS Ronald Reagan

"That's an order, Red. Put the helmet on."

Boyce looked to see if Hightree was serious. He was. Hightree was already wearing his battle helmet and float coat. A pair of binoculars dangled from around his neck. Boyce almost laughed. Hightree looked like Admiral Spruance at the Battle of Midway.

Boyce sighed and removed his piss-cutter uniform cap. He replaced it with the gray battle helmet.

A voice was booming over the speakers throughout the ship: "General quarters, general quarters! All hands man your battle stations. This is no drill. All hands man your battle stations."

The order was redundant, Boyce realized. They *were* at their damn battle stations. They'd been at them for the past two hours.

"Forty miles," called out Chief Lester, the petty officer manning the situational display command console. The three blips—Kh-77 Krait missiles—were tracking directly toward the *Reagan* at something close to Mach three. They were fanned out, separated by about a quarter mile.

They had already cleared the outer ring of the Strike Group's missile defense system. Three Aegis destroyers—*Gaddis*, *Evanston*, and *Warner*—had thrown up a wall of RIM-7 Sea Sparrow and RIM-116 Rolling Airframe antimissile missiles.

None had scored a hit.

Fucking wonderful, thought Boyce. The Aegis system automatically detected and tracked incoming threats and delivered electronic guidance to the antimissile missiles and the CIWS—close-in weapons system—to destroy them. The system cost half a billion dollars a copy. And it had just missed all three incoming missiles.

More Sea Sparrows and RIM-116s were launching from the cruisers *Bunker Hill* and her sister ship, *Ticonderoga*. More twenty-millimeter lead from the CIWS, which the gunners called the "Sea Whiz."

"Splash one Krait!" yelled Chief Lester. "*Bunker Hill* got one with a Sea Sparrow."

Boyce nodded his approval. The Sea Sparrow was a surface-to-air derivative of the air-to-air Sparrow missiles they carried on fighters. But one out of three wasn't good enough: Two of the ship killers were still coming like meteors from hell.

Boyce had never felt so exposed. He'd seen his share of

combat, but it was always in the air, and he was always armed. Now he felt like an ant on a mound.

"One minute," said a voice beside him.

Boyce turned to look at Hightree. "One minute for what?"

"In one minute those things will be here. Or they won't."

"You're making me feel a hell of a lot better," said Boyce.

Hightree grinned. "Relax, Red. A walk in the park, remember?"

Boyce had to shake his head. It was a role reversal, Hightree, the most nervous old lady in the fleet, telling *him* to relax.

He felt the deck sway under him. The carrier was in a hard turn to port. Sticks Stickney, the *Reagan*'s captain, was bringing the maximum number of guns and missile batteries to bear on the northwest quadrant. The formation of escort ships around the *Reagan* was turning with her.

"Twenty miles," called Chief Lester.

Boyce gazed out through the heavy plate glass. The two surviving missiles had gotten past the Aegis cruisers.

6,200 feet, South China Sea

Stalemate, thought Maxwell.

The jets were so evenly matched that neither was gaining an angle on the other. With each nose-on pass Maxwell could see the upturned heads of the *Dong-jin* crew looking at him. Maxwell had a hundred feet altitude advantage on the *Dong-jin*.

He remembered the old maxim: *Put yourself in your opponent's mind*. It was a rule they hammered into you in every air combat course.

Maxwell forced himself to think. *What would you do in Zhang's place?*

Zhang had to know he was running out of options. In a few more turns, they would both run out of altitude. But Zhang would run out slightly before Maxwell. He would either hit the water or level his wings and give Maxwell an opportunity to shoot him.

Zhang knew this, and he wouldn't wait. While he still had altitude, he would do something unexpected. *What?*

He saw the *Dong-jin* curving toward him again. The Black Star was a hundred feet higher than the *Dong-jin*. As before, the two jets crossed noses. After the cross, each jet would reverse and come back for the next cross.

What you do in Zhang's place?

The answer came to him.

Maxwell reversed his turn and craned his neck over his shoulder to pick up the *Dong-jin* in its own reversal. The *Dong-jin* wasn't there.

"I lost him, Boss!" called Gypsy. "Where'd he go?"

Maxwell knew, and he could almost admire Zhang's boldness. Instead of matching Maxwell's turn, Zhang had rolled his jet inverted and plunged into a split-S—the lower half of a loop. He would pull through the bottom and come up into a vertical climb. And have the Black Star in his sights.

"What do we do now?" said Gypsy.

"Watch."

He held the Black Star in its level turn for an agonizing two more seconds. Then he abruptly rolled inverted and pulled, hauling the Black Star's nose straight down toward the water.

If he was right, the *Dong-jin* would be there. If he was wrong—

"Three o'clock low!" yelled Gypsy. "See him?"

Maxwell blinked, refocused, and saw it through the green haze of the goggles. There it was. The shimmering bat-shaped craft just bottoming out of its dive.

He pulled hard, cutting across the *Dong-jin*'s turn. The extra two seconds he'd waited put him higher and slower than the *Dong-jin*. Now he was looking straight down at the top of the *Dong-jin*.

But the angle was still too acute. It would be a high-deflection shot, something close to sixty degrees. If he missed, they'd finish the fight on the water. His advantage would be gone.

"Extend the flaps," he ordered in the intercom. It was an old fighter pilot trick, putting out the landing flaps to tighten your turn radius. Never mind that they were a hundred knots over the Black Star's maximum flap extension speed. He needed Gypsy to extend them so he could stay locked on the fuzzy image of the *Dong-jin.*

"What? We're too fast to put out flaps. They're going to—"

"Just goddamn do it!" This was no time for a committee meeting.

Gypsy got the message. "Yes, sir." An instant later the flaps extended.

It worked. With the increased turning margin, Maxwell pulled the nose behind the *Dong-jin*'s tail. Then he reversed and pulled hard in the other direction, working the lead-computing gun sight up to the shimmering image of the *Dong-jin.*

He grunted against the high G load. Rivulets of perspiration streamed from inside his helmet into his eyes.

The pipper was still behind the *Dong-jin.* He pulled harder. He felt the Black Star's airframe shuddering.

A little more. The flight control computer was overriding his inputs, keeping the jet at its maximum allowable G for the airspeed. But the advantage of the extended flaps was allowing him to pull tighter than the Chinese jet. The pipper of his gun sight was almost touching the tail of the *Dong-jin.*

The range was decreasing too fast, less than a thousand feet now. In a few seconds he would overshoot the *Dong-jin*'s flight path and go outside.

The gun sight pipper was inching up the tail of the *Dong-jin.*

Range eight hundred.

He nudged the sight a bit further. He had a clear view of the *Dong-jin.* He saw vapor trails spewing off the wingtips as the jet pulled its maximum G load. Maxwell could see the two helmeted figures in the cockpit. They were looking at him.

He squeezed the trigger.

Zhang wasn't afraid. The *gwai-lo* didn't have a shot. The deflection angle was too great. He would have to pull too much lead—aim his cannon too far in front of the *Dong-jin*. In any case, the American had just overplayed his hand. His diving pursuit turn would take him deep and outside the *Dong-jin*'s turn. All Zhang had to do was return to the vertical, reverse, and he'd—

"Tracers!" yelled Po. "He's firing."

Zhang saw them too. It had to be a desperation shot. The *gwai-lo* had no more than a couple of seconds' firing opportunity, then it would be over.

The tracers seemed to be floating downward. It was an impossibly high lead angle. The tracers were arcing toward the tail of the *Dong-jin*. And missing.

Exactly as he expected. The deflection was too great to score a—

Something hit the *Dong-jin*. It felt like hammer blows against the airframe. The blows were coming from the aft fuselage.

A red light was flashing on the warning panel. Something in the engine bay was damaged. Zhang had no time to deal with it. He had to escape the *gwai-lo*'s cannon.

"We're hit!" screamed Po in the backseat. "We have a fire in the—"

Po's words were cut short. A gelatinous red spray gushed from behind Zhang, splattering his canopy and windshield. It took a microsecond to comprehend what he was seeing.

The remains of Lieutenant Po.

A roaring air noise filled the cockpit. The canopy behind him was shattered, exposed to the wind.

More red lights flashed on the warning panel. From the *Dong-jin*'s aft fuselage came a rumbling sound, like the bellow of a wounded beast. An ominous vibration rattled the airframe. The jet was rolling to the left. Zhang tried to counter the roll by shoving the stick all the way to the right. There was no response.

He had one option left. His hands moved by instinct, reaching for the handle of the ejection seat.

The *Dong-jin* was in a nearly vertical bank. Zhang could see the textured surface of the South China Sea below.

He pulled the handle.

USS Ronald Reagan

"There they are," said Hightree. He was pointing through the thick glass to the northwest.

Boyce didn't see them. He blinked and looked again. It wasn't possible to spot something that small. Not at that distance, not moving at over two thousand miles per hour.

But there they were. They looked like tiny cigars floating in space. They were silhouetted against a tableau of detonating missiles and a gray curtain of twenty-millimeter fire.

Coming closer.

Boyce was aware of a deep moaning noise. As he listened, the noise was joined by another, then another. The moaning swelled in his consciousness—until he realized what it was.

The Sea Whiz. He was hearing the combined sound of all the portside CIWS guns. Each six-barrel Gatling gun was spitting 4,500 rounds per minute. They were the ship's last-ditch defense.

As if on cue, the Kraits entered their programmed evasive maneuvers. The missiles pitched up in a vertical zigzag, then resumed their trajectories to the *Reagan*.

The hail of lead from the Sea Whiz followed the zigzagging Kraits. The moaning sound deepened. A volley of Sea Sparrows leaped from their launchers beneath the aft port flight deck. The horizon to the east of the *Reagan* blurred into a wall of gray.

The Kraits kept coming.

Boyce shook his head in wonder. How could *anything* penetrate that fence of steel?

Then he saw the answer. It couldn't.

One of the Kraits disintegrated. The warhead exploded, spewing a cone of dirty smoke and fire toward the sea. Pieces of the weapon glanced off the surface, then kicked up geysers of spray for several hundred more yards.

The last Krait was still coming.

Boyce had a good view of the incoming missile. It was untouched by the defensive fire. It was so close that Boyce could see the ugly brown shape, the blurry torch of its ram jet engine, the large aft guidance fins.

And he could see now where the Krait was aimed.

"Don't forget to duck, Red," said Hightree.

CHAPTER 33

PROJECTILES

1,200 feet
South China Sea
0710 Monday, 7 May

"*YeeeeeHaaa!*"

Gypsy Palmer's cheer hurt Maxwell's eardrums.

"You got him! You nailed that sonofabitch."

Later, thought Maxwell, in a quieter moment, he would replay the cockpit tape for her. He wanted to see her face when she heard herself yelling like a deranged wrestler.

They bottomed out of the vertical maneuver less than five hundred feet over the water. They had overshot the flight path of the *Dong-jin*, but it didn't matter. The *Dong-jin* was in a rolling dive, streaming flame as it plunged toward the sea.

Maxwell kept his eyes on it. He wanted to see it die. He wanted visual confirmation that Zhang was dead.

There was a momentary orange flash. A geyser of water shot into the air, marking the *Dong-jin*'s crash site.

Gypsy's voice came over the intercom. "Hey, Boss, check eight o'clock level."

He tore his eyes away from the spot where the *Dong-jin*

had crashed. He peered over his left shoulder. He blinked, then shoved the CFD goggles up so that he could see more clearly.

There was something out there. The pale, hemispherical canopy of a parachute. It was descending through five hundred feet.

"What are you going to do?" said Gypsy.

Maxwell didn't answer.

PLAN Submarine Yuanzheng 67

Captain Wu Tsien-li was perplexed. What was happening on the surface?

The U.S. destroyers on the outer screen of the U.S. Strike Group had lost their contact with *Yuanzheng 67*. He knew this by the direction and pattern of their active sonar search. Instead of tracking *Yuanzheng 67*, they had shifted to a systematic sweep of their perimeter.

But something was different. The destroyers had just changed their formation. Wu's sonar operator had reported that the American ships were firing surface-to-air missiles.

Firing missiles at what? Wu was perplexed. Had the war resumed, perhaps escalated to an open sea battle?

This sparsity of information was frustrating. The PLA Navy's undersea communications network was not as sophisticated as that of the Americans. Wu had no way of receiving updated information from the PLA high command unless he ascended to a shallow enough depth to raise his satellite communications antenna. Such an action would make him an instant contact on surface radar screens.

Wu's last orders were to shadow the American carrier strike group but avoid provocative gestures. Which was causing Wu a feeling of great disappointment. He and the crew of *Yuanzheng 67* had covered themselves with glory. His exploits in the South China Sea had earned him huge recognition in the high command of the PLA Navy. He was the highest-scoring submarine commander in modern history—six enemy patrol boats, two freighters, and a U.S. submarine.

"Undersea message traffic," reported his communications systems officer. "U.S. coded message traffic. It appears to be urgent one-way communication to a submarine in this vicinity, Captain."

Wu frowned. This was bad news. It meant there definitely *was* a U.S. submarine somewhere close, probably an SSN fast-attack submarine. The Americans wouldn't use the noisy extra-low-frequency communications band in a possible combat situation unless it was an urgent one-way signal to the submarine's captain.

Wu was getting an uneasy feeling. In their game of hide-and-seek, he could locate each of the American surface ships. If he chose, he could put a torpedo into each of them. But he was unable to locate his most dangerous adversary—the U.S. submarine. It was the reverse of the situation when he had detected the American submarine that was stalking the convoy out of Guangzhou. He remained undetected until he fired the *Shkval*, and then it was too late for the Americans. Their slower-moving MK 48 torpedo could not cover the distance between the submarines before the *Shkval* struck home.

Wu loved the *Shkval* rocket torpedo. Its guidance system was primitive, more on the order of an unguided missile, but it was deadly at close range. The Russians called it the "revenge weapon" because it could be fired down the bearing line of an incoming torpedo. It would either kill the torpedo or the submarine that launched it.

All this was on Wu's mind when he heard the high-pitched voice of the sonar operator. "Torpedo! Bearing 050, incoming."

Wu's mind snapped back to the present. He had rehearsed this moment a hundred times in training. He was on the defensive, and there was only one appropriate response.

"Stand by tube number two. Set target bearing 050, and update on the incoming contact."

"Yes, Captain, tube number two ready."

"Update bearing and fire when ready. Hard left, steer 230, depth eighty meters, full ahead."

The fire controller and the helmsman both acknowledged. A rumble shook the frame of the *Yuanzheng 67*.

"Tube two fired, Captain."

The *Shkval* was on its way. And the *Yuanzheng 67* was barreling away at full speed in the opposite direction. It was contrary to the old PLA Navy and Russian doctrine, which taught that you should turn *toward* your opponent, trying to force his torpedo to overshoot. But that was before the *Shkval*. They were in a race now, and the *Shkval* was the fastest of the competing weapons. Wu wanted to get as far away as he could from the incoming MK 48 while the *Shkval* closed the distance on the American submarine.

A new, relentless pinging came over the sonar. It was audible through the steel frame of the submarine.

"Active homing," said the sonarman. "The torpedo is tracking us."

Wu could see the incoming torpedo on the master display. It was close, less than two thousand meters, moving at twice the speed of the *Yuanzheng 67*. Everything depended now on timing. At the last moment, he would evade and deceive the enemy torpedo.

He watched the relentless oncoming blip on the display. He waited until it was within a thousand meters.

"Hard left, full rudder, 140. Deploy decoys."

Behind the hard-turning *Yuanzheng 67* streamed a trail of acoustic decoys. The torpedo would track one of the decoys. Or else it would turn to pursue the *Yuanzheng 67*.

500 feet
South China Sea

A miracle, thought Zhang.

The Russian-built Zvezda K-36 was the best ejection seat in the world. For the second time in his career, it had saved him from a destroyed *Dong-jin.* The device had functioned perfectly—the chest protector deploying in front of him, the two stabilizing booms behind. He had separated from the seat cleanly.

Now he hung suspended in the harness. He was less than a minute from splashing into the sea. The sea state didn't appear rough, waves lower than a meter in height. The survival pack attached to his harness included a life raft and signaling equipment. The PLA Navy would come to rescue him.

Only seconds after his parachute deployed, Zhang had watched his jet crash into the sea. A feeling of intense bitterness swept over him. He no longer had any doubt about the identity of his adversary. From the moment their engagement began, he knew it was Maxwell.

The descending parachute made a rustling noise in the thick air. The shroud lines were vibrating softly like the strings of an instrument. The gentle sounds were peaceful after the din and roar of the air battle. Zhang was close enough to the surface to hear the lapping noise of the waves.

And something else.

He cocked his head, listening. A deeper noise, not from the sea. Definitely not from the nylon canopy of his parachute.

Jet noise.

A jolt of anxiety shot through him. *The Black Star.* It was still out there. And Zhang couldn't see him.

A cold, unreasoning fear seized him. *Would the* gwai-lo *strafe him?*

No. Americans had no stomach for such things. They could be vicious in warfare, but they had a naive, sentimental attitude toward the defenseless. They worried about trivial things like endangering noncombatants, collateral damage, humane treatment of prisoners.

The jet noise swelled.

Zhang squinted in the direction of the noise. He was only about a hundred meters from the sea. In less than a minute he'd be in the water.

He saw it. The object was indistinct, swimming in and out his vision, but he recognized the flat, tailless shape. It was low, nearly level, flying directly toward him.

Zhang peered into the haze. He saw the blinking yellow light, like a flashing strobe. He stared at it, not willing to believe what he was seeing.

He glanced down. He was only seconds from the wave tops. If he could make it to the water, he had a chance.

He felt the blunt impact of the bullets tearing into him. In his last moment of awareness, he glimpsed the ephemeral shape of the Black Star flying toward him. The yellow light was still blinking.

What was left of General Zhang Yu's shredded body plunged into the South China Sea.

USS Ronald Reagan

Boyce didn't move.

He stood at the heavy glass pane, hands on his hips, eyes fixed on the brown object off the *Reagan*'s port beam. If these were to be his last few seconds of life, he was damn well going to watch the show. The missile was about five hundred yards out. It was on a direct course for the *Reagan*'s island structure.

Boyce saw a piece fly off the missile. Then another. The moan of the CIWS guns deepened.

"They're getting hits," said Hightree. "The Sea Whiz is hitting the missile."

A larger piece flew off. In the next instant the warhead exploded, and the Krait separated into a shower of fragments.

Time seemed to freeze for Boyce. Flaming pieces of shrapnel were suspended in the air. In slow motion, fragments of the shattered missile struck the water, skipped across the surface, smashed into the steel hull of the *Reagan*.

A piece the size of a car hood floated across the flight deck. It ripped through the fuselage of a parked F/A-18. The fuel-laden fighter flipped onto its back and exploded in an orange pyre.

A whirling fragment sailed behind the *Reagan*'s fantail and caught the blades of the plane guard helicopter, an SH-60 Seahawk hovering on station. The mortally wounded chopper flopped end over end into the foaming wake behind the carrier.

More shrapnel sliced across the deck. A jagged piece cleaved through a tug vehicle, decapitating its driver. Another slammed into a gun bay on the port side. A fountain of smoke and torn steel erupted from below the deck edge. Another hunk ricocheted off the forward flight deck, barely missing the parked jets, then soared back into space off the starboard side.

A flaming projectile was arcing over the deck. As in a dream, Boyce watched the object fill up his view through the window. It didn't appear to be moving, just swelling in size.

At the last instant he dived for the deck. He heard a sound like a steel door slamming behind his ear. Something struck him from behind. A flash of light ignited in Boyce's brain, followed by blackness.

USS Daytona Beach

The *Shkval* was coming at them like a rifle bullet.

"Ahead full," snapped Commander Al Sprague, watching his BSY-1 console. "Left full rudder, down twenty."

The helmsman acknowledged.

"Rudder amidships," Sprague ordered. "Deploy decoys one and two."

"Decoys deployed one and two."

Sprague stared at the BSY-1 console, watching the progress of the fast-moving blip on the console. It was incredible. Who would have dreamed something could move at such speed through water?

The *Shkval* was tracking straight ahead. It was emitting a steady pinging noise. Its onboard active sonar was searching for *Daytona Beach*.

And then the pinging changed tempo, becoming more frenetic.

"Active homing, Captain. The torpedo's turning right, tracking . . . tracking."

Sprague held his breath. For the next five seconds, no one in the control room spoke.

"Still turning . . . turning . . . *Missed*! The fucker missed us."

The *Shkval* shot past *Daytona Beach*'s stern and kept running mindlessly to the northeast. The sound of its propulsion system grew fainter.

Sprague said nothing. It was too soon to celebrate. Their MK 48 was still running after the Kilo.

PLAN Submarine Yuanzheng 67

Captain Wu stared at the display. The incoming torpedo was turning. Ignoring the decoys. Tracking the *Yuanzheng 67*.

The impact came from the stern, just forward of the aft planes. Wu felt the concussion, then swung his attention to the pressure bulkhead that separated his compartment from the aft section. He knew with a dreadful certainty what he would see next.

He saw it for only a moment. The lights flickered, then

went out. An instant later, he heard the steel bulkhead yield to the crushing pressure of a hundred tons of seawater.

USS Daytona Beach

"Detonation, bearing 235," called sonar. And then, after a moment, "It's the Kilo, sir."

The sonar was picking up the lonely, clattering, tinkling noise of the *Yuanzheng 67* collapsing in on itself, settling to the bottom.

After a silence of several seconds, cheering erupted in the control room. Sprague peered around at his ebullient crew. They were yelling, high-fiving, grinning like baboons. It was an extraordinary display of emotion for the crew of an SSN—and a breach of discipline in the middle of a combat operation.

Sprague didn't mind. Finally they had something to cheer about.

CHAPTER 34

BATTLE DAMAGE

USS Ronald Reagan
South China Sea
0740 Monday, 7 May

He tasted blood.

It was warm and salty, trickling into the back of his throat. In the distance he heard garbled voices, barked commands over a speaker. None of it made sense. It was drowned in the ringing that filled his ears.

Something hard was pressing into his cheek. He tried opening his eyes, and his vision returned in an expanding cone of gray. He was lying facedown on something cold and rough. A steel deck, he realized. It was covered with the ubiquitous pebbly, nonskid Navy paint.

Someone was kneeling beside him. Boyce raised his head, and a stab of pain shot down through his shoulder. He felt something trickling from his nose. He wiped at his nose with the back of his hand and saw that his nose was bleeding.

"He's alive," yelled the figure beside him.

He rolled over, then sat up, trying to ignore the pain in his shoulder. He recognized the man beside him. He was one of the flag staff yeomen, a first-class petty officer. He was wearing a helmet and float coat.

"You're gonna be okay, Admiral. Just don't move, okay?"

Boyce nodded. The petty officer unfastened Boyce's chin strap and removed the helmet.

"Holy shit," said the petty officer.

He held the helmet up so Boyce could see it. Boyce stared dumbly. It took him a few seconds to understand what the man was talking about. The left side of the helmet looked like it had been walloped with a sledgehammer.

"That thing saved your life," said the petty officer.

Boyce nodded, still not sure what had happened. His right shoulder hurt like hell. A haze of gray smoke filled the compartment. The deck was littered with jagged hunks of heavy plate glass.

He saw that one of the two communication consoles was smashed. Something had torn a jagged hole through the front of the console. The plasma screen on the bulkhead was still glowing, displaying the icons and symbols of the *Reagan* Strike group.

There were others in the compartment. Chief Lester was standing by the far bulkhead talking into a sound-powered telephone. Boyce couldn't understand anything he was saying.

A sailor in a blue chambray work uniform—Boyce saw that it was another member of Hightree's staff, a third-class petty officer—was kneeling over something on the deck. Boyce stared at the object on the deck for a minute, trying to comprehend what he was seeing.

Then, through the haze and his own dulled senses, it came to him. Boyce wobbled to his feet and lurched across the cluttered deck to where the sailor was kneeling.

The sailor looked up at him, then moved out of the way. He was shaking his head. "I tried," said the sailor. "I tried to get him out of the way, but he wouldn't move."

Boyce knelt on one knee. The ache in his shoulder was

worse in this position, and he guessed that it was his collarbone. He ignored the pain.

For a long while he knelt there, gazing down at the man
on the deck. He looked like he could be asleep. Boyce
guessed that the sailor had closed his eyelids. Whatever it
was that hit him—the missile fragment, Boyce guessed—
had taken him squarely across the chest.

Hightree had died instantly.

"Goddamn it, Jack. You were supposed to duck."

19,000 feet, South China Sea

Gypsy broke the silence in the cockpit.

"Was it Zhang?"

"Does it matter?" said Maxwell.

"Yes."

Neither of them had spoken since they'd left the site of
the *Dong-jin* shoot-down. They were climbing back to altitude, en route to the Super Hornet tanker on station fifty
miles east of the *Reagan*.

The sight of the man in the parachute was fixed like an in-
delible print in her mind.

"Yeah, it was Zhang," said Maxwell.

Gypsy thought for a moment. It still wasn't good enough.

"What makes you sure?"

"I saw the tracers. Our last burst got the aft cockpit. The
wizzo was dead meat. I doubt if his seat even worked. The
guy in the chute was very much alive. Had to be Zhang."

She knew all that. She'd seen the tracers too. She wanted
to hear it from Maxwell.

A flood of emotions ran through her. God knew she
wanted to see Zhang die. She wanted the sonofabitch who
murdered Sharp to die in the most gruesome way possible.
And so he had.

She knew she should feel lousy about it. Guilty, filled
with self-recrimination. In her inner being resided a civi-

lized person who revered life. She was a woman who rescued turtles and refused to kill spiders. Shooting a defenseless human while he dangled in a parachute was a heinous
act. She should be overcome with self-loathing.

She wasn't. Gypsy felt fine. She couldn't remember when
she'd felt better.

But she'd been wrong about one thing. Someday, maybe
over a couple of drinks, she would apologize to Maxwell.
He wouldn't even understand what she was talking about,
but she'd do it anyway. She'd admit that she was wrong. She
had thought that he was too much of a Boy Scout to kill that
sonofabitch Zhang.

The White House

Unbelievable, thought President Hollis Benjamin.

He listened to the Chinese translator on the speakerphone.
There was a break, then he heard again the frenetic, high-
pitched voice of President Xiang Fan-lo. This went on for
three more minutes, making no sense at all to Benjamin.
Then the translator returned to deliver Xiang's explanation
of why three supersonic missiles belonging to the PLA Air
Force had been fired at the largest warship of the United
States Navy.

It was all very simple. A misunderstanding.

When silence finally came to the line, Benjamin didn't
know whether to laugh or scream in rage. *A misunderstanding.* The reckless little bastards had just tried their level best
to sink a hundred-thousand-ton aircraft carrier. Instead, they
only destroyed three valuable aircraft, inflicted millions of
dollars in damage to the *Reagan*, and killed thirty-nine men
and women, including Rear Admiral Jack Hightree.

Benjamin tried to suppress his anger. The call from Xiang
had come within minutes of the missile attack. Xiang had
been eager—almost frantic—to declare the PRC's innocence.

The People's Republic of China, he insisted, had no wish to go to war with the United States.

The Chinese president went on. He wanted to make it clear that this unfortunate misunderstanding was not his fault. The chain of events that resulted in the launching of the missiles was triggered by a disloyal senior officer of the PLA. He had conducted certain unilateral military operations without the direction or immediate knowledge of his superiors.

In the pause that followed, Benjamin said, "Could you tell me this officer's name?"

After a pause, the translator said, "No. The president wishes to deal with the officer in a confidential manner."

Benjamin nodded. He already knew the officer's name. General Zhang had been the subject of several recent videoconferences with Admiral Boyce on the *Reagan*. And he had no doubt that Xiang already knew that his disloyal general was now shark food.

"Very well," said Benjamin. "Then perhaps the president could be specific about *what* certain unilateral operations this officer conducted?"

There was a silence, and Benjamin knew that Xiang was conferring with his advisors. The translator came back on the line. "No. The president believes it would not serve our purpose to be specific about such things."

Benjamin shook his head. Xiang was being too damned evasive. They both knew who had shot down Ambassador Joe Ferrone's jet at Gia Lam Airport. Zhang had killed Ferrone in a move to trigger a reprisal attack by the U.S.

And he had succeeded. During Xiang's long explanation of the PRC's innocence, he had scrupulously avoided any reference to the Black Star strike on the Lingshui base. Which was diplomatic of him, Benjamin thought. Instead of castigating each other for their various acts of war, the two nations could get on with implementing a truce.

Benjamin stifled a yawn. His eyes felt red and scratchy.

He looked over at Secretary Greenstein and General Matloff. They looked as haggard as he did. The events in Asia had taken place on the back side of the clock. The tension of the operations in the South China Sea had left all their nerves twanging.

Xiang's singsong voice was crackling over the speaker again. When he finished, the translator said that the president was eager and willing to sign the peace accord that had already been drafted in Hong Kong. In light of the recent circumstances, it would be a most stabilizing influence on the region.

"I couldn't agree more," said Benjamin.

With that, the two presidents agreed to an early summit meeting that would include the president of Vietnam. The nasty little conflict over the Spratly Islands would be resolved in a diplomatic fashion.

The connection to Beijing went dead. Benjamin sat for a while staring at the silent telephone console. He looked over at Greenstein. Something that resembled a grin was spreading over the defense secretary's deeply lined face.

"You know what this really means?" said Greenstein.

"No," said Benjamin, "but I presume you're about to tell me."

"It means that you get to keep your job."

Benjamin nodded. In the frenetic activity of the past few days, he'd stopped thinking about Wagstaff and the impeachment threat.

Despite his fatigue, a feeling of contentment seeped into Benjamin's body. It was going to be sweet. More than sweet. He would invite Wagstaff to the White House press conference tomorrow morning. He'd see to it that the senator was positioned where Benjamin could see his face when he announced that he had orchestrated a peace accord between Vietnam and China. The U.S.'s intervention had prevented a major war in the Far East.

Benjamin had been right, Wagstaff had been wrong.

But the best would come later. After the conference he'd find an opportunity to talk to the senator one on one. No reporters or staffers nearby. He'd smile and put his arm on Wagstaff's shoulder and tell the senator that he could take his impeachment initiative and shove it up his ass.

USS Ronald Reagan

Maxwell and Gypsy walked in silence down the long passageway to the SCIF—Special Compartmentalized Information Facility—where the most-classified intelligence debriefings were conducted. The SCIF was buried deep in the interior of the ship, guarded by emission-proof bulkheads. Two armed Marines stood outside the door.

A familiar figure was waiting for them. His right arm was in a sling. A bandage covered his right cheek. An unlit cigar jutted from his teeth.

"About time you two showed up," said Boyce.

"It's good to see you, Admiral," said Maxwell. "We heard you took some battle damage."

"No big deal. Busted collarbone, a light concussion, that's all. Sorry I can't say the same about Jack Hightree."

Maxwell and Gypsy exchanged glances. They'd seen the blackened paint and the shattered glass on the island structure when they landed back aboard an hour earlier. And they'd heard about Hightree.

"What's our defense condition?" said Maxwell. "Are we expecting more attacks on the Strike Group?"

"No, but we're ready. We'll hit back hard enough to make the ChiComs wish they'd never screwed with us."

Maxwell had taken his time getting to the SCIF for the after-action debriefing. He wasn't looking forward to confronting Harvey Wentz, the intel officer. Wentz would grill them about the strike on Lingshui and the encounter with the *Dong-jin.* He'd want the details about what happened to the *Dong-jin* crew.

That was the sticky part. Maxwell had no regrets about shooting Zhang in his parachute. He had exterminated a monster. The world was better off without Zhang.

But Maxwell might very well be accused of a war crime. His first priority was to establish that it was his action and no one else's. Gypsy Palmer must not be implicated.

"Does that mean we're standing down, Admiral?" said Gypsy.

"It means that what happened to the *Reagan* today was some kind of military aberration. It wasn't supposed to occur. Those are the president's words, not mine. And by the way, I briefed him on your recent performance out there."

Maxwell nodded. "Ah, Admiral, before we go into the debriefing, there's something you should know about—"

"I've already seen your HUD videotape," said Boyce.

Maxwell felt a rush of uneasiness. He'd almost forgotten about the digital videotape that recorded everything in the Black Star's cockpit, including the view through the gun sight. It would capture the death of the *Dong-jin* crew.

"Yes, sir. Then I want to make it clear that—"

"Too bad about the tape," Boyce said. He was giving him a look that Maxwell had seen before.

"If you saw it, then you know—"

"The damned thing quit running just after you shot down the *Dong-jin.*"

Boyce was still giving him the look. Gypsy was peering at them both quizzically.

"What about Zhang?" she blurted.

"Who?" said Boyce.

"General Zhang. The Chinese pilot we shot down."

"Oh, him. Dead as a dog turd. His wizzo too. Wedge Flores got there with a SEAL team about twenty minutes after the shoot-down. He found a helmet, remnants of a parachute, and some bloody flight gear. And lots of sharks. Forget Zhang."

Boyce was still giving them the look.

Maxwell made eye contact with Gypsy. He moved his lips almost imperceptibly. *Forget Zhang.*

She nodded.

"Shall we go to the debriefing?" said Boyce.

CHAPTER 35

BOY SCOUT

USS Ronald Reagan
South China Sea
1705 Monday, 7 May

"Purely medicinal," said Boyce. He held up his glass. "Flight surgeon's orders."

Maxwell didn't have to ask what was in the glass. He watched Boyce sip the drink and sigh with pleasure. His right arm was in a sling, bound to his side. Stolichnaya vodka was Boyce's medicine of choice.

"Sure you won't have one?" said Boyce.

"I wasn't wounded today."

"Today, yesterday, what the hell? There's no statute of limitations."

They were in Boyce's stateroom. The intel debriefing had been surprisingly short. Even Harvey Wentz had been uncustomarily civil. He had displayed little interest in the events following the shoot-down of Zhang's *Dong-jin*.

Boyce was tilted back in his bunk, cradling the glass against his chest. He was looking woozy, which meant that the painkiller Knuckles Ball, the flight surgeon, had given him for the broken bone was kicking in. The medicinal vodka, Maxwell assumed, was for something else. Losing Jack Hightree was a blow to Boyce.

"Have you seen Dr. Boudroux?" asked Boyce. His words were coming slowly.

Maxwell looked at him in surprise. "No. Why?"

"Oh, just wondered. I would have thought she'd be, you know, sort of curious about what happened today."

Maxwell didn't reply. He'd been wondering the same thing. He thought he'd glimpsed Dana at the edge of the hangar deck as they climbed down from the Black Star after the mission. When he looked again, she was gone. He tried calling her lab, then her stateroom. No answer either place.

That figured. Dragon Flight was history, and so was any relationship between them. Dana was headed back to Groom Lake, and he was going to Fallon—or wherever Boyce decided to send him. For all he knew, Dana had left already. And that was fine with him.

No, it wasn't, he thought. It wasn't fine at all.

Boyce's eyes were closed. Maxwell removed the drink from the admiral's hand and poured it in the sink. He turned the light out as he left.

Hanoi, Socialist Republic of Vietnam

"So good to see you again," said Li Che Kim.

"It is entirely my pleasure, Madame Ferrone," said Trunh Bao. "You have been much in my thoughts."

Kim stood at the head of the reception line in the garden of the Presidential Palace. At her side was the president of the Socialist Republic of Vietnam, Van Duc Chien. Standing at her other elbow was Mike Medford, Joe Ferrone's deputy and now the acting U.S. ambassador.

Kim had remained calm and dry-eyed throughout the memorial service for her husband. President Van had delivered a eulogy in surprisingly good English in which he described the unusual friendship he had struck with Joe Ferrone. The two of them, Van said, were old soldiers who could put the past behind them. Their countries could now do the same.

Mike Medford read a letter from the president of the United States about his old mentor and skipper. An honor guard presented Kim with both an American and a Vietnamese flag.

The reception line had dwindled to only a few remaining guests. Trunh was one of the last to pay his respects.

"I've been thinking about you, Trunh," said Kim.

"In what respect, madame?"

"Wondering what you've been doing since the death of the ambassador."

Trunh shook his head sadly. "It was very difficult for me. Not until yesterday could I bring myself to return to Hanoi."

As they spoke, Kim was aware of President Van's wrinkled face watching them both. He was nodding his head, following their conversation.

And then Van interrupted. "But you are Vietnamese, Trunh. Why did you remain in China?"

A look of alarm flashed over Trunh's face. It was obvious that he did not expect to be addressed directly by the president. "Because I . . . was overwhelmed with grief, Mr. President. As Madame Ferrone knows, I was very fond of the ambassador."

Van nodded. "So fond, in fact, that you signaled the news of his departure from Hong Kong to a PLA officer in Lingshui."

Trunh's eyes widened further. "I do not understand your meaning, Mr. President. What officer would I—"

"You knew him well. His name was Zhang. General Zhang Yu."

Trunh's eyes darted from the president to Kim. "What are you suggesting? That I had something to do with the ambassador's death?"

"What is your rank in the *Te-Wu*?" said Van.

"I . . . I do not know what you mean?"

"Of course, you do. You are an agent of the *Te-Wu*, the

PLA secret police. General Zhang was your superior officer. It was you who directed the assassins to the two Americans, Maxwell and Boudroux, when they were in Hanoi."

"I . . . I know nothing about that, Mr. President."

"And it was you, Trunh, who informed Zhang of the precise time of Ambassador Ferrone's arrival at Gia Lam Airport. Zhang then intercepted the ambassador's jet and shot it down."

Fascinated, Kim watched the exchange. Earlier that day Medford informed her that they had connected Trunh to her husband's death. She refused to believe it. It simply wasn't possible.

Now she believed it. The proof was in Trunh's darting eyes, the contorted face, the nervous twitch in his hands.

"I will not be subjected to such questions," said Trunh. "I must leave."

Abruptly he turned from them and strode toward the gate that led through the south wing of the palace and out to the street.

Medford started to go after him, but Van stopped him. "Let him," said Van. "He won't go far."

And he didn't. A half dozen green-uniformed Vietnamese soldiers were moving from either side of the garden to close the gateway. The officer in charge of the soldiers held up his hand, signaling Trunh to stop.

Trunh stopped, still twenty yards from the soldiers. For several seconds he studied the officer advancing toward him. Then he whirled back to where Kim and Medford and Van stood in a cluster. He slid his hand inside his coat and pulled out a semiautomatic pistol.

With both hands he aimed the pistol at Kim.

Kim stared back at him, transfixed. None of this was real. It wasn't possible that this young man whom she once trusted was about to put a bullet into her.

She saw the pistol recoil, and at the same instant she felt an impact. In some remote part of her consciousness she heard the sharp crack of the shot. It sounded like the back-fire of an automobile.

She was aware of more pistol shots, at least three of them. She felt the soft earth pressing into her face. A dull ache was spreading across her upper body. It occurred to her that dying was not all that agonizing. Uncomfortable, but without agony.

But she wasn't dying. She was sure of it. The ache in her upper body was not from a bullet. It was from being slammed by another body, which still lay atop her.

She rolled over and gazed into the face of Van Duc Chien. His eyes were closed. He appeared to be sleeping. His face wore an expression of utter peace.

She couldn't hold back the tears. Through her blurred vision she saw Trunh Bao lying facedown on the grass. The officer who had shot him was standing over him, keeping his own pistol trained on Trunh's body.

Mike Medford was kneeling beside her, looking worried. "Are you hurt?" he said.

She shook her head. "Van," she said, fighting back the grief that was welling up in her. "He threw himself in the way so that I wouldn't be shot."

At this, Van Duc Chien's eyes popped open. He sat up and plucked a wad of grass from the front of his jacket.

"Of course I did," he said. "Joe would never have forgiven me if I let something happen to you."

Kim stared for a long moment. Then she seized him and planted a kiss on the wrinkled face.

USS Ronald Reagan

The first clue came when he tried to unlock the door to his stateroom. It was already unlocked. Maxwell stood there for a moment, trying to remember whether he'd locked it when he left in the early morning.

The second clue came when he opened the door.

"Leave the light off."

He left the light off and closed the door behind him. Music was coming from the compact hi-fi on the desk. He recognized it—a Brahms violin concerto, one of the CDs he'd brought with him to the ship.

"I don't suppose it would do any good to ask how you got into the room," he said.

"That's right," she said. "It wouldn't."

He heard something that sounded like the rustling of nylon.

"I thought you said you didn't want a relationship with another fighter pilot."

"That was then," she said. "This is now."

"What's changed?"

"Everything. And nothing. Dragon Flight is finished. You're alive."

That much was true, Maxwell thought. Unless the Chinese reneged on the agreement and unless there was another nutcase like General Zhang to sabotage the peace, the Black Stars—and the Dragon Flight team—were going home to Nevada.

He was definitely alive, and liking it more by the minute. But a bothersome thought kept inserting itself in his mind. It was a breach of protocol for a senior officer to be alone in his room with a woman. As a squadron skipper aboard the *Reagan*, he had been scrupulous about setting the right example for his junior officers.

Of course, he wasn't a squadron skipper any longer. And Dana Boudroux wasn't in the military. But those were technicalities. The rules applied to everyone.

"It was the admiral," she said.

"Excuse me?" said Maxwell. "What about the admiral?"

"You asked how I got into your room. Admiral Boyce gave me a key."

"Oh."

"He said that you wouldn't mind. But he warned me that you were a Boy Scout. You had a thing about rules."

Maxwell nodded. Boyce again. Brilliant, meddlesome, presumptuous. Some things never changed.

"The admiral should mind his own business."

His eyes were adjusting to the semidarkness. In the sliver of light from beneath the door, he saw that she had undone her ponytail. Her hair was splayed on the pillow. He could see her tanned body silhouetted on the bed.

"Are you going lock the door?" she said.

"Sure," he said. Actually, it was already locked. He'd gotten over the bothersome thoughts. Some rules were meant to be broken.

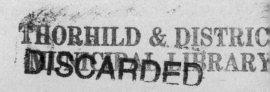

CLASSIFIED MATERIAL—TOP SECRET

Specifications: YF-27B Black Star

Contractors: Lockheed Martin/Northrop-Grumman
Power Plant: Two General Electric F404-GE-102D engines
Wingspan: 44.0 (13.41 meters)
Length: 38.4 (11.7 meters)
Height: 9.15 feet (2.8 meters)
Speed: High subsonic
Ceiling: 55,000 feet (16,764 meters)
Takeoff Weight (Typical): 52,000 pounds (23,587 kilograms)
Range: 810 nautical miles (1,500 kilometers)
Armament: Cannon, air-to-air missiles, internal bomb bay
Payload: 7,200 pounds (3,266 kilograms)
Crew: Two
Unit cost: Approximately $1.89 billion (2006 constant dollars)

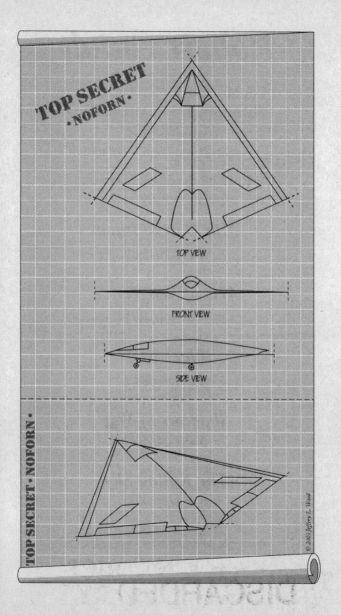

TOP SECRET
• NOFORN •

TOP VIEW

FRONT VIEW

SIDE VIEW

TOP SECRET • NOFORN •

© 2005 Jeffrey L. Ward